Praise for *Wrong Chance*

By E.L. Myrieckes

"*Wrong Chance* is a gripping glimpse into what makes a loving husband tick...and, unfortunately, what causes him to explode. Compelling momentum right up to the end."

—MRS. OASIS, COAUTHOR OF *White Heat*

"Mind-bending."

—RAFEALA BARBOUR, AUTHOR OF *Many Hats of a Woman*

"Brilliant. *Wrong Chance* is a phenomenal read. E. L. Myrieckes is an outstanding writer."

—BRENDA HAMPTON, BESTSELLING AUTHOR OF *Too Naughty*

The coppery smell of blood and rotten flesh raped his nose. His belly tried to crawl up his throat and out his mouth. He forced the bile down as his heart feloniously assaulted his chest. Decay and the residue of anger tainted the air. It was a funk that promised to cling until he scrubbed it clean. But Hakeem knew he'd still smell it in his mind.

Like a thoroughbred bloodhound he sniffed and followed the funk to its source, stomach protesting every step of the way. Just beyond the main sanctuary a man lay on the floor. Shirt open, pants and underwear gathered at his ankles. Blowflies circled his body like hungry vultures. Blood pooled around his body; it had turned brown and thick like meringue.

Hakeem pulled out his Palm Treo 750 and snapped a barrage of crime-screen photos. The victim's face was covered with the Metro section of yesterday's newspaper. Ancient Egyptian hieroglyphics were carefully carved into every visible part of the victim's skin. Hakeem ventured to lift the newspaper some. The victim's eyes were bulged from heat-expanded tissues and were filled with maggots. His mouth was frozen open as if he died screaming.

"Son of a bitch."

Dear Reader:

In this installment of a new mystery series, E.L. Myrieckes introduces us to Hakeem Eubanks and Aspen Skye, homicide detectives who team up to track a serial killer who is terrorizing residents in Ohio.

The author cleverly weaves this spine-tingling tale that is full of twists and leaves readers guessing what's to come next. A group of college students never realized that years later, their prank would lead to deadly mayhem. Mix in County Attorney Scenario Davenport, who has her own surprises, and courtroom drama supplements the spice.

Myrieckes, also known as Oasis, is an author who focuses on creating memorable characters and stimulating story lines. I'm sure once you start reading *Wrong Chance*, you'll want to continue this thrilling ride with a psychopath to the very end. Check out his other titles including *Duplicity*, *White Heat*, *Push Comes to Shove* and the ebook *Eternal Flame*.

Thanks for supporting the authors of Strebor Books. As always, we strive to bring you amazing stories from prolific authors. We appreciate the love. You can find me on Facebook and Twitter @AuthorZane, on Instagram @planetzane and you can join our text service to be aware of upcoming titles and events by texting Zane to 51660.

Blessings,

Zane

Publisher
Strebor Books
www.simonandschuster.com

ZANE PRESENTS

WRONG CHANCE

A DETECTIVE EUBANKS NOVEL

E.L. MYRIECKES

STREBOR BOOKS

NEW YORK LONDON TORONTO SYDNEY

Strebor Books
P.O. Box 6505
Largo, MD 20792
http://www.streborbooks.com

ISBN 978-1-59309-560-4
ISBN 978-1-4767-5863-3 (ebook)
LCCN 2014931190

First Strebor Books trade paperback edition July 2014

Edited by Docuversion

Cover design: www.mariondesigns.com
Cover photograph: © Keith Saunders Photos

10 9 8 7 6 5 4 3 2 1

Manufactured in the United States of America

For information regarding special discounts for bulk purchases, please contact Simon & Schuster Special Sales at 1-866-506-1949 or business@simonandschuster.com

The Simon & Schuster Speakers Bureau can bring authors to your live event. For more information or to book an event, contact the Simon & Schuster Speakers Bureau at 1-866-248-3049 or visit our website at www.simonspeakers.com.

For Billy Williams Jr.

ONE

Death was the only solution. Killing herself was more humane than facing the truth of how she destroyed their family. She authored the suicide letter in an admirable script, which explained each and every sickening detail, and left it neatly folded on his junky desk. She purposefully placed the suicide letter between his self-proclaimed Bible, *The 48 Laws of POWER*, and his *Animal Lovers* magazine. Without the shadow of a doubt, she knew for certain her husband would find it there.

When he was home, he spent more quality time at that damn desk—smoking marijuana, frolicking with the computer, playing email tag with his burnt-out animal enthusiasts, updating his Facebook account—than he did doing anything else, other than trying to get her pregnant.

She stood in the doorway of their nursery with a .45 automatic dangling at her side. A tear rolled down her face. Despair swallowed huge chunks of her soul without chewing first. She wondered how he'd found the time between the long hours he put in at the veterinarian hospital and traveling the country to participate in moral protest to design such an elaborate nursery for their unborn child. Then the next thought slammed into her gut like a fist: He would be the epitome of the "World's Greatest Dad" cliché. But she robbed him of that honor, which was part of the reason she knew killing herself was easier than taking on the truth.

She raised the .45 automatic to her temple and quickly realized the weapon was much too heavy to hold there while she choked up the raw nerve it took to pull the trigger. Switching positions, she gripped the polished handle with both hands and shoved the barrel under her chin like she had seen on TV. Better. Comfortable. *I can do this.*

There was no way she could come clean and stick around for the aftermath. He would snap; it most certainly would be nasty.

She clicked the safety off like a pro.

Tears rimmed her eyes, obscuring her vision of the baby crib.

She eased the hammer back, building up the grit.

She curled her trembling finger around the trigger.

She swallowed the lump in her throat and swore to herself that she'd do it on the count of three. End the lies. Escape the consequences. Get it over with. Check out. Her armpits were soaked with anxiety.

One.

She squeezed her radiant golden eyes shut.

"Two." This time she counted out loud, as if that would make the transition to three easier.

The phone rang once and frightened the shit out of her. She almost shot herself too soon. Their answering machine took the call. Her recorded voice said, "Hello, this is Cashmaire Fox." His: "And the one and only Chance Fox." Together, the perfect couple said, "We're not home. Leave us a message at the sound of the beep." Then the machine beeped.

"Cash, I've been sort of poking around with a few thoughts." It was him on the line: Chance Fox. "Since I'm a career moron, thinking isn't my most effective suit."

Cash opened her eyes. A single tear leaked and splashed onto her hand, as she visualized Chance while he spoke: blond dreadlocks pulled into a neat ponytail that pronounced a face so handsome that everyone considered him a pretty man.

"You're right about me not spending enough friggin' time in the dungeon. I just get caught up in my work and missing you bums me out…"

Cash listened to the rhythm of his breathing while he searched his mind for more words.

"While our crumb snatcher bakes in your oven, I'll be beside you the entire time. You're all I have and I love you." He sighed. "So I'll be at doctor visits, Lamaze class, and the whole nine yards." Then: "I leased a building ten minutes away from the dungeon. I'm opening my veterinarian practice there so I can always be near you and our little dude."

Cashmaire wished he would shut up. He was making it difficult to get to number three. She had to pull the trigger. She just had to, didn't she?

"Honest to goodness, dudette, you're the chick I've dreamed about my whole life: honest, intelligent, and gorgeous. Damn, I'm getting a serious boner just telling you how I feel. I mean…your idea of a perfect world—strange, I know—coincides perfectly with mine. Forgive me for not being attentive to your needs. You are important to me. Family means everything. I love you and our son so much. There are no lengths I won't go through to keep our family together or to eliminate anyone who tries to destroy our perfect world." Then: "Law 15: Crush Your Enemy Totally."

Cash dropped the .45 automatic and crumpled into a pile of tears and regret.

TWO

Cashmaire Fox was an extremely gorgeous bitch. The problem was she knew it. Her mannerisms and attitude and personality oozed *top-notch* bitch. Her black hair was perfect by everyone's standards. Lustrous, controlled, not a split hair or strand out of place, and it flowed down to her tramp stamp, the ankh tattoo on the small of her back. Her body was magnificent. A case study. A prototype. Not-so-blessed women envied and tried to imitate her God-given curves and delicate shape with expensive plastic surgery. Cash was the chick that other women hated, wishing they were fortunate enough to be born with good looks, a great ass, and a set of to-die-for tits.

And powerful men did their damnedest to exploit and acquire her feminine gifts. She turned down *Playboy* two years in a row, stalling for a multimillion-dollar paycheck. Anything less was an indecent proposal for a bitch of her caliber. Back in 2008, she and Chance attended a party at the Playboy mansion. Hugh Hefner went on and on about how Cashmaire looked like Paula Patton to the highest superlative. "Pure estrogen," Hugh had said about seven times in under two minutes. He promised Cashmaire that he wouldn't give up until she became *the* centerfold of all time. Hugh had never lain eyes on unadulterated beauty until Cashmaire sashayed onto his property.

Now Cashmaire turned away from her reflection in a Barnes & Noble showcase window and flipped up the collar of her shearling to keep the October chill at bay. She was no fool. None of her physical attributes would save her pretty little ass now. Speaking into her cell phone with an unsteady voice, she said, "I screwed up, Jazz. Everything is falling apart. Please tell me it's safe for you to talk."

Her best friend sighed. "Leon isn't around me, but—"

"Good. I hate that abusive bastard. Jazz, I'm really falling apart."

"Girl," Jazz said in a rushed tone, "sit your high-yellow tail down somewhere. You're not falling apart. Let me call you back. I'm at the Convention Center in the middle of a book signing."

Cashmaire focused on Jazz's new novel, *Two Weeks' Notice*, through the bookstore's showcase window. Her suspense thriller's presence in the establishment flaunted her *New York Times* bestseller status, pushing other new releases of the genre to mere obscurity. A life-size picture of Jazz holding the book towered over Cashmaire. Jazz was a slender beauty with an espresso complexion and a milk-colored smile. Her silky black bob cut framed her pretty face. Her mesmerizing eyes lured fans and new readers into the store. Cashmaire couldn't believe a picture like this existed of Jazz. Made Cash wonder what Jazz's publicist did to get her to agree to the photo shoot that inspired such a memorable picture. It was a complete makeover from Jazz's uninspiring norm. Things had really changed since their college days. Back then it was Jazz who showcased her beauty and Cash who hid hers behind drab clothing. Their roles flipped when Leon broke Jazz and Chance empowered Cash.

Cashmaire thought about Chance and turned away from her best friend's adorable image into a cold breeze that reddened the tip of her nose. An icy finger crept up her spine. She started pacing because her nerves were kicking a huge dent in her ass.

"You can't call me back," Cash said.

"And why not?"

"Because I'm at Hopkins International Airport."

They sparred in silence; Cashmaire felt herself winning.

"Excuse me? You're here in Cleveland and didn't tell me you were coming?"

"News to me too," Cashmaire said barely above a whisper.

"Are you serious?"

"I'm in trouble. Come get me before I lose it."

"Well, this is a plus. This means I won't be getting my butt kicked tonight. Leon won't hit me when witnesses are around." Jazz sighed. "Chill out. I'll be there in twenty minutes."

"Hurry, okay?" Cashmaire shoved the phone in her deep pockets and bundled herself against the cold. There was no turning back now. In nineteen minutes, she would reveal the secret she was certain would destroy her marriage, devastate a good man's life, and perhaps interrupt her loving friendship with Jazz. Cashmaire headed inside the terminal in search of a coffee shop. She wanted to be good and hopped up on caffeine while she figured out the best approach to lift the burden of such a nasty secret.

THREE

Something foul strangled the pit of Jazz Smith's stomach and sent an irritating sensation along her nerve endings. She masked her absorbing brown eyes with a pair of dollar-store sunglasses and put her foot on the accelerator. The sleek automobile followed the command without effort. When Jazz turned into the airport's arrival-and-pickup section, the foulness in her core turned sour. Cashmaire, her best friend of eleven years, the only soul who knew what had happened to her July 22, 2001, was nothing close to a "spur of the moment" woman.

Cashmaire's typical Type A personality didn't allow for any spontaneity. Her meticulous planning was downright anal. So this unplanned visit absolutely scared the heebie-jeebies out of Jazz. And what had Cashmaire meant by she was in trouble? As Jazz eased the car to a stop, she prayed that everything was alright.

As usual, another unanswered prayer; it was no fucking surprise, though. Jazz knew her petition had been rejected when she looked through the throng of travelers and internalized the pitiful look etched in Cashmaire's face. Jazz sighed and shook her head. She wished she could write a formal grievance to God for neglecting His responsibilities as far as her prayer requests were concerned. This God relationship was totally unfair. He was nothing but a damn control freak.

Cashmaire's beautiful manila complexion was minus its ever-present luster. That gave Jazz the creeps. Cashmaire's body language didn't sing, didn't demand the spotlight like normal. Something had Cashmaire spooked.

Jazz tapped the horn, then she reached across the seat to open the passenger's door as her friend reluctantly approached. Cashmaire eased into the seat and burst into tears. Jazz couldn't help but notice that Cashmaire was still the prettiest woman she'd ever seen, even when she was sad and mascara-stained tears ran down her face.

I can handle whatever this is, Jazz thought.

FOUR

Not many blocks away from Howard University, Chance Fox hit a joint he'd scored off some street kids as he strolled up North Capitol and rounded the corner onto Seaton Place. He held his breath as the powerful reefer smoke saturated his lungs, then tossed the roach into the wind before it burnt his fingertips again. His wife found reefer burns to be unattractive and she closed her legs every time she saw them. Still, he should have hit the joint once more. He told himself to grab another bag before he caught his flight home.

A fantastic high was a satisfying self-indulgence after a long and grueling day of protesting against human atrocities on Capitol Hill. He shook his head in disgust as a cold breeze nibbled on his ears and reddened his white cheeks. How could the nitwit policy-makers consider passing bills in support of legalizing gay marriages when God declared same-sex relations forbidden? Didn't the jerks know that the Lord rained brimstone and fire on Sodom and Gomorrah for the same indulgences? Surely the shitheads didn't think their congressional power was superior to God. Families didn't come from loins of the same gender. Two patriarchs had no moral right raising an impressionable child in a homosexual family structure as if it were normal and the child wouldn't be affected. The fucks. And that pissed Chance off, so he protested every chance he got.

Chance pulled his backpack off and stepped through the door of Liberian Orphanage. Immediately he spotted the reverend chatting it up with an acne-face receptionist bimbo with platinum blonde hair and cheap clothes. He and the reverend made eye contact and smiled. Chance crossed the room and shook the reverend's hand. "Nice to see you again, Reverend." Chance removed a football from his backpack, a well-worn copy of *The 48 Laws of POWER* stuck out the bag. "Where are the little dudes? I wanna toss the pigskin around with them before it gets dark."

"Come sit with me a moment, son." The reverend led Chance to a set of soft leather chairs in front of a defunct fireplace. "You reek of marijuana and your eyes are glassy."

"You know me, dude." Chance shrugged.

The reverend nodded. "Yes, I have come to know you. We purchased a new furnace and had the roof repaired with the last check you and your wife donated. Thank you, and don't forget to thank the missus for me."

"Oh shit, dude, I almost forgot." Chance dug in his backpack and fished out an envelope stuffed with cash. "Here, take it. I know you'll put it to good use for the boys. And that's between me and you, if you get my meaning."

The reverend nodded while fingering the envelope. "Why do you do it, Chance?"

"Gee whiz, dude, it's only money. We have more than—"

"I'm not speaking about the money, son. I'm referring to the causes you involve yourself in and showing up here every month to spend time with these children."

Chance shrugged a *why does it matter?* "I believe in what I believe in and that's all there is to it. The boys here have no family. I grew up without a father, so if I can come here and put a smile on their face, do things that a man would do with them so they'll have memories of someone giving two shits about them, then it'll take a security guard to keep me away from here. But I'll just kick a dent in his ass and make him quit."

The reverend cracked a smile. "You're gonna be a great father. How far along is Mrs. Fox?"

"She isn't showing yet. That means a lot coming from you, dude. You believing I'll be a decent dad." Chance rose from the chair. "Where are they?"

"Right through those doors. They just finished supper and are now watching *Avatar.*"

Chance pushed through the door with the football in hand. "Who's up for a game of catch?"

"Chance, you came back." A little black kid from West Africa jumped in his arms as the other boys rushed to hug him.

FIVE

Cashmaire did her damndest to stop her hands from shaking. Coffee spilt over the rim of the Starbucks cup. When Jazz's shiny Mercedes SL600 crawled to a stop, Cashmaire seriously considered becoming a coward, tucking tail, and fleeing back to Denver where she could keep her secret safe. Hell, she'd kept it under lock and key for the last eighteen years of her ambiguous life. Then she'd only have to lie her way out of the lies she'd already told Chance.

The car horn was blown.

Cashmaire's legs were rebellious, downright uncooperative. She walked as if she were dragging two stubborn concrete pillars. The first time her secret came out as a teenager all hell broke loose, which she felt would be the same result now. She climbed onto the soft leather passenger seat—body and nerves in complete protest—and crumbled into a ball of crocodile tears.

Jazz burst into a fit of tears too. "Why in the hell are we crying like this? Cash, what's wrong?"

"Just drive, okay?"

Twenty minutes and several miles later, they exited Interstate 90 just ahead of rush hour. Cash remembered the last time she was home in Cleveland. Jazz was in the hospital after falling down a flight of steps. At least that's what Leon forced her to say. Cash dug a napkin from the glove compartment and dabbed at her swollen eyes. "I should have told him years ago."

"Uh, being privy to the subject of this conversation would really help me follow it." Jazz half-assed kept an eye on the road, the other glued on Cash.

Cash hated that. Hated that Jazz had the tendency to pay more attention to her passengers than she did the road. Cash started imagining she could control the car from the passenger's seat with her make-believe steering wheel, accelerator, and brakes.

"And where's your luggage?"

Cash shrugged an *I don't know.* "Left in a hurry. Panicking. What are we going to tell Leon?"

"That he won't be kicking my ass tonight."

"You got that right. Not on my watch." The message Chance left on their answering machine trickled through her mind. "You know how obsessed Chance is about the white-picket-fence, American dream cliché. Starting a—"

"Especially the part about having kids and buying them puppies." Jazz nodded. "He takes that shit way too far if you ask me."

"He—"

"Where is Mr. American Dream anyway? He doesn't know you're here, does he?" Jazz picked up speed for no apparent reason.

Cash hated that too. In fact, she hated riding in a car with Jazz if she wasn't doing the driving. She eased her foot off the imaginary accelerator, hoping Jazz's foot would do the same.

Jazz said, "Did he… If he hit you, we're gonna fuck him up. I take enough abuse for the both of us. Chance is hip to the Emancipation Proclamation whether he's in total agreement with it or not."

Cash shook her head. "He won't put his hands on me." She wasn't so sure that would still be true if he knew the truth. "He's in D.C.

lobbying against gay marriages and same-sex couples adopting and foster parenting children."

"Figures." Jazz smirked. "His ass never agreed with the concept 'to each his own.' What if people were still tripping about inter-racial relationships? Then y'all would be under scrutiny. Besides, what does he want to be, a veterinarian or an anti-gay advocate?" Jazz turned her nose up. "No disrespect, but I might write a book and put Chance in it. I'd kill him in the title: *Chance is Dead*." Jazz laughed.

Cash's insides did a somersault. She really wished she had gone through with her suicide ambitions. "He hired a contractor to build this high-end addition on our home. A nursery; it's really beautiful." She waited for Jazz to chew and digest that. And they were still moving too fast for Cash's comfort or for what was deemed lawful.

Jazz frowned; her thin brows went southward and ducked behind her sunglasses. "You're pregnant?"

Did Jazz already know her secret? Cash contemplated the question. It sounded like Jazz was *really* asking *if* pregnancy was even possible instead of questioning if she was. Maybe Cash was just being paranoid, so she brushed her thoughts off. "No, I'm not, but Chance thinks so."

Now Jazz's brows shot northward. "You didn't."

"The truth wasn't an option; it would break his heart. He wants to start a family so bad." Then: "And he's been trying so hard, eating all types of supplements that are supposed to make his sperm potent. For the last three months we had sex every day, multiple times a day. He fucked me sore. I couldn't take it anymore. So I lied."

"Ooh-wee, you're dead-ass wrong for that one. That's some foul shit, Cash."

Cash finished her coffee. "I know."

"Then straighten it. Chance is way too fanatical in his quest for a family for me. Even though y'all are mismatched as hell, ebony and ivory, and it's crazy how much y'all look alike being from different ethnicities, but he loves you and he deserves the truth. You know that fool is borderline retarded. Can't you tell Chance is one of those crazy white boys? He might snap and get primitive if you let this go too far."

"It's gone too far." She'd known that the morning the contractors showed up at their house ready to punch the clock. "And they do say people who've been together a long time start looking like each other."

"Straighten your issues with him out."

"Can't."

"What do you mean by *can't?* Tell him why you lied, he'll understand." Jazz made an *I'm thinking* expression. "Then again, he might not."

"I can't have children." Now the truth was starting to flow. "I've known since puberty." Cash felt the car pick up more speed. "Everything Chance and I share, all that we are, is built on lies. Selfishly I married him knowing I couldn't give him the very thing he wants most in this world." After a deep breath, she whispered, "A family."

Jazz was flying down Lakeshore Boulevard and looking directly at Cash. If Jazz kept up this nonsense, Cash knew for a fact they would be pulled over by Bratenahl police.

"Slow down, Danica Patrick." Cash tapped her imaginary brakes.

"Girl, I'm not driving that fast." Then: "Whoa, back up. How come you can't have babies? What's the matter with you?"

Cash swallowed. The moment of truth was upon her. Not once

had Cash doubted the authenticity of their friendship. Today, however, she hoped that she wasn't about to share her secret with the wrong person. Her vision blurred with tears. "It's complicated." She blinked her sight clear. "I'm—Jazz, watch out!"

A huge pit bull-looking dog stood in the middle of the street, frozen in the path of the Mercedes' onslaught. Cash stomped on her imaginary brakes and braced herself for impact. Jazz stood on the real brakes. The Mercedes careened to the left, Jazz's best effort to avoid hitting Scooby-Doo. The last thing Cash remembered was her head going through the windshield.

ands down, today, October 17, 2010, was the worst fucking day of Chance Fox's life. On second thought, it was a toss-up between the day Nirvana's lead singer, Kurt Cobain, got juiced up on heroin and shot himself to death in a Seattle hotel.

Chance's blond dreadlocks were pulled into a stringy ponytail. With his hair out of the way, he knew people would focus on his eyebrow piercing and the Marlboro tucked behind his ear. He didn't smoke cigarettes. The cigarette behind-the-ear thing was edgy and he always thought it looked cool. He wore a quarter-length leather over a Guns & Roses T-shirt and cutoff camouflage pants, as if it wasn't damn near winter. He reeked of marijuana and his fluorescent orange high-top Adidas proved the weed was good.

Chance had been languishing at Metro Hospital on Cleveland's west side for nine solid hours while the trauma team worked diligently to save his wife's and unborn son's life. All he knew for sure as of this moment was that the air bag on Cash's side of the car had malfunctioned. He had a buddy, a personal-injury lawyer, who was going to ram one hell of a lawsuit up Mercedes' tight rectum.

Doctor Shoemaker, young and exhausted-looking, probably from a nineteen-hour shift and a going-nowhere relationship, Chance thought when the man trudged into the private room hospital administration had stuck Chance in to worry himself sick. Shoemaker wore green scrubs and crepe-soled shoes. He pushed his fingers through his blond hair, removed the surgical mask, and shook Chance's hand. "Hi, Mr. Fox, I'm Doctor Andrew Shoemaker."

Chance's bowels knotted. His mouth instantly went dry as the Mojave. To be honest, Chance wasn't sure if he should take a break or keep pacing a groove in the floor. "Dude, give it to me even. Will she live?"

"It's up in the air, but it doesn't look too good." Chance watched Shoemaker work the tension out of his neck. "Do you have a relationship with a higher power, Mr. Fox?"

Shoemaker's prying and impersonal tone didn't sit too well with Chance. He had a good mind to blow off some steam and ring Shoemaker's scrawny fucking neck. Instead Chance let his anger simmer and said, "For crying out loud, dude. You've got to be kidding me. What goddamn difference does it make?"

"Your wife suffered major head trauma. She'll never look the same. Close, but not the same. She's undergone extensive reconstructive surgery. On top of that, she suffered some iffy internal injuries in the abdominal region. So if you're acquainted with something greater than yourself, now's the time to ask for help. Mrs. Fox needs it."

Chance almost bolted from the room to find his wife when Shoemaker referenced Cash's stomach area. "What about our baby? Were you able to save him?" No one could tell Chance that their unborn child wasn't a boy. From the moment Cash announced the news of her pregnancy, he intuitively knew. He had gotten carried away—according to Cash—and had the nursery constructed to resemble a boxing ring, a discipline that he was considered a pro in. Like father like son would become. Chance often imagined himself teaching his son the art of fighting. The room had life-size murals of legendary UFC fighters—his niche—splattered across the walls. He'd even gone out and bought a two-stroke minibike and a gas-powered go-cart knowing it'd be at least five years before Chance Jr. could learn to ride them. That didn't matter to Chance Sr., he was having a boy! Nothing was too good for his boy.

Chance penetrated Shoemaker with bloodshot eyes. It dawned on him that Shoemaker was a spitting image of the late '80s sitcom character Doogie Howser. "Dude, please tell me that my son is alright."

"Mr. Fox, uh—" Shoemaker scratched his head. "—you don't know, do you?"

"Know what?"

"You should sit down for this."

SEVEN

For the last nine days, Chance—pissed, unshowered, nine years sobriety shot to hell—sat vigil beside Cash's hospital bed praying she'd die a painful death. But the resilient bitch just wouldn't croak. She held on to life like she had something to prove. The entire nine days Chance tried to drink himself numb, but not even Cash's morphine drip could numb his pain.

And for that, she deserved more than a coma. Today he would see to it that she got everything she had coming to her. Chance sensed a presence enter the room; then he heard the squeak of soft shoes; then he smelled Shoemaker's Herbal Essence shampoo. Chance didn't budge. His focus was on Cash, on the electrocardiographic contraption, wishing the oscilloscope screen would read *flatline*.

"You should reconsider this," Shoemaker said with a strained voice. "She isn't brain dead. Life support will prolong your wife's life without curing or reversing her underlying medical conditions."

Shoemaker's concern earned him a dark glance; Chance set his jaw in an uncompromising line and said, "She has no Advanced Healthcare Directive or a living will. That leaves the decision to withhold or withdraw artificial life support up to me, dude." Chance pawed at his irritating, overgrown beard. He was dying for a shave. And the tensed energy pouring out of Shoemaker wasn't making his irritation any better. "Just butt out, Doogie, and hand over the consent forms."

Shoemaker moved toward Chance. "They're here."

"Give 'em up." Chance held out his hand, still watching Cash's vitals, still wishing a flatline into existence. Whoever had told him that your frame of mind becomes your reality was full of shit, a goddamn liar, because Cash was still alive.

Shoemaker said, "It is my duty to inform you of my professional opinion. You're being vindictive and you'll regret it." Then: "My personal belief is that she was wrong for keeping a secret of such magnitude. But two wrongs don't make a right, Mr. Fox. Allow her condition to naturally stabilize, if that's possible."

Chance put his John Hancock on the forms, then he dug deep and hog spit in Cash's swollen face. "Law 9: Win Through Your Actions, Never Through Argument. Always remember that, Doctor Shoemaker. Pull the plug." To Cash's unanimated body, he said, "Now we're even, douche bag."

EIGHT

Jazz's lean body still hurt like hell. But this hurt was nothing compared to the many physical pains Leon had caused her to endure over the years. Every time she moved, she found something else that ached, but that wasn't going to deter her from putting a stop to Chance's bullshit. She would never be able to live with herself if she didn't at least try to stick up for her best friend.

Jazz was a slender spark plug. Not much in the way of tits, though. Her ass, however, was just right, an attractive little tush. She was an elusively good-looking black beauty, the kind of woman who was pretty without a drop of makeup. Elusive because she hid her naturally long hair stuffed in ball caps of the country's worst sports teams. Sports fanatics scrunched their faces as if something stunk when they read the insignias on her hats. Think Detroit Lions and L.A. Clippers. She hid sensationally long lashes and deep amber eyes behind $1.99 convenience store sunglasses. Always: indoors, outdoors, day, night. Her jaw-dropping dainty body was always obscured by dark, oversized clothing. The only visible signs of her outward beauty were her shamefully flawless, chocolate complexion and her kissable lips. The way Jazz had been conditioned to hide her God-given beauty was downright heartbreaking.

Because of the bumps and bruises, it took her eleven minutes to accomplish the three-minute walk from her hospital room to Cash's. She hobbled into the room, using her IV stand for support, wearing a flimsy hospital gown that made her an exhibitionist of sorts, at least to anyone who was blessed enough to be behind her.

Chance wiped his mouth with the back of a hand. "Now we're even, douche bag."

Jazz waved Shoemaker away when he rushed to assist her. "Chance, you psycho, what is your problem? You can't be serious. What if a medical miracle happens that can cure her? What if a miracle beyond medicine is possible?"

Chance was unresponsive. He looked put out. That's how she would describe him right now if she were writing this scene in a novel. His silence was loud and unnerving and working its magic. Out of the corner of her eye she saw Jaden lingering in the doorway, leaning against its frame. She'd distinctly told his hardheaded ass to stay put, but that was like talking to a brick wall. So there he was, behind her, clutching that damn basketball. She tried to close the back of her gown, but it was useless.

She lifted her sunglasses and gave Jaden the evil eye, warning him to behave, and then turned to Shoemaker. "Dammit, even I'm familiar with your Hippocratic Oath. In the interest of life or death, can't you do something to stop this fool? Call Al Sharpton, Jesse Jackson, Farrakhan, Michael Baisden. Get an injunction— anything but stand here looking like a donkey." It was this moment that Shoemaker reminded Jazz of someone, but she couldn't put her finger on it.

With a brow raised, Chance finally spoke up, "Dudette, wait a minute, you knew. Didn't you?"

That was a tentative question, she thought. Then she thought about how much she loathed being referred to as *dudette*. So white boyish. Anything she said at this point would only rub salt in his wound. "Lying about the baby was cruel, Chance."

"Cruel? You haven't seen cruel. I'm such a dope," he said to himself. Then his ominous blue gaze cut through the room like sophisticated laser beams and landed on Jazz. "You're so in for it if I find out you knew."

Was that a threat or a declaration that he'd be disappointed with her as well? How was she supposed to know Cash was stringing him along about a baby? She slid the sunglasses from her hair and eased them back on her face to break the intensity of Chance's blue-eyed gaze. "I can't imagine how you feel. I'd be lying if I said otherwise. But nothing—nothing—can justify you taking her off the life support." She faced Shoemaker and found Jaden standing beside her, which was cool because she was uncomfortable with the idea of him seeing her lace-flavored panties. "You're a doctor. You have no right helping him play God. So are you just gonna fucking stand here? That's my best friend lying in this bed. At least pretend like you believe in your oath and talk some sense into this nut case." The recognition hit her. The resemblance was spooky. Shoemaker looked like that guy who used to be on TV, Doogie Whatchamacallit.

"You're being very rude and asking for help in the same sentence. Hell of an example you are," Jaden said, the basketball wedged under his armpit.

"Shut the hell up, Jaden. Nobody asked you. Stay out of grown folks' business. If you would have stayed in my room like you were supposed to, you wouldn't be dipping." She pointed an authoritative finger. "And don't bounce that ball in here."

Chance looked at Jazz like she had blown a fuse and was a breath away from heavy medication, but she didn't care. Shoemaker gave her a look that she blew off too.

"You're warped," Chance said, shaking his head.

"Mr. Fox," Shoemaker said, "terminating someone's life isn't a decision you want to rush into."

That's it, Jazz thought, grow a set of balls.

Chance laughed.

The sound made Jazz's skin crawl. Jaden eased to Cash's bedside—opposite of Chance, facing them all—and held her limp hand.

Shoemaker said, "Please reconsider this, Mr. Fox. Three neurologists conclusively agree that your wife isn't in a persistent vegetative state. Her condition is minimal consciousness at best."

"This is wrong, Chance, and you know it. You remember exactly how she felt about the Terri Schiavo situation—she didn't fucking agree with Schiavo's husband, Michael. You even flew down to Florida with her so she could stand vigil."

"You're poking around in my spousal business," Chance said. "Buzz off, would you?"

Jazz was having a hard time believing that her best friend's life was hanging in the balance and would be over in the matter of hours because this punk couldn't keep his anger and immature emotions in check. She and Cash had discussed most of life's *what ifs*, but this scenario was never examined eleven years ago in their dorm room over butter pecan ice cream, Swiss Rolls, and episodes of *Ricki Lake*.

"I'll see what I can do about starting the proceedings for an injunction," Shoemaker said, as he all but bolted out the room.

"Come on, Jaden. Let's get the hell away from this mistake of a human being."

Jaden squeezed Cash's hand. Her eyes fluttered open. Jazz could tell that Cash was seriously studying Jaden. She weakly attempted to smile at him around the breathing tubes.

Jazz frowned at Chance and went to Cash's side. "See, you fucker. Do you see this, motherfucker? See what you would have done." Jazz silently thanked God for showing up.

The instant Cash opened her eyes, October 26, 2010, turned out to be worse than the day Kurt Cobain ate a shotgun round for dinner. A shiver crept down Chance's spine as a scream left his mouth. This time he screamed louder than he had when Shoemaker let him in on Cash's little secret.

NINE

Eventually everyone must face the consequences of their misdeeds. Cash remembered that was the theme of Jazz's latest work in progress. Cash had no doubt that she was finally about to tangle with the consequences of her misdeeds. She grimaced as she tried to sit up, then figured it was better to just stay put.

Chance's cold blue eyes grew more intense. She felt him scrutinizing her as if she were a complete stranger. The bitterness poisoning his body language was disturbing. She felt his anger tingle the marrow of her bones. His normal fluid motions were stiff and hard like a stubborn tumor. His high energy was now humid and acrid.

Cash's thoughts spun out of control like a car with bald tires doing ninety on a sheet of black ice. It didn't take a brainiac to know that Chance had questioned the doctors about Chance Jr. and learned more than his fragile sanity was capable of handling. She forced herself to straighten her mental steering wheel and reestablish control of her private thoughts. "You've been drinking." She coughed, short of breath. "Your eyes say things that I'm terrified to hear."

"Guess this explains the hair missing from your snatch that you tried to explain away." Chance looked at her with disgust. "And you were faking the periods."

She nodded.

"Should have gone with my first mind when we met: left a daycare center in your mouth and moved on." Then: "You gross me out. How come you didn't just die?"

His words raised the short hairs on her neck. Silence soaked in the room while the bond connecting them splintered and shattered. He had never spoken a cruel word to her. Now she regretted not ending it all back in Denver. Right then her life turned into a series of *should have nevers*. She should have never accepted the payment to go out with him back in college. Should have never fallen in love with him knowing her situation. Should have never lied in the first place. Should have never gotten on that plane or allowed Jazz to drive.

She whispered, "I'm sorry, Chance. I'm so sorry. Please find it in your heart to forgive me." She reached up to catch her tears and felt a series of stitches distorting her good looks. She felt him watching her as she traced the wounds.

"Serves you right. Hope you heal ugly." His sneer matched his words. "You were never gonna tell me."

"Don't you understand I couldn't?"

"Baloney." Then: "You're a lying, conniving, cunt bitch."

"It didn't start out that way. Never was my intention to deceive you."

"Why didn't you tell me then?"

She coughed, then she steadied her breathing. "The truth?" After all this, the truth still felt like an impossible task.

"That would be swell for a consummate liar, but you're not capable."

She found the contraption to manipulate the bed, made a show of adjusting the bed to her desired taste. *God, I know we aren't familiar, but please give me the words.* "My self-esteem was low. I isolated myself from my peers because of it. Wasn't sure if I was able to…you know, function in a relationship. Then you came along and gave me life, validated my existence as a woman."

"That's fuckin' absurd. You're a monster. Here's a promise: buzz the fuck off or I'll be detrimental to your health."

"But…. I still love—"

"For crying out loud, go fuck yourself." He headed for the door.

"Chance, wait, please. What can I do to make this right?"

He stopped in his tracks and lingered there for a moment. With his back to her, he said, "Drop dead, you nasty nigger bitch."

TEN

Buank. Buank. Buank. Buank.

"For the last damn time, Jaden, stop dribbling that ball in this house," Jazz said, scowling at him through her sunglasses. She calmed her nerves with several deep breaths, then she poured Cash and herself tall glasses of homemade tea.

"LeBron James practiced like this every day when he was my age. Look what it did for him. Daddy didn't have a problem with me practicing, so why are you tripping?"

Buank. Buank. Buank. Buank.

"Bet LeBron didn't practice in the house."

"How would you know?" Jaden's narrow face and big eyes were a clear indication that he would be a heartthrob when he grew up and matured. He was frail and definitely tall enough—six-one—at fifteen to have NBA ambitions. And Jazz knew he was hardly done growing yet. His baggy urban clothing and long cornrows gave him thug appeal, but Jaden was a suburbanite who didn't have a clue about the mean streets.

Buank. Buank. Buank. Buank.

"Honey—" Firm eye contact. "—I'm sorry. Never in a million years would I want you to be apart from your father. If there were some way, any way, to put things back the way they were—" She snapped her fingers. "—I would, that fast." Then: "Family means everything. Everything else comes second."

"My daddy was going to practice with me every day after work until I went pro. Because of what you did, that's not possible anymore, is it?"

Despair surged through her veins and found a home in her heart. "You're making me feel terrible again."

"You should."

"Can we please finish whatever this is later, after Cashmaire leaves?"

"It's not like I can up and leave if I wanted to." He pinned her with his eyes. "I'm stuck here with you, remember?"

She bit her tongue and bolted from the kitchen before he could spew more venom. She didn't know how to deal with Jaden's anger. She'd lost plenty of sleep trying to figure it out, and she was sure tonight wouldn't be any different.

Buank. Buank. Buank. Buank.

"It's hard to believe it's been six months since the accident," Jazz said, setting a cup of tea in front of Cash, then settling herself on the couch with the other.

Cash drifted off for a moment as if she were revisiting something unpleasant from times past. "That day changed so many people's lives." Cash nodded blankly. "No matter how you slice it, it's my entire fault. Do you have any idea of how hard that is to live—"

"We've been down this road too many times before. Damn, girl, if you apologize one more time, I'll go crazy." Jazz laughed— alone—at her weak attempt at humor. She was sure that people thought she was touched, evident from the way they behaved around her after the accident. Everyone except Cash and her literary agent. After all, "crazy" was one of the terms Leon loosely threw around during the disposition of their divorce.

Cash got quiet; silence saturated the room.

"I know what you're thinking." Jazz sipped her tea. "It wasn't your fault, you know? I was only involved in that marriage. I was never committed." She pulled her ponytail through the back of her Washington Wizards cap.

Cash smirked. "Like there's a big difference, Jazz."

"In a bacon and egg breakfast," Jazz said, "the chicken is involved, but the pig is committed."

"Yeah, you were just barely treading water. I'm not thrilled about how it happened. I'm just glad the divorce happened before he drowned you."

"Tell me about it. The accident threw me a life jacket."

Buank. Buank. Buank. Buank.

Always four irritating bounces, Jazz thought. Then she thought about how Jaden felt that she had taken him away from his father. "My only hope is that Leon does right by his son." Her gaze fell on Cash, who immediately turned away. "I wasn't staring at your scar."

Cash traced the scar that crawled from her earlobe to the corner of her mouth. "I know. I'm not really self-conscious about my looks."

"No lie, it's like you've been blessed twice. You look totally different, but you're still the prettiest woman I've ever seen. Nothing can flaw what God has given you." Jazz waved nonchalantly. "You can hardly even see the scar anyhow."

Cash perked up and grinned. "Think *Playboy* will still take me?"

Jazz nodded. "And pay you a million dollars. Girl, do you hear me? You got it going on."

"So," Cash said, changing the subject, "when will the new book be done?"

Books were a subject Jazz wanted no part of. She shrugged an

I'm not sure. "Can't find the mental strength to write." In fact, she didn't believe she would ever write again. Eric, her literary agent, was pressing her to get her ass in gear because Simon & Schuster was screaming about a breach of contract. With everything she was going through on the day-to-day basis, Eric, Simon, *and* Schuster could kiss her natural black ass.

Cash nudged Jazz. "Come on now, we have to regroup, redirect, and recommit."

"That day in the car," Jazz said. "You never told me why you couldn't have kids."

"Let it go. It's no longer important."

"So what about Chance, anything?"

"Not a peep since he walked out on me in the hospital."

"Fuck him," Jazz said with conviction. "Y'all were an odd couple anyway. But it still intrigues me how much y'all used to look alike. Look at the bright side, though, you've moved back home. Now we can hang out like best friends are supposed to. You've got yourself a brand-new start, and you've landed yourself a great job with the district attorney's office." Then: "Even though Cuyahoga County residents view you as a carpetbagger."

"About that."

Buank. Buank. Buank. Buank.

"I could scream! That boy and that damn ball." Jazz shifted toward the sound. "Jaden, would you please stop." She faced Cash, feeling awkward. "Excuse me."

"Take your sunglasses off."

Jazz withdrew and sat back on the couch. "For what?"

"Because you're not a vampire, Jazz. I want to see your eyes."

"It's that serious?"

"What I have to say, yes."

Jazz sucked her teeth, removed the sunglasses, and bulged her eyes. "Satisfied?"

"Your eyes are so attractive. I don't know why you still insist on hiding them. Leon is gone. Hard to believe you and your author photo are one and the same."

"Whatever. Talk."

"The new start thing." Cash threaded her fingers with Jazz's.

"What about it?"

"The person you once knew as Cashmaire Fox—" Cash touched her scar. "—she died in our car accident. With my new look, now I can start over as Scenario Davenport and leave Chance and my past behind."

Jazz thought about what Cash said for a long moment then nodded. She understood Scenario Davenport's position perfectly well. "I understand." With the apropos of nothing, Jazz said, "Girl, did you hear about the hieroglyphics serial killer murdering all those people in Denver?"

"Yeah, honey child, that's awful. As long as he stays out of Cleveland, Ohio, I won't have to prosecute him."

ELEVEN

She pushed through the rental office door like a stormy wind. The gray-haired blind man sitting behind the desk smelled and committed her expensive fragrance to memory. His nose was better than a bloodhound's; it never failed him.

He sniffed the air. "Never smelled that perfume before. What is it?"

The urgent clicking of her heels came to a stop in front of the counter he was holed up behind. "You wouldn't have. It's called Thin Air. Had it designed for my personal use." Then: "Heard through the grapevine you would help me."

He tried to pinpoint her ambiguous accent. Midwest with a touch of West Coast. "Depending on what kinds of help you's in the business of needing."

"A safe apartment. Off the radar."

He said, "I stock those. What's your name?"

"Uh, Ca—umm…Marie. No last name."

"Wells, Ca-umm-Marie, I recons you needs to take your troubles elsewheres. Don't like or gives my help to liars." He stuck his stubby fingertips back on a Braille copy of *Push Comes To Shove* and ignored her.

"I'm not leaving," she said, her voice taut with tension. "There is no other place for me to go."

"Hiding from someone, Ca-umm-Marie? The likes of the law? Don't fool with lawbreakers."

"It's my husband." She paused for effect, letting the implications of a defenseless woman hiding from her husband trickle through the man's mind. "He's clever. He'll find me if I use my real name."

"That bad?"

"Worse." Then: "He's killed before."

"Supposing you wanna pay cash and not leave a paper trail."

"Yes, yes." She breathed a sigh of relief. "I knew I came to the right place."

"Not ifens I don't know your real name." He snapped the book closed. "Ms. Ca-umm-Marie, I can't see a lick. Borns that way. And I don't keep records or receipts of anything. So I only operates on *real* names and what my nose smells. Surely you heard that through the grapevine, too."

Winner winner chicken dinner, she thought, then she leaned forward and whispered her name.

TWELVE

On April 21, 2011, Chance's research led him to the unsavory end of Cedar Road. The elderly brick buildings were hunched over like they had suffered a lifetime of abuse. Some of the crippled buildings had broken windows that made them look snaggle-toothed. He had obviously been fed bad information. He looked at the lowercase lettering—*stormie bishop, esq.*—on the stained-glass door and started to say fuck it. A man who didn't think to capitalize his name wasn't worth Chance's time or hard-earned money. But a pack of dangerous-looking thugs bopping in his direction urged him to go inside. No use for unnecessary violence and troublesome attention.

Stormie Bishop, the best damn criminal defense attorney in the Midwest, at least that's how the source who'd referred Stormie to Chance described him. For days Chance tried to imagine what the "best" looked like. He sure didn't figure on Stormie Bishop being such a casual man: Old Navy T-shirt and well-worn denims, loafers and a diamond earring with hair as white as an Antarctic blizzard.

Stormie covered the phone. "Just be a sec; take a seat." He gestured to the phone. "Granddaughter wants a new car with subacceptable grades. Generation Y." He flagged his hand. "Move the junk."

Chance looked at the *Federal Supplements* and other law books stacked in the only chair facing Stormie's desk. He wondered why this jerk-off would refer to his professional tools as junk. "I'll stand. I won't be poking around long." He adjusted the bulky book bag on his shoulder, then he took in the office.

It wasn't decked out with all the expensive trappings he expected the best would have; it was the exact opposite: Unimpressive. Cluttered. Dirty. A minifridge and a food-stained microwave were shoved in the corner. The area looked like a rest haven for roaches. A drip coffee maker sat on the desk next to the computer. Its Home Row keys were stained brown. Chance couldn't figure that one out. Maybe Stormie stirred his Folgers with his fingers and didn't wash his hands before getting on the computer. The only window in the room offered an ugly view of the senile brick building next door.

Piles of *Criminal Law Reporters* and law briefs occupied every available crevice. From the looks of things, Stormie Bishop was far from high-powered. More like static electricity. Chance started to shove off and take a look at his alternative research options now that the thugs outside were more than likely gone. But the Marc Newson Lockheed lounge chair Stormie's narrow ass was parked in told a different story. Chance knew the chair was worth a couple million easy. Who could afford an ass parking space like that but someone who knew their shit?

Stormie hung up the phone. "Sorry about that." He stood and offered Chance a hand. "How can I help you, Mr....?"

"Fox. Mr. Fox, but call me Chance." Chance noted Stormie's firm, confident grip.

"So what brings you, Chance?"

"How many limbs do you charge to defend a capital murder case?"

"Depends."

"On?"

"Whether I'm pleading it down to a lesser charge or taking it to trial."

"Going the distance."

"Three hundred thousand," Stormie said.

"Does that cover multiple bodies or only one?"

"Depends."

"On?"

"If the bodies were killed together in one location or if they were killed separately in different locations."

Chance said, "Different."

"Per par share."

Chance tossed him the book bag. "It's all there."

Stormie unzipped the bag and took a peek. "Who…who am I defending?" He slowly and carefully set his eyes on Chance. "There hasn't been a capital murder case around here since that fellow Anthony Sewell murdered those street girls and buried them in that house on Imperial Avenue."

"I haven't whacked them yet," Chance said without a glimmer of humor, then headed toward the door. "Dude, I'll give you a buzz when I've done the deed."

Scenario Davenport watched the volley of subtle insults bounce from one sibling to the other. She sat in uncomfortable silence in her boss's office, not believing she had a front-row seat to this family feud.

"It's unethical," County Prosecutor Marcus Jefferson said and set his square chin. His tone wasn't kind; it suggested a history of contempt and inflexibility.

"But we're family," Miranda Brooks, a bejeweled woman with coiffed hair, said.

"Like that amounts to much. Funny, the *family* word only comes out your fat mouth when you need something. This time it works against you because it's a conflict of interest."

"You seem to act like you don't know we're talking about George, your only nephew."

"Who robbed a convenience store and carjacked a senior citizen to flee the scene of the crime." Then: "I can't prosecute his case because George *is* my nephew. It's called conflict of interest. It's the same reason why husbands and wives can't be forced to testify against each other."

Miranda Brooks said, "If Mother were alive—"

"She'd what, Miranda? Force me to break the law and risk my job and freedom to give your junkie son a break? Side with you as usual and beat me if I don't comply? We're not kids anymore, and she's fifteen years dead and I'm thrilled about it."

Scenario could tell from Miranda's facial expression that Marcus's words cut to the quick and set her temper on edge. Their moment of silence was everything but amicable; it was almost intolerable to inhale the fumes.

Marcus said, "I've pulled all the strings I am going to pull for poor George. He got those breaks while he was a juvenile. He crossed the adult line this time. He chose his path."

Scenario figured Miranda was too proud and hateful to cry. Instead she kept her tears in check and dabbed them with a fancy handkerchief.

"You're never going to change," Miranda said. "Mother was right about you. You're a selfish self-centered bastard, Mar Mar."

"Don't. Ever. Call me that again or I'll make you eat your words and lick your fingers when you're done."

"Isn't there anything you'll do for George?" She made an imaginary crucifix on her body. "He's my son."

"This is what I can do for you, Miranda," Marcus said. "Meet Ms. Scenario Davenport. She's my new assistant county prosecutor, my successor when I retire in a few years."

Scenario flinched when her boss said her name. She felt like he'd just thrown her under a bus. From the sheer look alone, Scenario could tell that Miranda was regarding her with as much contempt as humanly possible. Marcus's office was too small for the bitterness being stuffed into it. Scenario wanted to open the door but was certain she'd be blown into the hallway when the enormous pressure released. Scenario swallowed and offered a hand. "Nice to meet you, Mrs. Brooks."

"And?" Miranda looked at Scenario's hand like it was covered in shit. And she had the audacity not to hide her upturned nose.

"I'm assigning George's case to her," Marcus said with a smug smile.

Miranda stood up so fast it made Scenario woozy.

"She's an outsider," Miranda said. Her eyes burned with outrage.

"Assistant County Prosecutor Scenario Davenport is impartial, which is the only way to achieve justice with this sensitive matter you find yourself faced with."

Miranda stormed out without uttering another word and slammed the door behind her.

Marcus put his penetrating turquoise gaze on Scenario. "If anyone in this office ever calls me Mar Mar, you're fired. Are we clear on that?"

"Crystal."

"Conflict of interest is a fucked-up thing when you want to nail someone. Show me exactly why I hired you and throw the fucking book at my nephew. I hate that little bastard." He gave Scenario George's criminal file.

THIRTEEN

I t was a seedy place called The Kennel, and it was overflowing with idiots. A portable radio with a hanger antenna played the static version of Christina Aguilera's "Not Myself Tonight." A raggedy fan stirred the stale air. The place smelled awful, just like its namesake. Chance hopped up on a barstool between a big-tit bimbo with a bad dye job and a redneck that looked like a surgically altered version of Vin Diesel. Diesel look-alike had the tough look down to a science. *What is this world coming to?* Chance questioned himself as he rubbed his new bald head. He was going to miss his dreadlocks.

He placed a ten-dollar bill on the scarred countertop and glanced at the Budweiser clock behind the barkeep, 3:55 p.m. "Give me what it'll take. Pour it neat and make it tall."

"What are you into?" the bimbo said.

Chance knew that ass and tits were all that anyone ever noticed or remembered about her. "I'm into having magic sex," he said.

She wiggled her eyebrows. "Oh, really? How do you do that?"

"We fuck then you disappear. Wanna have a go at it?"

"Stranger, I knew you were a wild one when you came through the door. Aren't you gonna ask me my name first?"

Chance threw back his drink. The cognac burned going down. "I already know your name. It's Tits and Ass." He tucked a Marlboro behind his ear.

"You're a mess, stranger. Meet me in the bathroom in a couple of minutes. I need to freshen up before we do magic." Tits and Ass strutted off toward the can.

Chance checked the Budweiser clock, 3:58 p.m. Revenge was only thirty-two minutes away, so he had a few minutes to blow off some steam doing a little grab ass.

Diesel belched, then he leaned over. "Mind if I get sloppy seconds?"

Chance shrugged a *suit yourself* then followed Tits and Ass into the shitter.

FOURTEEN

A knock-down-drag-out fisticuffs, that's how their last encounter ended eight months ago, and Yancee Taylor had gone home that day to his family with his ass thoroughly kicked. Nevertheless, now, Yancee was excited to hook up with his homeboy Chance Fox. Yancee just hoped that they were able to keep their hands to themselves this time.

Africa, Yancee's wife, often commented that he and Chance were engaged in a sadomasochism relationship because they weren't happy unless they physically or verbally abused each other. Nothing new. These knuckleheads had been carrying on like this since elementary school: fight about something childish, then the stubborn bastards would wait to see who'd give in first and apologize so they could do it all again.

Yancee laughed to himself as he nosed his '67 Camaro to the Wood Chips, their old neighborhood meeting place that sat on the corner of Sidney and E. 276 Street. He, Leon, and Chance used to hang out there when they were kids, doing all the things mannish little boys did. *The stories that outdoor jungle gym would tell if it could talk.*

Yancee shook his head, disappointed in himself. Worm or lure? He still couldn't believe that their last fight was over fishing bait. Chance was pro worm; he was pro lure. Yancee peeked at his watch as he parked in front of the Wood Chips, 4:29 p.m. Right on time.

Chance was sitting on top of the monkey bars swinging his feet in a pair of peep-toe pumps when Yancee strolled up. Yancee squinted and shaded his eyes from the sun as he gazed up at Chance. "What's up with the wig and dress?"

"Dude, my psychiatrist said I should get in touch with my feminine side."

"And looking like Cash is your answer?" Yancee shook his head.

"It's a start," Chance said. "Besides, I know you won't hit a girl."

"You're stupid, you know that?"

"You gonna stand down there giving me goo-goo eyes or are you gonna come up here?"

"We're not exactly young bucks anymore, Chance."

"Dude, stop crying. Geez."

Yancee settled down beside Chance and smelled marijuana and liquor. "You've been drinking."

"Wow, you're such a genius. It's fascinating how intellectually gifted you are."

Yancee said, "Here we go with the bull—"

"Dude, you're the one who started smarting off at me first, talking about 'you've been drinking.'"

"Forgive me for thinking it was worth mentioning. Last time I checked you had nine years' sobriety under your belt."

"And I'm still taking it one day at a time. Today I'm drinking."

"And you're wearing a wig and a dress. For God's sake, you're wearing fake tits." Yancee threw his hands up. "Good luck with that. What's up with it, though? Saved any abused pets lately?" He thought it best to get Chance open on a subject he was passionate about before cutting in to him to find out what was really going on.

Chance frowned. "People are dims wads."

"Chance."

"What, dude?"

"You're tripping. White people don't use terms like dim wad anymore. If I'm not mistaken, that went out with the eighties."

"I'm a retro white boy in a class of my own."

Yancee shrugged a *so you say*.

"Anyway," Chance said. "Who gives people permission to cage animals that are meant to be free?" Then: "I could never harm any animal, and people who do deserve to die. Violently."

"You know how it is. That's why we have animal enthusiasts like you in the world." Yancee squeezed Chance's shoulder and really took in their surroundings. "This is like looking twenty years into the past. I thought this place would have been torn down."

"Those were the good old days." Chance pulled out two bottles of Mickey's Big Mouth from the purse he was carrying. He forced one on Yancee. "So many dames got a piece of my boner right here. Adrienne Edwards put out right over there on the sliding board."

"Straight up?"

Chance nodded. "Did a little grab ass with Sahara Lawrence under the sliding board. Gave her the T-bone right in the chips."

"Get out of here. Leon loved the hell out of her, but damn, she was a freak." Then: "If our parents only knew the things we came here to do. I smoked some of the best weed in my life right here on top of these monkey bars. What are we doing here in the past?"

"Nitwit, it all started here."

Yancee frowned. "I don't follow."

"Dude, you, me, and Leon made a blood pact to have one another's back, to be best buds for the rest of our lives. That was the night before my mother moved me to Cleveland Heights. You know me; I took our pact to heart."

Yancee closed his eyes and thought back to the day they pricked their fingers and touched them together. Foolish young boys on a quest to become real brothers. "Yeah, I remember. We hated that you had to go to Monticello Junior High." He smiled. "We scrapped that same day because I cracked on your shoes. Learned real quick that you hit hard for a Caucasian."

"Hey, shithead, don't call me Caucasian. Sounds too bourgeois, too sophisticated. Call me trailer park, white trash, dirty foot. Anything along those lines is suitable." He swigged his Mickey's. "Thanks for the birthday card. Moron, you should have just called and apologized instead of disguising it with a corny card."

"That wasn't an apology; it was a birthday card."

Chance made a show of surrounding by throwing up his hands. "Dude, I'm just saying I accept your apology."

"Thanks," Yancee said. "I'm sorry about you and Cashmaire separating."

"Don't be. Shit happens."

Yancee put his gaze on the Infiniti M37 in the parking lot. "I see you're driving her car."

"She left it behind when she split. No sense in letting it sit."

"So what happened?" Yancee hoped he hadn't overstepped his bounds. He'd learned from an episode of Oprah that marital discord was a touchy subject even among close friends.

"You don't know?"

Yancee shrugged. "All I know is she was supposed to have lied about being pregnant."

"We'll get to that later."

"So what brings you to town? Thinking of moving back home?"

Chance shrugged an *I'm not sure.* "You up for some fishing? Did some on the Colorado River last week. It was great."

"I'm down. When?"

"No better time than the present."

"You're wearing a dress."

"Like that makes a difference," Chance said.

"Can't. Africa's at home catching hell with the twins. They've been asking about their Uncle Chance, by the way. And my mother… she's deteriorating. We're all catching hell with her dementia. She'll be eighty-four this year."

"Dude, I got a change of clothes in the car. Another few hours won't hurt."

Yancee made a face while scratching his head. "She'll kill me; she's waiting for me to relieve her." He stated that as if their household ran in eight-hour shifts.

Chance said, "You were right, you know? Lures are better."

"Let's go out on the lake tomorrow. I know a spot in Mentor where sheephead and pike are practically jumping on the line."

"Tomorrow's not promised to either of us, dude." Chance eyed him skeptically. "You did like I asked, right?"

"Didn't say a word." He looked at the amateur tattoos covering Chance's arms and neck.

"What about to Africa?"

"No one knows you're here. What's up with the secrets and this dress and wig thing?" Then Yancee noticed something strange and leaned in closer to Chance.

"What?" Chance said.

"Where's…Did you cut your dreads off? Oh, you're really tripping."

Chance tossed the Mickey's bottle, then he climbed to the ground. "Come on, I wanna show you something."

"What is it?"

"Come see for yourself, shithead."

Yancee followed Chance to the Infiniti. Chance popped the trunk and Yancee saw a ten-gallon Igloo cooler.

"Open it," Chance said with a grin.

FIFTEEN

Africa Taylor felt like throwing in the parental towel and saying "fuck it." No, she wasn't an unfit mother; but, as far as she was concerned, she damn sure had unfit children. She wished there was a hotline where parents could report abusive children.

She was a disheveled young mother—by force not choice. Looking good and styling the latest Gucci wasn't for women like her anymore. Her once to-die-for hair was pulled into a mangled ponytail. Kool-Aid stains were such a norm, she sported her sons' grape-flavored fingerprints on her clothes like they were fashion trendy.

Her anger bypassed simmer and went straight to boil. She was so pissed she was shaking and having hot flashes like they were contractions. She'd signed up to raise loveable children, not midget devils. Her smoldering glare landed on her six-year-old son standing on top of her refrigerator. Her kitchen curtain was tied around his neck like a cape. He wore his tighty-whitey Fruit of the Looms with a pair of tube socks pulled over his hands like gloves. And what pissed Africa off even further was the silly-ass grin plastered on his face.

She said slow and deliberately, "I'm gonna kick your motherfuckin' ass if you don't get down from there, Rasheed." She'd specifically told Yancee that the comic books were a terrible idea, because he wouldn't be home to deal with their interpretations. "Rasheed—" She pointed to the floor. "—I said get down."

"My name ain't Rasheed, Mommie. I'm Superman and I'm fixin' to kick the Hulk's green ass."

Her blood pressure spiked. "Down, dammit! And watch your damn mouth. Where the hell is your brother?" She wondered how Rasheed had gotten on top of her refrigerator. Then she thought it was best she didn't know the details.

Rashaad, the other twin boy, rolled from under the table. His brand-new school shirt was ripped to shreds, green finger paint—she hoped—covered his face, and he had their fire extinguisher in hand. "Kryptonite, motherfucker."

"You better not, goddammit," Africa warned with the point of a finger as a tear leaked from her eye. "You better not spray that. You better not."

"Don't worry, Mommie," Superman said. "I'll save you from that no-good green bastard." He leaped off the refrigerator like the cape actually worked.

Hulk fired the kryptonite, blasting Superman in midair, coating the entire kitchen with white soot. Hulk flexed his muscles and growled. The twins laughed as the dust settled.

Africa stormed out of the kitchen without a word—livid, lump in throat, unsure if she should all-out cry or just fucking leave. She had it. Yancee was going to deal with this shit on his own as soon as he got home, because she was going to her mother's.

In the living room, she found Ms. Gail Taylor, her mother-in-law, whispering into the phone, mischievousness in her cataract-ridden eyes. Africa knew immediately things had taken a turn for the worst. Wiping her tears, she said, "Madear, who are you talking to?"

Madear crinkled her face and shushed Africa. "The CIA is gonna give me a job after this one."

"Hang up, Madear." Africa wept. "Please hang up the phone, Madear. I can't take this shit anymore."

"What's a phone? That sounds familiar."

"It's the thing you got stuck to the side of your head you're talking in."

"Oh." Then Madear got indignant: "No, I will not hang up. They're gonna personally put Barack Obama on the phone for me."

"Hang up right now." Then: "Please, Madear."

Madear shushed her again, then she spoke into the phone: "Yup saw it with my good eye, the right one. One of 'em is about four-two and green, an ugly sum bitch." Madear smiled a toothless smile at Africa. "The other one calls himself Superman; and my so-called daughter-in-law, Africa Taylor, went in there a fairly attractive black woman and came out white. Talk about super powers." Madear raised her eyes to Africa. "So how long before you send in the military? Barack—"

Africa unplugged the phone and prayed that Yancee would hurry home.

SIXTEEN

Chance knew exactly what the Janus-face butt wipe would do next. He counted on it. Yancee always had a problem with keeping his dick beaters off things that didn't belong to him.

Yancee shifted his gaze between Chance and the cooler. "On everything, my sons will love these." He dug in the cooler and scooped up one of the tiny eight-armed creatures and balanced it on his palm. "What are they?"

Winner winner chicken dinner, Chance thought, then said, "Law 8: Make Other People Come To You—Use Bait If Necessary."

Then it happened.

"Ouch!" Yancee dropped it back in the Igloo. "The little fucker bit me."

"Dude, you're such a dupe."

"What?" Yancee pressed down on the bite.

"The bite. That's how it starts," Chance said. "Reason I choose a Blue-ringed octopus is because their poison works immediately and it won't be found in your system once you're dead."

Yancee rubbed his mouth.

"First you feel a tingling sensation in your lips, like you are now." Chance shrugged a *sorry buddy*. "Next you'll go into a state of paralysis. Lose control of every muscle, dude." Then: "Hope you don't shit and piss yourself. You're too old for that."

Yancee's eyes darted around. He started to fall until Chance guided his limp body into the trunk. It took some doing, but Chance managed to twist and turn Yancee's sculpted body until he was on his back. Chance wanted to see Yancee's dark eyes.

"Chance...what are..." Yancee's eyes darted back and forth. "What—"

"Difficulty speaking is a side effect," Chance said, looking down on his frightened friend. "Save your energy because you have a lot of explaining to do. You need to think long and hard about how bad of a friend you've been." He slammed the trunk closed.

SEVENTEEN

The silent treatment really got beneath Jazz's skin in the worst way. She hated when someone igged her and put her on ignore status, especially someone who was highly animated like she was and could run their mouth and talk plenty shit like she could.

Jazz plopped down on the sofa beside Jaden, going out of her way to disturb him. "Really, are you gonna sit here all day spinning that ball on your finger?"

He kept the ball's momentum going with strict concentration.

"Dammit, Jaden, talk to me."

Silence.

She said, "Tell me what I can do to make this better."

He gave her an *I wish you were dead* look.

"Jaden."

More ball spinning. More ignore status.

"I know you're angry with me."

"No shit."

She smiled, satisfied she made a breakthrough. "Before the—" She glanced at Jaden, thinking twice about proceeding. "Before the accident I was working on a novel where the protagonist has anger issues. In one sense, he's his own antagonist."

"I'm not listening."

"But you're responding so you hear me."

"Smart ass," he mumbled.

"Would you rather I be a dumb ass?" Then: "Terrance—that's the protagonist's name—reminds me of you. He's older than you by two years."

"You act like you can't see I'm ignoring you," Jaden said. "I'm exerting all my energy trying to be nice, but you're starting to push my buttons." He went to the other side of the living room.

Buank. Buank. Buank. Buank.

"Through Terrance I discovered that the problem with poisoning by anger is it eats away your insides. Everything Terrance does and says is poisoned." She thought about their situation and sighed. "After a while a person who poisons themselves with anger feels nothing. I don't want that to happen to you, Jaden."

"You have a lot of nerve preaching the choir to me about an unfinished, undeveloped character. You couldn't possibly know how Terrance's personal conflict is gonna unfold because you're too weak to discover an ending, to close the story. He can't go any further than he's been like I can't." He stomped across the room and stood over her. "I have every right to be angry. You—nobody else—ruined everything and took me away from my dad in the process. I'll never forgive you. And I promise to remind you of that fact every day."

Buank. Buank. Buank. Buank.

EIGHTEEN

He stared into Stygian darkness. It was getting harder to breathe. And being stuffed in the trunk of an Infiniti didn't have a damn thing to do with it. Yancee didn't know what was happening to him or why. He did Number One and Number Two on himself, and the stench was turning his stomach. He couldn't move a lick. His motor skills had taken a permanent lunch break. But oddly he could feel every agonizing inch of pain each time his head slammed against the rim of the spare tire. He didn't know what had gotten into Chance. This was way beyond the perimeter of their normal fighting and bickering. But he realized that Chance had dedicated himself to playing bumper cars with every pothole in the city.

After listening to the thrum of tires cruise against different textures of road for an undetermined amount of time, the tires crunched over a long strip of gravel, then the car stopped.

The engine was shut off; he could hear it tick.

Apprehension set in; his heart sounded like a bass drum in his ears.

The car door was slammed shut.

What had Chance so pissed? Yancee tried to swallow the lump in his throat, but the stubborn thing wouldn't go down.

Urgent footsteps fell on gravel.

A key slid into the trunk's lock.

Yancee couldn't move. So the urge to attack he had was no good.

The trunk opened and without preamble, Chance said, "You stink." Then: "Dude, you're gonna die of respiratory failure if I don't inject you with this." He showed Yancee a syringe. "But not before I make you feel all the pain I'm feeling."

Yancee's eyes moved right, left, up, and down. Wherever he was there was a tree-leaf canopy covering them. He looked through the leaves and saw the sky had darkened. Africa was going to kill him for being late. She was going to swear up and down he was out fooling around on her again, he thought, totally blowing off the seriousness of his immediate predicament. He smelled hints of rain mixed with a pine-needle breeze and his bowels.

Then his eyes pinned Chance and reality sucker-punched him, putting things in proper perspective. "Why are you doing this?"

"Hunch," Chance said, grabbing two fistfuls of Yancee's UPS work shirt. "But my sixth sense tells me you know exactly why." Chance tugged Yancee from the trunk and let his body hit the gravel with a thud. "Time to get your comeuppance."

"Aahg!" Yancee howled in pain, hoping someone would hear him.

"It's only us, dude. Scream like a pregnant bitch if you wanna." Then: "Now you understand why I chose to zap you with the venom of a Blue-ringed oct." Chance started dragging Yancee across the gravel. "You're completely paralyzed and fully conscious. You're gonna love this part, dude: the beauty about this contradiction is you can feel all the hell I'm about to put you through. Well...up until the point your breathing stops."

Now, in typical Chance fashion, Yancee realized that Chance wore thread-bare jeans, scuffed Vans sneakers, and a bleach-splattered Nirvana T-shirt. After Yancee endured the punishment of a flight of concrete stairs, the dragging was over. He wasn't sure of how far Chance dragged him—ten, fifteen feet maybe—but judging from the burning sensation of his chest and face, it was farther than a hop and a skip.

Yancee lay face down—skin on fire—against a cold floor, another contradiction. He was still clueless as to where he was, and he couldn't get the sight of Chance's bald head out his mind. All he knew about his whereabouts was he was indoors and the place smelled like it had been bottled up for years.

Chance kicked him onto his back and showed him a large surgical scalpel. "Dude, I'm not horsing around." His voice echoed throughout the building.

That meant the place was definitely big and probably empty, Yancee assumed. "Chance, man, what the fuck?" His eyes darted back and forth, taking in as much of his surroundings as his limited field of vision would allow. From the architecture and stained-glass windows, he thought he was in a church. Only he couldn't locate a reference or likeness of Jesus Christ. Somewhere in the distance he could hear a choir of crickets, the rustling of trees bringing up the background, and traffic, of all things. Then he felt a faint draft push across his face.

Chance didn't waste any more time. He jabbed the scalpel into Yancee's thigh and twisted the blade to get a good flow going.

Yancee screamed.

"Nice comeback." Then: "Been thinking about it for the last six months. Dude, you knew about Cashmaire all along."

Click.

Now everything fell into place. Chance must've known about what they had done or he was fishing for answers. Yancee's guilt catapulted him back to 1999 when Leon had shown him an article written in a medical journal. Yancee could still see the evil smirk Leon had on his face as Yancee had read the article.

Yancee was jerked back to the here-and-now when he saw the shiny blade lunging toward him again. First everything went from 88 rpm down to 3 rpm, and then his surroundings went mute. In slow motion he studied the deliberateness of the asymmetrical-shaped blade, the audacity of its precision point. He anticipated the inevitable pain it would cause but couldn't flinch or brace himself to soften the impact. Primal fear instructed him to survive, instructed his body to take flight or fight, instructed his hands to reach up and stop the dangerous blade from hitting its mark.

Nothing happened, though.

His brain transmitted, but his body didn't receive the messages. During the slow motion, he examined Chance's face: anger and vengeance had replaced easygoing and laid-back. Chance had to know, but how? Who had broken their pact of silence?

Then the blade sliced into his flesh; a guttural scream leapt from his mouth at 100 rpm.

"If I'm right, you got some huge gonads screwing around with my life." Chance twisted the scalpel. "Dude, you're leaking plenty good."

Yancee lay there in pain, motionless. He knew he was bleeding to death. "Why are you…what you want from me?"

Chance put his face uncomfortably close to Yancee's. "The truth."

"Don't let me die like this." Yancee felt his fear crystallize.

Chance laughed. "Of course not. We're buddies, dude. You can count on it."

Yancee heard the duet of crickets and trees again. His breathing was labored. He did his best to speak through his agony. "The truth about what?"

"Shithead, why didn't you stop me from hooking up with my wife?"

"Come on, Chance. It doesn't—"

Chance showed him the bloody scalpel. "I'm not in the mood."

As the sound of traffic filtered in, Yancee relived that day in his dorm room and did his best to tell Chance all about it. "It started on a Wednesday back in February of ninety-nine."

NINETEEN

"In breaking news this afternoon," the newscaster said from the television set, *"The charred bodies of Carole Sund and Silvina Pelosso were found in a rental car. Sund's daughter's body was found thirty miles away from Yosemite National Park where the women were last seen alive. Police and the FBI—"*

Yancee shut the television off and turned 93 FM on. Mad Cobra's voice came through the speakers: "Girl, flex time to have sex…" *And Yancee went back to what he was doing.*

"Boy, stop it." The gold-digging tramp slapped his paws away from her crotch. "Do you always put your hands on things you ain't earned?"

"Bad habit I've had since I was a kid," Yancee said, easing up on the bed while kissing her neck, positioning himself to dry-fuck her. "I like touching things, baby, to see how they feel. You feel—"

"I. Said. Stop!" She elbowed him in the gut. "Next time I'll go lower."

"Girl, flex time to have sex."

Yancee swung his feet around to the floor, frustrated and horny. "What are you tripping on?"

She climbed off the bed and straightened her designer clothing. "Just like you thought you was about to get some of these goodies, I thought you was paying for my hair and nails to get done." She crossed the room, purposefully teasing him with the sway of her handlebar hips and lovely ass, and reached for the doorknob.

Yancee sprang to his feet, erection straining against his khaki Dockers. "Girl, what are you trying to do, leave a brother with blue balls?"

Mad Cobra said, "Girl, flex time to have sex."

She dug a trial-size bottle of Jergens lotion from her purse and tossed it to him. "Hope that works for you. My new appointment is tomorrow at eleven." Then: "I need a pedicure too since you played me and made me reschedule."

The door burst open, nearly knocking the tramp on her lovely ass, and Leon charged in their room like Serious Trouble was chasing him with two loaded .9mm Glocks. Their dorm room measured up to a one-room efficiency apartment with a small kitchenette and an even tinier bathroom that sat on Euclid Avenue above the infamous Rascal House and catty-cornered to Cleveland State University.

"Excuse you," she said, sucking her teeth and rolling her over-the-counter hazel eyes.

Leon looked at her with 100% disgust. He possessed a deep-rooted hatred for anyone who bled once a month for an average of five days straight. "Fuck you. Get out. Don't no drug dealers live on these premises."

"One day I'mma have somebody put a foot in your ass, Leon. Wait 'til my brother comes home from prison." She slammed the door so hard behind her it bounced back open.

"Africa," Yancee yelled, "wait a minute. I was just playing. I got the money."

Leon literally crossed the room in nine steps and blocked Yancee's exit. Leon's broad chest heaved beneath the CSU sweat shirt. While trying to catch his breath, he shoved a 1993 issue of The New England Journal of Medicine *into Yancee's hand. "Page twenty-six. Man, you gotta read this article."*

"Not now. I'm trying to let Africa get my dick out the dirt before my next class."

"Bros before hoes." Leon stood his ground in Yancee's path. "I'm not letting you go after your little slut until you read it."

Sighing, Yancee flipped the magazine open and plopped down on the empty bed—God, he wished Africa was naked right now—then started to read.

Yancee frowned with the lurch of his stomach.

Leon smiled.

Yancee turned his nose up and glanced at Leon over the magazine.

Leon grinned and rubbed his hands together as if he were absolutely up to no good.

When Yancee finished the article, he looked pale and sick. "Condoms can't preempt this. I gots to be more careful. How would I know to look for something like this?" Yancee questioned himself. "Do they even have a way for us to test for something like this? Like a pregnancy test but for gender?" Yancee let out a confused breath, forgetting all about Africa. "So it's really girls out there who are really boys?" Yancee was having a hard time wrapping his mind around that.

"I researched it at the library," Leon said. "It's called Androgen Insensitivity Syndrome. Pussy, ass, tits, and a pretty face on the surface but undescended nuts and XY chromosomes underneath. Genetically, AIS pseudo-females are boys." Then: "It doesn't have ovaries, grow pubic, or underarm hair. It doesn't menstruate or have kids."

Yancee said, "I call that nasty. A girl with balls, literally." He shook his head as if he had no clue what this world was coming to.

"I call it reverse homosexuality." Leon said that like he was proud of himself. "And now I'm about to pay Chance back for..."

Chance heard the beating of his own heart and excited breathing as he buried the scalpel deep in Yancee's thigh for the third time.

When Yancee finished hollering, Chance said, "You passed out on me. Don't quit. Come on, spit the rest out. What did the shithead wanna get me back for?"

"I'm dying, man, oh, God."

"No, not God. It's just me, Chance Fox."

Yancee fought to breathe. "Shit, help me, Chance. Don't let me die like this."

Chance put his face in Yancee's. "My bet is you'll bleed out before respiratory failure claims you." Chance wiped the blade clean on Yancee's UPS shirt. "I'm not helping you make it home to your reformed whore and the terrible twosome until you tell me what Leon wanted to get me for."

"For—" Yancee coughed. "—taking Sahara Lawrence from him."

"For crying out loud, he could've taken a spin. She was a sperm pit stop."

"But Leon…he had a real thing for her. You crushed him when you slept with her. He never trusted a woman after that, turned into a cold-blooded misogynist." Yancee gulped down a breath. "I asked him how he planned to get you. Chance, it was a joke."

TWENTY

L eon looked at Yancee like he was a mental midget, like he had rid-
den the short bus to school growing up. How could he not be catching
on? Leon plucked the magazine from where it lay on the bed. He
pointed to the cover photo of an androgynous-looking teenager. The left
half of a male's photo was perfectly joined to the right half of a female's
photo. The caption accompanying the photo read:

IS CASHMAIRE JONES A BOY OR GIRL?

Leon folded the magazine down the center, covering the left side of the
teenager, leaving only the female side visible. "She look familiar?"

After studying the girl for a moment, Yancee shrugged a not really.
"No."

Leon popped him upside the head with the magazine. "You try to
screw her every time you go in the campus bookstore."

"Cash, the part-time girl?" Yancee's eyes liked to jump out his head.
"Get the fuck out of here. Let me see that again." Yancee really studied
the female side of the photo this time.

"She-slash-he is one and the same," Leon said.

"Damn, I'm glad she ain't give me none." Then: "She doesn't even
date anyone; that girl's self-esteem is shot to hell. She's scared of her own
shadow."

"With a secret like this, do you blame shim?"

"It isn't a secret if you know about it. Who else knows?"

"Nobody. Shim doesn't even know I know. This article is seven years old. I came across it while helping Professor Wolstencroft clean out an office in the administration building."

"So what does this have to do with you getting Chance back?" No sooner than he posed the question, warning bells went off in Yancee's head, as Leon's intent dawned on him.

"I paid her to go out with Chance on Valentine's Day and to give him a kiss. I mean tongue and all. And I'm gonna be right there with my camcorder. It's gonna be the funniest shit ever." Leon laughed. "He should have never crossed me."

Yancee shook his head. "That's not a good idea. If Chance finds out—"

"What's not a good idea?" Anderson Smith said, walking into the room with a gorgeous, tall girl trailing closely behind him.

Yancee took note of the way the predator showed itself in Leon's face when the long-legged queen wearing a Baltimore Ravens skull hat stepped into the room.

"Breathe, shithead." Chance smacked Yancee across the face. "Who was the bimbo with Anderson?" Then: "I gotta get every prick involved."

Yancee didn't respond. His pulse was gone. Chance roared into the night like a rabid dog, then he went to work with the scalpel.

TWENTY-ONE

Hakeem Eubanks just couldn't shake the cloud of grief that was quite literally smothering him to death. It had been lingering over him like a funky odor for six solid months now, and it wasn't showing signs of letting up any time soon. He shook himself dry, flushed the toilet with the toe of his Prada shoe, then he stepped out the stall to find the full-bodied stunner Aspen Skye standing in front of the mirror, poking her stomach out. He knew she was imagining how she'd look if she were pregnant. Embarrassed, she blushed and leaned against the counter of sinks. God, she's beautiful, he thought. Hakeem tried to keep it professional and not look at her like *that* but it was damn hard, because secretly he loved her.

Aspen was dressed in Yves Saint Laurent from her apple cap, which her curly locks tumbled from and framed her girlish face, to her peep-toe pumps. Her Chanel No5 scented the air, and her diamond tennis bracelet was a nice complement to her pecan complexion. Yes, beautiful, Hakeem thought.

"So what do you say?" she said, flashing her expensive smile that showed off two adorable dimples.

"That I'm getting old." He bumped her aside and washed his hands. He couldn't help but notice her perfect evocative ass perched on the sink through the mirror. He quickly averted his gaze to his own image before she caught him looking. It was difficult to ignore his reflection: an impeccably tailored two-button Gianluca Isaia cashmere suit, four-figure cuff links, and a Rolex Explorer sat on an athletic six-foot-one frame. His handsome face was highlighted by hints of worry lines, but Hakeem had the sturdy, relaxed posture of a man who could kick some serious ass. "When I was in my prime, I could take a leak and that stream would dash out like a thoroughbred race horse. That piss hit the water so hard it sounded like thunder, made a whirlpool in the toilet. Now it just drips out. Barely makes a splash."

"Be serious, Hakeem. Damn. You know I'm sensitive and irritable."

"And moody and touchy and explosive and volatile and capricious, tell me something I don't know." He looked into her limpid brandy-colored eyes with striations of hazel streaking through them longer than he intended, longer than what was comfortable. "I'm serious. I'm getting old."

"You know what, fuck it. Forget I even asked you." She started for the door.

"Wait a minute, Aspen. Just wait a minute. If you just insist on knowing what I think, I think you should find you a man and start a family. You're a good woman, temperamental, but good. Family means everything. Life isn't even worth living if you can't share it with family."

She looked at herself in the mirror and poked out her flat belly again. "You know what, you're right. Thanks."

"And as far as being an organ donor, I used to entertain those thoughts, but I changed my mind."

"Oh, yeah, why?" She fired up a Newport.

"Came to the conclusion that if they know I'm a donor, the doctors might not work as hard to save a black man knowing some white man in Kentucky needs a heart."

"Interesting. I never thought of it like that," she said. The end of her cigarette glowed red as she puffed.

Hakeem watched her lips form a small *O* as she blew smoke out. He loved her pouty lips. Also he knew that having a baby and deciding whether to become a donor or not were important issues to her. But cigarettes had a harmful effect on both decisions, didn't it? "I thought you gave up nicotine."

"Weaning myself." Smoke floated from her lips. "I only smoke every six hours now."

"Then you didn't quit."

Her intense gaze sat behind thick, ebony lashes and beautifully arched brows. "That's preparing to quit."

"Keep it up and your lungs won't be good to anyone." He held the door open for her.

She paused in the threshold. "About that other thing."

Hakeem knew the *other thing* was coming. He'd been trying to duck that conversation for the last month.

"She's a nice girl," Aspen said. "You've been cooped up in that house since—"

"Don't." Hakeem didn't want that topic in his head. "It seems like I'll never get over what happened or feel normal again. So I really don't care how nice your friend is."

"I'm worried about you, Hakeem. You've withdrawn from social activities and me. We don't even play chess anymore. Listen, it'll do you some good to get out and start living again." She found his tired gaze and held it.

A uniformed officer walked past the bathroom and saw them looking goofy at each other. "Black Ken and Barbie, get a room."

"Kiss my ass, beat-walker." Aspen flipped the officer the birdie when he glanced over a shoulder. "You switch like you played with dolls growing up."

"Nice, real nice," the officer said. "Real ladylike, Detective Skye."

Smiling a mouthful of white teeth, Aspen said to Hakeem, "So, are you going to go out with her?"

"Right now I'm just not feeling it. I'd much rather pay for a shot of pussy. That way I'm paying for a good time and for her to leave me the hell alone in one transaction."

"Do that and I might have to bust you for soliciting a prostitute."

Hakeem said nothing.

"I told her you'd meet her at the View tonight at ten."

He sighed knowing that she'd keep bugging him until he at least attempt to get on with his life. "Can't do old broads, Aspen. They'll give you the worms."

"Young women, nowadays, have HIV and herpes…and they come with a lot of drama."

After a moment of considerable thought, Hakeem said, "On second thought, give me a case of the worms. But she can't be over thirty-five. What are two dead batteries gonna do? She at least has to be young enough to recharge me."

"Check, younger than thirty-five," Aspen said as they strolled down the hallway of the Cleveland Homicide Unit. "You'll like her; I'd give her an eight point eight."

"Round it up, she's a nine." He yawned, hadn't slept a wink last night. "I'm in love already. Someone that pretty, I might not know how to act. Never had anyone over a three because I've been cursed with ugly-girl energy."

"You're terrible." She burst into laughter. "And funny."

Hakeem said, "She can't be over a hundred twenty-five pounds either. I draw my line in the sand there when it comes to women—pretty or ugly. If she's heavier than that, she can't do a thing for me but point me in the direction of her slim friend." He noticed Aspen's facial expression change. "Can't believe you tried to hook me up with a fat girl."

"She isn't fat and you're not old. Not many thirty-eight-year-old men can stand next to you."

"Aspen, is she heavier than a buck a quarter?"

She made a small gap between her thumb and index finger. "A wee bit."

"Forget about it."

"Hakeem, she's about a hundred twenty-eight."

"Forget about it."

"Hakeem, stop acting an ass."

"Tell her to lose *about* three pounds and we got a date."

"Detective Eubanks, Detective Skye," a raspy voice called out from behind them.

They turned and faced Sergeant Morris—nicknamed Urkel because he was skinny and often wore high-water slacks with annoying suspenders and a pair of unfashionable glasses.

"What's up, Urkel?" Hakeem said, glad to be away from the conversation about Aspen's nameless friend.

Sergeant Morris cringed and scowled all at once, proof he still despised his nickname today just as much as he did yesterday. He gave the detectives a serious look. "There's been a murder. The mayor wants you two to personally handle it."

TWENTY-TWO

It pissed acid rain on Cleveland in one steady stream. Hakeem rode shotgun in Aspen's latest sex-appeal complement, a BMW 760Li luxury sedan, while she plunged the V-12 toward the scene of the crime. He no longer made comments about the things she bought because it was useless. She changed vehicles like he changed watches, which was every day.

"How about this," Aspen said with her musical voice. "Muslims are required to shave their pubic and underarm hair. The males and females."

"You're kidding," Hakeem said, not interested at all. He was thinking about calling Ms. Drew Felding, his neighbor, and asking her to let Keebler out and keep an eye on her because a fresh homicide promised late working hours. Especially when he wasn't getting started until after five post meridiem.

"Seriously. Ran across it online last night. Get this: Back in the day of the Prophet Muhammad, they practiced that because they rode camels without proper underclothes. Shaving was their answer to the flea and tick problem in those times, which is understandable. But today people wear Victoria's Secret and Calvin Klein underwear. We drive beautiful machines like this baby here." She gripped the steering wheel. "So it's crazy for shaving to still be a mandate, right?"

"You sure know a lot about Muslims."

"Thought about signing up to give my children a religion and to tick my father off. Changed my mind when I found out Muslim women didn't have equal rights, have to starve themselves for thirty days during the month of Ramadan, and have to shave. You have no idea of how irritating it is to walk around with an itchy coochie."

"Nope, wouldn't have a clue." Then: "Looks like you have to find another way to piss off dear old Dad." He pulled out his Mont Blanc pen and pad and started writing.

"What are you doing?" Aspen said.

"Adding become a Muslim and shave my pubic hair to my bucket list."

Aspen rolled her eyes. "You and this bucket list."

The rain had moved on to piss on the southern part of Ohio by the time they turned off Mayfield Road into a parking lot cluttered with Cleveland Heights municipal marked and unmarked police cars, emergency personnel vehicles, news satellite vans, and the one vehicle that caused Hakeem's hemorrhoids to flare: a neon-green Honda. That meant the incorrigible Gus Hobbs, a reporter for the *Cleveland Plain Dealer*, was lurking. Hakeem hated all reporters. They used people's tragedy and misery as a means to get a Pulitzer Prize. As soon as he and Aspen stepped out of the car, everyone on the unofficial side of the crime-scene tape stopped what they were doing to stare at them.

Hakeem knew they stood out like sore thumbs, the only pair in any group. Their clothes were ridiculously expensive. Not like other detectives who depended on department-issued clothing vouchers, whose outdated blazers boasted holes in the linings from years of their gun hammers rubbing against the fabric.

No. Hakeem and Aspen stunk of privilege and six-digit educations.

To the majority of their colleagues they looked like two rich ass-holes that got bored and stepped off the pages of *Vanity Fair* and came to the inner city to play cop because it looked fun on their seventy-two-inch plasma screens. But, in fact, they had a hundred percent case clearance rate and their pedigrees were as sharp as the pleats in their slacks. Him: heir to Empire Energy & Natural Gas Company; her, twenty-eight percent stake holder of her father's eighty-six-million-dollar trust fund.

As they neared the crime-scene tape—sectioning off a throng of Pine and Maple trees—Sharon Reed, a reporter for *Live On 5*, winked at Hakeem as she spoke into the camera. "Fear grips a suburban community this evening. Just beyond these trees officials are saying is the most gruesome murder scene in the history of this city. The unidentified victim is a black male…"

When Hakeem and Aspen ducked under the crime-scene tape and breached the tree-lined perimeter, the building's sentries, they looked up at a Jewish synagogue. It was an overbearing building with a wide set of concrete steps that sat beneath huge pillars that stretched to the sky swollen with clouds. Hakeem wondered what type of monster would kill a person in a sacred place of worship. He needed to know. It was that thirst for unanswered questions that drove him.

A burly man with a thin goatee and receding hairline came over and shook Aspen's hand, then Hakeem's. "Heard the mayor assigned you guys to this. It's nice to finally meet the infamous Dynamic Duo. I'm Officer McNally."

Scanning the area with his intense gaze, Hakeem said, "McNally, I'm taking it you were the first officer on the scene."

McNally nodded. "Dispatch assigned me the call at four thirtyish."

"Push the perimeter back another ten feet," Aspen said. "Until someone relieves you, you're solely responsible for keeping my perimeter secure. Within the next forty minutes, this place will be a circus." She took in their surroundings. "No one gets past you, not even the person who signs your paycheck unless I authorize it. We clear?"

McNally nodded like a little boy who'd gotten in trouble.

Aspen had recounted to Hakeem about how she'd learned the hard way about keeping foot traffic inside a crime scene to a necessary minimum. Back in Los Angeles when she worked in the legendary Glass House with Homicide Special, she was processing the crime scene of Nicole Brown Simpson and Ronald Goldman, which was overrun with reporters. While bagging and tagging evidence, she caught a break, or so she thought. She bagged a cigarette butt that everyone assumed belonged to the killer or killer's accomplice. After wasting several weeks waiting on DNA evidence to come back on the butt, it turned out to match a reporter who had contaminated the scene. Now as a veteran detective, she prevented the unconscious removal, addition, and/or destruction of evidence by keeping nosey folks out.

Hakeem appreciated her thoroughness.

TWENTY-THREE

Aspen nudged the thin strip of soil beneath her with a pump. "Where does this path lead to, Officer McNally?"

"It, uh, winds behind the synagogue for about thirty yards and comes out on Euclid Heights Boulevard. The path's mouth is obscured by overgrown shrubbery. To know it's there you'd have to know it's there. Years ago the neighborhood kids created it as a shortcut to get to school. Four generations later, kids still use this path to get to school."

Hakeem gestured to another potbellied officer who stood at the entrance of the sanctuary. "Your partner?"

"Eight years straight," Officer McNally said. "He's manning the logbook."

Aspen said, "Never knew this place was here."

"Been here since the sixties," Officer McNally said. "The Jewish community stopped using it as a place of worship about eleven years ago. It's so well hidden by the trees, like the path, you wouldn't know this building was here unless you knew it was here."

Hakeem said nothing.

Aspen had already noticed that on first visual, the area looked like it was a dense patch of woods until they cut through the tree perimeter guarding the synagogue and found its hollow bowels.

McNally pointed to their left. "Just behind that evergreen there's a hidden driveway. The killer probably used it unless they walked in here."

"You're real familiar with this place." Aspen nailed him with her suspicious cop eyes.

"Used to be one of those kids who rode my bike through here every morning. I went to Monticello Junior High."

Aspen said, "Who found the body?"

Hakeem cringed. Aspen knew Hakeem hated how real people were reduced to insignificant "bodies" once they expired.

"Uh…Mr. and Mrs.—" McNally whipped out his notepad. "—Walter and Mary Williams."

Hakeem's—ever the pessimist—radar went off. What would a married couple be doing inside the building if it's been closed down for eleven years? "Williams isn't a Jewish name."

"A couple?" Aspen said, picking up on Hakeem's frequency. "Thought this place hasn't been operational, that the most action it sees is kids using this path to get from Point A to B, right?"

"They're senior citizens; they work, housecleaning and maintenance, for the Hebrew Academy of Cleveland up on Taylor Road. The academy uses this old place as a warehouse for the school. They came down here to pick up supplies and found our victim."

"So they have keys to this place?" Hakeem looked at his Rolex and thought about Keebler.

"Yeah," McNally said, nodding. "But I believe the killer got in through a window. There's a window broken out in there." McNally jerked a thumb toward the building. "Mr. Williams is certain it wasn't broken out two days ago."

On first observation of the place, Hakeem noticed a tree limb reaching out and flirting with the building.

"I'm guessing this broken window is on the third floor, east side of the building," Aspen said, always on point.

"How'd you know?" McNally had the I'm-puzzled look down to a science.

She shrugged a *lucky guess*, slid her peep-toe pumps off, and then said to Hakeem, "I'll check around back. Sign me in the log; I'll initial it later." She strutted away carrying her shoes.

"McNally."

Nothing.

"Officer McNally." Hakeem shook him back to the here-and-now.

"Huh?" McNally said, coming out his trance.

"I asked you about the Williamses. Where are they?"

"Oh, the old man had medication to take, and they had to let their grandson in after school. I took their statements and let them go home." McNally gave Hakeem a copy of their statement.

"Give me a minute," Hakeem said, stepping off to the side, pulling out his Palm Treo smart phone. He pulled up Ms. Drew Felding's information and dialed her number. "Hi, Drew; Hakeem here."

"I have caller ID, Hakeem. But it's good to hear your voice." She was always as cheerful as ever. "Your car isn't in the driveway. What's going on?"

"Ran into a little situation at work."

"It wouldn't have anything to do with what Sharon Reed is talking about on the news, would it?" Then: "She's scaring the bejesus out of me, and I'm sure she's scaring the rest of the good people in this city."

"Don't listen to Reed. Her paycheck is based on putting panic and fear in people's lives. She wants network coverage. Ratings. She gives a story legs. So how can you believe anything she says?" He peeped Officer McNally checking him out on the sly. "But I am working the case she's speculating about, so I'll be home late. I was wondering if—"

"Hakeem, you just make this city safe and I'll take care of Keebler until you get home."

"Thanks, Drew." He hung up and dropped the phone in his pocket. He turned to McNally. "Take me to the deceased."

McNally aimed his Maglite and led Hakeem up the concrete steps and froze at the door. "This is as far as I'm going. Once was enough. Hope you got a cast-iron stomach."

TWENTY-FOUR

What a fucking dummy, Scratch, a heroin addict, thought as he peeked through the Camaro's window. The lame with that pretty broad from yesterday had left his keys in the ignition *and* an iPhone on the seat. Scratch looked around, confident he wasn't being watched, then climbed inside the ride and fired it up. The rumble of the engine was powerful. It made him feel tough. Without a doubt, he was about to get a bankroll for this beautiful machine. He gripped the steering wheel eager to see what the car was made of when flashing lights lit up Sidney Avenue. *Fuck.* There goes his fix. He hadn't even stolen the damn thing yet and already Euclid cops were coming. He jerked the car back in Drive, snatched up the iPhone, and hustled out the car and over to the Wood Chips.

He sat on a rung of the sliding board ladder, trying to catch his breath as a tow truck rounded the curve in the street. A tow truck? He panicked and blew his high behind a tow truck? He was pissed with himself for not pulling off as he watched the tow truck back up to the Camaro. At least he got a phone out the deal. That would definitely get him a bag or two. He took the iPhone out to check its applications and saw that the display screen read *92 Missed Calls*. This lame must be important, he told himself.

He slyly shot up his last bag of dope as he watched the tow truck driver hook the Camaro up to its hoist. Just as the dope hit his system, the iPhone rang. He hit the Send button and listened.

"Yancee...Yancee, hello?" Then: "You black motherfucker, I hope she's worth it 'cause we're through. Come get your crazy-ass mammee and these rotten, penitentiary-bound kids and take 'em to that bitch's house. Fuck this marriage and fuck—"

Scratch hung up. With a woman with a mouth and attitude like that, he understood why the lame drove off with another woman yesterday.

TWENTY-FIVE

he synagogue gave Hakeem the creeps; it reminded him of a setting that Wes Craven would use in a horror flick, a building that would have scared Hakeem shitless as a child. He pushed his hands inside a pair of leather gloves, slipped shoe covers over his shoes, and stepped through the domineering double doors. Everything good and wholesome inside him whispered, "Fool, turn your ass around."

He took a few more steps into the building's guts and waited, waited for the nausea to grip him and knot his innards. It was a feeling he counted on, one that screamed "I'm still normal." He'd vowed to Aspen that when he became desensitized to death and the nauseous feeling divorced him, he would turn in his gold shield and spend the rest of his days on an exotic beach in Dubai with half-naked women.

The coppery smell of blood and rotten flesh raped his nose. His belly tried to crawl up his throat and out his mouth. He forced the bile down as his heart feloniously assaulted his chest. Decay and the residue of anger tainted the air. It was a funk that promised to cling until he scrubbed it clean. But Hakeem knew he'd still smell it in his mind.

Like a thoroughbred bloodhound he sniffed and followed the funk to its source, stomach protesting every step of the way. Just beyond the main sanctuary a man lay on the floor. Shirt open, pants and underwear gathered at his ankles. Blowflies circled his body like hungry vultures. Blood pooled around his body; it had turned brown and thick like meringue.

Hakeem pulled out his Palm Treo 750 and snapped a barrage of crime-screen photos. The victim's face was covered with the Metro section of yesterday's newspaper. Ancient Egyptian hieroglyphics were carefully carved into every visible part of the victim's skin. Hakeem ventured to lift the newspaper some. The victim's eyes were bulged from heat-expanded tissues and were filled with maggots. His mouth was frozen open as if he died screaming.

"Son of a bitch."

TWENTY-SIX

spen climbed through the third-floor window with the straps of her high-heels clenched between her teeth. She eased her small feet into the shoes, then she removed a fingerprint kit from her clutch and dusted the window.

Nothing.

The killer had concealed his prints. The stench of human tissue crept up her nose. It reminded her of Pete's Butchery. When she was a small child, she and her mother visited Pete's every weekend to get the following week's supply of fresh meat. Her mother wouldn't allow the hired help to purchase their meat. She insisted on handling that herself. Aspen hated the weekly visits to Pete's, and she hated the smell even more.

When Aspen clicked her heels to the end of the hallway and rounded the corner, she came to a balcony that overlooked the ground floor. A marble flight of steps unfolded from the balcony to the floor. She looked down and saw Hakeem kneeling beside a naked body. Her first concern was Hakeem. "How are you feeling?"

His tired eyes found her voice. "Sick."

"Good to hear," she said, coming down the stairs. "What did Officer McNally do when I walked off?"

"Checked out your ass."

"I still got it."

"How'd you get in?" He snapped off a few more pictures.

"The oak tree outside invited me in." Then: "It's how he got in."

"Our unsub is a he?"

She knew Hakeem wouldn't miss a beat. "Not many girls can climb a twenty-six-foot tree and scale across a nine-foot branch and break in through a window. And I did it barefoot."

"You're the exception to the girl rule."

Aspen stood beside him and looked down on the dead man. She couldn't believe what she was seeing. The implications of the elaborate markings carved into the body was a threat to every citizen in Cuyahoga County. "Looks like a serial killer has come to town."

"Maybe it's a copycat," Hakeem said.

"Maybe not."

"If not, I sure hope he isn't planning on staying too long."

She said, "I feel you."

"Aspen?"

She already knew where his head was at. "I want to catch this guy too."

"Then let's get him before he does it again."

Aspen whipped out her BlackBerry and put in a call to Forensic Pathologist Aura Chavez MD—the trusted Alfred to their Dynamic Duo, then they began to process the scene of the crime.

TWENTY-SEVEN

Forensic Pathologist Aura Chavez MD was over-the-hill and did her best to disguise it with too much CoverGirl. She was one of those women who found it necessary to whack her eyebrows off and draw them back on in such a way that made her look like she was in a constant state of surprise. "The Hieroglyphic Hacker is a pretty salty fellow," she said with her thick Spanish accent while looking down on the enigmatic symbol system cut into the victim's skin. "What type of hate, what type of mind does it take to do something like this?"

"An unstable one," Aspen said, firing up a Newport three hours before scheduled. "The type of hate our death penalty will cure."

Hakeem said, "What's your preliminary thoughts on the cause and time of death?"

"It's way too early to talk cause; it could be anything. Speculation without an autopsy in my line of work is unprofessional, Detective."

"Well, I don't have a problem with speculating," Aspen said. "Judging from these three stab wounds in his thigh, I'd venture to say he bled to death and the hieroglyphics were postmortem."

"Possible," Dr. Chavez said. "Full rigor is set. The buildup of internal gases is purging fluids from his nose and mouth. In combination with lividity and liver temp, this man has been dead for approximately sixteen, seventeen hours. On record I'd say he was murdered around eight-fifteen, eight-thirty yesterday evening."

She shook her head. "So does anyone have a clue who this young man is?"

Smoke flowed from Aspen's mouth as she spoke. "No cell phone, wallet, or keys."

"Only thing we can infer is he works for UPS by his shirt, so we'll start there." Hakeem put his arm around Dr. Chavez's shoulder. "In the meantime, after you check his hands for trace, fax me his prints. I'll run them through IAFIS. Maybe he has a record."

Dr. Aura Chavez considered the victim for a long moment while her criminalists busied themselves in the background video taping, collecting evidence, and snapping hundreds of photos along with the crime-scene techs. As a little girl she was taught that dead people could talk. Her grandmother, a Yoruba priestess, told her that sometime people's souls stayed earthbound so they could help someone heal or to warn them about something. She was taught that sometimes souls even stayed behind because they needed help themselves before crossing over. Her grandmother once shared a story with her about their cousin who didn't cross over when he died. He stayed behind so he could help his wife accept that his death was an accident, that it wasn't her fault.

"But why doesn't she understand, Grandma, if he's there to help her?" Aura had said in Spanish so many years ago.

The Yoruba priestess had held her granddaughter's tiny hand. "When she learns to listen to him with her heart, they'll heal each other. Right now, my sweet child, she's only listening with guilt."

Now, as an adult, Dr. Chavez never had any personal run-ins with ghosts, but she knew exactly how to listen and interpret what a dead body had to say. She kneeled down beside John Doe and slipped paper bags over his hands to protect any trace evidence. "When I get back to my office, I want you to tell me who did this to you."

TWENTY-EIGHT

akeem's head was swarming with questions. Nothing but death would stop him from getting the answers. He had an eerie feeling about this murder, something that strangely bordered on nostalgia. By the time he and Aspen left the scene of the crime, his energy was hovering just above zero. He knew he needed sleep or he wouldn't be any good to himself or this case. He just wasn't sure of how to get some sleep. He was literally scared to close his eyes now. Each time he did, the gruesome images were there. As he and Aspen reached her BMW, Gus Hobbs approached them smiling like a game show host.

Gus was a dusty blond who had a surfer's swagger and the boyish charm of someone who grew up in Southern California. But his jaded blue eyes inferred a rougher upbringing. Gus's byline was attached to just about every crime story in the city. Hakeem frowned. Gus was the last person he wanted to be bothered with.

Gus nodded at Aspen like a professional philanderer. "Detective Skye, you're looking as scrumptious as ever."

"I'm not sure if I should be flattered or insulted."

"We can always work it out over a biscuit and a pillow," Gus said.

"I'm a direct descendant of Nat Turner," Aspen said. "I'm loyal to my hard-wiring. What I got for a white man won't make you come."

"What a pity." Then: "Detective Eubanks," Gus said, shoving his hands in his jacket pockets, "you could at least pretend that you're happy to see me. You know it takes more muscles to frown than it does to smile. Can't we let bygones be bygones?"

Hakeem started getting agitated. Never would he forgive Gus for running a smear campaign in the paper about his family's tragedy. He blasted Gus with a gaze that had turned many tough guys into cowards. "What do you want?"

Gus shrugged a *nothing really*, avoiding direct eye contact. "Just trying to do my job. Some of us actually have to work to put biscuits on the table."

"You boys play nice or you'll get jumped, Gus." Aspen started the car with a feature on her BlackBerry.

Gus threw his hands up, surrendering. "Okay, okay." Then: "How about giving me something, Eubanks?"

"How's this? We're in the business of hunting killers, not encouraging them through incorrigible journalists," Hakeem said.

"The Homicide Unit," Aspen said, "is not making any statements at this time. Come on, asshole. I mean, Gus. You know the routine. You get no special privileges; you'll wait like every other reporter."

"Okay, I'll play fair." Gus pulled a mini tape recorder from his pocket and shut it off. "Off the record then, Eubanks. I'm hearing whispers on this side of the crime-scene tape that the victim was taken out by the Hieroglyphic Hacker. Is there a serial killer stalking our city?"

"I don't know where he is or anyone else for that matter," Hakeem said on the verge of strangling Gus for old and new. "If you let me do my job without running interference under the Freedom of Press Act, I can find the murderer and put him behind bars where he belongs." Hakeem and Aspen turned into a slap of cold air, heading for the car.

"Chill out a minute, Eubanks, would you?"

Hakeem spun on his heels and faced Gus.

"Tell 'em to kiss your ass and let's go," Aspen said and kept going to the car.

Gus sighed. "Come on, Eubanks, let me get the inside track. I need this story. You can give me something without compromising your investigation. All I'm looking for is an angle to get ahead of the pack."

Hakeem imagined his hands around Gus's neck squeezing until he turned beet red and the blood vessels in his eyes broke. "The department will issue a statement in due time."

"Okay, okay. I screwed up. Is that what you wanna hear me say, Eubanks? I'm sorry, okay? I'm sorry for sensationalizing the story about your personal tragedies after you asked me not to."

"Goodbye, Gus."

"Wait a minute." He pushed his fingers through his hair. "How about letting me work with you?"

"Give it up and stay out my way or I'll have you arrested."

"Can't. I have a job to do and the public has a right to be informed."

Hakeem stepped so close to Gus that he felt the man's trepidation. "You mean scare them with your half-cocked assumptions, twisted words, and stories that aren't always fact checked. Stories that have no regard or sympathy for the victim's family. And if you somehow do get the facts from a leak in the department, you'll print them and give the killer the advantage by telling him everything we know. All you reporters are inconsiderate liars and snitches." Hakeem worked himself up a good dose of anger. "Get your pad out. Here's something you can quote."

Gus fumbled with his notepad and pen. When Hakeem saw that he was ready to write, Hakeem said, "No comment, you son of a bitch."

TWENTY-NINE

The Cleveland *Plain Dealer* and other national newspapers and networks were going to have a field day with this turn of events. Aspen took a furtive look at Hakeem, then put her eyes back on the road as her heart filled with empathy. She wished Hakeem would summon the strength to pull out of his rut. It was obvious to anyone with a set of eyes that Hakeem was suffering from post-traumatic stress and was burying himself in work to self-medicate. She checked him out from the corner of an eye as she maneuvered the BMW through Public Square. He was exhausted and trying to pretend as if he wasn't.

"Have the sleeping pills worked for you?" Aspen said.

"I'm immune." He yawned. "I need tranquilizers."

"You look whupped. I'll go back to the office and write the report; you go home and try to get some rest."

"You know that's not my style. There's no way I'll dump all the grunt work in your lap like that."

"Hakeem, you're no good to me running on fumes. Go home and rest so we can approach this from a fresh perspective tomorrow."

Hakeem settled his head against the headrest, relaxed, and closed his tired eyes. "I've been following this story since CNN broke it fourteen months ago. By all news accounts, the Hieroglyphic Hacker has exclusively stalked Denver, Colorado. He's never strayed from his hunting ground. So why now?"

"I'll find out who's the lead in Denver. See what we can learn about this guy's MO. See if any of their suspects or victims have any connections to Cleveland."

Hakeem massaged his temples. "It's oddly uncharacteristic for a pattern killer to change patterns this late in the game. Our victim makes number eight. Three more and he'll be tied with Anthony Sowell."

"Maybe the Hieroglyphic Hacker is evolving or changing geographical locations to elude capture."

He opened his eyes and gave her a serious look as they rode by Stouffer's Inn on the Square. "This guy is no stranger to Cleveland Heights."

"You're thinking the Hieroglyphic Hacker is a native?"

"All I'm saying is he didn't find the synagogue by accident. Like McNally said, 'you wouldn't know the place was there unless you *knew* it was there.' If I were a betting man, I'd put my money on the unsub being Jewish. He also knew he'd have privacy for a long period of time." He yawned. "Can you imagine how long it takes to do what he does to his victims?"

"He's definitely not an opportunistic killer. He plans, which means his victims aren't random. Now we have to find out how he selects them."

"I'm thinking we'll find some answers in yesterday's paper if everything he does is as meticulous as his hieroglyphics."

"Possible," Aspen said, not sounding too convinced. "Maybe he knew the victim and covered the face because of his conscience. Maybe he felt like he was being watched as he did something awful to a friend or loved one."

"Gave that angle some thought too. But, Aspen, this guy has no conscience. I need to see the crime scene photos from his previous victims." Hakeem stretched. "In the meantime, let's see if the prints and trace Chavez's criminologist and the crime-scene techs collected gives us a break."

"Nope," Aspen said, shaking her head as she pulled into the Justice Center's underground parking structure. "That's way too easy. This monster plans; he's smart. We have to assume that the prints and trace belong to the Williamses." She stopped behind Hakeem's Range Rover HSE, then reached across his lap and pushed the door open. "Hakeem, go home and get some sleep. We have a long day ahead of us."

THIRTY

Bratenahl, the epicenter of Cleveland's wealth, boasted an abundance of 6,400-square-foot homes that ranged from Italianate architecture to Victorians with imported marble, angular rooflines, and formidable wrought-iron security gates. Its blue-blooded community held the lakefront properties in their grips since the nineteenth century.

It was after two in the morning when Hakeem Eubanks eased the Range Rover into the Veranda entrance of his swanky home. He tried not to look like always, because mirrors always reflected haunted brown eyes that were glassy with pain, but he couldn't resist. Fixing his gaze on the side-view mirror, he saw it. The battered light pole on his tree lawn. Hakeem downloaded. Burst into tears. He lay his head on the steering wheel and sobbed. What had he done so bad to deserve this type of cruelty from a loving God? How could He justify taking away the people he loved most in the world? As far as Hakeem was concerned, God wasn't fair. He was full of shit.

Then there was the sound of claws against glass. It startled Hakeem. He jerked away from the steering wheel and saw the huge paws of his hundred sixty-pound Presa Canario, Keebler, on the driver's side window.

He stared at her.

Keebler whined then barked. Hakeem powered the window down as Ms. Drew Felding strutted up the driveway wearing a pink bandana, matching terry-cloth housecoat, and bunny-eared slippers. Cute, really cute, he thought, then quickly tried to dry his tears. But he'd learned months ago that Drew didn't miss much.

Keebler barked.

"Missed you too, girl," Hakeem said, stroking Keebler's massive head through the window. "You been good for Ms. Drew?"

Drew said, "She saw your headlights and went berserk with excitement."

Hakeem said nothing.

"Thought she'd tear my door down. Soon as I opened it, she took off."

"Thanks for keeping an eye on her." He stepped out the truck; all six-feet-one of him towering over her.

Drew Felding was nouveau-riche according to their motor-mouthed neighbors. He never fueled the gossip machine; it wasn't his thing. He only nodded his head and pretended to listen when a gossipmonger managed to corner him. Some things were interesting like the Thompsons being swingers, but he didn't agree with the lip service offered up on Drew. True, she recently came into wealth as a result of selecting the right combination of lottery numbers, but she definitely wasn't ostentatious and she definitely had good taste. Didn't the bunny-eared slippers prove that?

"No thanks needed," she said. "We're cool; I mess with you like that. That's how cool peoples get down. I put the spare key back in its hiding place."

Hakeem said nothing.

"Is it true what Sharon Reed is saying about a suspected serial killer murdering that poor man?"

Rubbing Keebler's brindle coat, Hakeem said, "Afraid it looks that way."

"But serial means somebody is repeating the same criminal act. I ain't heard about no serial killers around here but Anthony Sowell. He's in jail, and I keep up with the news. So who are they talking about, Hakeem? All serial killers have names to identify them like they call Sowell the Cleveland Strangler."

"Those details are being withheld right now until the victim is identified and his family is properly notified."

Drew frowned.

"Don't worry. With nosey neighbors like ours, you'll be safe. And I won't rest until I bring this guy to justice or send him to the morgue."

"Oh, I know I'm gonna be safe." She pulled a .9mm Glock 17 semiautomatic from her housecoat pocket. "I'm from the hood, grew up in Garden Valley."

"Is that legal?"

"Boy, I'm legit."

"Well, it's illegal to conceal it in your pocket. Give me this." Hakeem expertly disarmed Drew, made sure the safety was on and the breech was clear. "Come on, Drew, me and Keebler are walking you home."

"What's wrong?" she said as Hakeem all but pulled her across their immaculately manicured lawns.

Hakeem said nothing.

"Hakeem, what's wrong?"

"Women."

"And exactly what's that supposed to mean?" she said, trying to keep the pace with his long strides.

THIRTY-ONE

"**Y**ou need a permit to carry a firearm so I'm carrying it home for you since you aren't allowed to take it outside your house." Then: "You keep up with the news so I'm sure you know about the Castle Doctrine."

"I don't."

Hakeem said nothing.

"You're upset with me. I'm sorry."

"I'm not upset. And there is nothing to apologize about." He pushed her front door open, and then gave her the Glock. "Thanks again for looking out for Keebler." He turned to leave, Keebler obediently at his side.

"Uh, Hakeem."

"Yeah," he said with his back to her.

"I saw the tears."

He faced her and staggered. Drew's housecoat was open and off her shoulders. Naked. Goddess. Breasts set up like a teenager's. His eyes fell to her belly-button piercing, then lower. Shaved clean. Absolutely beautiful, Hakeem thought. Drew was a hundred twenty pounds top. Just perfect.

She took his hand, pulled him inside the house. "Sometimes God takes people from us to give us someone else."

His lips found hers. Soft at first, then their mouths pressed hard against each other's. Hakeem kicked the front door closed, then he peeled her out of the housecoat. Flawless. His style. His type. She pulled him toward the sofa by his belt, knocking around furniture on their way. She pulled his shirttail from his slacks.

"Make love to me all night, Hakeem," she whispered.

A dead body flashed through his mind. It lay on a slab, a tag hung from its toe. Hakeem opened his eyes and hesitated. He took a deliberate breath and fought with himself to take several steps backward.

"What's wrong?" she said, lust in her eyes.

"Forgive me, Drew. You're a beautiful woman, but we can't do this. Not now." He fixed his clothes.

"Never seen a man turn down sex with a naked beautiful woman. Wish you weren't hurting so bad."

"Me too. Goodnight, Drew." Then: "Come on, Keebler, let's go home."

"Goodnight, Detective Hakeem Eubanks." She let out a disappointed sigh.

Hakeem called himself an idiot nearly thirty times as he and Keebler cut across Drew's lawn. When his Pradas hit his driveway, his Palm Treo rang. The short hairs on his neck stiffened. Anytime a homicide detective's phone rang at 2:42 in the morning, it wasn't good news. He took the phone from his pocket and found a text message from Aspen.

her: dr. chavez wants us in her office by eight. she stressed "both."

him: both? sounds scary.

her: tell me about it.

him: meet you there at eight sharp.

her: see you then. sweet dreams, hakeem.

He decided not to touch that text. He powered the phone off and went into the house to eat a Polish Boy smothered with coleslaw, French fries, and barbecue sauce, and to take a cold shower.

THIRTY-TWO

It was a ballsy move. Chance thought long and hard about the importance of it. Law 31: Control the Options. Get Others to Play With the Cards You Deal. He lurked in the shadows and watched the glass door of Edgewater Towers, a high-end high-rise occupied by some of the city's bureaucrats and dignitaries. But Chance knew that even ass-kissing uppity people were creatures of habit. This morning Marcus Jefferson's habit would prove fatal. There was no other way for Chance to exact revenge and win at the end of the day.

Beneath the Nike running suit, Chance's skin was cool. His pulse was even. No worries. He pulled a skull cap on his bald head. He had yet to get comfortable with his dreadlocks being gone. Not his cup of tea, but his feet felt good in the black Air Maxes. Black like his running suit. Black like the Raybans covering his calculating blue eyes. Black like his leather gloves. Chance was more than ready to sacrifice his lamb.

The lobby door of the high-rise swung open.

Clockwork. Chance pushed his hand inside his jacket pocket and stroked the handle of a silenced .45 automatic.

Marcus Jefferson stepped out the building into the darkness, haloed by the light pouring from the lobby. He was a fifty-something white man with thinning hair, a pockmarked face that highlighted a square chin, and palsied hands. He made Chance think of Nick Nolte without the makeup. Marcus Jefferson did a series of warm-up stretches in preparation of his five-mile run through Perkins Beach, a man-made beach and picnic area that sat on the city's west side along the shore of Lake Erie, which he did every morning before work.

Poor schmuck, Chance thought, you'll be punching out this morning.

Marcus waited as a tremor passed through his hands, then he set the lap counter on his Ironman watch and took off, feet pounding the pavement in a steady rhythm. Chance took off running thirty yards behind the lamb, his arms and legs pumping like Hemi pistons. Marcus reached the end of his block in under a minute and made a left turn into the mouth of Perkins Beach.

Twenty yards.

Marcus hit the joggers' path that unfolded parallel with the beach.

Ten yards.

He followed the path while watching the first hints of dawn stretch across the lake's horizon.

Five yards.

Chance didn't know if it was the thump of his Air Maxes or intuition that caused Marcus to look over a shoulder as Chance fell in step with him.

"Good morning," Marcus said with a gritty voice.

Chance whipped out the silenced .45 automatic and unloaded it in Marcus' chest. "Dude, there's nothing good about that."

THIRTY-THREE

akeem Eubanks hadn't slept a wink. By the time 6:45 a.m. rolled around, his alarm clock started making a bunch of noise for nothing. He—red-eyed—lay in his ultra California king staring at the vaulted ceiling while nursing his stress. When he tossed left, there were sweaty visions of Drew's naked body locked in the throes of passion with his. When he turned right, there was the vision of John Doe with his mouth frozen open and a language carved into his skin that Hakeem didn't understand. And when he closed his eyes, there was another body waiting there that he couldn't stand to look at. How could he sleep under those conditions?

Keebler stood in the doorway with a leash in her mouth.

"You want to go outside, girl?"

She whined and wagged her tail.

Hakeem planted his feet on the hardwood floor and picked his way through the house to the marble and stainless steel kitchen with Viking appliances and a set of Tiffany cookware that hung from a wire rack suspended from the ceiling. The kitchen was his wife's favorite place to be. He enjoyed hanging out there with her, talking, while she cooked. Now, the only reason he bothered with the kitchen was because it reminded him of their friendship.

"Don't be mad at me, Keebler. Promise I'll take you for a walk later." He let Keebler into the backyard, then put on a pot of imported coffee. He dug through the recycling bin and took out Thursday's edition of the Cleveland *Plain Dealer*.

As the aroma of expensive java filled the kitchen, Hakeem sat at the island on a cozy stool and read the Metro section for the second time. Minutes into the read, Keebler barked and stood on her hind legs to look at him through the screen door.

"I let you out," Hakeem said, looking up from the newspaper. "You're gonna have to let yourself in. Nice try, girl. I'll take you out for a walk later."

Keebler lifted the door handle with her nose, popped the screen door, and came inside as Hakeem filled her bowl with Eukanuba. Hakeem finished the paper while sipping from his favorite #1 Dad mug. He stared at the paper. There had to be something he missed, something hidden in plain view. All he read was the everyday run-of-the-mill stuff: fugitives wanted, heroin dealer arrested, robbery suspect, shoplifter busted, rapist sentenced. All summed up with a caption of Mayor Nesto Balfour, Chief of Police Dwight Eisenhower, and the new Assistant County Prosecutor Scenario Davenport. They were at a press conference where they vowed to reduce the city's crime wave with community watches, swift police action, and stiff prosecution. Nothing new. So why did the Hieroglyphic Hacker use this section of the newspaper?

The house phone rang.

"Keebler, bring me the phone."

She left the room, returned with the cordless phone in her jaws, then dropped it in Hakeem's hand.

"Communicate," he said into the receiver.

THIRTY-FOUR

Aspen Skye's hair stuck to her forehead, sweat glued her tiny wife beater tee to her skin—tight nipples magnified—and her panties crawled in her ass crack. She hated that shit, but she pressed on. She powered the digital treadmill up to 8.5 and was now in a full sprint. She ran wide open for seven minutes before she powered the machine back down to 5.3 to calm her heart rate and breathing. When she got her wind together, she took out her BlackBerry and called Hakeem.

On the third ring, Hakeem said, "Communicate."

She imagined his handsome face: square jaw, sharp goatee, seductive eyes, dreamy smile that she often got lost in. An erotic sensation swept through her stomach as she pictured him. "Did you see the morning paper?" She jogged like she was born to run.

"Not yet. I was wrapping my mind around Thursday's again. Why, what's up?"

"Put it this way: you'll be hearing from Chief Eisenhower." Translation: *Boy ole boy, I'd hate to be you 'cause your black ass is in big trouble.*

Hakeem said nothing. Translation: *Damn, what did I do this time?*

Aspen said, "So what did Thursday's do for you?"

"Nothing as far as I can tell."

"Didn't do a damn thing for me either." Then: "We're back at covering the face implying that the victim and the killer aren't strangers."

"I'm not fixed on anything."

Aspen said, "A detective by name of Leonardo Scott is flying in from Denver today."

"He wants to see if John Doe was murdered by his guy."

"Yep. Won't budge a lick on sharing any info with us 'til he's sure." Aspen stepped off the treadmill and popped a fertility pill in her mouth. "He doesn't believe the Hieroglyphic Hacker has left his jurisdiction. He thinks we have a copycat on our hands."

"A cop with instincts, knowledgeable about pattern killers."

"Hakeem, I've been thinking about the victim all night." She went into the bathroom and turned the shower on. She poked her belly out in the mirror, imagining herself pregnant, and frowned. "We've got to identify this guy. His family must be worried."

"I feel you. I really do. But I also want to pick someone's brain who has a Ph.D. in Egyptology."

Aspen considered his statement.

"It came to me while laying in bed this morning," Hakeem said. "The Hieroglyphic Hacker wrote on John Doe's body in a language I don't understand. I want to know what he's writing."

THIRTY-FIVE

Hakeem wondered what Aspen had given him the heads-up about. He also wondered what spurred her to hit the tread-mill this morning. He heard the *thump...thump...thump... thump* of her sneakers hitting its pad as they spoke, heard her elevated breathing, imagined the rise and fall of her breasts. The muscles in his stomach tightened. He put the cordless phone on the countertop and forced himself to stop thinking of her before his imagination went too far. One cold shower was enough.

He spied through his kitchen window to make sure the coast was clear. It would really be awkward bumping into Drew right now. He hurried out the kitchen door and went around the house to his front porch so that he could purposefully avoid going through the living room to the front of his house. Hakeem hadn't been in that part of the house since *it* happened. It was still too painful to see the family photos lining the living room's and entrance hall's walls. The framed memories sitting on the mantelpiece over the fireplace were turned face-down like he did all others.

He plucked the morning's paper from the shrubbery—the paper-boy missed the porch as usual—as a black couple came out of the Thompsons' house. The black woman French-kissed Mr. Thomp-son while the black man tongued Mrs. Thompson. Some gossip is true, Hakeem thought. He unrolled the paper and his hemorrhoids flared when he read the bold headline:

HIEROGLYPHIC HACKER HUNTS HEIGHTS

The alliteration told Hakeem that Gus Hobbs was the author behind this morning's headline. He scrolled down the article and found the two independent clauses that Aspen alluded to:

An official source very intimate with the case confirms that the unidentified black male was slain by the Hieroglyphic Hacker, and he swears by his badge that he won't rest until the killer is brought to justice.

"Son of a bitch!" Hakeem said in desperate need of his tube of Preparation H. "You flat-out lied. You should've just quoted my name in the piece."

"Outside the fact that I'm really feeling you," Drew said, coming up behind him, shaking her head, "I tried to give you some empathy pussy to help you get back on track, but talking to yourself is beyond my help." Then she peeked at the headline and her eyes grew wide. "That's who Sharon Reed was talking about?"

Hakeem said nothing.

She pointed. "I live in that big house by myself."

"You'll be fine." He took in the view of Lake Erie while mentally kicking himself in the ass for not sending Keebler to get the newspaper.

"Do you know what this fool does to people? I can't stay by myself until someone figures out how to catch him."

He whistled. "Keebler, come."

Keebler, obedient, came and sat beside him.

"Keebler will keep you company. She's a man-eater and a highly trained police dog. Trust me, she won't fail you." Hakeem knelt beside Keebler and stroked her coat. "Protect Ms. Drew, girl," he said, pointing at Drew.

Keebler barked, then sat beside Drew. Hakeem stormed off.

Empathy pussy? Am I that bad?

Drew said, "When are you coming back?"

Hakeem didn't look back or break stride. "When I catch him."

Hakeem was dressed in a two-button—always two buttons—summer-weight Givenchy suit, a silk shirt, and a pair of alligator shoes when he left the house. While threading his customized Hummer H1 through traffic, his Palm Treo rang.

"Communicate," he said.

"Have you lost your goddamn mind, Eubanks?" It was Chief Eisenhower.

"No, sir."

"You don't talk to the goddamn press unless I okay it."

"Yes, sir."

"This thing was supposed to have a goddamn lid on it."

"I know, sir."

"Who do you work for, me or the goddamn *Plain Dealer?*"

"You, sir."

"Then toe the goddamn line or I'll throw you out on your fancy pansy ass."

"Okay, sir."

"Do I make myself goddammit perfectly clear?"

"Yes, sir."

Chief Eisenhower hung up.

Hakeem thought about how much he hated Gus Hobbs.

THIRTY-SIX

Aspen Skye stepped off her Honda 1200 VFR motorcycle looking like a superstar, as Hakeem pulled onto the parking apron of the Cuyahoga County Coroner's office. The sun was her spotlight. The cigarette dangling from her lips was strangely attractive. It was hard for Hakeem to look at Aspen as just his partner and not identify with her as a gorgeous woman, to not admire her feminine attributes, to ignore the confident sway of her hips. He thought it cute how she religiously wore one designer from head to toe. She wouldn't be caught dead wearing mismatched fashion designers. This morning she was clad in Dolce & Gabbana, evident by the D&G logo repeatedly printed on her apple cap.

Hakeem eased off the car seat and took even easier steps toward her. The Preparation H wasn't doing a damn thing. His heart pounded in his ears as he approached her. He had an impulse to tell her how good she looked to him but chickened out. That was his problem. He never said the things that needed to be said to the people he cared about. He assumed they automatically knew, an assumption he'd spent many sleepless nights regretting. Instead of conveying his inner feelings, he said, "Good morning."

She worked her supermodel strut up to him, nodded, and got right to it. "County Prosecutor Marcus Jefferson was gunned down this morning."

"Caught the tail end of it on FM-108 a few minutes ago."

"Detective Omar Madison is heading up the investigation. Large caliber. They're thinking a forty-five. Did a lot of internal damage." Then: "No eyewitness. No suspect. Professional hit." She thumped the cigarette.

Hakeem said nothing. Translation: *That's fucked up.*

"Doctors don't expect him to make it through the day."

"No one assassinates prosecutors these days except the Zetas cartel. The mob doesn't even pull stunts like that anymore."

Aspen shrugged. "I don't know. Between the Long Wood boys, the Seven All crew, and them hustlers from West a Hundred Thirtieth, I'd place my bet on local drug dealers. They're still bitter about how things played out with the Lee Lucas scandal."

"Sure hope this new assistant county prosecutor, Scenario Davenport, has a huge set of nuts on her. If Jefferson doesn't live through this, it'll be her dog and pony show. She'll need a lot more than good looks to pursue justice in this city."

"Talk to Chief Eisenhower?" Aspen said, eyeing him.

"Seven goddamns in under a minute."

"That's a new record."

"Yeah." Hakeem nodded. "I had to be the one who managed to piss the chief off the worst during his tenure with the department behind Gus' lies."

"Your hemorrhoids are acting up again."

Hakeem clearly understood that as a statement and not a question. "I don't know how I feel about you knowing me so well." Then: "How'd you know?"

"You walk like it hurts."

"Gus Hobbs is a literal pain in my butt."

"No, post-traumatic stress and insomnia are the cause of your hemorrhoids. Learned it on a medical online chat room."

"My hemorrhoids are not a subject open for discussion."

They went inside the squat-brown building. The air conditioning chilled their skin. It had to be set on Arctic Circle. An ominous scent deceptively lingered beneath a pleasant industrial deodorizer. The sensory ambiguity was dizzying. Stephanie, the twenty-something receptionist with black lipstick and an eyebrow piercing, spoke and waved them through. They navigated the narrow halls to the autopsy suite.

Here, the presence of death and flesh rot didn't linger; it overpowered. Aspen grabbed a bottle of mentholatum sitting on a stand near the entrance and rubbed some under Hakeem's nose to mask the scent, then rubbed it beneath her own nostrils. An internal speaker system played Bruno Mars' "Die For You." The autopsy suite was colder than the rest of the building. Aspen hugged herself and rubbed her bare arms. Hakeem, eager to offer her comfort, wrapped his suit jacket around her slender frame. Forensic Pathologist Aura Chavez, MD was hosing blood and bodily fluids—the leftovers of a drunk driver—down the drain of a soiled autopsy table while eating a turkey club sandwich. Her age showed itself with each chew.

Chavez snapped off her rubber gloves. "Top of the morning, Detectives. I was just finishing up breakfast." She popped the last bite of turkey club in her mouth.

Hakeem and Aspen greeted her.

"Terrible, terrible thing about Marcus Jefferson," Chavez said. "I always wanted to see him naked, but doing an autopsy on him wasn't what I had in mind. From what I'm hearing, looks like that's how things are going to play out."

Hakeem said nothing.

"Let's hope not," Aspen said. "He's one of the good guys."

"Well, don't be bashful. Come over here and let me tell you what Mr. John Doe told me." Chavez led them across the stainless steel room to a gurney. She sang along with Bruno as she unzipped the body bag.

THIRTY-SEVEN

C hance extracted thirty cubic centimeters of tetrodotoxin from the Blue-ringed octopus—more than enough venom to down an elephant—then put the creature back in the aquarium with the others. He carefully capped the syringe and placed it with his murder tools. Next, he changed into clothing more his speed: a *Free Lil' Wayne* T-shirt, loose-fitting jeans with no underwear, and a pair of Vans sneakers. No socks. Then he went to the building's incinerator to dispose of his previous outfit. After he watched the Nike get-up burn to ashes, he returned to his apartment for his murder tools. Now it was time to pay another so-called friend a visit that he'd never forget.

Chance sat at an RTA bus stop directly across the street from the Yoga Wellness Center on Superior Avenue. While keeping an eye on the center, he read about Yancee's murder in the newspaper. He hoped it was Detective Hakeem Eubanks who was the "official source" who had sworn to put him behind bars. Hakeem doesn't have enough intelligence quotient to catch me if I purposefully made mistakes, Chance thought.

A top-heavy sister with even heavier knockers sat down on the bench beside Chance. She was sweating and wearing a Burger King uniform and smelling just like the Hamburglar. She stuck her nose in Chance's newspaper like they were buddy-buddy. Chance peeped her out through his peripheral vision and thought, fat ass.

"Now that's just a damn shame," Fat Ass said. "They ought not waste taxpayers' dollars. Soon as they catch that lunatic, they should shoot and kill 'em on the spot. Get it over with; that's what I'd do."

"Then your position is no better than his." Chance watched as Anderson unlocked the center.

Fat Ass snorted. "What you mean?"

"You share the same morals as the person who whacked this twit."

"Boy, you done lost your mind." She rested her arms on top of her knockers.

"For whatever depth of pain is driving this guy, it's obvious it's his way of righting a wrong done to him. And your way of righting a wrong is to kill. You said that."

"You act like you support 'em."

"Morally, so do you, Fat Ass."

She was taken aback. The bus rolled to a stop in front of them; its doors hissed open. Fat Ass hauled her wide load off the bench and onto the bus.

Chance tossed the newspaper and pushed his hands inside a pair of leather gloves. Two minutes later he slipped into the Yoga Wellness Center. He secured the door, closed the blinds, and hung a sign he had written last night that read: *Closed, Family Emergency.* The place was nothing more than an empty room with seven rows of mats across and six back on the floor. Paneled walls boasted vanity-driven pictures of Anderson in the scorpion position, downward dog, sun salutation, and numerous other yoga positions that Chance didn't give a fuck about. The few windows were blocked by venetian blinds for intimacy and privacy, because Anderson offered naked yoga to his more spiritually free clients.

Perfect.

A single mat was front and center. That's where Chance found Anderson sitting in the lotus position with his back to the entrance. He was deep in meditation and chanting: "Om namah shivaya." Translation: *I honor my own inner self, that part of me that is the unchanging witness of everything I do, think, and say.* Ocean sounds poured from a CD player. For crying out loud, Chance thought, this is fucking absurd. Anderson was just as Chance remembered: rail thin, skin blotched with exanthema, long face, teeth bucked and gapped like a claw-headed hammer, all capped off with a bald head. He was barefoot and wearing a pair of sweat pants and a loose-fitting white T-shirt. By Anderson's fifth Om mantra, Chance was so close, he cast a shadow on Anderson.

"Appointments only, and I'm not open until ten." Anderson never opened his eyes.

"Dude, a Smith & Wesson forty-four magnum doesn't need an appointment."

Anderson's eyes popped open. He found himself looking down the wrong end of a gun.

THIRTY-EIGHT

John Doe lay dead with a Y incision cut into his torso. The hieroglyphics cut into his skin looked like a tribute to the ancient pyramids in Giza, Egypt.

Mr. Doe's physique, however, was the result of years of hard work in the gym. Every muscle was defined and pronounced. Ghostly X-rays of Mr. Doe's skull and teeth were clipped to an exam box near the autopsy table.

Chavez turned on a fluorescent exam light that hovered above Mr. Doe. "Got some prelims in before breakfast. All the blood evidence found at the crime scene belongs to Mr. Doe here. An examination of his teeth puts him at approximately thirty-two, thirty-three years old. Still waiting on toxicology. Since I'm certain of my conclusion, toxicology won't provide any new evidence. And I sent the hair sample to the lab for a DNA profile."

Hakeem said nothing. Aspen considered what was said.

"The hair sample my criminologist collected, I can definitively say doesn't belong to Mr. Doe. It has a bulb, but most I believe we'll learn from it is race. So don't count on it to break the case."

"What was the cause of death?" Aspen said, studying the Anubis cut into John Doe's forehead.

"Be patient, Detective Skye," Chavez said. "We'll get to that. Let me walk you through this."

Hakeem started sweating. He felt it happening again.

"No semen and no tearing or bruising of the anus."

Interesting, Hakeem thought as he tried to calm himself. Serial killers who mutilated their victims were usually sexually motivated. So what inspired John Doe's killer if not sexual gratification?

And then it happened. The body haunting him flashed in Hakeem's mind's eye. The tag hanging from its toe. Its thin legs and scarred knees. Hakeem stumbled into a tray, knocking over Chavez's tools. He gasped for air, unloosening his tie.

"Hakeem…Hakeem." Aspen went to him.

"Detective Eubanks, are you all right?" Chavez said.

Hakeem took a deep breath and wiped the sweat from his forehead. "I'm…I'll be fine. I'm all right. Please forgive me." He started picking up Chavez's tools with Aspen's help. "Please continue."

"Are you sure, Detective?"

"He said he's good," Aspen said, shifting into defense mode.

Chavez shook her head. "No alcohol or any type of drugs in John Doe's blood or urine." She pulled a specimen bottle from her lab coat pocket and held it up to the light. Inside was a tiny bug that looked part crab-part beetle. "This was found in Mr. Doe's hair. It's a grieter, a predatory bug that belongs to the Heteroptera group. But what on God's green earth is it doing here in Ohio? You have to ask yourself that when we don't have these here. They can't survive here."

Aspen shrugged. "No biggie. Someone unknowingly carried it here, but from where?"

Chavez smiled, a gold tooth front and center. "I've always admired your inductive reasoning skills, Detective Skye. They're keen. The grieter is a native of Colorado that thrives in the high altitudes of the Rocky Mountains. Every April it leaves the mountain and goes to the banks of the Colorado River to breed."

Hakeem said, "Then we're not dealing with a copycat murderer. The Hieroglyphic Hacker is from Denver." But why did he switch his pitch now? Hakeem thought.

Aspen hugged herself tight in Hakeem's suit jacket.

"Now that we've got that established," Chavez said, "here's where things start to stink worse than a dead body."

THIRTY-NINE

Aspen highly doubled that. Nothing real or figuratively she ever experienced stunk worse than dead human flesh. So she wasn't buying into that hyperbole.

Chavez said, "There are no ligature markings or defensive wounds. With the condition of Mr. Doe's body, you have to ask yourself, why is that?" She moved down to Mr. Doe's thighs. "Detective Skye, you were right in part with your assessment last night. The hieroglyphics are postmortem, but he didn't bleed to death from the stab wounds." She stuck a latex-gloved fingertip in a stab wound. "Yet this man was stabbed *three* different times before he died."

Hakeem jotted some notes in his Mont Blanc day planner. "A guy built like this—anyone really—would have fought his attacker during and/or started fighting after the stabbing."

"There isn't a sliver of evidence to support a struggle." Chavez paused. Aspen knew it was to let them absorb that tidbit. "That baffled me but not for long."

Aspen played it out in her head. "Maybe John Doe had a strong incentive not to fight. Someone else's life might have depended on his compliance."

"Nothing is stronger than self-preservation," Hakeem said. "Let's say you're right, Aspen. Someone else's life was being bargained with. Even then, at the bare minimum, you'll raise your hands to block a knife coming at you. It's a natural reflex. Just like you'll raise your hands and beg for your life if someone threatens you with a gun."

Anderson threw his hands up. "Please don't shoot me. Chance, think about this. You don't want my death on your conscience."

"Dude, if I don't kill you, it'll be on my conscience."

"But…but why do you have a gun in my face? I haven't seen or spoken to you in over ten years."

Chance clicked the hammer in place. "You took part in ruining my family."

"I don't know what you're talking about." Anderson started sobbing. "But whatever you're thinking, I don't deserve to die. Please don't kill me."

"Stop your sniveling, you prick. 'Cause I got a soft spot, I'll do you a solid."

Anderson eagerly nodded. "Anything you want for my life."

"Tell me everything about February third of ninety-nine and I won't punch your clock, shithead."

"My point exactly. Self-preservation," Chavez said. "I began wondering if this was a cult killing and Mr. Doe offered himself as a sacrifice until I found this." She moved to the upper part of the corpse. She pointed to a series of vertical scratches, fine scratches. They stretched from the left side of John Doe's chiseled face to the bottom of his chest. "You're probably thinking these scratches run from the face downward, which is a logical assumption, but it's the exact opposite. They begin below his pecs and end here on his face."

Hakeem said nothing.

"Someone dragged him," Aspen said.

Lady Gaga's "Born This Way" replaced Bruno Mars. *Who was next*, Aspen thought, *Justin Bieber?*

"Correct. He was dragged indeed," Chavez said. "But what concerned me was what he didn't *instinctively* do while being dragged." She pronounced *IN-STINGK-TIV–LY* very deliberately so it would hit its mark. "Mr. Doe was on his stomach. The Hieroglyphic Hacker lifted his legs leaving only his chest and face on the ground, and dragged him from outside the synagogue to where he was found inside. Found gravel particles and soil in the scratches consistent with the gravel and soil composition outside the crime scene." Then: "But you have to ask yourself, why are there only scratches on one side of Mr. Doe's face? Why aren't soil and gravel particles under his nails?" She looked from Hakeem to Aspen. "Because he was unable to turn his head or claw the ground in an effort to stop himself from being dragged to his death."

"Okay," Aspen said. "He was unconscious."

"We factually know Mr. Doe wasn't drugged unconscious because his urine and blood work says so. There's no scientific evidence to prove he's been hit with anything. No contusions or hemorrhaging. You have to be physically struck with a fist or an object to be knocked out without the aid of drugs, right?"

Aspen wasn't going to dignify a rhetorical question.

Chavez moved to Mr. Doe's face, pulled his eyelids back, and shined a penlight into what was left of his black irises. There appeared to be red dots around his eyes and inside the eyelids. "The red hemorrhage specks you see are called petechiae, which occur in death when a person is strangled or suffocated."

Hakeem leaned in to get a closer look. "Scientifically you ruled out strangulation."

"There are no cloth fibers in Mr. Doe's mouth or nose. Nor was there any adhesive substance on his face."

Aspen said, "So the Hieroglyphic Hacker didn't tape John Doe's mouth or smother him with something or put a plastic bag over his head because there's no ligature markings around his neck, which there would be because he would naturally struggle against the bag. Self-preservation."

"You got it, kiddo," Chavez said with a smile, clearly pleased with her teaching skills.

"Hey, wait a minute," Hakeem said. "Petechiae can only happen when someone is strangled or suffocated to death."

"Correct, Detective Eubanks. Yet this man still died of suffocation, respiratory failure." Chavez zipped the body bag and handed Aspen and Hakeem each a copy of her autopsy report. "Mr. Doe's fingerprints are along with my findings. In light of all the evidence, there are only two ways I know Mr. Doe could have died of respiratory failure under these circumstances. He was either injected with an anesthesia such as succinylcholine, but there are no injection markings on his body that I can find, or he was bitten by a Hapalocheana maculosa."

Hakeem said nothing.

"Now you know damn well we don't know what the hell that is." Aspen rolled her eyes.

"A Blue-ring octopus. But rule that out because they are only found in Australia. Both, however, render a person totally paralyzed but fully conscious. Both, if not treated immediately, will kill a person via suffocation. And both vanish from the system in the matter of minutes. Sometimes traces of sucs can be found but never the toxins of a blue ring."

Aspen thought about John Doe's stab wounds. "Can a person talk under the influence of sucs or a blue ring?"

"It's difficult, very painful, but yes."

"Painful?" Hakeem said. "They can still feel pain?"

Chavez nodded. "Every bit of it." Then: "And let me leave you with this: There's a difference in cutting and being professionally trained to cut, Detectives. The wounds on Mr. Doe are not regular cuts made with a nonserrated blade; they're surgical incisions that cut through the skin and into the superficial fascia. The methodical sequence of incisions wasn't learned by practicing to cut on his victims. He has experience. The hieroglyphics on Mr. Doe's body were cut with a scalpel by the hand of a professional." She gave them a plastic bag with John Doe's UPS shirt in it. Through the bag they saw the blood-stained shape of a scalpel blade on the shirt.

Anesthesia? Scalpel? Aspen knew what type of person they were hunting.

FORTY

S cenario Davenport enjoyed her view of the Rock 'n' Roll Hall of Fame from her office in the county courthouse. She was finally moving forward with her life without having to worry about the person she used to be. She leaned back in a high-back leather chair and spoke into the phone. "Detectives Eubanks and Skye."

"What about them?" Sergeant Morris said.

"Detective Eubanks hasn't been tight-lipped."

"Haven't spoken to him yet, but I'm sure there's more to it."

"From a legal standpoint, I hope this isn't the level of profession- alism he'll give to the investigation. I've never worked with him or Detective Skye, so I don't know their MO. I'm concerned because their investigation is what I'll use to prosecute this case should it ever go to trial." Then: "It has to be solid."

"Mayor Balfour handpicked them," Sergeant Morris said. "I'm sure that tells you a lot."

"That tells me nothing, Sergeant Morris. The mayor's selection has nothing to do with my job description. This is a high-profiled murder so I need to be certain that I have competent investigators working on this. And I'm just not convinced judging from this morning's paper." Scenario tossed the paper in her wastepaper basket. "I'm not being a bitch, Sergeant. But because of the tragedy this morning, this situation was dropped in my lap and it's my responsibility to see it through."

"I know you're new and all and it must be hectic over there in the DA's office with Jefferson being gone, but let me tell you something about my detectives, Ms. Davenport."

"I'm listening."

"Detectives Eubanks and Skye have a hundred percent case clearance because their hard-wiring makes them the perfect combination."

A hundred percent? Excellent, Scenario thought.

Sergeant Morris continued: "They clear cases because Eubanks needs answers and Skye needs to set things right. They're expert trial witnesses. Eubanks is a grade-three detective who has worked on every multijurisdictional task force you can name. Skye used to be an FBI profiler. She was taught by the nation's leading serial killer investigators. And she worked on the FBI-LAPD unsolved murder team. If this guy is nabbed in Cleveland, they will hand you everything to send him to death row."

"Have them available for a briefing before the press conference this afternoon. Any official statements made to the public in regards to the Hieroglyphic Hacker from this day forward will be examined by me first."

"Not a problem, Ms. Davenport."

Scenario forgot her manners and hung up without warning. She took in her view for a moment—loving how her life was coming together—then swiveled her chair to face Jazz leaning against the doorjamb. Jazz wore a trendy pair of jeans, sunglasses, and a New York Knicks ball cap.

"This is a pleasant surprise," Scenario said, thinking of how the Knicks had the worst season ever.

"Thought you might need a dose of your best friend, considering everything that's going on."

"Who would ever think that I'd make county prosecutor by default? That's a big responsibility I'm not sure I can handle." Then: "I was perfectly fine with *Assistant* County Prosecutor Scenario Davenport."

"Let's go somewhere," Jazz said, "and talk. You had breakfast?"

"If you consider a banana protein shake breakfast," Scenario said, thinking of how convicting a case like the Hieroglyphic Hacker's would put her career on easy street.

"Come have breakfast with Jaden and me."

Jaden? Scenario thought and shot to her feet. "Where's Jaden?"

Jazz glanced somewhere down the hallway. "He's sitting down there by the elevators spinning that darn basketball on his finger."

Scenario slipped into her suit jacket before Jazz could say another word and headed for the door. "Where are we having breakfast?"

"Jaden is crazy about Benihana. His dad always took him there."

FORTY-ONE

A hibachi grill sizzled their French toast golden brown. The grill sat inches from their table. The chef, a pudgy man with a unibrow, juggled a trio of eggs.

Jaden watched with something close to amazement. That pleased Jazz. Suddenly, the chef cracked each egg in midair with a Santoku knife. The yolks fell to the grill as the chef expertly caught the shells in his smock pocket. Jaden skinned and grinned as the chef entertained them with the preparation of the gourmet meal. Jazz was happy to see Jaden smile.

Scenario snapped her fingers and cleared her throat. "At some point this has to stop. It's worrying me, Jazz."

Reluctantly, Jazz took her attention off Jaden and put it on Scenario. "Girl, I'm good. One thing I know is we can't have testimony without being tested by adversity."

Scenario sighed.

"Everything will work itself out," Jazz said.

"Have you even tried getting back on your grind and write?" Scenario said as the chef diced green peppers, mushrooms, and onions.

"Yeah right," Jaden said. "She's too busy bugging the heck out of me all day."

"No one asked you anything, Jaden. Hasn't anyone ever told you to stay out of grown folks' conversations?" Jazz peeped the chef ear hustling and trying to make heads or tails of their dialogue. To Scenario, she said, "I'll get things on track."

"We all fall on our face; it's how we get back up that's important. You haven't gotten up since the accident."

Jazz thought back to the day she watched the paramedics peel Scenario off the hood of her car. She frowned, hating that she was responsible for changing the course of all their lives.

"Everyone has something they need to lay to rest," Scenario said. "That's what I had to do with Cashmaire Fox; it was the only way for me to move forward." Then: "I was watching *Ghost Whisperer.*"

"A sitcom, Scenario? Really?"

Scenario rolled her eyes and turned up the corner of her mouth. "You of all people know that art imitates life."

"Whatever."

"There's a lot of truth in entertainment and you know it," Scenario said. "Anyway. Jennifer Love Hewitt's character said something that resonated: if you want to lay your ghost to rest, you should revisit the scene of the accident since it changed your life so much. It'll help you let it go."

"I'm ready to go," Jaden said.

Jazz said with a brow raised above the frame of her glasses, "But… but we haven't eaten yet."

"Now! I'm ready to go now!" He pounded his fists on the table so hard that Scenario jumped. He scooted his chair away from the table and stormed out of the restaurant.

"Jaden, wait a minute." Jazz took off behind him, as she heard Scenario say "Sorry" to the bewildered chef.

Outside of Benihana Jazz found Jaden standing next to her BMW X6. "What happened in there?"

Buank. Buank. Buank. Buank.

"Jaden, I'm talking to you."

Buank. Buank. Buank. Buank.

"What is going on with you?"

Buank. Buank. Buank. Buank.

Scenario came out the restaurant as the BMW's engine started. Its lights flashed and the horn blew.

"I. Said. I'm. Ready. To. Go." *Buank. Buank. Buank. Buank.*

FORTY-TWO

O utside the coroner's office, Aspen handed Hakeem his suit jacket. "He tortured him, Hakeem. The Hieroglyphic Hacker questioned Mr. Doe and stabbed him for the answers."

"What about those answers were important enough to kill over?"

"That's what we have to find out."

"He used the tools of his trade to murder John Doe with." Hakeem stroked his chin. "We're looking for a doctor. He's smart."

"Extremely. And he's a fucking psychopath." Then: "A dangerous combination."

"You have a psychological fingerprint worked up on this nut yet?"

"I got a little something-something put together," she said, straddling the motorcycle. "It's a preliminary profile based on the information we have."

Hakeem said nothing. Translation: *Drop it on him.*

"Definitely a male, white. More than likely he's in his early to mid-thirties. We can reasonably conclude that he's very detailed-oriented from the mastery of the hieroglyphics. He's antisocial and shuns public attention. That's why he keeps things personal between himself and the police, flaunting his intelligence by writing on the victims in brilliant codes instead of sending simple letters to the press. He's an egocentric who's prone to boredom and wields superficial charm. He spends a lot of his private time thinking, planning, which is why he hasn't been caught. According to Mr. Doe, the Hieroglyphic Hacker isn't sexually motivated, so he's a sadistic murderer, who lacks remorse, which probably means his choice of music ranges from rock to heavy metal. The sadistic nature of his murders suggest his aim is to inflict the pain on his victim that he feels himself. A transference. A punishment. It's like he's saying, 'see how *it* feels.' And now we know he's been educated in the medical field."

"I wanna know what *it* is and *what* Mr. Doe told him." He fell silent until his Palm Treo rang.

"Communicate."

"Detective Eubanks, Tony Adams here." Tony was the head crime scene technician.

"What you got for me, Tony?" Hakeem said, watching Aspen pucker her pouty lips in the motorcycle's mirror and gloss them. She had no idea how much of a distraction she was.

"The shoe prints were made by a Vans sneaker, size nine. The distance in the stride between the left and the right shoe prints makes the killer approximately five-nine, five-ten inches tall."

"Assuming our unsub made the prints." Hakeem never validated a point without conclusive proof.

"Yes, assuming."

"Give me some good news on the latents."

"We're still running them, Detective Eubanks." Tony sounded disappointed. "There are hundreds of them. Probably every Jew in Cleveland Heights has a set of prints in that place. The ones I can positively identify right now are Mr. and Mrs. Williams', which were located in the appropriate areas consistent with their job description."

And their story, Hakeem thought. "Thanks, Tony. Call me when you get anything."

"Okay, Detective Eubanks."

"Anything, Tony. I don't care how small. I wanna nail this guy." Hakeem ended the call and the phone rang right back. "Communicate."

"Marcus Jefferson didn't make it," Sergeant Morris said. "Died twenty minutes ago."

"Sorry to hear that, sir. I know the two of you were friends."

Aspen mouthed the word *Jefferson?* And Hakeem nodded.

"Be in the Homicide Unit by two," Sergeant Morris said. "Since you yapped your gums, the mayor, chief, and the ACP are trying their hand at damage control with a press conference this evening. You and Aspen need to brief them."

"Okay, Sergeant. See you later." Hakeem hung up, then filled Aspen in.

Aspen said, "Scenario Davenport is worried. With Marcus gone, she ultimately knows that this case will be up to her when we bring this guy in."

"You sound sure of yourself."

"I'm an optimist. Davenport wants to be briefed to test the legality of what we have."

"Which is nothing but a preliminary profile."

Aspen smiled. "It's a start. I'm going to the station and have Tony run Mr. Doe's prints. And I have a hunch I want to follow."

"A hunch?"

"Yeah, I'll hip you on later."

"While you're doing that," Hakeem said, "I'll check out the Williamses' story, then I'll go pay an old friend a visit."

FORTY-THREE

Anderson smiled his bucked-and gapped-tooth smile. "My friends are a little thrown off like everyone else, but they're cool. Jazz, you'll like them. Trust me," he said as they walked the narrow dormitory hallway toward Apartment 619. "While I take my insulin, you make yourself comfortable."

"You don't know how happy I am to finally be away from the country. I swear to God the State of Maryland doesn't ever have to worry about Jazz Smith again." Jazz was a slender beauty, all legs and charisma. By all definitions, she was considered a dainty dime. She wore a pair of Guess jeans like a second layer of skin and a girly sweater under a fly leather coat. She stepped with confidence in a trendy pair of boots and a Baltimore Ravens skull cap.

"Sell one of your manuscripts and you can live anywhere in the world you want."

"Think I really have what it takes to make it as an author?"

"Lil' cousin, you're gonna be a New York Times bestseller. They're gonna study your works in prestigious universities like they do Tolstoy, Hemingway, Dickens, and Dumas."

"That would really be something." She turned up the corners of her mouth into a gorgeous smile.

When they rounded the corner, the door of Apartment 619 was wide open. They entered as Yancee was saying, "That's not a good idea. If he finds out—"

"What's not a good idea?" Anderson said to his friends.

Yancee and Leon looked up. Jazz and Leon locked gazes, communicating something that only they understood.

Yancee was pissed. He said, "This fool wants to set Chance up with a girl who's kinda like a hermaphrodite. All for laughs because he's still hurt about Sahara."

"There isn't such a thing as a hermaphrodite," Anderson said. "It's a purely mythical creature from ancient literature. It was said to have a completely functional set of…It was supposed to have a dick and a pussy."

"Yeah," Jazz said, "the medical community adopted the fictional term 'hermaphrodite' to describe a condition where a female has an abnormally large clitoris."

"I don't know anything about any of that." Yancee passed Jazz the article. "This is what I'm talking about."

"Excuse me for being rude," Anderson said. "This is my cousin Jazz Smith from Maryland. She's going to school here now. And you guys are looking at a world-famous author in the making."

Jazz blushed. "Stop it. You're embarrassing me."

"I'm Yancee." He shook her tiny hand. "And this fool looking at you all goofy is Leon."

Leon took her hand and held on to it, sensing a weakness within her. "Nice to meet you." He looked at her with disgust. "I would be honored to show you around campus."

Jazz blushed, mistaking Leon's gaze of disrespect for admiration. "I'd like that."

"No way, Jose." Anderson injected himself in the thigh with a dose of insulin. "She's my first cousin, Leon."

"But I'm not your little cousin anymore, Anderson. I'm a grown woman."

"Say no more." Leon squeezed her hand harder than necessary, then reluctantly let it go, not convinced that he had established his dominance.

Jazz read the article aloud, getting comfortable with the group. When she finished, she closed the magazine. "Never heard of this."

"Me neither," Anderson said, looking at the cover of the magazine. "I'm in total agreement with Yancee. Hooking Chance up with someone like this is not a good idea, Leon. Did you forget that we all got a gay-bashing conviction because Chance started that fight in Best Steak House last semester?"

"It's none of my business, Leon," Jazz said. "But you shouldn't play that type of trick on a person, especially someone who's averse to gays. Somebody could get hurt like that guy did on the Jenny Jones Show.*"*

"Talk some sense into him then," Yancee said. "Keep that up and you're gonna fit right in."

Leon said, "She-slash-he isn't gay, though." Pissed that Jazz had challenged him.

Yancee shook his head and tightened his jaw. "That's not the point."

"I swear AIS is some top-secret stuff. I've never heard of it," Anderson said. "What does someone look like who has it?"

"You know the girl this article is talking about," Yancee said.

"No, I don't." Anderson emphatically made that statement like he would be ashamed if he did know her.

"The bea— Whoa, I almost said beautiful, but that doesn't sound right anymore," Yancee said. "It's Cash, that reclusive girl who works in the school bookstore."

Anderson's brows lifted. "Stop playing. She's probably the most gorgeous girl I've ever seen."

Leon nodded, proud of himself. "And she-slash-he has a Valentine's date that ends with a tongue kiss with Chance. Bought and paid for. I'm gonna laugh my ass off and record the whole kiss part. Chance is finally gonna get what he has coming to him for sleeping with and stealing people's girls."

"*Chance is a little off. Like* needs medication *off, if you somehow haven't noticed.*" *Anderson stared at Euclid Avenue from the window.* "*He might pull a Jenny Jones if he finds out. No matter how you slice it, Leon, Chance will think that going out with Cash and kissing her is a homosexual act.*"

"*You sound like you're gonna snitch on me.*" *Leon gave Anderson a hard stare.*

"*I don't have a thing to do with it. Now I wish I didn't know.*"

Leon turned his ominous gaze on Yancee. "*What about you, champ?*"

"*It's your world, Leon; it's all on you. And even if I were so happenly to laugh at the situation, which I might, that doesn't mean I condone your bullshit. So don't misinterpret nothing.*"

"*Before you even look at me,*" *Jazz said.* "*I told you once already that it ain't my business. I don't know this Chance dude or y'all. But I do think this AIS business is an interesting subject matter to research and write about. Leon, think you can introduce me to Cash?*"

"*Sure, but she doesn't know we know her secret.*"

FORTY-FOUR

"**D**ude, don't confuse my willingness to postpone your death sentence with compassion. I didn't give you permission to stop running your fucking mouth."

"It's my sugar, Chance," Anderson said, sweat spilling off him. "I need my insulin."

Chance thought about that for a long while. "Where is it, shithead?"

"In my tote bag hanging there." Anderson pointed to a wall-mounted coat rack near the door.

After looking across the room at the tote, Chance focused back on Anderson. "Move that turd cutter of yours an inch and you're gonna be in humongous trouble." Chance went to the tote bag and swapped Anderson's syringe with the one he brought in his murder kit.

Then two things happened: some illiterate asswipe knocked on the door and Anderson screamed for help like a bitch. Chance was fucked.

By 9:15 a.m. Detective Aspen Skye had dropped off John Doe's fingerprints to be run through the system. When she entered the cool ambience of the Homicide Unit, she walked in on the tail end of a conversation between the notorious male chauvinist Detective Omar Madison and Tony Adams. There was no doubt in Aspen's mind that Madison was trying to proselytize Tony Adams to his fucked-up views about women.

"See, Adams, there's absolutely nothing like it," Detective Madison said, gnawing on an imitation Havana. "But the irony about a decent blow job is that you've got the chick on her knees where she's supposed to be, submitting to you, but she's got you by the balls."

Madison's pseudo-Havana made Aspen crave a cigarette, but she headed to the coffee maker for a fix instead. "Madison, why don't you tell Tony how magnificent women like me have super powers."

"You wish you had super powers, Skye. You wish women had any real power at all," Detective Madison said as if Aspen was way out of line for opening her mouth and butting in without an invite.

"Trust me, Madison, I do have super powers. I can get soaking wet any time I want to without water. I can bleed without being cut. I can make boneless meat hard as a rock, and I can make you eat without cooking whenever the fuck I feel like it." She saw Madison's eyes light up as if he were thinking something lewd. "Tony, the victim's prints are on your desk. Get me something on them soon."

She felt the men watching the sway of her hips as she walked away.

"Yup, she has super powers," Tony said.

Aspen settled in behind her desk and turned on the computer. She began by checking her email account, then she made a call to Monticello Junior High School, who transferred her to the Cleveland Heights Board of Education.

"Board of Education, how may I direct your call?"

"Records." She sipped her coffee hoping it satisfied her jones.

"Hold please." After a few aggravating minutes of bullshit phone music, a male voice said, "Records, Brendyn Harris speaking."

Aspen heard the youthfulness of his voice and figured that Brendyn wasn't older than twenty-one. "Brendyn, this is Detective Aspen Skye with the Cleveland Police Department."

Brendyn was quiet for way too long. "Ah." He fumbled again. "Ah…how can I help you, Detective?"

Aspen was very intuitive. She peeped Brendyn's apprehension. He must have, for some reason, figured that this call was in direct relation to him. So you're a bad boy, Aspen thought. "I'm investigating a murder and I'm wondering if you can help me compile a list of names. Male students who attended Monticello during the years of—" She did a quick calculation of the years the killer would have been in junior high based on her profile. "—ninety-two through ninety-five."

Brendyn let out a deep breath. "That has to be a huge list." He sounded so relieved.

I wonder what you're hiding, Brendyn, Aspen thought. "I can narrow it."

"How so?"

"Only the males who lived between Cain Park and Euclid Heights Boulevard, roughly a twenty-block radius."

"That simplifies things, but I'll have to check with my supervisor and he won't be in until Monday."

"Brendyn, did you read the headlines this morning?"

"No, ma'am. But I know what you're talking about. Everybody is worrying about it."

"Then we don't have time for the mumbo jumbo. I'm not asking for their file, just names."

Brendyn hesitated. "How do I know you're really a cop?"

"Because I know all about the mess you're caught up in."

"Detective Skye, I swear to God it wasn't my weed. I was just giving those guys a ride to the Steel Yard." Then: "If my mother finds out, she'll take my car and I'll have to catch the bus to school and work."

"You know what, Brendyn, I'll forget about your marijuana troubles if you give me the names."

"You swear?"

"Girl Scout's honor."

"It'll take me at least an hour to search the records."

"Got a pen?"

"Yeah, shoot."

"My number is 216-619-2009. I'll expect those names in an hour."

FORTY-FIVE

The entire world around them was mute. It was nothing more than images, colors, motion, perception, and touch. They stood in front of the Wellness Center dressed for a rigorous yoga session. After reading the "Family Emergency" note stuck to the door, the man turned to his wife and spoke to her in sign language. She frowned, disappointed, then knocked on the Wellness Center's door for good measure anyway. When no one answered, they strolled up Superior Avenue holding an intense conversation in sign language.

"Please help me! Somebody help me," Anderson screamed. "He's got a gun!"

Through clenched teeth, Chance said, "Open your pussy eaters again and I'll go out in a blaze of glory starting by killing you. Then I'll shoot through this door and kill whoever's on the other side of it." He raised the gun to Anderson's head. "Choose."

Anderson remained silent.

"Good answer, shithead." Chance's heart was giving him a good pounding. He hadn't punished everyone involved with plotting to ruin his family life yet. Now was not the time to get caught; it would defeat the purpose and spoil the spectacular ending. He eased to the window and to his amazement, he watched a hearing-impaired couple through a slight opening in the venetian blinds, as he realized he had broken out in a sweat. When the couple walked away, he turned back to Anderson. "I don't think they heard you. Dude, you're gonna pay for that big-time."

"I'm terrified." A tear ran down Anderson's face.

"You should be."

"I don't know what got into me."

"Knock it off." Chance tossed the syringe on the floor in front of Anderson. "Don't touch it or I'll plug you one."

"I need it."

"Moron, I need all the answers. Talk before you really upset me."

Anderson thought back to his college days. "A week after Valentine's Day you announced that you and Cash were getting married."

FORTY-SIX

"They're getting what?" Jazz was outraged. Her smoldering gaze landed on everyone in the room. "They don't even know each other well enough to get married."

"She didn't tell you," Yancee said, tying on a do-rag.

"No, we've only been hanging out for a little over a week." Jazz flopped down on the futon between Anderson and Leon. She held Leon's hand so everyone could see as he had instructed her to. "Cash isn't exactly trusting of people. She hasn't told me much of anything. She's a real piece of work the way she isolates herself." Then: "I can tell this, though, I notice she's changing. It's like she's coming to life, unthawing or something since she went out with Chance. When she does talk to me, Chance is the topic and her face lights up."

"Hate to admit it," Leon said, "but Chance is the same way. He's living and breathing Cash."

"Then you need to fix this mess, Leon," Anderson said. "Your little joke backfired. People stand to get hurt behind this if the truth comes out later than sooner."

"Why does it have to come out at all?" Leon stood and paced. "Cash obviously isn't telling him, why should we?"

"I know you're not that fucked up. First of all," Yancee said, "it ain't a we thing; it's a you thing. And you can't let this go on. You couldn't possibly feel good about it. What part of they're getting married this weekend at the courthouse don't you understand?"

"*Then you break their hearts, Mr. Morals,*" Leon said. "*Go ahead and snatch Cupid's arrow out.*"

"*I didn't put them in a fucked-up position, you did.*"

Anderson said, "*Yeah, this is on you. Man up, homeboy.*"

Jazz didn't open her pretty mouth. Translation: It wasn't her business when it started; it still ain't her business now.

"*Everyone is focused on what I so-called did wrong and not on what became of it.*"

"*You're so full of shit. I don't believe what I'm hearing.*" *Yancee shook his head.* "*You're manipulative and you know I know it. So don't sit here and try to justify this. It's wrong, plain and simple.*"

"*Sometimes you can turn a negative situation into a positive,*" *Jazz said.*

"*I ain't trying to hear that. You and Leon like each other. If you knew what I know, you'd find somebody else to like. But since you don't know no better, you're amorously sticking up for him. For all we know, y'all might run off to the courthouse and get married.*"

Jazz rolled her beautiful brown eyes at Yancee.

"*No way Jose,*" *Anderson said.* "*That ain't happening. Aunt Alice will kill me.*"

"*You know what, Yancee? Your opinions about me don't make me shit. And you and Anderson need to stay out of my business with Jazz. She made it clear that she's grown.*" *Leon looked between the two of them.* "*Now that we have that straight. All I was trying to say is no matter what the circumstances, Chance and Cash found love. The real gift. The wrong thing to do is interfere with that. I'm not. If I do that, then I'd be doing the same thing he did to me.*" *He paused.* "*Naw, I'm not down with that.*"

They all stared at Leon with rapt attention.

Leon said, "*If either of you wants to be their killjoy, be my mother-*

fucking guest. But I'm warning you that I'm taking this to my grave. Should either one of you moral crusaders bring it to light before then, I'll deny it and make you look like the bad guy."

"Sometime I'm ashamed I even know you," Yancee said. "You're seriously fucked up."

"To the grave." Leon held out a fist.

"Only 'cause you leave me no other choice," Anderson said and bumped his fist against Leon's. "To the grave."

"One day, Leon, I swear your hesitation to do the right thing is gonna get somebody killed." Yancee put his fist on the pile. "To the grave."

Everyone looked at Jazz.

"How many times do I have to tell y'all that this ain't none of my business? I met Chance once. I'm new, remember? I unknowingly walked into this because my cousin introduced me to y'all."

Anderson said, "But this situation is how you and Cash became friends, and you're part of our circle now."

Leon gave her an intimidating stare that made her look away. "You are down with me, right?"

"This is crazy." Jazz added her tiny fist. "To the grave."

"That's how it went down. Please let me take my insulin. I'm sick, Chance."

"Sure, buddy, go ahead."

Anderson quickly grabbed the syringe as if Chance would change his mind. "Thank you." When he saw Chance put the .44 Magnum away, he said with much relief, "God is good. I'm really, really sorry, Chance. We all wanted to tell you, everyone except Leon."

"God has absolutely nothing to do with this, shithead. You've been a terrible friend."

"Please forgive me."

Chance stood over Anderson and waited. Anderson pulled his sweat pants down far enough to expose his thigh, then he injected himself.

"Winner winner chicken dinner," Chance said, quoting a line from his favorite movie, *21*. He whipped out his surgical scalpel. "Law 2: Never Put Too Much Trust in Friends. Dude, this is gonna hurt. I promise."

FORTY-SEVEN

Scenario didn't have a clue about what to do with Jazz. The accident had taken its toll on her best friend to the point she was contemplating a crisis intervention. Scenario wasn't in her office a good ten minutes before her secretary, Jamillah Woodard, an ambitious three-year law student who had her eye on the clerk's office, came in with a Xerox box filled with files.

"Sit it here." Scenario cleared a spot on her desk. "And do me a favor."

"Not big on favors, but what is it?"

"Knock before you come in. I like a heads-up."

"Habits are hard to break, so don't count on it." She offered a clinical shrug. "These are the cases County Prosecutor Jefferson was working that'll need your immediate attention. They're all on the docket for this week." She touched the top folder. "And this one here is information on the Hieroglyphic Hacker that Detective Skye faxed Jefferson at four this morning. She and Detective Eubanks always shared info with Jefferson on cases he would eventually prosecute." She wiped away the tear that lost its grip. "Anyway, I thought you'd like to go over it."

"Thanks, Jamillah. That was thoughtful of you."

"You have an eleven o'clock in front of Judge Ronald Adrine. Ohio versus Prater. It's a possession of cocaine over the bulk amount with intent to distribute. The press is on line one, two, three, four, and five. And there are two reporters in the lobby."

"Hang up on the press," Scenario said, "and kick the reporters out."

"We're gonna get along just fine with an attitude like that." Jamillah left Scenario to handle her business.

In truth, things were moving way too fast. Scenario just wanted things to slow down so she could catch her breath and gain some control of the mess that blindsided her. She pulled out the Hieroglyphic Hacker murder file and flipped it open. She thoroughly read Skye's report concerning the circumstances surrounding the unidentified murder victim. Then she came across the first of many crime scene photos and the earth fell out from beneath her. She knew the victim personally. She sat at his dinner table more times than she could count. Ethically, she was up shit creek in a boat full of holes. Morally, she was fucked.

Anxiety tightened her chest; she was on the outskirts of a panic attack. This was not happening. Was the world really that small? Of all the people in Cleveland, how come the victim had to be someone she knew? Now Scenario was faced with a choice: identify Yancee Taylor and burn her new life and the seventy-thousand-dollar identity change or keep another secret.

FORTY-EIGHT

Aspen hung up the phone with Tony Adams then looked down at the information she had spent all morning gathering from her Facebook and Google search. Finally some progress. She picked up her landline to call Hakeem just as Detective Omar Madison appeared in front of her desk.

He frowned. "Hate to use this as a point of reference," he said. "Remember the day you got the call that Eubanks' wife had succumbed to breast cancer?"

"Why?"

"We were on the computer at some web site you were showing me that could help me with my investigations. What's the URL of that site?"

"Obviously it's not important to you if you didn't commit it to memory, Detective."

"Come on, Aspen, don't bust my balls."

"Faces of the nation dot com," she said in a curt tone. "Next time it'll cost you."

"Thanks." He disappeared as easy as he had appeared.

She punched in Hakeem's number.

"Communicate."

"It's me," Aspen said, looking at his empty desk and the framed picture turned face-down, among some domestic murder case files they still needed to clear. "What you come up with?"

"A blank. The Williamses check out. Sweet people. I'm on I-77 headed to Lorain Correctional to see Butter Bean."

"He's an asshole. You're looking to draw another blank with the little professor."

"Maybe, maybe not." Then: "You turn up anything?"

"The prints on John Doe come back to a Yancee Taylor, thirty-one. Caught a hate crime back in ninety-nine, been clean since."

"Who does he hate?"

"Homosexuals."

"Got a current address on him?"

"He stays on Avalon."

"I'll be back in an hour. I can't stomach more than thirty minutes of Butter Bean, so let's do the notification together."

"One hour, Hakeem. Mr. Taylor's family has to be worried sick."

"I'll be there."

"My hunch turned up some good leads."

Hakeem said nothing. Translation: *Give it to me.*

"Officer McNally stressed that you had to know the synagogue and path were there."

"True that. I've been thinking the unsub is or was a resident of Cleveland Heights myself."

"My line of thinking is a kid who used to use the path to get to school."

Hakeem said nothing.

"The only kids who would use that shortcut to get to and from Monticello Junior High come from a twenty-one-block radius, between Cain Park and Euclid Heights Boulevard. Every kid past Cain Park goes to Roxberry Junior High. The path starts on Euclid Heights Boulevard or on Mayfield Road depending on which way you're coming from."

"I'm with you."

"My profile of the Hacker puts him in his early thirties, which means he would have attended Monticello between ninety-two and ninety-five."

Hakeem said nothing.

"There were only twenty-six males from that radius who attended Monticello during those years. Seven are in prison. Five are dead. Three are in mental wards. Three are serving their country in Afghanistan. Two have been handicapped all their lives and therefore couldn't have pulled off any crime that requires physical strength. One lives overseas and hasn't touched United States soil in six years. The other five are medical doctors of various sorts."

"Who would reasonably know about the path and the synagogue," Hakeem said.

"Bingo. They had to know because Cleveland Heights didn't start busing students until ninety-six." Aspen shuffled through her notes. "Douglas Brown, Juan Goggins, Kevin Petit, Peter Glover, Chancellor Fox."

"How many are Caucasians?"

"Two. Peter and Chancellor. Peter is a neuropathologist, and Chancellor is a veterinarian."

"Let's dig in their business; see what dirt we can uncover."

"Hold up. It gets better, Hakeem."

Hakeem said nothing. Translation: *Please give it to me.*

"Chancellor Fox moved to Denver in 2001."

"Maybe he's come home to roost."

"Had my informant out at Hopkins check the plane manifest for Chancellor's name. You're not gonna like this."

"Shoot," Hakeem said.

"Chancellor Fox came to Cleveland on your boy's birthday."

FORTY-NINE

Every state penitentiary-bound felon from northeastern Ohio got a taste of Lorain Correctional Institution's twenty-three and one-hour lockdown before they were processed and classified then shipped to various prisons throughout the state. Cadre prisoners, a selected group: high-profile snitches, rogue witness protection inmates, model inmates, and government classified inmates, were housed in Lorain to work landscaping, maintenance, and food service.

Matthew "Butter Bean" Allen was a government classified cadre whose IQ made extremely intelligent people look like retards. Flat-out, Butter Bean was a genius, which was probably due to his Asperger's Disorder or the "Little Professor Syndrome," as Aspen liked to call it. While Butter Bean's intelligence was far-reaching, he possessed an unusual ability to decipher symbols, ancient languages, and impossible calculations. The powers that be didn't approve of Butter Bean's abilities if they weren't benefiting the Power, which was why Butter Bean was serving an indefinite prison term for being a threat to national security.

Hakeem's hemorrhoids were raw and inflamed, and the metal chair didn't help. He impatiently waited in a small interview room— a table, two chairs, a camera mounted on the wall—for the CO to bring Butter Bean in. After eight uncomfortable minutes, the door swung open and there stood the little professor. His aging face was set in a perpetual frown. He was much rounder than when Hakeem had seen him last in Judge Ronald Adrine's courtroom. Butter Bean's male-pattern baldness had crawled back three more inches. Pretty soon he would have a bald mohawk. And his teeth were just crooked enough to be considered interesting. But what stood out more than anything to Hakeem was the complete and utter aggravation lingering behind Butter Bean's turquoise-blue eyes.

"You should have never arrested me if you desired to pay me social visits, Detective Eubanks. The irony is quite insulting." Then: "We could have discussed world views on my open-air patio with tall glasses of homemade tea. I'm really averse to the confinement of concrete and steel."

"If you didn't hide top secret documents and accounts behind some elaborate algorithmic formula while I was with Homeland Security, I wouldn't have cuffed you."

"I resent the accusation; I'm not hiding anything. The government is stealing money from United States citizens on top of taxation. I only seek to give hard-working people their misappropriated funds back."

"You're too intelligent, Butter Bean, not to understand how wrong you are."

Butter Bean laughed. "Detective Eubanks, you're too morally stupid to see how right I am. The Constitution is a beautiful archetype for a wholesome and productive society. Its beauty is marred when your government uses it for its own personal growth against the people it was designed to protect and help prosper."

"Butter Bean, you chose to sit here for the last seven years. Give me the algorithm and you can leave with me today." Then: "All the government wants in lieu of prosecution is for you to work for them. Show them how you made thirteen billion dollars and classified documents disappear in thin air, and create a system where no one else can do it again."

"We find ourselves at an impasse again, Detective Eubanks." Butter Bean shifted his gaze toward the camera. "Now that you see my position hasn't altered, what in the hell do you want?"

"Have a seat, Butter Bean." Hakeem pushed a bottled orange juice to the center of the table. "It's your favorite. Hundred percent natural."

"It's the least you could do. Should have brought me a two-dollar whore and a condom to go with it since you were being sensitive to my favorites." Butter Bean took a seat across from Hakeem. "They served tacos today." He sighed. "No cheese. How the fuck do decent human beings serve tacos without cheese? Never seen nothing like it in my life."

"It's psychological, the no-cheese thing. It's a way to get in your head."

"They painted all the bathroom stalls black. Do you have any idea of how peaceful it is to take a dump surrounded by total blackness?"

"That's one I have to put on my bucket list and try out." Hakeem wrote it down on his notepad.

"Try white bread," Butter Bean said. "It works." He moved the orange juice to his left, exactly where he wanted it.

Hakeem frowned. "You lost me."

"That's not hard to do. I'm speaking on those hemorrhoids you're sitting over there wrestling with. Treat them with white bread."

"Didn't come here for your medical advice." Hakeem moved Butter Bean's juice.

"I'm not going to help you with what you did come here for, so take the gift I'm willing to give." Then: "Stop moving my juice. I like things in the place and order *I* set. My feng shui." He put the juice where he intended it to stay.

At that very moment Hakeem became tired of Butter Bean. "You don't know why I'm here."

"Don't be stupid; you'll only get me mad. Getting the algorithm would have been like finding an extra prize in a box of Lucky Charms. There's a serial killer running around our beloved city carving hieroglyphics into modern and civilized people." Butter Bean pointed to Hakeem's Mont Blanc folder. "I'll bet the algorithm that it's crime scene photos in that pricey folder of yours. Photos of which you want me to tell you what the hieroglyphics say. Assuming they say anything comprehensible. I never welsh on a bet."

Hakeem reached for the juice.

Butter Bean smacked his hand. "Stop!" He swallowed half of the orange juice in one gulp. "It's front-page news; it's on all the television and radio stations, and you show up here."

"What can I do for you," Hakeem said, "in exchange for your help?"

"Nothing. I'm in sole possession of thirteen billion dollars. I have empathy for your feeblemindedness, but surely you didn't forget that."

Hakeem laid the crime scene photos of Yancee Taylor in front of Butter Bean. "He was an American citizen protected by the Constitution."

"You gain no leverage frolicking with my patriotism."

"Innocent people are in danger until I nail the guy behind this."

Butter Bean cast a tight gaze on the horrific images for a moment. Hakeem knew it was only because the verbal tussle failed to intrigue him. "Thanks for the orange juice." He chugged the bottle empty then stood to leave.

"I need to know what it says, Butter Bean."

His tight gaze sharpened. "Trust me, Detective Eubanks, you don't want to know what this says." Butter Bean pushed the photos back and walked out.

FIFTY

"**O**h no, anything but this." Sweat broke out on Butter Bean's bald spot. His big ass shook like he'd come down with a severe case of Tourette's syndrome. Literally. He held on to his cell door to keep from collapsing. He craved an ibuprofen to preempt his imminent migraine. He couldn't believe his eyes. His once pristine clean and obsessively compulsive orderly cell was in total fucking disarray.

Detective Eubanks, he thought.

It was downright cruel and uncivilized for Eubanks to resort to mind games. "Fix it back," he whispered, thinking of how he could get Eubanks back for violating the rules of engagement. Butter Bean started banging his head against the cell door over and over and over while repeating "Fix it back."

"Get used to it, Butter Bean," the CO said. "We've got the green light to toss your cell every day."

"Can't function…without order." Butter Bean started hyper-ventilating. "You…can't…do…this."

"Calm down and breathe," the CO said.

"Make it go back to normal. Make it like it was." More head banging.

"Only Detective Eubanks can call it off. Relax some and maybe you can catch him before he leaves."

Between breaths, Butter Bean said, "Take me to him."

Hakeem flipped open his Palm Treo. "Communicate."

"Where are you?" Aspen said, sounding like an angel.

"Prison interview room." He peeped at his Patek Phillipe, 10:43 a.m., and sighed. "I give Butter Bean ten more minutes, then I'm on my way."

"How did it go?"

"He shot me down and stormed out of here, but I'm certain he'll warm up before I leave."

With concern coating her voice, Aspen said, "Why? What did you do, Hakeem?"

"Had his cell destroyed. Rearranged his stamp collection. You know, scrambled his whacky world, and agitated his acute obsession with order."

"That was dirty. Bet the little professor threw one hell of a temper tantrum. Hope you can sleep at night knowing you're the reason he'll spend the next sixty days going to pill call trying to get back right."

"I'm not sleeping anyway." Hakeem didn't consider himself a great man—not even slightly. He just had a set of morals and principles that he wasn't sure what kind of person they categorized or qualified him as. Always respect and never strike a woman; beat the shit out of a disrespectful man. Always tell the truth; scheme and lie through his teeth to discover the greater truth. Be loyal to a fault; betray whoever initiates the cross. "He forced me to use his Asperger's to my advantage."

The door swung open and banged against the wall. "You dingleberry," Butter Bean said, soaked with sweat.

"Speak of the devil," Hakeem said to Aspen. To Butter Bean he said, "Back so soon?"

"Call your mutts off."

Hakeem held the phone to his ear and said nothing.

"Give me a pen and paper."

Hakeem tore a sheet of legal paper from the Mont Blanc folder and offered him a matching pen. "You need to see these photos again?"

"I have a steel-trap memory, dick head. He's smart. He converted the hieroglyphics to translate to pig Latin. A code within a code."

In his ear Aspen said, "What's he doing?"

"Writing."

"Here's the English version." Butter Bean pocketed the pen and shoved the paper at Hakeem.

Family is the sacred right of
passage. Death to evildoers who
alter the course of man and
woman, the creators of child,
the key to life. Stay out of
my way, Detective Eubanks.
Law 33: Discover Each
Man's Thumbscrew.
I know yours.

"Son of a bitch."

FIFTY-ONE

A few ticks past noon Hakeem damn near limped out a convenience store on the corner of Euclid and Avalon carrying a loaf of white bread and a Slim Fast for Aspen. What did she need a diet drink for when she was already perfect? *Women, I'll never understand them.*

When he eased onto the Hummer seat, Aspen said, "What's up with the bread?"

"Medicine." He nudged the Hummer down Avalon while Aspen browsed through a catalog of baby clothes.

She looked up from the catalog and frowned.

"Don't even try to wrap your mind around it." Then: "What's a dingleberry?"

"I like to had fell out when Butter Bean called you that." She laughed, giggled some, then smiled. Sheer amusement poured from her eyes.

"Mind telling me what's so funny?" he said as he parked in front of an ailing two-story brick house with a slated roof and rusted-out gutters.

"Take your pick." She laughed again as they got out the truck. "Either he was calling you a piece of shit stuck on an ass hair or an inept fool."

He gave that and the Hieroglyphic Hacker's deaths threat some serious thought as they walked onto the front porch. "Knowing

Butter Bean it was both."

When Aspen rang the doorbell, a Monte Carlo with twenty-four-inch rims turned into the driveway. Its stereo system was pumping Young Jeezy's "Go Crazy." The music abruptly stopped. A lady with an unattractive ponytail bound together with a yellow scrunchie stepped out the car. Two handsome twin boys climbed out the back seat and dashed up the street.

The lady looked Hakeem and Aspen up and down. "What y'all want?"

Then the front door swung open. An elderly woman with a milky film on her irises said, "Barack Obama send you with my stimulus social security check?" She flashed a toothless smile.

"Go back in the house, Madear. I got this." To Hakeem and Aspen, the lady with the bad ponytail said, "I said what y'all want? Y'all deaf or something?"

Hakeem pulled back the lapel of his Givenchy suit so the gold badge clipped to his crocodile belt would speak for itself. Aspen flashed her badge as well.

"We're detectives with the CPD," Hakeem said. "Hakeem Eubanks, and this is my partner, Aspen Skye." He offered his hand.

"Aw shit," Madear said. "I'm busted. I've been through this before. Give me a second."

"Are you Mrs. Taylor?" Aspen said.

"Yeah, I'm Africa Taylor. Is this about Madear calling the CIA the other day? She doesn't have much left upstairs if you haven't noticed already."

"Mind if we talk inside, Mrs. Taylor?" Hakeem was a veteran. He knew to never inform a family member of a homicide until after he conducted an interview and garnered as much info as he possibly could. Once a person became emotional, there was no point in trying to extract useful information.

The inside of the Taylor home starkly contrasted with the outside. It boasted a motif of money-green Italian leather furnishings, mahogany wood grain, and frameless tempered glass. The hardwood floors were polished to a mirror shine. Beautifully woven asymmetrical rugs were strategically placed throughout the dwelling. An overstuffed sectional with mink throws draped over it hugged the khaki-colored walls and faced a large plasma TV. Hakeem and Aspen relaxed on the sofa in front of a glass coffee table with a built-in saltwater aquarium stocked with a spectacularly colored coral reef that served as a backdrop to robust triggers, clownfishes, damselfishes, and lionfishes.

"Forgive me for being all ghetto outside," Africa said, placing ice-cold bottled waters on coasters for the detectives. "I've been stressing lately. Between my senile mother-in-law, my bad men children, and my cheating-ass husband, I don't know what to do anymore."

Hakeem and Aspen made eye contact, understanding that they possibly had another woman to investigate. Hakeem watched Africa with pessimistic eyes. She showed no obvious signs of deception. Her eye contact was firm. Confident. Concerned. Nothing like the gaze of a woman who was a cold-blooded killer. But then again, maybe she's just a good liar, Hakeem thought.

"Mrs. Taylor, boys will be boys." Aspen sipped her water.

"Girl, call me Africa. Mrs. makes me sound like I got grandchildren."

Hakeem said nothing.

"About Madear calling the Secret Service or the CIA," Africa said, "She—"

"Okay, you busted me red-handed. I won't put up a useless fuss," Madear said, coming into the living room as naked as the day she was born eighty-four years ago. Her loose skin was wrinkled and distorted like a crumpled brown paper bag. "I know the drill. Been arrested plenty enough when I marched with Dr. King and the Civil Rights Movement." She opened her mouth so Aspen and Hakeem could see inside her toothless hole, pulled her ears back for them, and spread her fingers apart. Then she proceeded to turn around, spread her cheeks, squat, and cough. Madear went through each step of a cavity search like a seasoned convict.

Hakeem couldn't take another moment of it. He skirted his eyes. Aspen's mouth fell open; Hakeem knew she had no desire to stop looking. Africa didn't seem surprised at all by Madear's behavior. Her face drew tight with anger.

She leaped off the sofa and wrapped Madear in a mink throw. "That's it!" she spoke through her teeth. "Pack your shit. I'm dropping your ass off at the nearest old folks' home. Let them deal with you 'cause I'm through." She led Madear to the sofa. "You hear me? I'm through with you embarrassing the hell out of me. You just don't let up." To Hakeem and Aspen, she said, "That's what I'm talking about. Madear didn't mean any harm when she made that call."

After the initial shock of Madear's lewd striptease wore off, Hakeem decided to do a little probing. "You called your husband Yancee a cheat."

"That's right. The fucker hasn't been home in two nights. I know he's creeping with this Terri chick that moved here from Philly. Ain't the first time he ain't come home because of that home-wrecking slut." Then: "Wait a minute. What the hell does this have to do with Yancee?" Now Hakeem could tell that Africa seriously contemplating their presence in her home and that her defenses had shot back to the roof.

"Will I be in jail before supper time?" Madear said, watching the aquarium as a clownfish frolicked with the stingy tentacles of a sea anemone.

Aspen said, "Africa, we're here to speak with you about your husband."

Africa's brows formed a single dark line. "What about him? Yancee stopped selling drugs when the twins were born. He ain't in jail, is he?"

It was too early in the game to dismiss Africa as a liar or a suspect, but Hakeem's cloud of suspicion started to thin. She definitely didn't strike him as the Hieroglyphic Hacker. Accomplice? Maybe. But she seemed genuinely clueless to the matter at hand. No artifices seeped from beneath her skin. "When was the last time you saw your husband?" Hakeem opened the Mont Blanc, a pen he borrowed from Aspen poised over the paper.

"Wednesday morning when he left for work. A little after nine. Why?"

"I'm gonna need commissary money when I go to jail."

No one paid Madear any attention.

Aspen leaned forward. "Bear with us. We'll explain everything to you. But it's very important that you do your best to answer all our questions first."

Worry crept across Africa's face. A moment of silence turned into a long minute of uncertainty. She studied them then reluctantly said, "Okay."

Aspen continued with her line of questioning. "Do you and Yancee regularly speak on the phone when he's away from home?"

"Yeah, unless he's screening his calls because he's laying up with that bitch Terri."

"You know Terri's last name? Phone number? Address? Where she works?"

"Yeah, Yancee doesn't know that I know, though. It's Dunlap." And she gave them the rest of the info she had on Terri Dunlap as Hakeem sat in silence and wrote it down.

Aspen said, "When was the last time you spoke to Yancee?"

"His lunch break, Thursday. He called me from his cell phone."

Hakeem jumped in. "What's his number?"

Africa rattled off the digits, then she said matter-of-factly, "You're starting to scare me."

"I'm scared too," Madear said, rocking in place, her bare knees poking out from the mink throw. "I don't want to go to jail. It's only a little pot I got from the boy on the corner for my cataracts." She gave Hakeem a conspiratorial wink and let the mink slip from her shoulders to expose her breasts. "Take me to my bedroom and we can work this out."

"Stop it!" Africa covered her back up. "Stop being nasty."

Hakeem could tell that Madear lived a full life, that she had marched for the equal rights of Blacks, and had endured the isms of the world long enough to see she hadn't marched in vain. He'd be willing to bet that when Barack Obama won the election for the presidency of the United States of America and the First Black Family filled her TV screen, she understood that the very definition of what it meant to be black in America had changed forever. That she knew it was no longer wishful thinking that her grandchildren would one day be judged and selected for the content of their character and intelligence and not dismissed for the color of their skin. There was no doubt in his mind that she now knew that her grandchildren could truly become whomever they aspired to be.

"According to the DMV," Aspen said, "Mr. Taylor has three cars registered in his name. You pulled up in the Monte Carlo. Where are the other two?"

Africa nibbled at a cuticle. "His sixty-seven Buick Riviera is in the garage and he drove his sixty-seven Camaro to work. He restores old school cars from the sixties. He's showing the Riviera next week at a car show in Detroit."

Hakeem wished that was true, but he said nothing.

"Why am I naked?" Madear said, looking down at herself. "Somebody broke in here and stole my clothes."

"Does Mr. Taylor have any enemies?" Aspen capped her water.

"No."

Her voice crawled to a tone that prickled Hakeem's body hairs.

She said, "I ain't answering another motherfucking question about my husband until one of y'all tell me what the hell is going on. It's that or get on the other side of my front door."

Africa took a firm stance and ended the interview before they could pry deeper into Yancee Taylor's life. Who were his friends? What type of person was he? Where did he hang out? Hakeem knew that the answers could somehow connect Yancee to his killer, unless Yancee was purely a victim of randomness. For now they would have to work with the information they did get. Hakeem hated to be the bearer of bad news, but he never let the burden fall on Aspen's shoulders. They naturally fell into pseudo husband-and-wife roles and played their positions because they cared about each other.

Hakeem pulled in a deep breath and let it go with a sigh. "Africa, I hate to inform you of this, but your husband was murdered."

Madear came back to the sane part of the world. Her eyes fastened on Hakeem and singled in on his eyebrows and goatee. "Damn liar. My son will be home any minute. Now get the hell out of my house with your hurtful lies before I call the cops." Then: "Damn liar. He called Africa's phone this morning and got disconnected."

FIFTY-TWO

The thrill of the hunt leaked endorphins into their systems like good dope. With their cell phones stuck to their ears, Aspen and Hakeem left the Taylor residence high on information.

Hakeem, always the chivalric gentleman, opened the Hummer door for Aspen and helped her inside as he spoke to a police dispatcher. "This is Detective Hakeem Eubanks of the Cleveland Homicide Unit. Badge number six-ten."

"Hold for verification," an overworked dispatcher said without much enthusiasm.

On the inside of the Hummer, Aspen spoke into her phone: "Tony, we may have something on the Hieroglyphic Hacker's whereabouts."

"Caught a break within the first forty-eight, huh?"

"Too soon to tell. I need you to triangulate a cell phone call for me and get me an address." She gave Tony Yancee's cell number and Africa's cell number and the time Yancee's phone last dialed Africa's. Tony would pinpoint the cell towers the call bounced through and then use Google Maps to locate the address the call was made from.

The weary police dispatcher said to Hakeem, "Go ahead, Detective Eubanks."

"Run a nationwide APB on a sixty-seven Camaro. Registered owner Yancee Taylor. Black on black. Vanity plate number, *ALL*

HERS." He hung up and looked at Aspen. "Are we thinking the same Terri Dunlap?"

Detective Leonardo Scott—fortyish, sinewy, sunburnt—looked like an old western gunslinger straight off the set of a *Gunsmoke* episode. His blond mustache was entirely too thick to be comfortable, and it had the nerve to be discolored from Red Indian chewing tobacco. He wore a Stetson hat with a high crown and an extra wide brim that must have cost him a week's wages. Even his cowboy boots were decked out with spurs. A .38 Smith & Wesson was holstered low on the hip of his denims. Aspen wondered if he had a stallion tethered to a parking meter out front.

Aspen and Hakeem sat quietly in the Homicide Unit's conference room while Detective Scott studied their file. After perusing the autopsy report and comparing their crime scene photos with a few of his, Detective Scott spat tobacco juice in an empty Pepsi bottle, then looked up at Aspen and Hakeem through a set of seaweed-green eyes.

"It's him," Detective Scott said. "It's our boy. After six months of silence, he's finally decompensating."

Hakeem said nothing.

Aspen stubbed out her cigarette. "What makes you so sure?"

"'Cause he's making mistakes. Seven flawless murders in Denver and not one piece of trace evidence until now." He dug into a leather cache bag and dropped his thick files on the table with a thud. "See for yourselves."

FIFTY-THREE

"Go away."

Jazz sauntered into the bedroom full of grace and confidence anyway. Had she known that she'd leave humiliated, she would have listened to Jaden and kept going. She came with the intention of finding a middle ground so things could be settled between them. Deciding how hard to push Jaden was the problem. Too much torque and he'd sink deeper into anger and drive the wedge between them to the hilt. Not enough pressure and he'd never take her seriously, leaving them in a never-ending state of dysfunction.

Buank. Buank. Buank. Buank. "You're still here," he said, bouncing the ball against the wall. "Too hardheaded for your own good."

"You ready to talk about the tantrum you threw this morning?"

"You ready to talk about the tantrum you *didn't* throw on July 22, 2001?"

Jazz flinched at the mention of *that* day. She almost choked on the lump that formed in her throat. She had the sensation of a broken fingernail running down her spine. Beneath her black, oversized clothing her skin rashed with goosebumps. Bile crept up her throat like a prowler. But all she could taste was despair, tasted regret, tasted excruciating physical and mental pain. Sweat beaded her brow as a taut silence kidnapped and strangled the room. She staggered on her feet, fighting desperately to maintain equilibrium.

"You look a little woozy," Jaden said. "Seems like you need to take a seat."

"How do you know?" she whispered.

"You'd be surprised at what I know." *Buank. Buank. Buank. Buank.* Jazz crumpled into the chair of the computer workstation nestled in the corner of the room because she had to. Her long brown legs were no longer reliable. Her blank stare fell to the window and the clear blue sky beyond it. She looked into a vision of what was supposed to be the happiest day of every woman's life. But for her, that day her self-esteem was torn into two irreplaceable pieces. Her self-worth was stolen forever. The horrific memory played across her mind like a video clip.

Over fifty law enforcement officers of various agencies gathered in a large conference room on the third floor of the Justice Center. A timeline was drawn on a dry-erase board to keep track of case developments since the discovery of Yancee Taylor's mutilated corpse. The main blue vein of the timeline had several arteries branching out in various directions and colors. At the end of a green artery, written in Aspen's ultra girly handwriting, was the message the Hieroglyphic Hacker had carved into Yancee's body. She underlined Eubanks' name twice because the threat bothered her twice as much. A large city map was tacked to a bulletin board. A blue-headed stickpin marked the spot where Yancee was found.

County Prosecutor Scenario Davenport walked in with a hell of a strut. The collective chatter stopped. She turned every head in the room. Her smile was easy. The scar on her face made her look like a beautiful battle-ready warrior. She wore a classy Oscar de la Renta number with a metallic gray python Nina bag thrown over her shoulder and matching shoes. She looked more like a *Show* magazine centerfold than a prosecutor. She took a seat in the front row next to Chief Dwight Eisenhower.

The corners of Hakeem's mouth turned up to a stupid grin. Aspen elbowed the silly smile off his face. She knew then and there that she didn't like Scenario Davenport.

FIFTY-FOUR

Jazz had done everything right. Believed in God and saved her virtue for her husband. She stood tall and proud like a princess in their Marriott suite. She felt beautiful in her long floor-skimming wedding gown. She felt worthy of standing before such a wonderful man, but she was a huge ball of nervous energy. Most she'd ever done was kiss a boy and done some exploratory touching. But now she was about to go all the way. She slowly turned around—imaging his tender touch—so Leon could un-button her wedding gown. Nervous giggles poured from her as his fingers freed each clasp.

Her dress hit the floor, exposing her slender frame, the sensual bra and panty set she picked out especially for him. She felt safe and sexy revealing herself to her husband. As his gaze eased along the length of her back, she prayed that she could please him sexually. What she didn't know, she promised herself to be open-minded so she could learn.

Leon turned up his nose with transparent disgust. "You should really be grateful for me. Life did you a favor."

A stone dropped in the pit of Jazz's stomach and ripped the lining out. The condescension in his tone was a brand-new being. One that she never witnessed within their union. She precariously faced him, afraid that if she tipped too far either way, her nausea would hit the floor. Jazz was vulnerable and visibly trembling. "What... what do you mean?"

"That someone like me felt sorry for you and actually married you. You owe me."

Those words knocked more than the wind out of Jazz. They tore out her beating heart. She was taken aback. Instinctively her mind retreated and her feet followed close behind as she stepped away from him.

Leon clenched a sturdy grip around her wrist, yanking her back in place. "Stand here and don't move again." Then: "And wipe that look off your face. I'm doing you a favor. Look at you, you're ugly and too skinny. Nobody in their right mind wants you. No tits. Your ass is flat. What am I supposed to do with any of this?" He snatched her bra off and shook his head.

Jazz wanted to cover her crawling flesh. This wasn't the respect Leon vowed to less than an hour ago in front of their minister, family, and God. The first time she showed her body to a man, he responded to it negatively. This wasn't what she dreamt her first time would be like. This was nothing like the beautiful description she internalized from the numerous romance novels she read. Jazz always imagined fireworks, shooting stars, an indescribable pleasure. She always thought her first time would allow her to experience the meaning of ecstasy. She never entertained the thought that she would be made to feel unloved and ugly.

She said, "What was all that lovey-dovey stuff you were whispering in my ear before we got married? If you felt like this, why even marry me?"

Leon reared back and smacked her face swollen. Jazz existed somewhere between shock and confusion. This betrayed the protection he promised her. Her eyes were frozen wide with fear.

Without thinking of her actions her fingertips found the raw skin of her face.

"Don't ever question me, and don't you ever fix your mouth to talk back to me," Leon said through his teeth. "Those are the first rules you'll learn to comply with, the easy way or the hard way." He squeezed her wrist to give her a true taste of his strength and dominance. "You're mine now. Good wives live according to their husband's rules." He appraised the value of her features again with unmixed disgust. "Your eyes are the ugliest things I've ever seen in my life. Stop looking at me with them."

She downcast her gaze and cried.

"I'll get you a pair of sunglasses so I don't have to see them again."

A cold emptiness of continental proportions surged through her veins like ice water. No, this wasn't love and honor; it was tyranny. She sobbed and covered her body with her arms as best as she could. Instantly she became self-conscious of her feminine attributes. No other soul would see her so exposed for as long as she lived.

"And do yourself and the entire world a favor," he said. "Don't hop your ass in another picture. You have no right. Ugly doesn't photograph well." Then: "Have I made myself clear, wife?" He loosened his tie.

Jazz was too horrified and too everything else to say anything. She was hoping to wake up and find that she was an unwilling participant of a nightmare.

Leon got pissed and raised his voice. "Am. I. Making. Myself. Clear?" He raised his hand, threatening to strike her if she didn't answer correctly.

Jazz flinched and nodded in one motion.

"Trust me when I tell you that I'm the only person who has the heart to attempt loving you. No one else cares about you. No other man will tolerate the likes of you."

She sobbed like never before.

"You are no longer allowed to speak with your family without my permission. I'm your mother, your father, your sister, your brother." He flung his tuxedo shirt to the bed. "You will keep my house spotless at all times and have my dinner prepared by four o'clock every day." He kicked his shoes off. "When your chores are done, then and only then can you write your imaginary stories. All your royalty checks come to me." He unzipped the fly of his tuxedo pants. "When I allow you the special privilege to be seen with me in public, you walk two paces behind me—always on my inside. I pray that you like to learn the hard way. That would really turn me on, because my rules have several consequences when broken." He stepped out of his pants, then took off his underwear. "Now let me see if this pussy satisfies her husband. It better if you know what's good for you. Take them panties off, bend over the bed, and hide your ugly face in the pillow while I break you in."

FIFTY-FIVE

Buank. Buank. Buank. Buank.

The ideal companionship Jazz shared with Leon died the moment she stood at the altar gazing into his seemingly innocent eyes. It all died the moment she said "I do." Getting married and losing her virginity were the two worst and most painful things that had ever happened to her. On her honeymoon she learned what the consequence was of not satisfying Leon in bed—his fists while he was inside her.

After the brutal ripping of her hymen, he cleaned the mess of blood from his penis with her sparkling white wedding gown, then beat her and told her it was a wedding gift. Through fear, intimidation, and the threat that her family would be harmed if she ever spoke a word of her abuse, Jazz became a submissive and obedient wife over the years. She had the trial-and-error scars to prove it. When Leon divorced her because she had snapped and gone crazy, all he left behind was a hollow shell of a woman.

Buank. Buank. Buank. Buank. "Read about people like you. You're the classic definition of a functional dysfunctional."

"You don't know a thing about me."

"I know you sublimate hurt and pain into bestsellers." He spun the ball on his finger. "You pretend to be happy living in a self-deprecating vacuum."

"Is that what you think is wrong with me?" Jazz raised a brow above her sunglasses.

"I know you have little regard for your worth. Be yourself—your real self. Not whoever this imposter is hiding behind dumb ball caps, ugly sunglasses, and those dark clothes that are way too big for you."

Be herself, she thought. If only Jazz knew whom herself really was. Ever since her wedding night, she no longer had use for an identity.

"Know what your problem is?" Jaden said.

"Nope, but I'm sure your smart ass has a theory." Jazz dismissively waved a hand and stared back out the window into the sky. She wanted to be pissed because he hit home and had read her true, but she couldn't zero in on the emotion. In the few minutes she had been in his room, he'd stripped her bare and left only her nerve endings exposed.

"You're afraid to live, afraid to love someone again. You compensate real life for fiction. The real you hides beneath the layers of your characters because you're running from yourself. Your real story. You pour so much emotion and love into your books, but you're afraid to express those feelings in real life where it counts. Pathetic."

"Watch how you talk to me."

Buank. Buank. Buank. Buank. "Or what? I'm not the person you should have taken a stance with. You know I'm right and that's what keeps you awake at night." Then: "And what scares you even more. Every time you look at me, you see the face of your greatest fear." *Buank. Buank. Buank. Buank.*

Jaden brought back memories too frightening to explore any further, but too intrusive to ignore. Jazz wanted to trust and feel safe and beautiful. She wanted to outwardly express love and know she would genuinely receive it in return. But her only relationship didn't support any of those notions ever being a possibility. She no longer believed Twin Flames existed. Happiness was a hot commodity that left her bankrupt when she'd invested. The only happy endings she'd ever known to be true were the ones she penned into bestsellers; the ones she imagined and fantasized for herself; the ones that didn't magnify her fear of death.

FIFTY-SIX

S cenario's skin crawled. She had an eerie feeling she was being watched; a feeling she couldn't shake. The short hairs on her neck stood like pine needles. She felt the heat of a familiar gaze on her. She jerked around in her seat—heart pounding—to the faces of complete strangers.

Brenda McGinnis, a sharp FBI profiler from Quantico's Investigative Support Unit, stepped to the front of the room. She was one of the few ISU agents who traveled the country profiling serial killers and giving professional advice to law enforcement agencies on how to apprehend them. Brenda got right down to business painting a psychological portrait of the unidentified subject.

"The unsub fits historical homicidal models like the Boston Strangler, Son of Sam, Unruh, Jeffrey Dahmer, and Ted Bundy to a tee," she said. "That means we can catch him because we can predict his movements, his state of mind. He's impulsive. Lacks normal anxiety. He has no behavioral control. His emotional deficit is his central flaw. He's a risk taker. The unsub is definitely a white male from a middle-class background with an above average IQ. The fact that he has targeted all African Americans suggest that he's either a member or supporter of a hate group or aberrant ideologies."

Scenario felt the sharp gaze tighten its focus on her. She rubbed the back of her neck hoping her hand would break the ray of heat.

Detective Aspen Skye spoke up: "The authorities in Denver haven't found any connection among their victims. It's too early in our investigation to know if Yancee Taylor has any connection to either of the Denver victims. So how do you think the unsub is selecting these people? Is it a build? A look? A particular act?"

"Among the two females and five males," Detective Leonardo Scott said, "none of the Denver victims are similar in build or complexion."

"An act?" Brenda McGinnis' brows pinched. "Interesting. That's an angle worth taking a thorough look at. It's highly probable that the victims offended the unsub in some way and he's seeking revenge through homicidal rages."

"That would mean he knows his victims," a uniformed officer in the crowd said.

"Not necessarily." Detective Hakeem Eubanks loosened his tie. "I turn on the news every day and get offended by people and their acts who I don't know."

Brenda McGinnis jumped back in: "If the unsub doesn't personally know the victims, he uses one hell of a credible ruse to lure people from safety to danger."

"Not just people," Detective Skye said, "risky people. He isn't killing addicts, runaways, or street people who won't be reported missing. He's killing taxpayers with solid family structures. People who start to be missed when they're an hour late."

"Are you implying that the unsub is using disguises, Agent McGinnis?" Hakeem said.

"I believe his ruse is his profession, which we know has roots in the medical field." Brenda McGinnis paused to sip water from a Dixie cup. "Maybe he's a doctor who treated abused children and now he's killing off their abusers."

For some reason Scenario's thoughts were tugged toward Chance. That gave her the creeps on top of the weird feelings she was already having. Was it a coincidence that Chance and Yancee were friends and now… She shut that mental picture down before it grew into something unruly. Chance wouldn't hurt a fly outside of a boxing ring. She was certain that Chance would be devastated when he caught wind of Yancee's death.

Detective Eubanks' voice pulled her from her reverie. "Whatever the case," he said. "In each killing, the Hieroglyphic Hacker has spent a lot of time in private settings writing on the victims with a scalpel without fear of interruption, certain that he could pack up his murder kit and walk away from the scene of the crime."

Chief Eisenhower stood up, his belly straining against the fabric and buttons of his shirt. "This is the first of many gatherings of this cross-jurisdictional task force until we nail this guy. And there will be no sleep until that happens, I promise you. We have established a tip hotline. County Prosecutor Scenario Davenport will make the number available to the public in a press conference within the hour." He had a brief coughing fit and then continued. "Brenda McGinnis will remain charged with advising us on how to nab this crackpot. Representing Denver, Colorado, is Detective Leonardo Scott."

Detective Scott tipped his Stetson in a "Howdy" fashion like a real-deal cowboy.

"Through him Denver's task force is coordinating their efforts with ours. And the press isn't in this room for one goddamn reason." Chief Eisenhower burned a hole in Hakeem with a laser stare. "Because they don't have a goddamn dog in this hunt."

A hand went up in the back of the room.

Brenda McGinnis said, "Go ahead, Officer…"

"Officer Raygor," the officer said, gesturing to the timeline on the dry-erase board. "It seems like we're overlooking the obvious. Find the unsub's connection to Detective Eubanks and we will find our killer."

That voice shot a cold chill down Scenario's spine.

FIFTY-SEVEN

A deluge of cops gushed out of the conference room and spilled into the guts of the Justice Center. Office Raygor didn't walk too fast or too slow. He stepped at just a smooth enough tempo to go unnoticed. The afternoon sun washed over him as he came out the building and stepped onto Ontario Avenue.

He carefully maneuvered—never a backward glance—around a growing mob of media people and eased down the avenue to his car. His police uniform was crisp and squeaked with each step. The squeaking abruptly stopped when he saw a parking ticket under the windshield wiper blade of his Infiniti M37. The meter still had two minutes to the good. Some fucking meter maid was trying to reach a quota, he thought.

He plucked the ticket from the windshield as a burst of lake-front wind blew it from his fingertips and into four-lane traffic. He watched the ticket ride the anxiety-free wind like a surfer planted her feet on a Ron Jon board and rode a crisp six-foot wave. That damn ticket could pose a serious fucking problem. He had a decision to make: chase it down, drawing attention to himself, and risk being filmed by the media thirty feet behind him or let it roll and hope the dice landed on a winner.

He slid behind the steering wheel of the Infiniti and drove away. He looked into his rearview mirror and peeled off the bushy eyebrows and mustache. At the next traffic light, Chance removed the synthetic skin from his nose and chin. "Law 25: Re-create Yourself," he said to his reflection. Chance knew he had become a master at hiding in plain sight.

Aspen pushed into the men's restroom as if it had "Unisex" written on the door. "Mind telling me what you came in here with a loaf of bread for?" She looked under the stalls until she saw his alligator shoes.

"Don't talk to me when I'm about to take a dump. I'm not as young as I used to be. I gotta concentrate, Aspen."

"In that case don't push too hard. You might pop a blood vessel."

"Get out. Let me take a dump in peace, would you, woman?"

"You're embarrassed, huh?"

Hakeem said nothing.

"I spoke with my girlfriend last—"

"Does this friend of yours even have a name?" He flushed the toilet.

"It's Phoenix Lovelace, and she wants to meet you."

"It's become quite obvious that you're not going to let me use the bathroom in peace, just like you aren't going to let this business with your friend go. I'll go on one date and one date only with her on the strength of you when we solve this case and not a moment before."

"One might turn into many. You might really be surprised."

"I doubt it." He flushed the toilet again and came out the stall with what was left of the bread.

"You know what? I don't think I want to know what the bread is for anymore."

"Thanks. I appreciate you not making me give up the details," he said and crossed the room to the sinks as Aspen's phone rang.

"Hello," she said.

"Tony here."

"Make it plain."

"Yancee's cell phone was used less than an hour ago. I have the address where the calls are coming from."

FIFTY-EIGHT

Scenario's internal alarm clock went berserk as she descended the Justice Center's steps to a podium swamped with microphones. All the major networks were present; their correspondents stood out like reality TV stars with thousand-dollar makeup. Local news people and newspaper photographers fought like runts for position and camera angles.

The media machine was nothing more than a pack or vicious black-bellied piranhas fiending for a feeding frenzy on murder, sin, corruption. Now that the most important case of her career had been dumped in her lap, Scenario knew the piranhas would scrutinize her every move and sink their jagged teeth in her flesh every chance they got until the case was brought to justice, until the case was severely prosecuted. Cleveland, Ohio, had become the focus of the nation, and she was moments away from becoming the face of Cleveland.

Scenario could only imagine how the information given today would be chewed, digested, and regurgitated on the evening's news and in tomorrow's headlines. She literally wanted to kill Marcus Jefferson for going out and getting himself killed on her. Now she didn't have a tabula rasa to work from but a precarious start to navigate.

Mayor Nesto Balfour, young and black—ever the pretentious

politician in search of a photo op—made a grand entrance with his entourage, the City Council. Balfour gnawed on a hundred-dollar Havana and wore a tailored suit that emphasized his broad shoulders. The enormous pack of piranhas before him was entirely too small for his ego, too insignificant to tame his media whore and power addiction.

It was as if Phillip Noyce had choreographed the scene for one of his blockbuster movies. This, however, was not art imitating life; this was the real deal and Scenario was in the hot seat. Brilliant burst of lights flashed as Mayor Balfour greeted Scenario and Chief Eisenhower. As Scenario placed her talking-point sheet on the podium, the piranhas fired a barrage of questions.

"Ms. Davenport, with such little experience as a lead prosecuting attorney, can you handle a case of this magnitude?"

"Has Detectives Hakeem Eubanks and Aspen Skye's investigation turned up any solid leads?"

"Are there any persons of interest?"

"What connection does Yancee Taylor have to the seven Denver victims?"

Scenario waved the flesh-eating piranhas quiet. She was confident and comfortable in front of the cameras. Her appearance represented the citizens of Cuyahoga County: innocent, trustworthy, family values, zero tolerance for bullshit. "Our fine city has been pushed to the edge by a psychopath. The Hieroglyphic Hacker's reign of terror ends in Cleveland, Ohio." Her voice was strong and angelic. She sounded impressive saying absolutely nothing. She knew to only say just enough because public criticism would fall on her. Official blame would point only to her if she blew it. Marcus Jefferson's death had fed her to the piranhas, but she wasn't scared. The Reynolds group home she'd grown up in didn't raise sissies.

Scenario promised the piranhas that once the killer was caught, she would aggressively prosecute him to the fullest extent of the law in honor of the victims and their families. She told them that she believed in the justice system and in her staff's ability to assist in achieving the goals of Lady Justice. She gave out a hotline number for anyone who had information that could lead to the Hieroglyphic Hacker's arrest. Then Scenario politely refused to answer any questions.

Mayor Balfour took the podium—eager to satisfy his publicity jones. "Our modern-day Joan of Arc." He made a show of winking at Scenario. "Myself, my cabinet, the City Council, and the police department, we're all counting on County Prosecutor Scenario Davenport to lead the state of Ohio to the conviction of the Hieroglyphic Hacker."

Mayor Balfour was a cunning bastard. He had just cleared every other city official of any responsibility and left Scenario solely culpable if things went wrong, if they ever caught the killer. Scenario cringed at the Joan of Arc analogy. Joan had led the French against the English in the Hundred Year War. By the end of the battle, Joan was captured and convicted of heresy and burned at the stake. Scenario instantly became uncomfortable as realization tugged at her soul. She was standing at a figurative stake there on the Justice Center's steps. She had just put the nails in her proverbial coffin when she gave the piranhas sound bites. She was literally standing under the sword of Damocles.

FIFTY-NINE

A flicker of raw emotion brightened Hakeem's exhausted face. Aspen recognized the look: pent-up testosterone amped up on adrenaline. With their weapons drawn, they gave Scenario Davenport a conspiratorial look. Translation: *Are you ready for this?* Scenario demanded that she accompany them during the arrest in order to monitor the legality of the process. She had all the props: bulletproof vest, badge, .40 caliber Sig Sauer holstered on her hip, and a no-knock warrant signed by Judge Adrine. She took a deep breath, unholstered the gun, then nodded.

Hakeem kicked the door in.

"Scratch, this is the police!" Aspen yelled as they rushed the apartment.

The place was infested with roaches. Flies buzzed around a garbage can overrun with spoiled trash. Fast-food containers with half-eaten food littered the table. Among the debris was a leather iPhone cover. Dirty dishes were stacked in the kitchen sink with enough blue mold on them to supply a pharmacy with penicillin. Other than the filth and the pest, the place appeared empty.

Then something fell.

Hakeem motioned to a closed door at the back of the apartment. Aspen covered him as they inched down the hall. His movements were painful. He was going to hurt Butter Bean bad. White bread on hemorrhoids was like treating them with Tabasco sauce. And his tush was literally paying the price. Bastard. Scenario fell in five steps behind Aspen.

"Scratch, old friend," Hakeem said just outside the bedroom door, "come out of there."

"Eubanks, that you?"

"Yeah, come out of there."

"I ain't going to jail, Eubanks. I'll be dope sick for days."

Hakeem reached for the doorknob. "I'm coming in."

"Don't know what the hell for. I don't get down like that," Scratch said. "Send your partner in here naked and then we're working with something I like."

Aspen shook her head. "Same old Scratch."

Hakeem pushed the door open. Scratch was straddled across the windowsill. One leg inside the apartment; the other outside. A twinkle of mischief was in his eyes. Aspen stepped into the room, assuming the Weaver stance, and training her gun on Scratch. Scenario lingered in the doorway with her .40 Cal pointed at the floor.

Hakeem holstered his weapon and pointed a threatening finger at Scratch like it was a loaded gun. "I swear you better not make me chase you. Not with all the pain I'm in. We just want to ask you some questions."

"My office hours are from nine to five Monday through Friday. It's Saturday, you assholes. Reschedule with my secretary and I'll get back at you later." Then: "Should've come alone, Aspen." He winked at Aspen and pushed himself through the window and took off in an all-out sprint.

"Son of a bitch." Hakeem dove through the window after him. He limp-ran, trying to keep the hemorrhoidal pain to a minimum, even though his long strides knocked chunks out of the distance Scratch had gained on him.

Scratch loss momentum as he hopped a fence and came out on 105th and Olivet. His lungs were about to explode. Hakeem blocked out the pain and hurdled the fence like he was nineteen.

The thoroughfare 105 was one of the most disenfranchised and disconnected blocks in the city. It was neatly tucked away from the rest of society and its inhabitants moved with complete lawlessness.

Hakeem chased Scratch past Big Daddy's, a monumental soul food restaurant in the hood. Hakeem had his hands full trying to gain on Scratch. Drug dealers and their groupies showed comradeship to the dope fiend by obstructing Hakeem's path and justice. He held up his badge and urged them out his way and even knocked a few people down. But for the most part, they didn't budge. Scratch cut the corner on Hampton Avenue, flipping Hakeem the birdie as he did, and Aspen clotheslined him off his feet and knocked the smug smile off his face. Hakeem bent the corner a moment later huffing and puffing.

Aspen gently patted him on the ass. "Thought you could use some help," she said as Scratch staggered to his feet.

Hakeem punched his lights out and noticed that Scenario Davenport was not pleased with brutality.

SIXTY

Scratch clawed at his neck for the twentieth time since he was escorted into the interrogation room. "Shit, man, I'm getting sick, Eubanks."

The fluorescent light suspended over the interview table cast a glow on Scratch that highlighted how bad of shape the heroin use had him in. The whites of his eyes and the hue of his skin had a yellow tint going on like he was suffering from jaundice. He was rail thin and his cheeks were sunken in so deep it looked to Hakeem as if Scratch was sucking on a straw.

"You're going to jail for murder this time for sure." There was an intense pounding behind Hakeem's temples. And he knew the last words he'd spoken were a lie. Scratch wasn't a killer. A theft, yes; but a cold-blooded murderer, no.

Aspen shook a Newport out and offered it to Scratch. "You know you're gonna have to make this right," she said, giving him a light.

Now he clawed at his arm. "I ain't kill nobody. Just like I didn't kill Monique. I didn't lie to you when I told you she had overdosed before I showed up. All I did was use the rest of the heroin since she wasn't gonna need it anymore."

"That was last year," Hakeem said. "And it has nothing to do with why we found a dead man's phone in your pocket today."

Aspen said, "You're just a magnet for dead people. Listen, Scratch,

I believe you, but the only way I can help you is you gotta tell me where you got the phone."

He cut his eyes to Hakeem. "I think you broke my nose." Then: "I should sue."

"I'll tell you where you got it," Hakeem said. "You robbed and killed a man so you can stick that junk in your arm and you were too stupid to get rid of the phone. Now you're on your way to Chillicothe State Penitentiary."

"You got it all wrong, Eubanks." Scratch stubbed out the cigarette. "That isn't true."

Aspen put photos of Yancee's body on the table. "Unless you tell me something different, it doesn't look like we're wrong."

"No." Scratch closed his eyes.

Hakeem jumped up and grabbed Scratch by the neck, then forced his face an inch away from the table. "Open your eyes. Look at what you did. Look at it."

"Talk to us, Scratch." Aspen lolled in her chair. "Help me make this right."

"I'm sick." Sweat dripped from his forehead. "You gotta let me out of here so I can get straight. Please."

Hakeem pushed Scratch's face on Yancee's picture. "Why did you have the phone of a man who's been murdered?"

"My nose, Eubanks. Watch my nose."

"Better talk," Aspen said.

Hakeem pushed harder.

"Okay, okay. I stole the damn thing, okay?" Then: "But I didn't know it belonged to a dead guy."

Hakeem let him go. "Talk."

"The other day, Thursday—" He rubbed his neck as his nose started running. "—I was out in Euclid going to hang out with this girl I freak and get high with sometime and I saw this guy." Scratch picked up a picture. "Yeah, this is the guy and he wasn't all cut up like this."

"You saw him where?" Aspen said.

With caution in his voice and uncertainty in his eyes, Scratch said, "Am I in trouble?"

"Murder spells out trouble," Hakeem said.

"I only stole something out the lame's car."

Aspen wrote something on her notepad. "So you were the last person to see Yancee alive?"

"No, there was a woman with him."

Hakeem's eyes found Aspen's as he recalled Africa describing her husband as a cheater. "You saw Yancee with a woman?"

Scratch nodded. "Yeah, they were sitting together like lovebirds."

"Where were they?"

"At the little playground on the corner of Brush and two seventy-sixth."

Aspen considered Scratch.

"You were in the playground?"

Scratch came down with a case of the shivers. "I'm in pain, man. I gotta get out of here."

"I swear I'll throw you in a holding tank and let that monkey break your back."

"You wouldn't."

"He would," Aspen said. "Seen him do it, and you're about this close from finding out for yourself." She made a tiny gap between her index finger and thumb.

"No, I wasn't in the playground. When I first saw the two love-birds, I was walking by. Told you that I was headed to a friend's house."

Hakeem pulled up a chair next to Scratch. "How did you end up with Yancee's phone?"

"My friend's apartment overlooks the playground. While she was in the bathroom getting ready for us to do our thing, I watched this Yancee guy and that pretty girl he was with through the window. They walked to a red Infiniti and messed around in the trunk. My friend said something to me and when I turned back to the window, the Infiniti was pulling off."

"They were in the car together?" Aspen perked up.

"Had to be. The Camaro I saw him get out of was still parked on the street." He wiped his nose with his shirt. "And when I left the next day, it was still parked there with the keys in the ignition and the phone on the seat, so I took it. Do you know how much iPhones are worth on the street? I can get straight for two or three days. There was no way I was leaving it."

Hakeem said, "Describe the girl."

SIXTY-ONE

Hakeem decided it was time to dig in Madam Terri Dunlap's business to see if she had any holes in her panties.

Aspen thumped a half-smoked cigarette to the sidewalk. "I'm telling you now, Hakeem. Don't be the cause of someone up in here getting the whore smacked out of them," she said as they stepped into the foyer of an east side massage parlor, which was merely a front for Terri's brothel. "Before your eyes get carried away roaming over every inch of flesh you see, remember you came with a lady on your arm."

Hakeem yawned, feeling the exhaustion hibernating in the marrow of his bones, and a little confused about why he was getting checked when he hadn't gotten out of line. "What makes you think—"

Aspen threw a hand up. "You're a man; you can't help but admire women. Just respect me enough while we're together to look, but be smooth enough to pretend like you're not looking. I'm not about to go in a place like this and be trumped by another kitten's meow."

"Yes, Your Majesty." Hakeem bowed, then opened a second door of the house whose first floor had been remodeled to resemble a hotel lobby. The lounge area, facing a register counter, was lined with cozy overstuffed armchairs, and an internal speaker system softly played make-out music. Three men, one of which Hakeem recognized from somewhere, dressed in business suits lounged while flipping through voyeuristic trade magazines. The cunning proprietor's way of engaging her customers in mental foreplay while they waited to experience the real thing. Velvet drapes covered the windows, blocking all traces of sunlight, low-wattage bulbs dimmed the ambience of the undercover brothel, and the air was scented with a powerful olfactory aphrodisiac that worked its magic on Hakeem's sexual desire.

A leggy brunette with the body of a sister winked at Hakeem as she sashayed by them carrying a serving tray with a bottle of red wine and tumblers on it into the lounge area. She wore six-inch heels, a white thong that made her tan sing, and pasties over the nipples of a set of perky breasts. Heeding Aspen's warning and feeling her piercing gaze on him, he fought the strong urge to take a second look so he could check out the white girl's ass and see what she was really working with.

"Damn, this Terri bitch knows what she's doing," Aspen said as they approached the register counter. "I can take a few lessons in the art of seduction from her."

Hakeem immediately realized that the place was working its magic on Aspen's desire too. He wondered if the temperature of Aspen's passion could—

"What masseuse are you two scheduled to see today, and are you seeing her as a couple or do you have separate appointments?" a dolled-up, brown-complexioned woman said. She wore lingerie and extra-long eyelashes. Her fingers were ready to type their response into the computer to fact-check it.

"We're here to speak with Ms. Terri Dunlap." Hakeem's gaze rose from the woman's cleavage to her inquisitive brown eyes.

"Uh." The woman made a face as if what Hakeem had said wasn't normal. "Ms. Dunlap, uh, isn't here. If you would like to leave her a message, I'll see to it that she gets it."

Aspen frowned. "Look, what we aren't about to do is bullshit each other." She whipped out her badge. "So I suggest you get on the phone and tell Ms. Dunlap that Detectives Aspen Skye and Hakeem Eubanks are here, or we'll back a paddy wagon up to the front door and arrest the whole house for prostitution." She shot the men in the lounge a look. "And for solicitation of prostitution."

Leaning on the counter, Hakeem eased his lapel back so the scantily dressed receptionist and everyone else could see his gold shield. "She ain't playing."

The men high-tailed it out the front door. Hakeem figured they couldn't stand the social embarrassment and the marital ramifications that were staples of the prostitution sting. The young receptionist's hands visibly shook as she whispered into the phone. Hakeem would bet the thirty bucks in his pocket that she was a newcomer to the sex industry because seasoned whores didn't frighten easily. She returned the phone to its cradle and Terri Dunlap appeared in a doorway to the left of where they stood.

"Detectives, please come into my office."

Immediately, Hakeem knew the description was all wrong. Scratch described a fair-skinned woman with yellow eyes and long hair. Terri stood five-ten in her flats, which was four inches taller than the woman Scratch had seen Yancee with. Terri's complexion was the color of the imported cappuccino he drank every morning before going to the office. Her black hair was cut short, styled to give her the appeal of a corporate American businesswoman. And her brown eyes had the glare of someone who hated cops. From the expression on Aspen's face, Hakeem could tell that she knew Terri wasn't their girl too.

When Terri closed the door behind them, she said, "Can I offer you all something to drink?"

"No thank you," Aspen said as Hakeem politely declined with a head shake.

Terri perched herself on the corner of her desk and folded her arms beneath her small breasts, bangles dangled from her wrists. Her hips fanned out from the way she positioned herself on the desk, straining the material on her dress pants. "So what was important enough for you to come here and run my clients away?"

Aspen looked her up and down. "The way your name is ringing downtown, a few missed tricks won't hurt."

"Detective Skye, right?"

Aspen nodded.

"The goal is always to turn the trick."

Hakeem said, "Does the name Yancee Taylor mean anything to you?" He watched her closely. "Was he a client of yours?"

She dropped her head for a moment, then looked up with glassy eyes. "Yes, I've known Yancee for a long time. Met him in Philly at a car show seven years ago."

"He was a loyal customer of yours then," Aspen said from her post by the door.

"Yancee wasn't ever a client. He was my lover."

"Ms. Dunlap," Hakeem said, "where were you on Thursday, April the twenty-first between four-fifteen and six o'clock?"

Terri flinched. "I'm a suspect? You couldn't possibly think...I loved Yancee. Trust me, Detectives, I'm not a bleep on your radar."

Aspen said, "Then where were you, Ms. Dunlap?"

"I was with a client. Thursdays, I'm a working girl. I'd have to check my appointment book to see who I was giving a massage to at the time."

Hakeem gestured to the leather bond ledger on her desk. "Mind if I take a look?"

"Of course I mind you looking at my trade secrets, unless you have a warrant." She flipped the ledger opened and chuckled when she finished scanning the page she'd opened it to.

"What type of car do you drive?" Aspen said.

"I have two. Gifts. A blue convertible Bentley and the white Mercedes parked outside." Terri stood straight up and closed the distance between she and Hakeem, holding his gaze as she approached. "This questioning is over, Detectives. I never kiss and tell, but you leave me no choice. If you want to verify my alibi for the twenty-first, check with Mayor Balfour. He'll clear me." She produced a business card from seemingly nowhere. "Detective Eubanks, if you find Yancee's killer, please let me know. And I have magic fingers. Looks like you can use a good massage. When the urge hits, give me a call." She smiled, then nibbled the corner of her lip as she blushed.

Aspen plucked the card from Terri's hand. "Sorry to interfere with your goals again, but that ain't happening."

Hakeem said nothing. He just wondered what that was all about.

SIXTY-TWO

There was a reason Scenario chose to meet her childhood sweetheart, GP, at Good Insults: she was on edge and needed to relieve some stress.

"What the fuck do y'all want to eat? And be quick about deciding 'cause I gots other shit to do." A slim waitress with lots of attitude stood at their table with a hand on her cocked hip.

Scenario said, "We'll order when we get good and damn ready."

GP laughed. Scenario knew that he couldn't believe that everyone around him was cussing one another out and having a good time doing it.

"What in the hell is so funny, you lanky fucker?"

GP laughed again. "She's really talking to me like that."

"Go ahead," Scenario said, reaching across the table and grabbing his hand. "Insult her back." She felt sexy touching him. She stroked his wedding ring wishing it was a commitment to her.

GP laughed. Scenario loved his laugh. The way it rumbled in his chest. Many nights when they were growing up in hell, she made it to a new day because his laugh carried her.

"Go ahead and try it, GP. That's what this place is all about, letting off frustration. Plus the food is good."

GP looked at the waitress. "Kiss my ass."

"Fuck you," the waitress said.

"No, fuck you."

Scenario stepped in. "Bitch, watch your mouth with my man. Now go get us a bottle of Chardon Blanc De Noirs and don't move like you got molasses in your ass."

"Assholes," the waitress said, walking away with a mean switch in her hips.

"I'm really surprised this place hasn't been shut down."

"This gimmick is getting the owners rich," she said, remembering their intimate time together. "I like coming here because sometimes you feel better after you cuss somebody out. Doing it here you don't have to actually worry about hurting someone's feelings or feeling bad afterward." Her eyes studied GP.

He was a handsome brother. Athletic build. Neat cornrows that hung past his broad shoulders. He wore a trendy pair of jeans with a sweat shirt that had the Street Prophet insignia blasted across the chest.

Scenario said, "I saw you on *The Mo'Nique Show*. Whoever would have thought that two kids who grew up in an abusive group home would be living their dreams."

"Yeah, we did real good for ourselves without any family," GP said. "I'm glad you got in touch with me. So how's the search for your parents going? Found any of your relatives?"

"I got exhausted with the hopelessness and dead-end leads and gave up my search nearly four years ago. What about you?"

"Finding my mother would really be nice. Have I made any attempts to do so? No, because it is what it is. I'm happy with the family I created with Kitchie."

"Well," Scenario said, blankly staring into the ambience of Good Insults, "I asked to see you because I needed someone to talk to. You're the closest thing to family I've ever had."

"We are family." GP flagged the foul-mouthed waitress and got a dirty look for his efforts. "You don't look that much different, not to me." He studied her face. "The plastic surgeons did a great job. No lie, you're even more beautiful. You still stand out in any crowd."

She fingered the scar.

"Even with that new beauty mark." Then: "I always question myself about us. I never thought life would pair us with different mates."

"Me neither. You couldn't have told me that we weren't going to get married and live a fairy tale. You'll never believe how I hit it off with Chance."

"Try me."

"Because of our love for animals. I told him about that time I beat the pudding out of Janice for kicking that stray cat we found."

GP said, "We named him Twinkles," they said the cat's name together.

"You remember?" She smiled.

"I remember everything about us."

"Me too. Anyway, Chance and I never looked back after that."

"I'll never forget it. I had to pull you off that poor girl. Still can't believe charges were pressed on you for a childhood fight."

"Bet Janice will never kick another cat or any animal for that matter."

GP flagged the waitress again.

"I saw you the first fucking time," the waitress yelled across the dining room. "Obviously I ain't got to you yet 'cause I don't fucking feel like it. Now sit there and wait."

"Get your narrow ass over here and take our order."

Scenario turned up the corners of her lips into a gorgeous smile. "That's it, GP. Now you're getting with the program around here."

"I'm hoping an explanation of your name change is a part of what you want to talk about, because you'll always be Cashmaire to me."

"GP, you know I spent my whole life lying about who I am because of my condition. You remember what happened when people found out when we were young. Kids are cruel. It was a horrible experience to learn you're not normal like everyone else. My parents probably knew it all along, which explains why I was left in a Dumpster as an infant. You were the only person around me who didn't change. You continued to love me." She paused, thinking. "With the accident and Chance leaving me when he learned the truth and the plastic surgery, it gave me the opportunity to leave my old life behind and start over with a new one. New face, new social security number, new name, new background." She took his hand and held it. "But a situation has forced me to lie under my new identity, and I'm afraid something really bad is going to happen if the truth comes out. I know a murder victim but haven't told anyone in order to keep my present separated from my past." She found GP's inviting eyes and sunk into them. "Can I ask you something?"

He nodded. "Yeah, Cash, anything. You know how we do."

She nibbled her bottom lip and stroked his hand. "I need to be touched in the way only you can. Take me home and sleep with me."

SIXTY-THREE

T he computer terminal lit up like a General Electric Christmas display. Kirsten Andrews, a stressed-out operator, hit the Enter key and adjusted her headset for comfort. "Crime Stoppers. How can I help you?" Kirsten read the caller's information on the screen.

"Is this the place to give information for the serial killer?" an elderly woman said.

"Yes, ma'am."

"Am I anonymous?"

"Yes, ma'am." Kirsten rolled her eyes.

"How you know?"

"If you would like your identity to remain private, I'll note it in my computer." Although Kirsten had the lady's name on the screen, she was a professional and knew not to use it since the lady already had reservations about her identity.

"That's what I want. What about my reward?"

"There's a twenty-thousand-dollar reward being offered for information that leads to the arrest of the Hieroglyphic Hacker."

"How you know?"

"Ma'am, do you have information you would like to give or not?"

"I know where he is."

Kirsten sighed. "Where who is?"

"The serial killer."

"And where would that be?"

"I trapped him."

Kirsten closed her eyes and chewed the inside of her mouth as she realized she was dealing with another quack job. "So you trapped him?"

"Sure 'nough did."

She shook her head and looked around the room at the other operators who were talking into their headsets. "Where? Where did you trap him, ma'am?"

"Got him right here in my bird cage. Get over here—"

"Okay, ma'am. We'll send somebody right over." She disconnected the call and the terminal lit up again. She pinched the bridge of her nose where the tension was, then took the call. "Crime Stoppers. How can I help you?"

A feminine voice said, "You wanna listen real closely to this."

The moment Hakeem stepped into the room, he knew there would be trouble. He felt it in the marrow of his tired bones. Or maybe his fatigued body was playing tricks on him because he'd spent another night alternating between walking the halls of his house and staring at his bedroom ceiling. Brenda McGinnis was monitoring the operators until she looked up and saw him. She crossed the room with confident strides. Hakeem pegged her as cute; she had too many boyish features to be considered beautiful.

"Detective Eubanks," she said, pumping his hand, "we've logged over four thousand calls since six this morning."

"Anything promising?"

"Every nut job in the city is calling in saying they've seen the

Hieroglyphic Hacker. He's been everything from somebody's pastor to the Emperor Haile Selassie reincarnated." Then: "Nothing worth following up."

Kirsten Andrews jumped out her seat. She flagged Hakeem and Brenda over. She gave Hakeem a printout with the logistics of the call. "It came from a pay phone inside Good Insults. She says she's the killer, and she left a message for you and Aspen."

SIXTY-FOUR

Chance sat in the back of Good Insults watching Cashmaire like a predator starving for satisfaction. He took particular note of her body language, of how she pawed GP's hands. He knew her well. The cunt wanted to fuck. The thought churned his stomach and carved a deep scowl in his face.

A waitress approached his table.

"Douche bag, get the fuck away from me. I'm serious. I play no games."

"Well, fuck you too and have a nice day." She turned up her lip as she rolled her eyes and strutted away.

He dug a sandwich bag from his pocket with a case quarter and dime in it, then made his way to the eatery's pay phone. He pushed his hands inside a pair of leather gloves and eased the coins from the bag, careful not to smudge them as he inserted them into the phone.

"Crime Stoppers." The woman sounded like she was having a bad day. "How can I help you?"

Chance thought, Law 38: Think As You Like But Behave Like Others. "You wanna listen real closely to this," he said, disguising his voice.

"Who am I speaking with?"

"The media calls me the Hieroglyphic Hacker."

"Is that right?"

"How does it feel?"

Kirsten said, "What?"

"To talk to a killer."

"You're just another wacko wasting my time."

"Hakeem Eubanks and Aspen Skye. Tell the detectives that I have a special gift for them."

Kirsten was quiet.

"So it's sinking in that I'm the real deal." Then: "About that gift for the ambitious detectives. Tell them that it's stinking up the Wellness Center on Superior Road." Chance hung up as Cashmaire left the club hugged up with the cartoon-drawing motherfucker GP.

SIXTY-FIVE

Hakeem flipped his Palm Treo open. "Communicate."

Aspen skipped all the bull and got right to what Hakeem knew concerned her the most. "How are you?"

"Sick to my stomach."

"It was true. Damn."

Hakeem stood on Superior with the posture of a prizefighter and the charisma of a contemplative Virgo. His keen eyes watched the growing crowd of spectators, wondering if the killer was mingling in the crowd watching him. Later he would review the video footage for signs of any odd behavior among the rubberneckers. He knew that serial killers got off on feeling smarter than detectives, and they would return to the crime scene to admire their work or to be helpful to the investigation. "Yeah, I'm afraid so. Dr. Chavez just pulled the deceased out. Anderson Smith. He owned the place. Crime scene techs found more trace." He scanned the crowd. "What's going on on your end?"

"I questioned all the employees. No one remembers anyone strange, out of place, or with peculiar behavior. Their surveillance ironically stopped working today. Didn't even know it wasn't operational until I asked to see the footage. Get this: the main feed on the roof was cut. And there aren't any other cameras in the area. City hasn't installed them yet."

"The pay phone?"

"Already on it. Tony pulled some prints, and I had our boys empty the coin tray. I want the change printed too."

"That's a long shot, but a smart one."

"Tell me about it. Best not to leave any stone unturned."

Hakeem said, "We're chasing our tails."

"What do we know about the caller?"

"Nothing." Then: "The operator thinks it was a female voice, but she won't swear on it because it could have been a soft-spoken man. But a feminine voice nonetheless. Listened to the call myself and I can't tell either. My guess would be a woman, though."

"I'm not feeling this, Hakeem. First the killer leaves a personal message to you on Yancee's body. Now it—"

"It?" Hakeem frowned.

"Yeah, *it* because no one can tell me if the call was made by a male or female. Like I was saying: now *it* calls a police tip line and speaks directly to you and me."

Hakeem stopped an officer coming out the Wellness Center. "Hey, I want everyone in this crowd identified. Get me field interview cards filled out on them."

The officer nodded.

To Aspen he said, "I swear I don't want to know what's written on this body."

"Me neither, Hakeem. Me neither."

He yawned and closed his eyes. Big mistake. Behind his eyes it happened again: The image of the small body flashed through his mind. Its lifeless form stretched across a stainless steel autopsy table; its dead eyes frozen open forever. Hakeem's cell phone hit the sidewalk. He opened his eyes, but his breath was gone. He struggled and gasped to get it back.

"Hakeem, are you all right?" Dr. Aura Chavez led him to the hood of a police cruiser that was parked at the curb.

He loosened his tie, sucking down cupfuls of air. "I'll be fine. Just give me a minute."

"I think I need to write you another prescription," she said, handing him his cell phone.

"That will really help." He powered off the phone, totally forgetting Aspen was on the line. "I'm scared to close my eyes. Every time I do, I see the body. I can't take it."

"It's a classic case of Survivor's Guilt. I'm starting to worry about you, Hakeem, and I swear this is the last prescription I'm writing you."

"I'll be fine." His breathing began to even out.

"Not if you're not sleeping." She scribbled his prescription on a medical slip. "I gave you an antidepressant for your post-traumatic stress."

"What about some stronger sleeping pills?"

"You're becoming dependent on them. The antidepressant will help."

"Aura, please, I need sleep."

"What's next, Hakeem? Are you going to start self-medicating with booze? This is getting out of hand."

Hakeem said nothing. He could tell from her tight expression that she was going against her better judgment as she wrote another prescription.

She stuffed the prescription in his breast pocket. "Got a DNA profile back on the hair from the Yancee Taylor murder. It belongs to an African American male."

"That was quick."

"Came from upstairs. They spent the money to get it done."

"I'll run it through CODIS and see if I get a hit on it." Thousands of genetic DNA profiles of convicted offenders and unidentified profiles collected from crime scenes throughout the country were stored in CODIS, a national database.

"What are the odds of it matching the eyelash we found here?"

Hakeem shrugged an *I don't know* as Aspen sent him a text message that read: *Are you all right?* He didn't know that answer either.

SIXTY-SIX

The way Scenario held her gaze on GP while unbuttoning her blouse took his breath away. They were each other's first, fumbled through their first orgasms together while they discovered the dynamics and joys of sex, experienced congress with each other like it was created only for them.

Scenario stepped closer to GP. "Take me right here. Bend me over the arm of the sofa."

GP bit his bottom lip, letting out a frustrated sigh. His mouth watered as he looked at her perky breasts, loving the way her flawless nipples were set in caramel areolas. "God, you're beautiful. Never seen anyone more beautiful." He turned his back on her, grabbed his head and sighed.

"What's wrong?" She wrapped her arms around his waist, pressing those perfect breasts on his back. "We can go in my bedroom if you want."

"I'm married, Cash." He peeled her soft arms away, begging his erection to back off.

"What difference does that make to me and you? We promised ourselves to each other no matter what, no matter who we're with. It's not like we haven't done it before. Kitchie won't know now like she didn't know then."

"I wasn't married then, and I'll know now, Cash." Then: "It's nothing personal against you."

"Then why are you talking to me with your back turned to me?"

"Because you're too gorgeous. I'm afraid if I turn around and face you, I won't turn back." Silence. "I didn't know that I still love you so much. You have everything inside of me going crazy."

"Then why aren't you inside of me where you're supposed to be?" He faced her.

She let her blouse slip from her shoulders and stuck her hand in his pants. "I want this. Don't you want to give it to me like you always have?"

He broke eye contact with her while her delicate hand stroked his desire. He could still picture all the times she straddled him and sucked a passion mark on his neck as they exploded together. He removed her hand. "No, Cash, what I want to do is say thank you."

Her brows knotted. "Thank me for what?"

"This test." He gathered his leather jacket from the sofa. "Us being here together gave me the perfect opportunity to honor my commitment to Kitchie and to truly understand what my marriage means to me." He leaned in and kissed her lips. "Thank you. I'll always love you and be here for you, Cash. For anything…but not this as long as I'm married." Then: "You wanted my advice. A lie is a lie. Just like a lie got you in trouble before, it'll get you in trouble again when the truth comes to light." He touched her face, then let himself out of her house.

Scenario locked the door behind him, horny, frustrated, unsatisfied. She paced and thought, stopping only when her landline rang. She stared at the phone until it stopped ringing. Then her cell phone came alive. "What is it?"

"Ms. Davenport." It was Chief Dwight Eisenhower.

"Yes," she said, softening her tone to sound more civil than she really felt.

"You better get down here." He paused and spoke to someone in his background. When his attention came back to her, he said, "We're on Superior at the Wellness Center. We've got another dead body courtesy of the Hieroglyphic Hacker."

She picked her blouse up. "Just what the fuck I needed."

SIXTY-SEVEN

S omething stunk about the whole situation and Aspen wasn't feeling it. The exhale of the air conditioner chilled the Homicide Unit to an uncomfortable temperature. She chugged down a Syntha-6 protein shake that guaranteed weight loss while keeping an eye on the fax machine. "It doesn't make any sense to me." She threw her hands up. "I'm completely thrown off."

Detective Leonardo Scott spat a wad of Red Indian in an empty soda can. "Profiles are pretty accurate. This guy is supposed to be a white male; it's textbook."

"See, now that's what puzzles me," Hakeem said, removing a folded piece of paper from the Mont Blanc folder. His eyes were getting heavier by the second. "The DNA found at the Yancee crime scene belongs to a black male. Nothing matching it in the database. And they're putting a rush job on the lash found at the Anderson crime scene."

"But," Aspen said about to light up a cigarette until Hakeem frowned at her, "Scratch saw Yancee approximately thirty minutes before his time of death with a woman, who didn't turn out to be Terri Dunlap." She glanced at her notes. "Driving a red Infiniti. And the voice on the tip line recording sounds like a woman to me."

"I'm with you, Aspen," Hakeem said. "I don't know if we're look-ing for a gorgeous woman, a white man, a black man, or all three."

"I like the Chancellor Fox fella for this." Detective Leonardo Scott stuffed a new batch of chew between his cheek and gums. Then, just like Aspen's, his eyes fell to the fax machine. "He fits: He's a veterinarian. Vets have skills with scalpels and stock medicine like succinylcholine. He lived in Denver during the time of the murders. Plane records show he's been to Cleveland as of recent, and he used to go to that school, uh—"

"Monticello." Hakeem yawned. "And he's fallen off the face of the earth."

"Or hiding," Detective Scott said.

Aspen finished her protein shake. "But we're back to him being white. And according to the plane manifest, he was here six months ago. The murders just started."

"They stopped six months ago in Denver, though," Detective Scott said.

"All of the reasons above are why I want to find him and bring him in for questioning." Hakeem closed his eyes and nodded off.

"The boys back home are searching high and low for him. His animal clinic has been closed for months." Detective Scott looked at Hakeem who was now asleep in the chair. "Detective Eu—"

"No, let him sleep, he needs it."

The piece of paper fell from Hakeem's hand. Detective Scott picked it up and tried to make sense of the words.

amilyfay isay ethay acredsay ightray
ofay assagepay. eathday otay ethay
vileay oersday owhay tersalay ethay oursecay
ofay anmay, omanway, ildchay. astlay
arningway, etectivesday, ackbay upay
or oinjay ethay eadday.

"Pig Latin is way above my pay grade," Detective Scott said, handing Aspen the paper.

"It says 'Family is the sacred rite of passage. Death to the evil-doers who alter the course of man, woman, child. Last warning, Detectives, back up or join the dead.'"

"Impressive. Where did you learn pig Latin?"

"Grade school. I think all little girls learn it so we can talk about boys in secrecy."

"So," Detective Scott said, "why would the Hieroglyphic Hacker lead us to a body and then leave a message on the body to ease off? Sounds like something personal between the killer and you and Eubanks."

"That's what I'm afraid all the taunting is about."

The fax machine came to life. Detective Scott twitched like he'd just had a premonition.

"The moment of truth," Aspen said.

Aspen wasn't the least bit surprised. Detective Leonardo Scott, however, stared at the fax as if he were the stupidest cop in the history of law enforcement.

"We just never thought the hieroglyphics actually communicated anything. Never considered it. I just thought he basically graffitied on people and the hieroglyphics were his calling card," Detective Scott said as they rounded the corner of Aspen and Hakeem's cubicle.

On the floor between a desk and chair lay Hakeem asleep.

Leonardo gave Aspen an uncertain look. "I'm afraid to ask."

"Then mind your business."

"Should we get him off the floor?"

"No, leave him be."

"I don't think I'm cool with this."

"Mind your *fucking* business." Then: "Did it register that time?"

He removed a pack of chewing tobacco from inside his Stetson, then readjusted the hat on his head. "I don't feel right leaving him here like this."

"Look, dammit." Aspen rolled her eyes; her nostrils flared. "He's going through some things. None of which is any of your damn business. He hasn't been sleeping so he needs this rest. Furthermore, if I say leave him the fuck alone, then leave him the fuck alone."

Her outburst didn't sway Leonardo either way. "Would this have anything to do with—" He gestured to Hakeem's desk. "—why his picture frames are turned faced down?"

"What you need to do is find out why you Denver boys are so incompetent. You need to find out why you assholes didn't have a clue the killer has been talking to you the whole time." She gestured to the fax in his hand. "On each of the Denver victims the killer wrote about the sacred rights of animals. What you need to do is find out what the fuck this has to do with animals so we can catch this psychopath." She lit a cigarette. "That will suit my temperament, Detective, because this not minding your business bullshit is rubbing me the wrong motherfucking way."

"You sound more like his woman than his partner."

"That ain't none of your damn business either."

SIXTY-EIGHT

Leon Page had a terrible habit of waking up with a hangover. Coupled with cirrhosis, it was enough to cause his life to be a painful living hell. Leon developed this despicable characteristic of alcoholism after he watched his partner get murdered in the line of duty and was too pussy to prevent it from happening. He'd just stood there frozen in fear while a golf club-wielding, cigar-smoking female lawyer split his partner's head open.

This Monday morning, however, was slightly different from all the other mornings he'd woken up after learning he was a coward. Today he had a nasty hangover; the cirrhosis was more painful than usual; he was still pissy drunk; *and* he was sincerely worried about Jazz. And to punctuate his issues, his cell phone wouldn't stop fucking ringing, amplifying the intensity of his hangover with each ring. He couldn't recall last night's events or how he'd managed to make it back home to his sofa with an empty bottle of Bacardi clutched in his hand. Leon closed his eyes, straining to remember anything that would validate his worthless existence.

And the damn phone continued to increase the volume of his hangover.

He sat up way too fast and his inhuman apartment started spinning. He settled himself against the sofa's back, dug his dirty fingertips into the cushions on both sides of him, and held on for the ride. When Leon's miserable world slowed to a reasonable pace that he could function in, his gaze landed on the Glock 23 sitting among the clutter of his coffee table.

And the phone rang.

He dug the annoying thing from his pocket. "What?"

"Leon," a muffled voice said, "you look like shit."

Chance, clad in an HVAC uniform, a curly wig, and a pair of sunglasses with built-in binoculars, stood on the rooftop of a downtown office building. He removed a Phillips screwdriver from the tool belt slung low on his waist and made a show of tinkering with a ventilation unit while watching Leon through the window of his low-rental apartment in a high-rise seventy yards away.

He whipped his phone out after amusing himself with Leon's discomfort and punched in the number of his next victim.

Eight rings later, Leon said, "What?"

"Leon, you look like shit."

"How the hell would you know what I look like?" Leon said, trying to place the voice but drawing a complete blank.

"'Cause I'm looking at you."

"Who's this?" Leon stuck his tongue out and turned the Bacardi bottle up until the last drip leaked onto his tongue.

"That's a nasty habit you got there."

"Who is this?" He staggered to his sixteenth-floor window.

"Doesn't matter." Then: "Guess what?"

"Do I get to buy a vowel? What?"

"You die next."

Leon did something he hadn't done in a year of Sundays—he sobered up. Instantly. "You'll only be doing me a real favor, you asshole. Alimony, my liver, Bacardi, and child support has already killed me." Leon glanced at his watch, 7:42 a.m. "Call me back when you got some bad news for me."

Leon hung up on the anonymous caller and thought about Jazz again. His thoughts compelled him to pick up the gun from the coffee table, figuring he'd make amends to Jazz for all the damage he'd done and make life simpler for everyone by driving a bullet through his brain. When he checked the clip in preparation of his suicide, he noticed a bullet missing—the same bullet that would have saved his partner's life if he'd had the guts to fire it sooner. In an instance the memories of his disgrace came rushing back as if it happened only hours ago.

He and his partner, Kirt Gilchrist, surrounded the cigar-smoking attorney with tactical precision. She held a golf club over her head. Sizing up her prey. Ready to strike like a seasoned predator. Leon, a rookie Hoboken, New Jersey, cop, stood behind the attorney with his gun drawn. Sweat inched down his forehead, headed straight for his eyes. Leon wanted to wipe the irritating sweat away, but he couldn't risk taking a hand off the gun.

She gnawed on the hundred-dollar cigar, swaying like a cobra.

Officer Gilchrist had said, "Ms. Daniels, you're under arrest for conspiracy to commit murder for financial gain."

She grunted. Smoke pouring from her nose. Pure defiance in her eyes.

Officer Gilchrist reached for his gun.

"Put. The. Club. Down!" Leon had said, as if he meant business and wasn't to be fucked with.

Before Officer Gilchrist could free his gun from its holster, she slammed the golf club into his wrist, crushing the bones with ease.

Leon froze; his feet rooted to the ground.

Within seconds, she struck Gilchrist again and split his skull easier than she had his wrist. Gilchrist was a corpse before his body hit the ground.

The arrest was supposed to be simple arithmetic: Serve the warrant. Secure her. Mirandatize the suspect. Deliver her to the county jail to be processed and await arraignment.

But Ms. Daniels had other plans. She spun around and squared off with Leon. She sucked in a thick cloud of smoke. "Always thought it would be the cigars that took me out." She lunged at Leon with the bloody golf club.

Leon thawed and pulled the trigger. As the bullet tore into her heart, Leon remembered Yancee's, his college buddy's, warning: *One day, Leon, I swear your hesitation to do the right thing is going to get someone killed.*

Four hours after Leon had frozen, he explained the events that led to Gilchrist's death to the department. Now all he needed was to relieve some stress. What better way to do it than to go home and punch out his wife?

SIXTY-NINE

Jazz cried out. "My baby. Please stop, Leon. You'll make me lose the baby." Heavy moans of deep pain leaked from her battered body. She lay on their bedroom floor, trembling, still feeling the sting of his fists; still hugging her stomach to protect her unborn child from another violent blow. This was the first time he'd drawn blood since the night he violently took her virginity. This was the first time he made his abuse visible to the naked eye.

Leon paced the room like an aggressive caged animal. "I told you to get rid of it. Every time I turn around, you do something to make me hit you." He kicked her in the belly as he passed her.

"Oh God," Jazz cried out. "My baby. You're hurting my baby."

"Get up so I can knock your ugly ass down again." Then: "Told your ass to get rid of it."

Jazz hugged herself tighter.

"I said get up, dammit!" He snatched her to her feet by her hair, then backhanded her to the floor again.

"I'm sorry," she said, spitting blood. "I'm sorry, Leon."

He kicked her and the baby again. "You know what? I'm gonna show you I ain't to be fucked with." He dragged her from their bedroom, dirtying her sparkling white jeans. He shoved her through the house and into their indoor garage. "Told you to stay off the phone. Think I wouldn't see the long-distance charges? I brought you here to keep you *away from the dregs of your family. Them people don't love you. Only I do." He pushed her into the front seat of his brand-new 2005 Mercedes-Benz CLS550—courtesy of her latest royalty check—and slammed the door.*

Jazz watched through the windshield as he ranted and raved, pacing. He disappeared from her line of vision. She was in too much pain to move, too afraid of his fists to try something daring to save her and the baby. She felt something warm and sticky between her legs. She glanced down and saw her crotch spotted burgundy.

The trunk slammed closed; Jazz flinched. Leon slid into the driver's seat, hit the automatic garage door opener, and backed out into the night. The clock on the dashboard read 3:22 a.m. Jazz wondered where he was taking her.

"I'm having a miscarriage. Take me to the hospital. Please, Leon. Please help me save my baby."

He pound on the steering wheel. "No one helped me save Gilchrist tonight when that bitch mashed his head in. No, honey, you don't need a hospital where you're going." He cut a hateful set of eyes on her.

It only took twenty-two minutes from the time they left home before they pulled onto a dirt road that winded two miles into an unkempt wooded section of Count Basie Park in Red Bank, New Jersey.

Leon threw the car in Drive. "Get out of my car."

When her swollen eyes adjusted to the darkness, she took in her surroundings. A dense knot of oak trees in the middle of…nowhere. "You're gonna kill me," she said in spite of a busted lip.

He reached across her lap, opened the door, and shoved her to the dirt road. "I said get the fuck out." Before he climbed out, he took his throwaway .32 caliber pistol from beneath the seat. He then removed a spade shovel from the trunk and threw it at Jazz's feet.

The shovel and its implication horrified Jazz.

He put the gun to her head. "Pick it up."

Through the pain and fear she did as she was told. By gunpoint he forced her deep into the woods to a clear patch of earth.

"Tonight we end this," he said with no feeling or inflection. "Dig."

The thought of her digging her own grave made Jazz give up. "I can't do this." She threw the shovel down as the October chill cooled the sticky fluid between her legs. "You want me dead, then kill me, Leon. Just do it. Dammit, do—"

He fired a bullet that whizzed by her head and left her ears ringing. "Honey, I'm serious. I advise you to pick the shovel up and dig without further procrastination."

She pushed the shovel into the earth and pulled out a rich chunk of soil like she used to do while helping her mother plant a bell pepper and tomato garden on a stretch of inherited land on the countryside of Maryland.

"Whatever I did to you, I won't ever do it again. Just tell me, Leon, and take me to a hospital."

"Don't stop digging until it's deep enough," Leon said. "I don't want the black bears and coons to smell you rotting and dig you up."

"I feel my baby dying, Leon. I swear I won't call my mother again. I swear." She pulled out another chunk of earth. "Take me to a hospital, please."

"Shut up whining and dig, you bitch."

"Eric will look for me."

"And I'll bring him out here and bury him beside you." Then: "You think I don't know your agent wants to fuck you?"

It took Jazz the better part of two hours to dig a grave in her condition suitable to Leon's liking. She stood in the hole, shivering, gazing up at him through tear-filled eyes.

"Hand me the shovel."

She was in too much pain and too exhausted to do anything other than comply.

"Now lay down."

She didn't budge.

Leon said, "I'll hurt your mother and let you carry that knowledge into the next life."

With her back against the cold earth and a dead baby in her belly, Jazz cried and screamed, "Kill me. Just kill—"

He threw a shovelful of dirt on her face. "If I ever have to speak to you again about anything, mark my words, this is where I'll leave your black ass."

SEVENTY

mpound lot. Now Hakeem worried that Yancee's Camaro wouldn't turn up any evidence that would identify the unsub or put them any closer to nailing the bastard.

He and Aspen watched as criminalist—with emphasized caution—loaded the Camaro onto a flatbed truck. Five days into the investigation and nothing made sense. None of the facts matched. The nation's elite profilers pegged the murders on a white male. Scratch witnessed Yancee with a stunning female of undetermined race a few hours before the time of death. "Maybe she was white or mixed or a fair-skinned sista," as Scratch had described her. DNA evidence collected from the crime scene belonged to an unidentified African American male.

"What if we're dealing with a serial killing team?" Hakeem said as a dumpy man with aggravated acne hustled toward them. "Three of 'em."

"That'll be one for the history books." She wiped traces of their breakfast from his mouth with a thumb. Their eyes locked. Their lips dangerously close. Hakeem held his breath.

"Here you go," Dumpy said, handing Aspen an impound invoice. "Yup, came in Saturday, April the twenty-third at twelve seventeen in the morning." Sweat dripped from his forehead; his breathing labored.

Hakeem and Aspen eyed each other, both understanding that they were at the scene of the crime while Yancee's car was being towed.

Aspen scanned the paperwork. "Has anyone touched the car or removed anything from it?"

Dumpy shrugged. "Sorry, Detective, that I can't say."

Hakeem knew what that meant: Dumpy was about to get a full dose of Aspen Skye. Poor Dumpy, Hakeem thought.

Aspen's eyes glazed over; her jawbone throbbed. She looked at Dumpy as if he were incompetent, retarded, or both. "So what in the hell do you have supervisor stitched on your shirt for? Point us in the damn direction of someone who *can* say."

"What I meant—"

"Exactly what the hell did you mean?" She tapped out a Newport as Hakeem looked on, wondering what was in her that made her go from zero to one hundred at the slightest irritation.

Dumpy said, "My employees haven't removed or touched the car after it was hauled in. There's a drug rehabilitation center and methadone clinic at the end of the block. We get vandalized weekly. Addicts climb my fence at night and steal car radios, TVs, and anything else they can carry outta here to get a fix."

Inside the police garage, the crime scene techs busied themselves gutting Yancee's Camaro and collecting potential evidence. Tony Adams excused himself from the others and went over to Hakeem and Aspen.

"Detectives," he said.

"Tony." Hakeem nodded.

In lieu of a greeting, Aspen said, "What you got?"

Tony glanced back at the car as the front seats were being re-moved. "Lifted seventy-two sets of latent that were made by five different people. Two sets were made by children. Got hits on another two sets as soon as we fed them to AIFIS."

Aspen's heart started pounding. "That's great. Who, Tony?"

"Of course one combination of prints belongs to Yancee Taylor. The other combination are—"

"Scratch's," Hakeem said, "if he told the whole truth."

Tony nodded.

"What about the fifth person?" Aspen said.

"Nothing in the database." Tony pulled out a plastic evidence bag and held it up. "We also found this stuck to the dashboard."

Inside the bag was a yellow Post-It note. Written in blue ink were the words *C.F. Wood Chips, 4:30, Thursday.*

"Does this mean anything to either of you?"

Hakeem said nothing.

"Dammit, I think it just might." Aspen snapped a picture of the note with her phone. "I could kiss you right now, Tony."

He blushed.

SEVENTY-ONE

They faced each other in the square of the kitchen like two prizefighters with their titles on the line.

Buank. Buank. Buank. Buank.

"I swear to God." Jazz pulled her hair into a ponytail and propped the sunglasses on her head. "I swear if you bounce that ball one more time—ever—in my house, I'll leave you here and never come back." She wore a jean skirt that showed off her long legs and a fashionable pair of sandals that highlighted her pretty toes. The tantalizing cover to her latest novel and the URL of her web site was printed on the front of her dainty T-shirt.

Fear flashed in Jaden's eyes. "You wouldn't."

Jazz saw it as plain as day. "So that's it, huh?" Translation: *I got you all figured out.* "You're scared to be alone."

He palmed the ball, feigning a dribble, testing her resolve.

She picked up her keys, eager to make good on her promise. "Try me. I dare you. You're hateful, mean, and rude as hell with your smart-ass mouth. I would love to leave you."

"You're lying."

"Bounce the ball and find out."

He pretended he would bounce it.

"Jaden, I'm so sick of you. Stop faking and do it so I can turn my back on you."

"You want to leave me for real?"

"I'm more than ready to go. You pushed and pushed me away. Now give me the reason I need to seal the deal." She set her chin. "My sanity is too precious to keep allowing you to put me through hell because you won't accept my apology."

"You can't leave me."

With a hand on her cocked hip, she said, "And why the hell not?"

"'Cause."

"Because what, Jaden?"

"'Cause you're more afraid of abandonment than I am. I got your number." *Buank. Buank. Buank. Buank.*

"Good riddance." Jazz's long, confident strides quickly carried her through the house.

"Don't leave me," Jaden said. "Take me with you."

She kept going straight toward the front door without so much as a backward glance.

"Okay, okay, okay, I'm sorry. Please don't leave."

"Should've thought about that before you disrespected me and did exactly what I asked you not to do."

"I won't do it again."

"Too damn late, Jaden. I'm gone." She snatched the door open and Leon was coming up the walkway.

Now she was in for a real fight.

SEVENTY-TWO

A gasp punctuated her surprise and got caught in her throat. Only her eyes blinked because it was an involuntary action. Everything else was too damn scared to move. She felt pure terror burrow deep into her heart.

He said, "Need to talk to you." He was sickly-looking and way too skinny. He'd lost at least thirty pounds since they sat at a conference table with their lawyers and signed divorce papers.

The sound of his baritone voice thawed her. She clicked the lock on the security screen door between them in a hurry.

"You can't leave me like this," Jaden said.

Over a shoulder, she said, "Shut up. Just shut up."

"Who are you talking to?" Leon stepped closer to the screen door, trying to see around her. His jaundice-colored eyes were sunken and distant.

"I know you didn't violate the restraining order to mind my business. What do you want?" Without permission, her heart tried to stab its way through her chest. In their twelve-year history, she never dared speak to him with such contempt. The thought of it now turned her into a nervous ball of energy.

"You can look at me." His once beefy shoulders slumped forward. Defeated.

Until Leon said that, Jazz had no idea her gaze was downcast.

The practice was beat into her so thoroughly, it became a natural reflex in Leon's presence—in any assertive man's presence. And now that he'd given her permission to look at him, she still couldn't find the power to lift her gaze.

"Do it," Jaden said. "Now's the time to get back everything he stole from you. Look him in his eyes."

She whispered, "Please be quiet." Then she eased the sunglasses onto her face, killing all possibilities of a personal connection.

"Uh," Leon said, taking a deep breath. "I'm sorry for what I did to you. I know that don't make my insecurities excusable or fix things, but I'm sorry. You didn't deserve my bull."

"Lift your head," Jaden said.

"You came here to say you're sorry for destroying everything good within me after all these years?"

"Yeah," Leon nodded. "And I risked you putting me in jail to do it." He blinked a tear loose. "I'm sorry, Jazz."

"Well, you said it. I'm shutting my door now."

"Wait, please," Leon said. "Hear me out."

"Look him in the face and say it."

Again she glanced over her shoulder at Jaden and whispered, "Say what?" Her expression softened toward him.

"Get mad and say what you need to say. Let it out." He spun the ball on his finger.

"Who are you talking to? Who's in there with you?"

Her head snapped back toward Leon. "None of your fucking business." That felt great...empowering.

Leon shrugged. "I deserve that."

"You're damn right you do."

"That's it," Jaden said, "get mad. Take a stance and reclaim everything he took."

She raised her head a smidgen, building confidence inch by inch. Anger intoxicating her.

"Do it," Jaden said. "What are you waiting for? Tell him."

"I was terrible to you." Leon scratched his beard stubble. "Can you ever find it in your heart to forgive me?"

"Forgive you? I hate you. You kicked my baby out my stomach."

"That's what I'm talking about," Jaden said. "Raise some hell."

"You beat me, you bastard, because I love my family. I'll never forgive you." Cinder block by cinder block, Jazz built a resistance to Leon, using hate and anger for mortar. She held her head high and proud. "You're a coward. A fucking poor excuse for a human being."

Jaden said, "Give it to him."

"Jazz, you don't know how bad I wish I could take it all back or how I wish I could've been a different man for you the day you walked into our dorm room." He shoved his hands in his pockets and lowered his own gaze. "I swear I wish these things."

"And I wish you die a thousand painful deaths. But we don't always get what we want, do we?"

"Knew you had it in you," Jaden said.

"Shut the hell up!"

Leon looked up. "Who—"

"What, Leon? What the fuck are you doing here?"

"I'm worried about you."

She burst into a fit of uncontrollable laughter. "I'm calling the cops."

Buank. Buank—

She spun on Jaden. "That fucking ball better bounce outdoors from this day forward or you will find yourself by yourself. Do I make myself clear?"

Jaden nodded, his expression saturated in shock. "Yes."

"Yes, what?"

"Yes, ma'am."

"And that's the way you better speak to me from now on." Jazz faced Leon again and couldn't contain herself. She burst into laughter. "You're too funny."

SEVENTY-THREE

Only a fifth of rum could momentarily stop Leon from feeling like a piece of shit. It had taken him two days to get over his suicidal contemplations and to choke up the nerve to step onto Jazz's porch.

"You can call the police if you want," he said. "But I'm serious."

Jazz was amused. Each time she tried to stop herself from laughing, she laughed harder. Laughed so hard he was sure tears clouded her vision.

He said, "It's Yancee's and your cousin's murder that has me worried about you."

That silenced her.

"What are the odds of both of them randomly being killed by the Hieroglyphic Hacker? There isn't that much coincidence in the world." He could tell that the conversation piqued her interest. Obviously she'd engaged similar thoughts. Novelists' minds clicked like that. Analytical. But he also knew she wasn't going to budge and be sociable. Not after all the hell he put her through.

She said, "I made funeral arrangements for Anderson."

"Got an anonymous call the other day from somebody telling me I would die next. What do you make of that?"

It seemed to Leon as if a pensive calm came over her. After two solid minutes of quiet, Jazz said, "Explains your conscience all of a sudden, whether it's real or fake. If that's all it took, I would've had someone send you a death threat years ago."

"Jazz, I'm talking about people's lives. Has anyone heard from Chance?"

Jazz's brow raised above the frame of her sunglasses. "Why are you asking about him?"

"Because my life was threatened. Because Yancee and Anderson are dead. Because we were all in my dorm room that day. Because Chance learned the truth about Cash after the car accident. Think about it, Jazz."

"But other people who weren't in the dorm were killed by the Hieroglyphic Hacker as well."

"They were all murdered in Denver. Chance and Cash lived there during the times of those murders."

"You're reaching," Jazz said.

"And if I'm not, your life is in danger. You were with us and agreed to keep your mouth shut that day too. I'm going to talk to Cash about my concerns, and then I'm going to the police. The paper says that Hakeem Eubanks and Aspen Skye are investigating Yancee's and Anderson's deaths."

"Good luck with Cash. I haven't heard from her in months."

"You're a terrible liar. I know Scenario Davenport is Cash. Ain't that much plastic or reconstructive surgery in the world when you know who you're looking at."

SEVENTY-FOUR

Without knocking, Jamillah sashayed into Scenario's office like she was *the* Queen Bee of the place. "Reporters are ringing the phone off the hook, getting on my damn nerves. They're an incorrigible lot. Attorney Vivian Green is on line two. She wants to work out a deal on the Brooks case."

Scenario was still in a funk behind GP turning her down. She yearned to be touched by someone meaningful. Someone she cared about. Someone she loved. Cheap fucks with strangers that only lasted long enough for her to get off weren't her thing. Only two men had ever understood the depths of her intimacy. And now she knew that if GP's marriage stayed solid, they would never share sexual understanding again.

"Thank you, Jamillah," she said, wishing the craving between her legs would go away. She picked up line two. "Good afternoon, Ms. Green."

"Let's talk dispo on George Brooks."

"Talk." Scenario leaned back in her leather chair and started clicking her pen.

"Two years and no probation is fair."

"You're out of your mind. Eight years for the robbery and car-jacking with a three-year gun spec, plus restitution. And that's me being nice, which only happens once a year. Take advantage of it."

Tension swelled in Vivian's voice. "But he's Marcus'—God bless the dead—nephew, and he cooperated."

"Which makes him and what he did even more despicable. Twelve years for all three counts of the indictment. The gun spec, restitution, and five thousand hours community service to an outreach program for troubled youth." She watched Jamillah being nosey.

"Okay, okay, okay, Ms. Davenport, I'll run the eight years with a spec by him and his mother. I can tell you right now that Miranda Brooks won't be pleased. With her political power, she's the wrong person to piss off. She expects a favor from your office."

"Don't do favors. It's that or suit up for trial so I can use *my* political power and throw the whole justice system at him." Scenario hung up, knowing that Marcus was smiling up from the grave.

The phone rang back.

"Let me," Jamillah said.

Scenario pushed the phone to the edge of her desk. "Be my guest."

"County Attorney's office. Jamillah Woodard speaking, how can I be of help to you?" Jamillah covered the phone and said, "It's somebody named Jazz."

"I'll take that in private. Thank you."

Jamillah passed Scenario the phone and left.

"Hey," Scenario said into the phone.

"He knows."

"Who knows what?"

"Leon." Then: "He knows it's you."

Sweat prickled her forehead. "Impossible. No one but you and GP—"

Leon lumbered through the door looking like a bum straight off the streets of downtown Cleveland. "Bet I'm the last person you wanted to see."

SEVENTY-FIVE

The confrontation happened outside of Cuyahoga County Justice Center on West Third Street. They argued in front of Quiznos sub shop where the courthouse and Justice Center staff gathered for lunch. And it seemed as if all of Scenario's colleagues were in Quiznos today staring at her through the restaurant's window. Judge Ronald Adrine and his frisky young secretary, who was rumored to sleep around for promotions and status positioning, sat inside at a window table facing Scenario and Leon on the sidewalk. The judge watched the commotion from his seat with sheer amusement, or maybe it was the foot Ms. Frisky was working between his legs. Scenario didn't know which one had the silly smirk on his face, but she saw it when she glanced into the window.

"I'm talking to you." Leon grabbed her arm.

She snatched away. "Don't you ever, ever touch me again. I'm not Jazz, you bastard."

"No, you're not. But I bet everyone in the county attorney's office would like to know they have an imposter amongst their ranks." His eyes found the judge's, then Leon started for the restaurant door. "How about I start spreading the news in here?"

Now Scenario grabbed him. "Fuck you, Leon. Fuck you, you hear me?"

He faced her. With pure contempt, he looked at her hand on his jacket. "You're obstructing a police investigation by not revealing that you personally know both victims. And you can't do that without you revealing who you are. Detective Hakeem—"

"Ma'am, is this guy giving you a hard time?" an obese man, wearing a Pepsi uniform with the name "Stan" stitched on his shirt, said. He stepped in their personal space.

"Push on," Leon said. "The lady's fine. Now kick rocks or I'll kick a hundred pounds off your fat ass."

"I'm fine, really," Scenario said. "Thanks for asking." She feigned a smile.

"You sure?"

"Dammit, she's sure."

Stan threw up his hands. "Okay already." He climbed into a Pepsi van and never considered them again.

Scenario's eyes turned to slits. "What do you want from me?"

"How 'bout we go for a little ride and talk about the details."

SEVENTY-SIX

Scenario was beyond irritated. Leon was a threat to every-thing she'd worked for. She wished someone would carve hieroglyphics on him or that she could drop him off the face of the earth and get away with it. "Which way?" she said, pulling her convertible Lexus out of the Justice Center's parking lot.

"Go to twenty-eighth and Cedar. You need to run in the liquor store and buy me a bottle of Bacardi. I'll pay you back after you get me a job."

"Job? What are you talking about?"

"You manipulated your way into the county attorney's office, so you're gonna do the same thing for me and get me a gig with the Cleveland Police Department, some type of law enforcement."

"I can't do that."

"You can and you will; it's the only way I'll keep quiet. You bitch, you started over and you're gonna give me a new start too."

Scenario took a deep breath. "Leon, it's not that simple; it takes almost a hundred grand to get a professional, untraceable identity change. And you still look like Leon."

"You're gonna pay for everything."

"Leon—"

"Bacardi first; details afterward."

Scenario decided at that moment that she hated Leon and she

was going to do whatever necessary to get rid of him. "You're pathetic."

"So are you, Cashmaire. So are you. We have something else in common other than us being men."

"You asshole, I am not a man. I'm a woman with an androgen disorder."

He shrugged. "Tomato, to-*mah*-to, it's all the same thing."

Scenario weaved the Lexus through traffic while plotting Leon's final downfall. She almost had it worked out in her head until Leon interrupted her and pointed and said, "Pull over right here."

She turned into a lot situated on the side of the State Liquor Store.

"Go in there and get me a bottle. And, Cash…"

"What, Leon?"

"Hurry back so we can have our business meeting."

"Don't get comfortable thinking you're pulling the strings."

"Shut up, bitch. That's your problem—no one has ever smacked you in your mouth."

"Fuck you, Leon." She slammed the car door behind her.

Bruno Mars' "Grenade" came on the radio. Leon leaned forward to hike the volume. When he sat back, he looked into the business end of a pistol.

Stan eased the Pepsi van into the lot as Scenario Davenport stomped her way inside the liquor store. His heart thumped his chest as he threw the van in Park, blocking the Lexus in. Stan hopped out with more grace and agility than an obese person possessed. Leon was fiddling with the radio when Stan tapped the passenger's window with the snout of a Glock 9.

Leon, true to form, froze.

"Dude, trust me, this is not a game. Get out of the fucking car, shitface."

Leon eased out and Stan tossed him a pair of cuffs.

"You know what to do with them. And don't bruise the skin or I'll hurt you really bad." Stan nodded to the opened sliding door of the Pepsi van after Leon cuffed himself. "Be quick about it, dude."

Leon stepped onto the running board and was knocked out cold.

SEVENTY-SEVEN

"**G**irl," Scenario said into the phone, "I don't know what to make of it. I came out the store and he was gone. It was like God answered my prayers. Leon just vanished into thin air."

"We need to talk about Yancee and Anderson," Jazz said.

Scenario cringed. "Thought we settled that already."

"I'm not comfortable with it, Cash, or should I continue to play this charade and call you Scenario? I think it's time I go to the police."

"And hang me out to dry?"

"It's not like that."

"Then what is it like? Tell me that, Jazz. I've never seen you and Leon bat for the same team before."

"You're just refusing to look at what's in front of your face."

"It's nothing more than a coincidence that Yancee and Anderson were murdered."

"Is it, Cash?"

Jamillah walked in the office. "Vending machine guy is here."

Scenario covered the phone. "I'll be there in a sec." To Jazz she said, "Don't make any move to do anything until I come over there."

"When are you coming, because something has to be said just in case this isn't a fluke."

"I'll be there no later than Friday."

"By Friday, Cash. I'm not playing."

"I'll be there. Just promise me you won't be Judas Iscariot until we have a face-to-face."

"I'm not a snitch."

"Then we'll talk later," Scenario said. "I have some business to take care of here at the office before I leave."

"Later." Jazz hung up.

Scenario went to the outer office. The vending machine guy was positioning a Pepsi machine against the wall. She said, "Stan, right?" remembering the name on his shirt. Good gosh, she thought, he's as wide as the Pepsi machine.

Stan turned around. "Hey, you're the lady from earlier."

"Yeah." She offered him a hand. "Thanks again for coming to my rescue. A regular knight in shining armor you are."

"No problem." He blushed. "Sorry I delivered this thing so late. My other runs took longer than expected." He glanced at his watch. "It's my quitting time and they want people like me out the building by five, so I'll get it up and running properly for you tomorrow."

Jamillah powered her computer off and rose from her desk. "I'm out of here too. See you in the morning, Ms. Davenport."

"Have a good evening," Scenario said, waving.

Jamillah headed for the door. "You too, and don't work too late. We always have tomorrow."

"Girl, I'm five minutes behind you."

Stan said, "I'm just gonna leave the dolly attached to this thing until morning."

"That's fine." Then something dawned on Scenario as she stared at Stan. "I wasn't aware that we were getting a pop machine."

"Hey, I just punch a clock and do what I'm told to keep the checks rolling in." Then: "Tell you what, Pepsi's on me tomorrow."

Scenario cracked a smile. "It's a date."

"Glad to see you smiling, Ms. Davenport."

"How'd you know my name?"

"The secretary just said it on her way out the door." He glanced at the door. "And it's stenciled on your door."

"Oh, forgive me. I've been misfiring here lately."

"Don't worry about it; it's no problem. Well, Ms. Davenport, I better get going. Rush-hour traffic can be nasty."

SEVENTY-EIGHT

Courthouse workers poured out the Justice Center, eager to bring their work day to a close. Stan eyed the day shift janitor he had pickpocketed a week earlier leaving the building as he ducked into a blind spot the security cameras couldn't see. During his reconnaissance of the Justice Center, he learned that the cameras switched positions every three minutes. So he knew for three solid minutes, twenty times an hour, there wouldn't be surveillance on the hallway outside of Scenario's office. His watch was set to know when it was and when it wasn't. When the camera rotated left to spy on an adjacent hall, Stan slid into a women's bathroom seventy feet down the hall from the county attorney's office. He hung an *Out of Order* sign on the door and locked it from the inside with a set of keys he'd stolen from the janitor during the reconnaissance mission.

Stan got right down to business in front of the mirror. He removed two tiny putty bags from his jowls, knocking the appearance of eight pounds off his face. That was a relief he appreciated. Those things ached the hell out of his jaws. Next went the wig. Then he proceeded to peel the synthetic unibrow and broad nose from his face, which was work. He made a note to himself not to use so much skin glue next time. He hummed a soothing melody as he scrubbed the makeup off. Slowly but surely, fat-ass Stan turned back into the cunning Chance Fox.

He removed the black contact lenses and replaced them with golden ones. He shed the Pepsi uniform to reveal an inflatable bodysuit that had a zipper down the front. After neatly folding the uniform, Chance pulled the plastic cork on the bodysuit's appendix and lost weight by the seconds. Chance laughed as air escaped the suit. If weight loss could be so easy, the world would be free of human lard. The thought really tickled Chance.

He stepped out the bodysuit, folding it as precisely as he had the uniform, and then removed a Chanel tote bag he had taped to his torso. Inside the bag was his murder kit and the next disguise he wanted to show off in for the security cameras.

SEVENTY-NINE

"Hope she keeps her clothes on this time." Hakeem shook his head as he and Aspen approached the Taylor residence. "Can't sit through a senior citizen strip show again. That was not cool."

Aspen thumped her cigarette butt and rang the bell. "Think old people still screw?"

"With Viagra for men and women, I'm certain."

Aspen thought about that and frowned. "I just imagined my parents getting busy and it was not pretty."

"When I get old-old, I'm still gonna want some. Viagra is a god-send."

"Psst," Aspen said under her breath and rolled her eyes. "You don't want no ass now." She rang the bell again.

"Huh?"

"If you *huh* you can hear."

The door opened.

"Aw," Aspen said, "he is so adorable, Hakeem, look at him. What's your name, honey?"

The little boy winked at her. "Rasheed."

Aspen's heart melted with the sound of his voice. "Rasheed, is your mother home?"

"Gimme a kiss and five dollars and I'll tell you," he said, looking over his shoulder.

Hakeem cracked a smile. "They're learning to be mannish younger and younger. Boy, go get your momma."

"Mister, I don't know what that meant or who you think you're talking to, but it ain't Yancee Taylor's son," he said, looking over his shoulder, obviously knowing he was doing something he had no business doing. "Now back to you, pretty. Make it ten and show me what first base is all about since your boyfriend got a big mouth."

"And you want kids," Hakeem said as Aspen cracked up with laughter. He gave Rasheed a firm look. "What you know about first base?"

"Everything my daddy taught me."

"Rasheed, what I tell your hardheaded butt about answering my damn door?" Africa came up behind him, wiping her hands on a dish towel. Her long hair was pulled into a modest bun with a few tresses dangling down her face. She wore a trendy pair of cut-off jean shorts, flip-flops, and wife beater T-shirt under a see-through blouse with ruffled sleeves. "Now go get your brother. Dinner's ready. And y'all wash y'all's nasty hands before y'all park y'all's behinds at my table." She scooted Rasheed along, then her facial expression changed from didactic to brusque when she looked into the faces of Aspen and Hakeem. "What is it now, Detectives?"

"Sorry to bother you, Mrs. Taylor," Hakeem said. "We came to inform you that we found your husband's car. Mind if we come in and talk with you for a moment?"

"Yes, I mind. My family has gone through enough. We're about to eat dinner, so now isn't a good time."

Aspen stepped in. "I understand you wholeheartedly, Africa. But this is really important to our investigation, and it'll only take a few minutes of your time. We're working really hard to track down the person or persons responsible for Mr. Taylor's death."

EIGHTY

Africa Taylor didn't want to be bothered. All she wanted to do was lick her wounds and find a way to move on and raise her bad-ass sons as a single mother. But every time she turned around, the media or the police were on her phone or on her doorstep. She looked from Aspen to Hakeem then back to Aspen. Africa pushed the screen door open and led them into the dining room where the rest of her family was gathered.

"We're having fried corn, homemade cornbread, collard greens, sweet potatoes, and barbecued chicken," Africa said. "And for dessert, I made Philadelphia cream cheese pie from scratch."

Hakeem hesitated at the threshold. Africa understood that he was checking out how well prepared the table was. "We can't impose like this. We'll come back."

Africa pulled out a chair beside Madear, who was dressed in a simple spring dress with her gray hair braided neatly to the back in two French braids. "No, you insisted on being here. So we're gonna eat and talk."

Rasheed nudged his brother. "Shaad, that's the one with the mouth right there."

Rashaad said, "Big man, you owe my brother ten dollars and your girlfriend got some kisses to pass out."

"Shut up, boy, and mind your manners." Madear glared at her grandson.

Africa said, "And I told y'all about being fresh with women. Come on over here and have a seat, Detective Eubanks."

Madear smiled her toothless smile and exaggerated batting her lashes as Hakeem settled in the chair. "We met somewhere before?"

Aspen said, "If you don't mind, I'll sit with these two handsome young men."

"That comes with a warning label," Africa said. "Do so at your own risk because I ain't liable for any negligence." She disappeared into the kitchen and returned with an ice-cold pitcher of red Kool-Aid.

"Are you a real police?" Rashaad said. "'Cause you don't dress like a cop."

"That's because I'm a detective and I don't have to wear the uniforms you're familiar with." She pinched his cheek.

Rasheed said, "So you have a gun?"

Aspen nodded.

"Can I hold it?"

"No, you can't see it or touch it," Africa said. "So stop thinking about it."

"Aw, Ma, you're no fun." Rashaad caught an attitude. "We just wanted to see it."

"Forget about it. Now shut up and bow your head so Madear can say grace."

"Naw," Madear said, easing her hand onto Hakeem's thigh. "I'll like it better if this fine man leads us in prayer tonight."

Everyone bowed their heads while Hakeem dodged Madear's roaming hand. "Dear Lord…" With those two words a deep sense of nostalgia instantly overcame him. He longed for the happy days of yesterday that he once shared with his family. He craved sentimental family settings like those that presented themselves around the dinner table with his loved ones. Now the personal association of the Taylor gathering with a tragic past that imprisoned him highlighted his need to let go and move on. Hakeem just didn't know how. "Thank you for blessing Aspen and I with an invitation into the Taylor home this evening for this delicious-looking meal. Please continue to bring the Taylors together with your blessings because there is nothing more important than family. Amen."

"Amen." Madear squeezed his groin. "Yes, Lord, amen for such a big blessing."

Hakeem jerked. His thighs hit the underside of the table, causing the silverware to rattle.

Africa said, "Is everything okay, Detective?" She eyed him as she passed the food around.

"Yes, it will be." He gave Madear a warning look as he eased her hand back where it belonged.

Madear said, "Africa, who are these strange people?"

EIGHTY-ONE

After the twins devoured dessert, Africa said, "Y'all make your-selves invisible so us grown folks can talk."

One twin left with his lip poked out; the other left the dining room as if he had better things to do anyway. Aspen's heart fluttered as the boys filed out the room. She dreamed night and day about being someone's mother, being called Mom. And she couldn't wait. She couldn't wait to potty-train them and plan birthday parties at Chuck E. Cheese's, help them with homework and go to parent-teacher conferences, make her children proud of her on career day, cheer louder than any other parent during school plays and sports events, watch their world light up each Christmas morning. All the while instilling in them her moral vision of the world and giving them the confidence and proper self-tools to create their own moral vision. She thought about what Hakeem had said while saying grace and agreed that family means everything—nothing's more important than family. She just needed to start hers.

Madear sat back and regarded Aspen and Hakeem as if seeing them for the first time. "You're here to take me away to that scary nursing home. I don't wanna go, Africa. Please don't make me go."

"No one's sending you away, Madear."

"Oh," she said.

Getting down to the nitty-gritty, Hakeem said, "I hate to keep sticking my finger on a sore spot in your marriage to Mr. Taylor, but I have to—"

"I'm a big girl, Detective. Say what you have to say." Africa gave him steady eyes and waited for him to continue.

"Was Mr. Taylor having an extramarital affair with anyone besides Terri Dunlap?"

"They do bad things to old people like me in nursing homes." Madear stared straight ahead, although Aspen didn't have a clue at what.

Africa said, "Madear, I'm really sorry I threatened to send you away. I never meant it." To Hakeem she said, "I'm sure there were others. Yancee was a pussy hound. He's been caught cheating so many times, but Terri was the only current one that I got wind of." Her gaze went from Hakeem to Aspen. "Why?"

"An eyewitness saw Yancee with a stunning woman, who doesn't fit Terri's description, thirty minutes before his estimated time of death." Aspen took out her cell phone and pulled up an image on its screen. "Whomever this woman is Yancee was seen with, we believe she was the last person to see him alive." She passed Africa the phone. "This is a picture of the note we found in Yancee's car. Does anything about it make sense to you?"

"It's my husband's handwriting. He wrote reminders to himself about everything." Africa then proceeded to read the note aloud. "C.F. wood chips, four-thirty, Thursday."

Madear said, "Told that boy the wood chips was gonna get him in a world of trouble one day. Never thought he'd mess with that girl."

EIGHTY-TWO

Hakeem felt like a bastard for what he was about to do, but if it kept Madear talking coherently, then so be it. He eased his hand onto her thigh and stroked it. "What girl?"

She blushed and bat her lashes at him. "His friend, Chance Fox's wife. Cashmaire Fox. C.F."

Africa stiffened at Madear's words. Africa's eyes went small and black. "I'll kill that bitch. Right under my damn nose."

Madear rubbed Hakeem's hand as he stroked her leg. "Yancee, Chance, and Leon used to do all kinds of stuff they didn't think I knew about at the wood chips."

Aspen considered Madear.

Hakeem said, "I don't understand what you mean by wood chips."

"It's just a little playground on two seventy-six and Brush Avenue in Euclid that they nicknamed the Wood Chips."

"Mrs. Taylor," Aspen said. "What makes you say Cashmaire when it was Chance who used to hang out with Yancee at the wood chips?"

"'Cause Chance would have come here to meet Yancee. But Cash and Yancee would have to sneak to see each other. You said my baby was there with a pretty girl. C.F. wood chips, four-thirty, Thursday."

Africa scooted her chair away from the table. "I have a picture you should see." She left the room and returned less than a minute later with a photo album. She cleared a spot on the table for it and flipped it open. "They all went to college together."

Hakeem went to Aspen and Africa's side of the table as Madear malfunctioned again. "Somebody go find my son and tell him I need to talk to him right now," Madear said.

Everyone ignored her.

Africa pointed to a picture taken outside of Jacobs Field. Each of the people in the photo wore some sort of Cleveland State University clothing. "This is Cashmaire and Chance."

Aspen nodded. "She's gorgeous."

"Matches our description of the woman Yancee was last seen with."

"Behind them," Africa said, "is Yancee's asshole friend Leon Page and that's Jazz Smith right there. She's a famous author now."

Hakeem turned pale. His breath left him. A vision of an innocent victim stretched out on an autopsy table with his young eyes frozen open popped in Hakeem's head. His knees went wobbly; he gripped the table to stay upright.

"Are you all right?" Aspen said, pulling out a chair for him.

He gasped for air. "I'm...I'll be all right."

Africa probably didn't know how to take whatever just happened to him. It was evident in her voice. "Can I get you something?"

"Just take him to my room," Madear said. "I'll make him better."

"I'm fine, really. Continue." He avoided Aspen's concerned eyes.

Africa pointed to the picture. "And these two clowns making stupid faces are my husband and their other college friend...uh, what's his name? Anderson. Yeah, that's it. Anderson Smith. If I remember correctly, he's related to Jazz."

"Son of a bitch."

"How close are you to this group of people?" Aspen said, on point with Hakeem.

"I'm not. Those were Yancee's college friends. I mean I met them all but Anderson. Me and Yancee didn't get serious until after he left college." She closed the photo album. "The only friendship he maintained from this group was with Chance and Cashmaire—can't believe that bitch was sneaking around and meeting my husband. My kids call them aunt and uncle."

Aspen said, "So you're close to—" She opened the photo album back and looked at the woman. "You and Cash are close?" Then: "Something about her looks familiar, like I've seen her somewhere before."

"Naturally," Africa said. "Yancee and Chance are best friends. Me and Cash talk on the phone a lot 'cause they live in Denver. Cash and Jazz are also close friends. But, yeah, we're cool, or so I thought. I helped Chance pick out a car for her last year for their tenth wedding anniversary."

Hakeem said nothing.

"What kind of car?" Aspen said.

"A red Infiniti."

"Son of a bitch."

"Africa," Aspen said. "I'll explain it to you later, but right now I'm ordering round-the-clock police protection for you and your family."

EIGHTY-THREE

Night covered the city and darkened everything good beneath it. Aspen watched Hakeem pace the length of the Hummer parked in the Taylors' driveway.

"This is where I get off the train at," Hakeem said. "I won't do this."

"I know what this is shaping up to look like, and I know how you must feel about—"

"No, you don't. So stop pretending like you do. I don't need your sympathy or anyone's pity for my misfortune. You don't get that, do you?"

"Calm down, Hakeem. Let's just look into it. Even though it looks one way, right now we're assuming until we confirm the information as fact."

"Assuming? Assuming my ass. No matter what, this leads our investigation to probe into Jazz Smith's life of all the people in this city." He paced. "We have two—two!—dead people in one photo. Both murdered by the Hieroglyphic Hacker. One of those people was last seen alive with a woman who fits Cashmaire Fox's description to a tee. Bet you that Scratch is gonna ID Cash. How strange is it that she and her husband just so happenly fell off the face of the earth?" He paused to look at her. "Or maybe she's hiding, Aspen, because she's the killer and the authorities in Denver haven't found Chance's body yet. And if I'm right, if I'm right, she's kill-ing the people in this photo for some revenge reason." He looked at the picture in his hand. "Or whoever the killer is, he's murdering these people for revenge. They did something to him or her. And that means two things: we'll find the Hieroglyphic Hacker through this group of people, and Leon and Jazz Smith are possibly on the killer's list, which is blessing enough for me to turn my back."

Aspen pulled out a cigarette and lit up. "You through venting?"

Hakeem took her lighter. "Let's see you light another one."

"You know what your problem is? You gave up. For the last seven months I sat and watched you—by force, not choice—sink into depression and insomnia while you claim everything is okay. It's not! What happened was terrible. But that grudge and the hate you're carrying in your heart is turning you into an ugly, despi-cable man that I don't like. And if you don't get it together, that hate is gonna cost somebody their life if your theory is correct." She drew on the Newport. "The fact that God threw Jazz Smith in this twisted mix is to give you the perfect opportunity to be the best person you and I know you are capable of being. It isn't vali-dation for you to justify abandoning your life, your friends, and your morals to become a complete asshole."

EIGHTY-FOUR

After Hakeem learned from the chief's wife that he was working late, Hakeem stormed into Dwight Eisenhower's office
unannounced. Hakeem knew the shit was about to hit the
fan, but that concerned him not. A face-to-face confrontation was
what he craved. Sergeant Morris, tired and stressed out, and Chief
Eisenhower glared at Hakeem as if he were a rabid dog foaming
at the mouth.

"Goddammit, Eubanks," Chief Eisenhower said, nostrils flaring
like an angry bull, "where's your goddamn manners?" He jabbed
a finger in Hakeem's direction. "Knock next goddamn time." He
sipped his glass of brandy.

"I want off the Hieroglyphic Hacker case." Hakeem aimed his
loaded gaze on his superiors like a throwaway semiautomatic.
"Reassign me."

"You've lost your goddamn mind, Eubanks."

"Good to know we finally see eye to eye about something."

Concern plagued Sergeant Morris' face, and it was apparent in
his voice. "Why do you want off the case?"

"Jazz Smith, that's why." He tossed the picture in front of them.
"I have reason to believe she's on the unsub's revenge list. Aspen
will fill you in. I want out."

The room fell silent as the men absorbed Hakeem's revelation
and pain.

"First of all, this isn't goddamn Burger King. You can't have it your goddamn way. I'm running a goddamn police department here." Eisenhower polished off his brandy. "If you have evidence or even a goddamn suspicion that Ms. Smith is in danger, it's your job to remove the threat of danger, Eubanks. The mayor hand-selected you because you're good at what you do. Now get over your hang-ups and get the hell out of my goddamn office and don't come back until you find your fancy manners."

"I don't care about this job if its value is measured against Jazz Smith. Far as I'm concerned, she should have been first on the Hacker's list, then maybe my—"

"Watch yourself, Eubanks, before you go too far," Sergeant Morris said. "I have empathy for how I imagine you must feel about these developments, but you're on the border line of insubordination and that won't be tolerated."

"Suspend me then, you little cowardly son of a bitch." Hakeem hated himself for saying that, but he'd lived with much worse clinging to his soul, which made it too easy to shrug off Sergeant Morris' hurt feelings and scuffed ego.

Eisenhower jumped to his feet and rounded the desk. "Nice goddamn try, Eubanks." He stood between Hakeem and Sergeant Morris. "We're not suspending you either. You're stuck with this until you and Skye close the book on this case. Now for the last goddamn time, get out my office and go do your job." Chief Eisenhower opened the door. "Do I make myself goddamn clear?"

Hakeem shoved his shield and gun in Eisenhower's chest. "I quit. Find someone else to help the famous author. Is that clear enough for you?" He turned to leave and Aspen was leaning against the door frame, shaking her head with disappointment.

EIGHTY-FIVE

Lakeshore Boulevard curved and twisted toward Lake Erie. Hakeem turned the Hummer onto Spring Bank Lane and nudged it into his driveway. He'd sworn months ago that he would go to his grave hating Jazz Smith and her stupid books. Just the fact that she was a big-shot author pissed him off and deepened his ill will toward her. She didn't deserve invites to late-night talk shows, books adapted to movies and translated to many foreign languages, or her inflated personage that transcended national boundaries. Not after what she'd done.

Hakeem tried to avoid the panoramic scene in his rearview mirror. Impossible. It called to him like a living thing with a nasty attitude. Its ominous presence lingered and lurked in the recesses of his mind when the rest of Cleveland was sound asleep. Now his eyes sucked in the painful details: tall and skinny, metal and gray, crippled and ugly. He turned away from the rearview, eased out of the driver's seat, and went inside the house without a backward glance.

Keebler rushed him at the door, throwing her huge paws on his shoulders.

"Thought you were at—"

"Didn't want to babysit her in my big house alone anymore," Drew said, coming into the kitchen. "I got bored." She wore a see-through lingerie number and wasn't the least bit ashamed about her exposed flesh.

"When I gave you access to my spare key, I wasn't expecting to come home and find you running around my house half naked."

"You told me you wouldn't be here, so I just made myself comfortable. But now that you're here, do you like what you see?" She modeled her risqué outfit.

"Is that a pimple on your booty?" Hakeem laughed to keep from breaking down in tears. Lust was in his voice, but he tried to joke it away.

Drew fought to hide her smile. "Boy, you wish. Not a blemish, Mr. Comedy Central." She closed the distance between them, keeping her eyes nailed to him.

Hakeem couldn't shake her stare; his eyes were firmly entrenched in hers. "Put some clothes on, Drew, before I bend you over this table and give you what you're looking for." He loosened his tie, anticipating the possibilities of a beautiful, undressed woman in his house.

"Then I just ended my search." She pushed the table fixtures aside, clearing a space for them on the island. "Right here?" She bent over the table. "Like this?"

He was drawn to her hairless petals. "You don't give up." He turned to Keebler, patting her head. "Get me a beer, girl."

Keebler pulled the refrigerator open by a dish towel tied to the handle. Lined across the bottom sleeve of the door were bottles of imported beer. Keebler brought Hakeem a cold one.

"Close it back, girl," he said as he rinsed the bottle off and cracked it open. He sipped the beer and watched Drew climb on the table and open her legs. Again, he was drawn to the split of her petals. A place he hadn't been since—

"What are you waiting on?" she said. "The table was your idea. I'm game."

Hakeem said nothing. He was too busy admiring her beautiful

body. He still had ripe memories of it from the first time she offered it to him. He chugged down the beer and decided to expand his memory to knowledge. Passing up the feel and gratification of her offering wasn't going to happen a second time.

"Stop imagining, Hakeem. Experience it." She held out her small wrists for him, submitting. "Cuff me and fuck me. I need you inside me just as bad as you want to be."

He took his suit jacket off. "We're about to make a mistake."

"At least we'll have fun doing it and there won't be any strings attached after we both come," she said, rubbing her clitoris through the see-through fabric of her panties.

"There are always strings attached." He tossed his shirt on the counter, then went to put the bottle in the recycling bin. That was when he saw what she had done. His family's pictures were back on the living room walls. Thoughts of sex left and anger returned with a vengeance. "What the hell did you do to my house? You had no right to violate my personal space like this."

Her legs snapped shut. "What are you talking about?"

He stared into the living room for the first time in months. "You don't know me or what I'm going through. And you can't fix me with a piece of pussy. You had no right to come into my home and put those pictures on the wall."

"I'm sorry, Hakeem. I only called myself helping you clean up. Showing you that I'm a good woman to have around. I thought you took them down to dust or paint the walls or something."

"That's the problem—you thought wrong."

Aspen walked through the kitchen door. Drew jumped off the table and hid behind Hakeem to cover herself.

Hakeem followed Aspen's eyes to the hard-on that strained against his slacks.

"No need, sister. I'm leaving," Aspen said. "Get back on the table and assume the position. I'll be out your way in one sec. *I'm* disturbing *your* groove." She fixed Hakeem with an anticlimactic gaze. "You should have just told me you had a woman. No wonder we don't play chess anymore."

Hakeem recognized the demeanor shift. Right now a slow burn was creeping up the back of Aspen's neck and scorching her attitude. "It's not what you think. She—"

"I would tell you to kiss my natural black ass, Hakeem, but from the looks of it, you have enough ass to kiss tonight." Aspen walked out the door as easy as she walked through it. Her fragrance wafted through the air and tugged at his heart strings.

"Son of a bitch." Then: "Aspen, wait a minute. Let me explain." He—bare-chested—went out the door behind her. "Would you please hold up a minute."

"Fuck you, Hakeem." She hit a number on her phone that started her car. "Fuck you."

"I'm confused. Why are you mad about her?"

Aspen laughed, shaking her head. "You know what? I'm not. I couldn't care less." She climbed inside the BMW. "You no longer owe me an explanation about a damn thing. You're obviously not the person I thought you were to me. And you're not my partner anymore. You quit, remember?" She backed out the driveway and yelled out the window, "Fuck you, Hakeem." She slid him a look that chilled him to glacial proportions.

When Hakeem went back in the house, he abandoned all pretenses of manners and said, "Get out!"

"Hakeem, I—"

Keebler stood on all fours and growled, showing Drew her teeth.

"Are you getting the point?" He held the door open.

EIGHTY-SIX

er expensive heels clicked against the marble floor to the melody of her sway. On the far end of the hall, under the surveillance cameras, the night janitor worked a mop in an easy side-to-side pattern. He bobbed his head and sang to the lyrics of "Ready for the World."

When he noticed her, he turned down his MP3 player and waved. "Burning the midnight oil, Ms. Davenport," he said loud enough for her to hear.

She adjusted the Chanel bag on her shoulder and waved back with the enthusiasm of someone who wasn't in the mood to be bothered. She hurried through the office door before he tried his luck at conversation again. Once inside the office, she secured the door with her gloved hands.

She unstrapped the dolly from the Pepsi machine and opened it. Leon was stuffed inside, sedated, but on the brink of consciousness. She put an ammonia capsule under Leon's nose and his eyes blinked open with a startle.

"Cash, what…what happened to me?" Leon said.

"Take a closer look, dude."

That voice stole Leon's attention. "Chance?" Leon said like he was blown away by how well Chance could make himself up to look like Cash.

"You got it, shithead." Chance pulled him out of the machine. "And I'm really pissed about you destroying my chance to have a family. That means I'm gonna make it hurt." He dragged Leon from the outer office into Scenario's office. He left Leon on the floor as he cleared the desktop. "You've been a terrible friend."

"You…you murdered Yancee and Anderson."

"Don't worry, buddy. I swear I won't leave you out. Scout's honor." Chance admired the night lights of Rock'n'Roll Hall of Fame as he removed the murder kit from the Chanel bag and prepared the syringe. "You fucking moron. Is that the type of joke you play on your blood brother?"

"We were—"

"*You* were. They were just too weak to tell you no, which made them just as guilty." Chance put his face inches away from Leon's. "Law 19: Know Who You're Dealing With—Do Not Offend The Wrong Person. I'm the wrong Chance."

"Please, man, I'm sorry."

"Come on, dude, be original. That's what all the others said when I was minutes away from punishing them. You watched the news; it didn't work. Neither did the *Oh, God* cliché." Chance thumped the air bubbles out of the syringe. "So you're not gonna scream, tough guy?"

"Please forgive—"

"You stole a real wife and children from me. You robbed me of a family. Unforgiveable." He lugged Leon onto the desktop and injected the blue ring venom into his system. "Family means everything, you idiot. Nothing is more important than family." He cut the buttons away from Leon's shirt with a scalpel and removed the handcuffs and leg binding.

Leon's arms fell limply to the side. "I…I can't move."

"Children are a heritage from the Lord, the crown of their father," Chance said as he stripped Leon naked. "Wives bear children, Leon. God created me in His likeness and image to reward me with the fruit of the womb." He grabbed Leon's flaccid penis and stretched it to its full length. "But you thought it would be funny to give me a wife without a womb and rob me of my rightful inheritance—a family."

"Please, Chance, accept my apology. Think about what you're doing."

"I have, dude." Chance detached Leon's penis with one clean cut. Leon screamed.

"I knew you had it in you, tough guy." Chance stuffed the penis in Leon's mouth to quiet him. Then he cut hieroglyphics into his body until long after he was dead.

EIGHTY-SEVEN

Buank. Buank. Buank. Buank.

Thursday morning Jazz smiled when she woke up and looked out her window to see Jaden practicing in the driveway. She leaned on the windowsill. "Good morning, Jaden."

Buank. Buank. Buank. Buank. He waved. "Morning."

The phone on the nightstand rang.

"Watch this," Jaden said, pat dribbling the ball low to the ground. His hands moved fast as he switched the ball from hand to hand and through his legs.

"That's great. Keep up the good work." She plucked the phone from the nightstand. "Hello."

"I tried to stay out of this, Jazz." It was Javenna Myrieckes, her friend and her literary agent's wife. Javenna was also an author's representative for Myrieckes Literary Associates.

"If you're calling," Jazz said, "that means Eric's upset."

"Pissed is a more accurate adjective. We're catching flak from the execs at Simon and Schuster. You're four months past your deadline and no one has seen even a rough draft. They're not happy."

"I know."

"They're threatening to terminate your contract and take you to court to recoup your advance. When people shell out a million dollars, they expect you to produce."

Jazz eyed her computer. She hadn't touched the thing in months. "They'll get their manuscript."

"When?"

"I'm not sure." She headed to the kitchen for her morning cup of room temperature water.

"Jazz." Javenna took a deep breath. "I can't pretend to say I can relate to what happened. But you have to dig deep and find the strength to move on."

"Honestly, Javenna, you're right." Jazz stood at her patio door. "You can't relate."

Buank. Buank. Buank. Buank.

"No one can."

"I'm sorry."

"Don't be." Then: "Tell Eric to use his charisma and clout to stall them. I'll get them a book."

"When? Give us something to pacify them with. A tentative date so we can dodge the courtroom."

Cash appeared at the patio door as if she came out of nowhere. *Buank. Buank. Buank. Buank.*

"Let me call you back, Javenna."

"Jazz."

"I don't know when, okay? I have to hang up now." She clicked off and slid the patio door open. "You're late for work, and you look exhausted. What are you doing here? I wasn't expecting you until tomorrow."

EIGHTY-EIGHT

Cash placed her purse on the counter and popped the refrigerator open. "You felt it urgent that we talk. Best we get it over with. Checked my schedule and I'll be tied up in court all day tomorrow." She sat at the table with a banana yogurt. "My first case isn't until one this afternoon so I didn't feel like being bothered with the office and a circus of reporters until then."

Jazz stared out the kitchen window with a gorgeous smile stretched across her face.

"What are you looking at?"

"Jaden. You had to walk right by him. He doesn't dribble the ball in the house anymore."

Cash dug into the yogurt. "Oh really? When are—"

"Don't start in on me," Jazz said, turning away from the window. "You need to look in the mirror and edit yourself. You're inconsiderate and a habitual liar, which also makes you selfish as hell."

"Inconsiderate?"

"You're damn right you're inconsiderate. We're supposed to be best friends. You haven't taken that into consideration. I was under the impression that the best friend title came with certain rights and privileges. My cousin is dead, but you'd rather lie to your colleagues to protect this Scenario Davenport character, which is a complete lie in itself, instead of helping me and my family get closure. Doesn't the institution of family mean anything to you?"

"You have a whole lot of nerve, Jazz. You know I only became Scenario Davenport in order to start my life over with a tabula rasa to build it on. And that way I could find a man who can accept my truth, and together we can adopt children and start a family."

"Yeah, I supported your grand idea if you were *actually* starting over. But you brought the same bullshit with you—lies, inconsideration, selfishness. I hate to burst your bubble, but the only things that have actually changed with you are your name and appearance." Jazz swallowed a mouthful of water. "I despise liars and you know it. But you've been consistently lying about everything and everybody since the day I met you. Yancee is dead too. His children think you're their aunt and you haven't said a thing to the police. Is being Scenario Davenport really worth betraying your friends, the people who consider you family?"

"You think I get a kick out of being in a position where I can't open my mouth? You got it all twisted if that's what you think. I'm losing sleep, and that ain't the half of it."

"Just like I told you when you were lying to that fool Chance about being pregnant—fix it! Tell the damn truth for once in your life." Jazz finished her morning cup of water, then put on a pot of tea.

"I can't."

"You mean you won't, so I will. I'm going to the cops. I'm through being your enabler and participating in the texture of your lies. It doesn't suit my morals."

"And you'll put me in jail. How considerate is that of my situation, *best friend?*"

They stared at each other in silence. In those few moments, something happened between them that neither could explain or label.

"I broke the law, Jazz. I obstructed justice by not saying anything to help the investigation, if my information holds any weight other than coincidence. If I expose that I personally knew Yancee and Anderson, I'd have to explain that I'm not Scenario Davenport, and how I defrauded the Bar under my new identity. I'll go to prison." Cash spooned out a heap of yogurt and geared up to tell another lie. Prison wasn't an option; winning and moving on with her life was all that mattered—no matter what she had to do or who she had to hurt to pull it off. She abandoned the spoonful of yogurt and stood beside Jazz at the patio door. "Just hear me out," Cash said. "I don't have to put myself at risk and say anything."

"You're uncorrectable."

"Listen, would you? The detectives are days away from fingering someone on this. I'm certain of it. I'm privy to most of the information and evidence gathered on Yancee's and Anderson's murders. They're going to catch the killer without me bringing harm to myself. I don't want to go to prison, Jazz." Cash's cell phone started ringing, but she ignored it.

"I don't want to see you behind bars. I'm not saying that. I'm not. I'm only saying that, categorically, you have both our lips sealed about my cousin and Yancee based on your elaborate lie." Jazz poured herself a cup of tea. "You can't be that blind. Don't you see something wrong with this whole picture? Two people who knew each other, who we also knew, were murdered by the same killer. I think it's our responsibility to tell the police that and not wait until they figure it out on their own." She blew her cup of tea. "Where's Chance?"

Cash glanced over a shoulder. "How would I know and why are you asking?"

Jazz watched her. "This police information you're privy to, did Chance's name come up in it?"

"No," Cash said matter-of-factly.

"Would you tell me if it did?"

"This is ridiculous. You think Chance has something to do with these murders?"

"You honestly don't? He didn't show up to Yancee's funeral. Chance is the last person anyone would expect not to show up for Yancee. Although the County Prosecutor Scenario Davenport showed up to Yancee's funeral, Cash wasn't there. Looks funny. Even Leon thinks Chance has something to do with what's going on. Didn't he tell you that when he came to your office yesterday?"

"No, the fucker tried to extort me." Cash started laughing. "Chance? Get out of here." Her cell phone started ringing again.

"Seems like it's important," Jazz said. "You should answer it."

"Not more important than what we're discussing, so whoever this is can wait." Cash pushed the cell phone away from her. "Anderson and Yancee are purely a coincidence, and because of that, you're way off base about Chance. It's as simple as that. But look, I swear that our friendship is important to me because we are family. Give the investigation two more weeks. Just two, Jazz."

The cell phone started up again.

"That way," Cash said, "I can protect my past and enjoy the future without the lies hanging over my head or creating any new ones."

And the phone rang.

"What happens if they don't find the killer between now and then?"

"I swear I'll go to them and tell them everything I know and face the consequences of my misdeeds. But you have to swear in return that you'll give me that long. Please."

After a few moments of thought, Jazz said, "Okay."

"Okay, what, Jazz?"

"I swear to it. Now answer your phone; it's getting on my nerves."

Cash stuck the phone to her ear. "What?"

"Ms. Davenport, this is Detective Aspen Skye. Where are you?"

"Why?"

"Because I'm sending a police escort to pick you up."

"I can drive myself if I have to. What's the problem?"

"The Hieroglyphic Hacker struck again."

Cash sighed and stepped out on the patio so Jazz couldn't hear her conversation. "Where's the body this time, for God's sake?"

Aspen said, "In your office."

he truth of the matter hit Scenario so hard, it gave her an instant headache. She abandoned her entire "coincidence" argument when she stepped inside her office and saw Leon's lifeless body spread eagle on her desk. There was nothing coincidental about that. The murders were connected. And without a doubt, she knew Jazz was right about Chance's involvement, which only meant she was damned if she came clean and damned if she didn't.

Aspen leaned on the wall farthest from the desk with her arms folded across her breasts. She watched Scenario like a hawk. Detective Leonardo Scott studied her from the other side of the room.

Leon's blood had dripped down the sides of the desk and soaked into the tan carpet. His blank eyes stared at the architectural decorations designed into the ceiling. Deeply cut into every visible part of his dark skin was an elaborate meandering of explicit hieroglyphics. The ancient Egyptian pharaohs would be proud of the killer's craftsmanship. From the permanent grimace on Leon's face, Scenario and everyone else processing the crime scene knew Leon had died a torturous death.

Scenario scanned Leon's body again and found herself on the edge of sickness. "My God, where is his—"

"Stuffed in his mouth," Dr. Aura Chavez said as she examined Leon's fingertips. "Wonder what point the killer is making." She looked at Scenario. "Would you like to see it?"

Scenario shook her head no. Uncomfortable with the way Aspen's suspicious gaze drilled into her, she turned to Aspen and said, "Why are you staring at me like that, Detective Skye?"

"Admiring your poise." Aspen stepped forward. "Detective Scott and I have a room set up across the hall. Let's go there and talk."

NINETY

They were in an empty storage room that the county planned to turn into a family crisis office. Scenario noticed that the two chairs facing each other were kidnapped from the waiting room area of her office. And the roll-away TV that she used to examine video evidence was plugged into the wall. Detective Scott sat in the corner with his Stetson pulled over his face as if he were sleeping and not really listening.

"You were seen arguing with Mr. Page yesterday. Who is he to you?" Aspen lit a cigarette and offered Scenario one.

Scenario declined while her wheels spun. She had to think on her feet, figure out what the detective knew and didn't know. She knew from Aspen's opening statement that she couldn't deny knowing Leon, but she damn sure wasn't going to confess the whole truth in case there was a way to wiggle free of this mess. "Someone I had a very brief affair with."

"What's brief?"

"You mean how many times did we fuck, Detective Skye?" Scenario glanced at Detective Scott, who didn't budge.

Aspen shrugged and exhaled a cloud of smoke. "Since you put it that way."

"Twice. Not that it's any of your business. Why am I being probed like I'm a suspect?"

"You have a dead man in *your* office, Ms. Davenport."

"And! My prints and hair and everything else is in that office. That doesn't make me guilty."

"Not a stitch of trace evidence or a print."

If that was the truth and not a trick to mislead her, Scenario knew there was promise. So she fished. "Come on, it has to be. My office has to be dirty with my prints and hair, as well as Jamillah's and Marcus'. Every judge and assistant prosecutor in this building has a set of prints in my office."

"Nope. It's been wiped clean. And the vacuum cleaner bag is missing," Aspen said with a smooth tone.

"Do I need a lawyer?"

"Only you would know that, Ms. Davenport."

"I've done nothing wrong."

Aspen said, "Then we move on. Why did y'all stop?"

"Stop what?"

Aspen stubbed the cigarette on the bottom of her shoe. The butt smoldered. "Fucking."

The thought of her actually sleeping with Leon made her feel sicker than she had when she realized his dick was cut off, but she was committed to the lie. "Because I met his ex-wife first. She and I have been to lunch a few times. The more I learned about her, the worse I felt about interfering with their mess. So I knew if I kept sleeping with him, I'd destroy a potential friendship with her if she found out."

"Who's Leon's wife?"

The fact that Aspen wasn't taking any notes told Scenario that Aspen already had the answers to her line of questioning. Aspen just wanted to see if her answers would match.

"Ex-wife," Scenario said. "Jazz Smith."

Aspen handed Scenario a copy of the photo she and Hakeem had gotten from Mrs. Africa Taylor. Scenario stared at herself ten years ago. Stared at Chance, Leon, Anderson, and her best friend, Jazz. She was cautious not to show Aspen or Detective Scott any emotion. Careful not to give them a questionable body language reading.

Aspen said, "Three people in that photo were murdered by the Hieroglyphic Hacker. One of which is lying on your desk as we speak. Chance and Cashmaire Fox are missing, and you're friends with Jazz Smith."

"Associates. I wouldn't have slept with Leon if she was a friend. I stopped because it looked like we could be friends."

"How long have you known Leon and Jazz?"

"I met Jazz a little after I moved back to Cleveland. About five months ago at her book signing. Met Leon two months after that indirectly through Jazz."

"Do you know any of the other people in the picture? Ever indirectly meet them or seen them—alive—anywhere other than in that picture?"

"No, why would I? Furthermore, I would have been forthcoming with that information at the previous crime scenes like I am now about Leon. I am an officer of the court, Detective Skye. Your line of questioning is implicative and it's pissing me off. Let's not forget we play ball on the same side of the fence."

Aspen considered County Prosecutor Scenario Davenport. "Relax. I mean no harm. What was the beef between you and Leon about?"

"He wanted to continue seeing me. He was upset that I wouldn't take or return his calls or make any effort to pursue a relationship with him. It was so embarrassing. He accused me in public of being a lesbian, of wanting to be with Jazz instead of him."

"Is there any truth to that?"

"Are you asking for the investigation or for yourself, Detective Skye?"

Aspen rolled her eyes. "Then what happened?"

"I promised to call Leon when I got off work so I could diplomatically end the confrontation. He walked me back to the Justice Center's lobby. I went to work and I assumed he left."

"What time was that?"

"Lunchtime."

"Did you speak with him last night as promised?"

"No. I had no intentions of doing so in the first place."

"You didn't come into work this morning. Why?"

"Because I didn't feel like it, Detective. One of the luxuries that comes with my job is my hours are flexible."

"Where were you last night between eleven p.m. and four a.m.?"

"At home in bed."

"Can anyone verify that?"

"My rabbit is battery-operated so no. But my doorman knows what time I came in the building yesterday and left this morning." Scenario leaned forward. "My turn to ask a question. Has the message on Leon's body been translated yet?"

"Yeah," Aspen said. "Law 37: Create Compelling Spectacles. Does that mean anything to you?"

"No," Scenario lied.

Aspen turned the TV on and pushed Play on the DVD player. "This is footage from the surveillance camera outside your office last night at eleven fifteen."

Detective Scott put his hat on his head and faced the screen. They watched Scenario wave at someone and then go inside the county attorney's office.

Aspen said, "That's a bad-ass outfit you were wearing."

"That's not me."

"The night janitor says he spoke to you."

"He spoke to someone pretending to be me. That isn't me."

"We're keeping this out of the press until we figure this one out."

"Smartest thing you've said since I showed up. The killer is making us look like clowns."

"For your sake, Ms. Davenport, I hope you're right."

"For your sake," Detective Scott repeated Aspen's words.

NINETY-ONE

As Jazz wheeled her BMW X6 down Lakeshore Boulevard she wondered why Cash left without saying goodbye.

"This ain't cool," Jaden said.

"If it'll make you feel any better, Jaden, I'm not comfortable with this either." Jazz knew she had to try this, even if nothing came of it. She turned onto Spring Bank Lane, the stretch of road that had changed her life last October. This time, though, she drove under the speed limit and her hands shook.

Jaden looked as if he'd seen a ghost. He held on to the basketball like it would jump out his lap.

Jazz took a deep breath. "Relax," she said to Jaden as she parked five feet away from where Cash was thrown through the windshield. Everything will be all right." She was really trying to convince herself while putting on airs of strength and confidence for Jaden's benefit.

Beneath the cheap sunglasses and drab clothing, her gaze was unreadable. Her body language didn't communicate. How could she have been so careless? Cash had told her a million times about her reckless driving. She even had the cigarette burns on her thighs from when Leon disciplined her for bringing home speeding ticket after speeding ticket.

She opened the car door.

"Don't go." Jaden's voice was as shaky as her hands. "Trust me."

She whispered, "I have to. I really have to." She climbed out the car and left Jaden where he sat. When she ran her hand over the deep dent in a curb-side light pole, the tears stinging her eyes lost their grip. In the crevices of the twisted metal was blue paint that transferred from her Mercedes's front end on impact. The pole lost its erect posture from the force of the collision. Now it leaned over like a tired old lady in desperate need of a cane.

Buank. Buank. Buank. Buank.

"I'm sorry," she whispered. "I'm so sorry."

"I think you should turn around," Jaden said.

She looked over her shoulder and found Chance Fox standing there with a Marlboro behind his ear. The morning sun shined on his bald head. He wore camouflage cargo shorts, a Creed T-shirt, Skechers sneakers, and he reeked of a marijuana and alcohol concoction. The look in his ice-blue eyes said it all. Jazz was in the vicinity of death. Her skin crawled. She'd seen this look before, the night she looked up at Leon from the grave he forced her to dig at gunpoint.

"What are you doing here?" she said.

"I always keep my word. It's a bad habit of mine."

Jazz stepped back. "You never gave me your word on anything." Even putting space between them didn't make her feel comfortable.

"Told you we shouldn't have come here," Jaden said. "Let's get out of here."

"You're a riot." Chance laughed, and then turned serious. "I friggin' told you that I better not find out you knew Cash had AIS. I found out. Now let's finish this."

"Come on, Jaden," Jazz said, "we're leaving."

Chance held up her car keys and then lifted his shirt, showing off the shiny butt of his gun. "You're leaving with me, and I'm gonna enjoy cutting up that sexy body of yours."

"This way," Jaden said and took off running up the driveway.

Jazz was right on his heels.

"Nice. Real nice, you ass ache," Chance said to himself and went after her.

NINETY-TWO

Keebler wagged her tail with excitement when Jaden burst through the kitchen door. "Hey, Keebler, girl," he said as Jazz hurried to close the door and lock it.

"I don't think so, missy." Chance rammed the door open, knocking Jazz backward.

"Get 'em, Keebler." Jaden pointed to the threat. "Get 'em, girl."

Keebler showed her loyalty and attacked.

Jaden led Jazz deeper into the interior of the house.

Chance leapt onto the island in the center of the kitchen in one motion and armed himself with two Tiffany skillets from the overhead rack. Had he reacted a second later he would have experienced Keebler's bone-crushing bite. That was a pain he wanted no part of. Keebler circled the island Chance was stranded on. The growl in her chest rumbled like thunder, warning Chance that lightning was preparing to strike.

"Tried to nibble on old Chance, did you?"

Keebler bared her teeth, then barked to let him know she wasn't fucking around. Chance studied her. Bulging muscles. Beautiful brindle coat. Massive chest. Huge head.

"You're an impressive beast," Chance said. "Dammit, I'd like to shake Detective Eubanks' hand. But unfortunately, your master's at work trying to catch me."

Keebler circled her prey.

"Gee whiz, poochie. You don't really wanna get a taste of the fantastic Chancester, do you?" He reached out to her, testing her temperament.

She snapped at him like an emotional bitch, then barked the roar of six angry dogs.

"Well, that's just swell, isn't it? See, poochie pooch, now we have ourselves a problem since you're hell-bent on this biting thing. We have to come to a compromise here because I refuse to hurt a beautiful animal like you. It goes against everything the Chancester believes in." He assessed the kitchen for an escape. "But on the other hand, poochie pooch, that bitch you somehow let get by you, I have to hurt her very bad for taking away my inalienable human right to a family. And now you're in my way. So what are we gonna do about that, poochie pooch?" Chance looked at the skillets and shook his head with disappointment. "I can't win with these. They're no match against you." He looked at the door and knew he couldn't make it. "We're spending too much time here. I can't let her get away, poochie. Letting her live is not an option."

Keebler bared her teeth.

"You're forcing me to go against my morals."

Keebler jumped onto the opposite end of the island and faced Chance. Chance thought, if it was that easy, why did poochie pooch taunt him so long? She hunched her shoulders and lifted the hairs between her shoulder blades.

Chance shrugged a *have it your way*. "So this is what it comes to?"

Keebler attacked. Chance raised his gun and fired as her teeth connected with his skin. Keebler fell off the island and yelped like a woman giving birth when the nine-millimeter slug tore into her chest.

"God, please forgive me for what I've done." He stroked Keebler. "God, please don't let her die." Chance crossed himself with an imaginary crucifix. "Poochie pooch, I'm gonna make that bitch hurt really bad for this. I swear." He went after Jazz with tears burning his eyes.

NINETY-THREE

"**K**eebler," Hakeem yelled, stepping out of the bathroom, "what are you making all that noise for?" He was bare-chested and wearing a pair of drawstring pajama pants. "Shut up or I won't take you for a car ride today. It's too early, Keebler, and I didn't sleep a wink."

He figured she must be barking at someone on the lake. She always acted a fool anytime a fisherman's boat or a jet skier wandered too close to their boat dock or shoreline backyard. He yawned and stretched then headed to his bedroom to lie in bed and stare at the ceiling awhile longer.

But Hakeem froze midway down the hallway.

All traces of fatigue vanished when he heard heavy breathing behind him. He spun around prepared to fight for his life. The person he saw standing at the mouth of the hall was the very object of his hate.

"Help me," Jazz said, trying to catch her breath. "Please help me, Mr. Eubanks."

"How did you get in my house?" Then: "There's no way Keebler would have let you pass her. What did you do to Keebler?" A second later he yelled, "Keebler!"

"Don't let him kill me. Please."

"I don't know who leaked information to you about the case,

but I'm off it. I will do nothing to help you. Now get out of my house."

Jazz pointed. "He's downstairs."

Hakeem started toward her. "Who?"

"Chance Fox, the Hieroglyphic Hacker." She put her arms around him and cried. "Please don't let him hurt me. I'm so sorry."

Hakeem didn't hug her back. His nerve endings were irritated. A million times he told himself that he hated this woman. That he wanted her to feel as much pain as he had. But now that she was crying on his chest, he was certain it wasn't hate that he harbored. He was just pissed and didn't know how to forgive her. Now here she was frightened to death. The way she trembled made him feel bad for all the foul things he openly said about her but didn't really mean; for all the terrible things he focused so much energy wishing would happen to her but really didn't want to happen. She didn't deserve that from him.

She balled. "I'm sorry."

He put his arms around her. "I know. I know, it was an accident."

A gun went off downstairs.

Jazz flinched. He held her tighter. Keebler yelped.

"Dudette," Chance yelled from downstairs, "don't make me come up there and get you."

Hakeem lifted her sunglasses and looked deep into her eyes. "It'll be all right," he whispered.

"You got this screwy puzzle all wrong," Chance yelled. "Don't hide from me. I'm not the person you gotta run from. We're buds. It's Cashmaire you gotta concern yourself with. She killed them all. I swear. I only followed you here to warn you that she's coming for you." Then: "You got your ears on up there?"

A tear rolled from the corner of her eye. "You don't know how sorry I am. Please forgive me and help me."

Hakeem put a finger to her lips to shush her, then led her to the nearest bedroom. He whispered, "Lock yourself in and don't come out. Call the police and tell them you're in my house and I need backup."

"Jazz, you cunt. I searched everywhere down here. Now I know you're up there. You're unraveling my friggin' patience. Stop hiding. You're only getting me madder." He started stomping up the stairs.

This time Hakeem removed Jazz's sunglasses and found her eyes again. "I won't let anything happen to you."

"Promise."

"You got my word. Now lock the door and call my friends." Hakeem ducked into the bathroom because there was no way he could make it to his gun safe in the bedroom.

NINETY-FOUR

Chance hit the crest of the stairs with sheer determination to write on Jazz with his scalpel and to watch her suffer as she bled to death. "Never liked this hide-and-seek shit, Ms. Writer Lady," he said, looking at the five doors lining the narrow hallway, wondering which door he would find his prize behind. "Eeny meeny miny moe. Caught an author by her toe. If she hollers, don't let her go. Eeny meeny miny…moe." He pushed open the door he pointed at.

Hakeem stood there armed with a can of Lysol and Aspen's lighter.

Chance said, "I must admit, I'm surprised to find you home this morning, Detective."

Hakeem sprayed the homemade torch in Chance's face, burning a layer of skin, singeing his eyebrows and mustache. Then Hakeem slammed into him like an angry elephant. The force of their backward momentum broke the oak banister, jarring the gun under Chance's shirt loose, sending it hurling down the stairs. Hakeem and Chance saw it slide to a stop at the bottom of the stairs.

"Dude, don't think that makes this a fair fight." He head-butted Hakeem, sending him backward a few feet with blood pouring out his nose, then he hit Hakeem with a flying knee to the sternum that blew the wind from his body.

Hakeem went down hard. The tight hall reeked of burnt hair.

"Ever had someone kick your ass, Detective Eubanks, and talk to you while they're doing it?" Chance grabbed Hakeem's head and rammed it into the wall.

Hakeem went down again and tried to crawl into the bathroom to regain his faculties, reclaim some sense of direction. Chance repeatedly slammed the door on Hakeem's leg. Hakeem howled each time agony jettisoned up his leg.

"I'm really disappointed, Detective," Chance said, standing over him. "I had you pegged as a worthy opponent." He stomped the injured leg. "If you plan on saving her, you're gonna have to take a better stand than this, dude." He shoved Hakeem's head in the toilet. "You gotta fight really hard for what you believe in. Right now I'm not convinced you believe in much of anything." He held Hakeem's face in the water. "Drink up."

Jazz placed the phone back on the nightstand beside a picture frame that was turned face-down.

Buank. Buank. Buank. Buank.

The room was neat but smelled like it had been bottled up for ages. Posters of LeBron James and Nicki Minaj covered the walls. The bed was made as if no one ever slept in it. Among a stack of *Hip Hop Weekly* magazines and an Honor Roll plaque proudly displayed on the dresser was the biggest remote control boat Jazz had ever seen.

She heard the bumps and bangs of a violent tussle outside the door. When she heard a grown man holler like he was dying—not sure if it was Detective Hakeem Eubanks or Chance—she opened the window overlooking the roof of the sunporch.

Buank. Buank—"What are you doing?" Jaden's nerves were shot. "We're not sticking around to see who wins and opens that door."

Hakeem had nothing left. Unconsciousness loomed in his immediate future. He coughed up water from his burning lungs as Chance dragged him from the bathroom by his injured leg into the narrow hall.

"Always liked fighting in tight spaces," Chance said. "It makes it personal, don't you think?" Chance came down on Hakeem's leg with an elbow.

Every nerve ending in Hakeem's body sent excruciating pain throughout his body. He expressed his discomfort through his mouth.

"Which room is she hiding in? Dude, you better tell me or I'll do it again."

"Hakeem," someone called out.

"Drew, get out of here," he yelled.

"I heard gunshots and Keebler's—"

"Who's this pretty thing joining our party?" Chance said as Drew reached the landing. He sprang to his feet like a cat. "And I'm diggin' the bunny-eared slippers."

"Run, Drew. Get out of here or he'll kill you." Hakeem tried to get to his feet. "Run, dammit."

Chance started toward her.

"Run for what?" She raised her Glock 17 semiautomatic. "I got my permit to carry, and I told you I'm from Garden Valley." She squeezed the trigger and stopped Chance in his tracks.

NINETY-FIVE

One hundred and ninety-nine. That's how many days it had been since Cashmaire was in the same room with her husband. That's how many days it had been since he wished death on her. The memory of it was fresh in her mind as if it were yesterday.

There was so much pain. Her lies had surfaced and ripped the fabric of their timeless love like the windshield had ripped the skin of her face. She desperately wanted the reassurance of his compassionate blue eyes, but he refused to connect gazes. She panicked when she saw her life walking out the door, the one man who validated her existence as a woman. "Chance, wait, please. What can I do to make this right?"

All he gave her was his back. "Drop dead, you nasty nigger bitch."

Her emotions were caught in her throat. She thought of that October day in the hospital every day since their separation, yet all she wanted him to do was hold her and tell her that everything would be all right; that all this could disappear and things could go back to the way they were when they were in love.

But none of that was possible now that Chance was sitting across from her in a police interview room dressed in county jail orange and wearing cuffs and shackles.

"You showed," Chance said, his voice edgy. "I appreciate that, Ms. Davenport."

"You demanded to see me." Then: "Anything you say to me will be used against you. I advise you to have your lawyer present."

"I know what I'm doing. Since he works for me, I insisted he take the day off." He tilted his head toward her. "It took you two weeks to come check me out. That's disheartening. Thought my popularity was up there with the death of my buddy Osama Bin Laden. You been catching the news? Isn't that terrible what SEAL Team 6 did to him?"

"I'm a busy woman, Mr. Fox. Why am I here?"

He nodded to the surveillance camera mounted on the wall. *"Law 5: So Much Depends On Reputation. Guard It With Your Life."*

She studied his addictive blue eyes. His third-degree burns had healed nicely since the day of his arrest, and he showed no signs of discomfort from being shot in his shoulder and side. Then she contemplated the camera and all the cons a recorded conversation between them could expose. She strutted out the interview room and into an adjacent office where a smorgasbord of officers were gathered around a monitor watching Chance give them the finger.

Chance stood in front of the camera digging in his nose. "Eat this, you fuckin' pigs." He smeared a booger on the lens and then waved. "Bye-bye, you eavesdropping shitheads."

"Ugh." Aspen turned up her nose. "That's nasty. He's an ornery motherfucker."

County Prosecutor Scenario Davenport broke through the gathering and shut the monitor off.

Aspen frowned. "What in the hell do you think you're—"

"Save it, Detective Skye," Scenario said, throwing up a hand. She then proceeded to take off the monitor's USB cord.

Hakeem struggled to hobble to the front of the crowd. He pushed through Chief Dwight Eisenhower and Detective Leonardo Scott. He winced and gritted his teeth as he maneuvered on the crutches. From the thigh down, Hakeem's leg was covered with a fiberglass cast with six titanium screws protruding from it. Four above the knee, two below it. Eisenhower rushed to help, but Hakeem backed him off with an icy glare.

"Goddammit, Eubanks, if you won't use the wheelchair until you're better like you're supposed to, then let somebody help you."

"I'll have a lame leg for the rest of my life, Chief. Let me live with it my way." Then: "Ms. Davenport, we have every right to hear what—"

"I'm not trying to hear it, Eubanks. There's no law that says you do. Find somebody else's shoulder to boohoo on. This conversation is between me and him." She heard someone question the meaning of Law Number 5 as she went to the door. "He quoted a strategic principle from Robert Greene's *The 48 Laws of POWER*," she said, closing the door behind her.

She went into the interview room and threw the USB cord on the table.

Chance clapped. "That was an awesome performance you did playing Ms. Scenario Davenport for the camera." His eyes shifted toward her. Nothing else moved. "So, Cashmaire, honey, how much did he pay you to ruin my life?"

NINETY-SIX

A cold chill ran through Cash. "I—" She cut herself off to swallow the aggravating lump in her throat. "Chance, I love you. Never would I intentionally set out to ruin your life."

"Love knows nothing but the truth." Then: "How much, Cashmaire?"

Shaking her head, clearly in the dark, she said, "I don't know what you're referring to."

"That prick Leon."

She saw where this was going, a road that was better left untraveled.

"He paid you to go out with me so they could sit back and laugh at us when you kissed me. How much did he sell you my life for?"

"Laugh at us?"

Sheer amusement danced in Chance's eyes. A smile tugged at the corner of his lips. "You don't freakin' know, do you?" He giggled. "This shit gets greater with each revelation. All of them knew, Cashmaire. They all knew you were a dude on the inside. Even that long-legged cunt girlfriend of yours."

So many thoughts penetrated her head as her husband's words found their mark. The memories played on the screen of her mind like a DVD stuck on fast forward. The voices of the starring characters in her mental production reminded her so much of Alvin and the Chipmunks. How did anyone learn of the secret she guarded as if its exposure was a threat to national security? Until now she had never viewed it like Chance's life had been exchanged for a tangible. There was no doubt that Chance would further be offended if he knew what Leon had actually paid her. Then one distinctive memory stood out like a Sunday matinee at a dollar show.

Cash sat alone in the CSU cafeteria, high on marijuana and shunned by her peers because of her gothic style. Extrovert by nature; introvert because of shame and low self-esteem. A beautiful, tall sister dressed to the nines put her lunch tray on the table and sat down in front of Cash. The sister's hair flowed down her back like a Dark and Lovely model, just long enough to be perfect. She had the prettiest cocoa skin Cash had ever seen on a human being. Cash almost lost her breath when she looked into the woman's radiant eyes that oozed intelligence. No one had ever voluntarily sat at the same table with Cash since her enrollment and she preferred it that way. She didn't want anyone to know she even existed. Cash looked around the cafeteria hoping the marijuana didn't have her hallucinating.

The sister offered a hand, an iron grip for a woman. "Hi, I'm Jazz. I'm new here, but I was thinking we could be friends."

"Jazz knew," Cash whispered more to herself than to Chance.

"You got it, kiddo. She only wanted to meet you so she could write about you, lab rat you in a book." Then: "It's eating me to know what my life and family dreams sold for."

She turned away, not believing what she was about to say. "I did it for a nickel bag."

"Five dollars' worth of weed?" His blond brows pinched together. "I killed my buds 'cause you wanted to smoke a couple joints?"

She wanted to justify, lie if she had to, but the words couldn't get past the lump in her throat.

He laughed. "Wifey, their blood is on your hands."

NINETY-SEVEN

C hance watched as Cash slumped into the chair. Serves her right, he thought. Even if she didn't get a full dose of the venom dripping through his veins, at least she got enough of it to make her woozy.

"Family means everything," Chance said, switching gears like an Indy 500 race car driver. "Mother sewed the theme into me from the time she squeezed me out her funky twat." Bitterness crept into his voice. He wanted her to understand his rage. "She tightened the stitch with a curtain rod after I became numb to the extension cords and being locked in the basement for days without food and water. Brownie, my Labrador, was the only one there to comfort me while I healed from the beatings." Then: "It sucked learning the meaning of family from Mother, but it stuck."

She was too quiet. He could tell she was contemplating several sympathetic responses. Her eyes bounced around the interview room, then landed on him as a tear fell.

"I'm sorry," she whispered. "I didn't know."

He shrugged a *don't be*. "Just comes down to what family means to you and how far you'll go to preserve your meaning, to protect your God-given rights. As I lay in that stinky cold basement, healing, I dreamed about the woman I'd marry and the children we'd have. I knew every detail of my perfect world, how we'd raise our children to be better people than we were, how we'd teach them a progressive meaning of family. I even knew the color paint that would be in their rooms." He took a folded sheet of paper from his pocket and slid it across the table. "They conspired and took that from us. When I met you, the details were complete." He gestured to the paper. "You should have told me the truth. We could have worked through it."

Cash's fingertips stroked the truth of her lies condensed into the suicide note she'd written so long ago.

"Cash," Chance said, "I've always known you're a pathological liar." Hearing him say it with such nonchalance cut her to the quick.

"Never had a problem with it," he said. "We all have our flaws. I only have a problem with it when your lying is directed at me, when it works against us and not for us."

"I didn't know how to tell you—if I could tell you and keep you loving me. How could I tell you that I was a genetic mess and I couldn't make your dreams come true by bearing your children?" She dropped her head, dizzy with shame. "How, Chance, after I married you fully aware of your family ambitions?" She was quiet for a moment. "You don't know how badly I want to have a family to belong to. You don't know how it feels to spend your whole life in group homes and not having anyone in this world and no one willing to adopt you because they think you're a freak. And you definitely don't know a thing about knowing you're going to leave this world without bringing your own family into it. I disappear when I go. Not a trace that I ever existed."

"Gee whiz, Cash. I'll never stop loving you. We could've freakin' adopted if you told me the truth. We still can." He paused, letting that statement hang in the air. "What does family mean to you?"

She raised a brow. "Huh?"

"Don't be a pain in the turd cutter. I hate it when you stall like that."

She thought for a moment. "To me…family is a group of people who will love one another no matter what. It means putting the people you care about first, being able to depend on one another regardless of favorable circumstances."

"Well put," he said as she crumbled the suicide letter in her fist and squeezed. "How about the Chancester, am I family, Cash?"

"Of course," she said. "You're all the real family I have. I have your last name."

"How far will you go to preserve your meaning of family, Mrs. Fox?"

This was a vacuous question she didn't have to give any thought to. "I'll do whatever I must for mine."

"Then now it's time for your lies to work for us."

NINETY-EIGHT

Cash's brows pointed inward. "And by that you mean what exactly?"

"You always wanted to go South Africa. I got us a cozy place on the shore of Port Elizabeth. We can ditch this trash dump and push the restart button. Adopt a whole bunch of little Chances. I really miss you, Cash."

"I miss you too, but none of that is possible now. The State of Ohio will prosecute you and convict you for the murders." Then something else jumped to the front of her mind. "My God, Chance, you killed those people in Denver."

"For crying out loud, the fuck faces had it coming. They deserved everything I did to them for abusing their pets," he said without a smidgen of remorse. "Let's focus on the case here. The idiot cops think I killed my wife and her body hasn't turned up yet, but here you are in the flesh. County Prosecutor Ms. Scenario Davenport. Throw the case. Leave reasonable doubt in the minds of the jurors, and my lawyer will convince the world that Cashmaire Fox is the culprit and we'll spend the rest of our days making love and raising crumb snatchers in South Africa."

"It's risky, Chance. You took a big gamble banking on me being your prosecutor."

"Not. Thought you'd be a little more appreciative of the promotion I gave you."

"You killed Marcus Jeffers, too?" That was a revelation, not a question. She got up and paced the length of the interview room. "You shouldn't have done that."

"According to Christians, today is supposed to be Judgment Day. Let's allow God to deal with it." Chance shrugged. "Marcus was an unfortunate schmuck. Good dude. Wrong game."

"And what part of the game is this? You hated me when you excommunicated me in the hospital. Now we're in the interview room and you're on the chopping block for murdering our friends and you love me again and want to run away together. What number law of power is this?"

"I missed one of our so-called friends. Still kicking myself in the turd cutter for that slip-up. Can you really blame me for the hospital? I was angry, Cash. Shattered. One minute I had a son and the next I don't and no possibility of a family. And there is no strategic law for love." He stood in her path, then kissed her. Their mouths locked. The kiss powerful and passionate. "Just like I remembered," Chance said, sinking back into his chair. "Getting a boner over here. Think we got enough time to do a little grab ass?"

The door swung open and in came Aspen. Pissed. "The mayor's on the line for you."

"Well, Mr. Fox," Cash said like a no-nonsense prosecutor, "if you're not going to inform me where we can find your wife's body, the death penalty stays on the table and I'll see you in trial this September."

Aspen turned her anger on Chance. "I have a good mind to kick your ass and make you clean my camera lens off."

"You stupid, stupid bimbo. Did you not see what I did to your partner when he tried to kick the Chancester's ass?"

NINETY-NINE

L abor Day. Jazz lounged on the patio of her ultra-modern Spanish-tiled home that was lined with ten-foot hedges and a backyard that was exposed to the shore of Lake Erie. She soaked up the warm sun while taking in the picturesque view and inhaling the hickory flavoring pouring from a traditional kettle-styled grill. She wore a cotton-blue dainty short set with a sleeveless top. The chocolate skin of her long legs and slender arms gleamed of good health. An hour ago she had treated herself to a professional manicure and pedicure, an indulgence she hadn't been allowed since her wedding night. She had forgotten how good it felt to be pampered until the nail technician showed up at her home. Her polished toenails and designer sandals made her pretty feet look simply adorable.

Buank. Buank. Buank. Buank.

Her shaded gaze left the ebb and flow of the lake and found Jaden making a layup off an NBA-sized backboard she had installed when summer kicked in. That boy loves him some basketball, she thought as Cash pulled into the driveway and stepped out a convertible Lexus, wearing an eye-catching sundress and a pronounced straw hat.

"Hey girl, you look good," Cash said, dropping her purse on an empty patio lounger.

Jazz blushed and waved her off, smile bright as daylight.

"Now if I can get you to shed that stupid ball cap and those un-inspiring sunglasses, we'll be on to something." Then: "I'm proud of you. And I'm looking forward to seeing that vibrant girl with gorgeous hair that I met in college."

Buank. Buank. Buank. Buank.

Cash made herself useful by tending to the slabs of baby beef ribs on the grill.

"You're really gonna do it next week, aren't you?" Jazz decided to address a more pressing matter. Conversations about her appearance, she still wasn't ready to entertain, even if the tone stunk of positivity.

Cash said, "Could we please not go there?" She rotated the meat, then based it with a barbecue sauce whose ingredients had been a secret in Jazz's family since the turn of the eighteenth century. "I just want to get me a plate, lick this sauce off my fingers, and enjoy this day. Hope that's all right with you."

"This Scenario Davenport business is tearing my conscience apart," Jazz said, ignoring her. "I'm afraid if you keep it up and go through with prosecuting Chance, you'll regret it. We're family. I care about you and I don't want to see you in trouble."

"Family?" Cash threw a look over her shoulder, then she went back to what she was doing.

Jazz saw something poisonous flash in Cash's eyes that dropped the temperature a few notches. Jazz rubbed her arms, coaxing the goosebumps away. She had to be sure she wasn't tripping, though. She needed to see Cash's eyes again to be certain. "Yeah, family."

"Tell me something, Jazz. What does family mean to you?"

The angelic sound and easy tempo of Cash's voice made Jazz think she'd been mistaken about what she saw in Cash's gaze. "Family is all anyone truly has in this life," Jazz said with a smile in her voice. "And not all family is blood related. Neither is all blood relative's family. Despite all the dregs and the dross, family means everything. Family is the reason I kept my mouth shut and didn't go to the police with my suspicions about Yancee and my blood cousin. Family is the reason why I'm worried about your high-yellow self and this Scenario Davenport bull, Cash."

Buank. Buank. Buank. Buank.

"Relax or you'll give yourself an ulcer." Cash made herself comfortable in the patio lounger and followed Jazz's gaze to the basket-ball hoop. "Everything will work out this way. Trust me. I'll let Chance think I'm helping him get off, but I'm gonna prosecute Chance and put him away forever. In the process, I'll get retribution for Anderson, Yancee, and that asshole Leon."

Jazz didn't flinch or become uncomfortable at the mention of Leon's name. She showed no emotion just like she didn't show any at his funeral.

Cash said, "This way I can personally save myself and the past can finally be the past."

"What happens if Chance tells after you convict him?"

"He'll sound like an insane serial killer saying anything and no one will take his ramblings serious. Just like no one's trying to hear anything Charles Manson has to say after the fact or Jeffrey MacDonald."

"Jeffrey MacDonald?"

"Murdered his whole family thirty-five, forty years ago. Said Charles Manson followers did it. Anyway, he still is coming up with media coverage today with tall tales about how it really happened. The same thing will happen to Chance if he says anything after conviction. And trust me, even if someone does listen to him, it'll be fifty years from now and it won't matter because we'll all be ready for the grave or already in it."

Shaking her head, Jazz said, "I don't like it." She got up. "Watch the grill for me. I'm going to pick up my mom and them from the bus station."

"Sure."

"Jaden," Jazz said, "you wanna ride?"

Buank. Buank. Buank. Buank.

ONE HUNDRED

On September 9, 2011, Criminal Defense Attorney Stormie Bishop watched with rapt attention as County Prosecutor Scenario Davenport made the young man in the witness box look like a Boy Scout who helped little old ladies cross busy streets. Her manila complexion exaggerated the color depth of her golden gaze, which sparkled and cut through the courtroom like a hypnotizing light show. Stormie liked her style. She was a formidable opponent, and her good looks and high-end clothing made Scenario a complete knockout.

She turned her back on him in such a way that Stormie understood that she was telling him to kiss her ass. He had used the tactic several times during his career. She calmly took her seat at the state's table and threw her golden gaze his way.

"Your witness, Counselor," she said.

It was nothing for Stormie to make the man in the witness box look like a complete liar and the dope fiend he really was, who couldn't be trusted, but Stormie would take a different approach. He consulted his notes as Chance whispered something to him. Stormie shook his head, then rose from his seat.

Stormie Bishop was a master at commanding attention and casting spells on those who observed his magic. His white hair made people assume he was older than his forty-one years, but the chic way he wore it slicked back made him come across as hip as a twenty-six-year-old. He wore a pair of jeans, a Ralph Lauren button-down, and a pair of expensive loafers. He knew that by presenting himself as laid-back and at ease in a formal setting, the twelve people he needed to persuade to deliver a not guilty verdict would be comfortable listening to him.

Stormie leaned on the witness box as if he and the young man were old buddies who were about to reminisce about the time they'd gotten pissy drunk at an Indians game. "Hello, Mr. Bradshaw," Stormie said, giving the audience his profile view and the jurors firm eye contact.

"Hi," he said with a shaky voice.

Stormie knew the young man was worried about if he'd be able to remember everything the prosecution had coached him not to say on record. His skin was so flushed from nervousness that he looked like a chemo patient.

"Your nickname is Scratch, right? Mind if I call you Scratch?"

"That's cool."

"Scratch, you just shared with the court how you came to be in possession of Mr. Yancee Taylor's cell phone, correct?"

"Yeah, I stole it out of his car."

"Other things happened that day, didn't they, Scratch?"

"Objection," Scenario said. "He's leading the witness, Your Honor."

"Don't worry about it, Your Honor. I'll rephrase." Stormie focused on Scratch. "On Sunday, April twenty-fourth of this year, you were arrested by Detective Eubanks and Detective Skye. Do you remember that day?"

"Yeah, somewhat."

"In an interview with the detectives you made several statements—"

"Objection, Your Honor." Scenario shot to her feet. "The record will show that *Scratch* was under the influence of heroin during the April twenty-fourth interview. Therefore the information gleaned from the interview is inadmissible and has no relevance to these proceedings."

"Your Honor, I am duty bound—not to mention it's my right—to prove to this court that my client, Mr. Chance Fox, is not culpable for the murders of Yancee Taylor, Anderson Smith, or Leon Page."

"Mr. Bradshaw and his interview with the homicide detectives are not on trial here," Scenario said. "Mr. Fox is. Therefore, the interview is not relevant."

Judge Ronald Adrine smacked his gavel down. "You're in my castle, Ms. Davenport. I am capable of running it and I will *run* it."

"Sorry, Your Honor."

"Objection overruled. Tread lightly, Mr. Bishop."

"Scratch, a couple of hours before Yancee Taylor's time of death, did you see him alive and well?"

"Yeah."

"Did you tell the homicide detectives this when they interviewed you?"

He nodded. "Yeah."

"You also told them you saw Yancee with someone. Share with the court who you saw Yancee with before he was murdered."

Scratch shrugged. "I don't know who she was, but she was a beautiful woman. Couldn't tell if she was white or mixed, but they drove off together."

"No further questions."

ONE HUNDRED ONE

Jazz left the witness stand forty-five minutes after Scratch. She was so blown away by Cash's disorderly conduct, Jazz knew it was time to restore order in her life. She settled herself in the seat of her computer station.

Buank—

She shot a look toward the room's threshold.

"My bad," Jaden said, entering her home office. "What are you doing?"

"Blowing the dust off this thing." She set her tea cup on the desktop.

"Straight up?" he said, fingering the spine of a Brenda Hampton book on the shelf.

"Yeah. It's time. I feel it." She pulled up a blank screen and positioned her fingers over the home row keys.

"Can I watch for a while?"

"As long as you don't start running off at the mouth and disturb my groove."

"I won't. Promise."

Jazz took in a deep breath and slowly let it go along with the hang-up that underlined the stagnation of her career. Her fingers started moving and it felt damn good.

HARM'S WAY

By Jazz Smith

CHAPTER ONE

Onica Everheart's life was in greater danger than ever before. She didn't know it, though, until she awoke to a raccoon clearing snow away from her face with its gross tongue. She screamed, then instantly started shivering from the thirty-seven-degree temperature. Then she screamed again through chattering teeth. The critter hissed and scurried away. Pissed that its lunch all of a sudden became uncooperative.

Onica couldn't feel her extremities; she was packed in snow the way meat was packed in a deep freezer to be kept fresh. Through her weakness and immense pain, a discomfort she didn't know the source of, Onica managed to pull herself free of the wintry grave. Although her head was smoggy and she definitely felt the side effect of a drug surging through her veins, she was acutely aware of the pounding of her heart. She heard it in her ears like a romantic whisper.

She was vigilant. Sepia eyes keen, scanning the woods for trouble. Then, Onica took off in a full-stride sprint. The fact that she was barefoot and naked didn't matter. She ran for her life and for the life of her unborn child, never once flinching when the forest floor tore into the pads of her feet. Adrenaline and the pure will to survive pumped her slender brown legs until she collapsed on the sleet-covered emergency lane of Interstate 90.

Jazz stopped typing for a moment to glance up at Jaden. He stood over her shoulder, reading. He smiled his approval.

ONE HUNDRED TWO

The tension in the courtroom smothered the air like the seconds before the execution of a death row inmate.

"Call your next witness, Ms. Davenport," Judge Ronald Adrine said in his thick rasp.

"The state calls Homicide Detective Hakeem Eubanks."

The audience burst at the seams with members of the press looking to sensationalize murder, transform the despicable act from a sin to an art form, and elevate Chancellor Fox to perverse stardom in the process. Hakeem hated the media. He glanced at Gus Hobbs and did everything in his power to bite back his anger. Aspen gave him a gentle rub as he rose from his seat. Except for Chance's, every set of eyes in the place were on Hakeem as he passed through the gate, backing a pitty-wielding bailiff off with a head shake.

Hakeem was overly self-conscious about his lilting gait. Because of Chance, his leg was no longer able to fully straighten, which made him dependent on a walking cane to do simple things like walk from his seat to the witness box, a journey he'd made more times in his career than he could count. And now that he was saddled with a few extra pounds because the lame leg slowed him down didn't help matters. Hakeem looked the part of a veteran detective and seasoned trial witness: stony expression, sharp haircut, and an even sharper four-figure suit, but lurking closely beneath the iron-clad exterior was an exhausted man, worn out by the demons that stalked him during the night.

After he was sworn in, County Prosecutor Scenario Davenport approached the witness box. "Detective Eubanks, would you please state your occupation for the record."

"I'm a homicide detective for Cuyahoga County. I work out of Cleveland's Homicide Unit." He wished that Aspen was on the stand. But since she couldn't control her temper, Davenport decided to call her *only* if necessary.

"And because of your job, you and your partner, Detective Aspen Skye, were charged with investigating the Hieroglyphic Hacker murders?"

"Yes." Hakeem couldn't help but to admire her beauty. Anyone in their right mind would take a few moments to appreciate the work God put into her creation.

"How did that investigation lead you to suspect Mr. Chancellor Fox is the Hieroglyphic Hacker?"

Hakeem fixed his stony expression on the defense table. Chance sat there with a gleaming bald head and a suit just as expensive as his own. "Ultimately the initials 'C.F.' made him good for it." He wanted to knock that silly grin off Chance's face.

"A set of initials? How so, Detective?"

"Early in our investigation, Mr. Fox became a person of interest. We traced him to the secluded area Yancee Taylor's body was found in." He saw Africa Taylor wipe her tears. "Only natives of the area knew it existed."

"Would you be more specific, Detective Eubanks?"

"Three decades ago, the middle-schoolers of Cleveland Heights cut through a wooded area that encases a synagogue as a shortcut to get to school. They made a path."

"Only kids used this path?"

"Yes, and it's still used as a shortcut today. Our profile suggested the killer was a white male in his early thirties, which means he would have used the path between nineteen ninety and ninety-five."

"What did you do with that information?"

ONE HUNDRED THREE

A lready Chance was sick of listening to the twit in the decked-out suit. He really wished he could kick Detective Eubanks' drawers up the crack of his ass in front of the whole courtroom and show everyone how easy it was. This time, though, he'd apply Law 15: Crush Your Enemy Totally. Chance whispered a very detailed set of instructions to Stormie, then he forced himself to tune into Detective Eubanks' baloney.

"Actually," the twit said, "it was Aspen who put us on the scent of Mr. Fox. We learned from Yancee Taylor's autopsy that the hieroglyphics cut into his body were done by a skilled surgeon's hand. Some sort of doctor. Detective Skye cross-referenced all the male students who went to Monticello Junior High School in the early nineties against those who turned out professions in the medical/health care field. One of the two white males who made the list was Mr. Fox, because he's a practicing veterinarian. But that dead-ended on us."

Aspen's a smart little cunt, Chance thought. He made a mental note to himself to never again dump a body anywhere that the location could come back and bite him on the turd cutter no matter how remote the possibility.

"Would you tell the court about the evidence discovered on April twenty-seventh of this year."

"We located Yancee's car." The twit paused for a brief moment, as if he were remembering the day. "Inside the car we found a note Yancee had written to himself."

"What was on the note?"

His wife played her role to a tee; it made Chance grin.

"It had the words 'wood chips 4:30, Thursday,' written on it. Yancee went missing on April twenty-first, which was a Thursday."

"Was there anything else?"

"Yes, he wrote the initials C.F."

Chance whispered to Stormie again as the star character of his production, County Prosecutor Scenario Davenport, collected a document from the state's table.

She approached Bridgette, the clerk of courts, a bimbo with bee-sting tits and a cottage-cheese complexion who wore a skirt too high above the knees to be considered appropriate. Chance had been imagining different ways he could fuck her ever since they led him in the courtroom. Each time he winked at her, she smiled. He dug her lip piercing, and the bottled auburn hair let him know that Bridgette had a little *wild* in her blood.

Scenario handed the object of his present lust the document. "The state enters People's Exhibit A into the record, the note Yancee Taylor wrote to himself." She turned back to the twit. "Detective Eubanks, what do the initials C.F. stand for?"

Chance elbowed Stormie.

"Objection, Your Honor." Stormie shot to his feet, biting back the pain. "Speculation. Without Yancee Taylor, no one can definitively know what C.F. stands for. It could stand for that new gentlemens club, Chocolate Factory, for all we know."

"Sustained."

"No problem, Your Honor. I'll rephrase," Scenario said. "What do the initials mean to you, Detective Eubanks?"

"Until Mr. Fox showed up at my house with the intentions of harming Ms. Smith, my partner and I thought the initials stood for Cashmaire Fox."

"Really? How so?"

ONE HUNDRED FOUR

Scenario Davenport felt the first bead of perspiration drip from her armpit. She knew this line of questioning was the first step in freeing her husband and burying Cashmaire Fox forever.

"It was confusing at first, because the wood chips is a playground that Chance, Yancee, and Leon used to frequent together as children. Ms. Gail Taylor, Yancee's mother, provided us with that information during the investigation. That connected the deaths of Yancee and Leon together and then to Chance, and then connected them all to their college roommate Anderson Smith. But as Scratch testified, Yancee was last seen with a woman. In the call log of Yancee's cell phone, there were several calls placed between Yancee and a number registered to Cashmaire Fox. One call was shared between them twenty minutes prior to when Yancee was last seen alive."

Scenario paced in front of the jurors while Hakeem talked.

"At seven thirty-six of the same morning Yancee didn't come home from work, a red Infiniti blew through the Ohio turnpike, entering the state with an expired E-Z Pass. The E-Z Pass cameras photographed the license plate. The car is registered to Cashmaire Fox. As Scratch testified, he saw the same make and model car being driven away from the wood chips later that day with a woman fitting Mrs. Fox's description."

"So you concluded that Yancee and Cashmaire drove away together in her car, and Yancee's car was towed by the city of Euclid because he left it illegally parked for an extended period of time, obviously because he had been murdered."

Hakeem nodded. "Yes, but that was just the beginning of our theory."

"Please explain, Detective." Scenario perched herself on the state's table and folded her arms. She couldn't wait until this was over so she and Chance could settle into their new home in their new world and adopt a family.

"Once we linked one body to Mr. Fox," Detective Eubanks said, "we linked them all to an intimate group of friends."

"Please share the names of that group with the court, Detective."

"Yancee Taylor, Anderson Smith, Leon Page, Jazz Smith, Cashmaire Fox, and Chancellor Fox. Two were dead when we discovered this web of people. Leon Page was murdered a few hours afterward. Our efforts or the efforts of the authorities in Denver couldn't locate Mr. or Mrs. Fox, but we had proof she was in Cleveland."

"Because of the E-Z Pass and where the cell towers put her when the calls were made between her cell phone and Yancee's."

"Yes, and as I stated earlier, the description of the woman Yancee was last seen with matches Mrs. Fox."

"But Mr. Fox is on trial here, not his wife."

"That's correct. Once we narrowed the deaths to one group of people, we knew that Jazz Smith was potentially in danger of the same fate, and we assumed that Mr. Fox was already dead and his body just hadn't been discovered."

She knew the jury and press would love to hear the answer to her next question. "What switched your focus to Mr. Fox?"

"Mrs. Fox didn't show up trying to kill Ms. Smith; Mr. Fox did."

"Why, what motive did he have to kill off his friends?"

"He doesn't need one," Hakeem said with energy. "Look at him, he's crazy. He carves messages in people's bodies, for God's sake."

"Objection, Your Honor," Stormie said. "I move to have that inflammatory statement stricken from the record."

"Sustained." The judge instructed the jury to disregard the comment. Then he said, "Watch it, Detective Eubanks."

"You sustained a permanent injury when Mr. Fox attacked you in your home in his pursuit of Ms. Smith."

"Objection," Stormie said. "My client was not the aggressor."

"I'll hear it," the judge said. "Overruled."

"Yes," Hakeem said, staring blankly at her, probably remembering the intense pain each time he felt his leg break under the force of the door. "My leg was broken in six places. My femur and tibia bones are held together by surgical screws and I have ligament damage. When I received these injuries, I also realized our theory was the exact opposite. That it was Cashmaire Fox who was missing."

"Where is Mrs. Fox today, Detective Eubanks?"

Hakeem shrugged. "We're clueless. Mr. Fox won't tell us."

"Thank you, Detective Eubanks." Scenario walked away from the witness box and avoided Chance's gaze. "Your witness, Mr. Bishop."

"**D**etective Eubanks, are you familiar with my client Chancellor Fox?" Stormie paced in front of the witness box with his hands in his pockets.

"Yes."

"How?"

"My investigation into the murder of Yancee Taylor led me and my partner to him." Hakeem found Africa Taylor in the audience and felt bad that she had to go through all this.

"Do you see Mr. Fox in the courtroom today?"

"Yes."

"Would you please point to him for us?"

He pointed. "That's him right there."

"What color is Mr. Fox, Detective Eubanks?"

"What?"

"What race is my client?"

"He's Caucasian."

"No, shithead," Chance interrupted. "I'm trailer park, white trash. Get it right." He blew Bridgette a kiss on the sly while some people in the audience snickered. Others laughed outright.

Judge Adrine banged his gavel. "Mr. Fox, I will not tolerate outburst from you, and you will not use sophomoric language in my courtroom. Do either of the two again and you'll find yourself in contempt." He looked at Stormie. "Continue, Counselor."

Stormie leaned on the witness box, stealing the attention back. "Let's talk about the murders, Detective. More specifically, the crime scenes."

"That's what we're here for."

"At the crime scenes of Yancee Taylor and Anderson Smith, was there any biological evidence found?"

"Yes."

"What specifically do you mean by *yes*, Detective?"

"At the Taylor scene our crime scene technicians discovered a hair sample in the crease of his neck. On Smith, we found an eye-lash."

"What is normally done with the evidence?"

"It's sent to the lab for DNA testing, as was done in these cases."

"Did the results yield DNA profiles?"

Hakeem nodded.

"Is that a yes, Detective?"

"Yes."

"Does either of the profiles match the DNA of my client?"

"No."

"Does each of the DNA profiles collected from the crime scenes match each other?"

"Yes, the DNA collected from the crime scenes match the same person."

"And neither DNA sample matches any of the victims, correct?"

"That is correct."

"Well, answer this for us, Detective. Can we reasonably conclude that the killer is the person who left their DNA at these crime scenes?"

"Objection, Your Honor. Speculation." Scenario shot Stormie a warning look.

"Sustained."

"Detective Eubanks, whose DNA was found at these crime scenes?"

Hakeem hated to admit it. "We don't know."

"What race and gender does this mysterious DNA profile match?"

"An African American male."

A fucking bug? For crying out loud, Chance thought. Three weeks into Chance's stage play and the prosecution rested with Forensic Pathologist Dr. Aura Chavez establishing that the Hieroglyphic Hacker had ties to the Denver area because of a bug. Chance hadn't calculated that mistake. Now he knew better. And he knew the shit was about to get explosive now that Stormie had taken center stage. Port Elizabeth, here I fucking come, Chance thought.

"The defense calls Cornell Livingood to the stand," Stormie said, sending Scenario into a state of confusion, causing her to shuffle through paperwork.

Chance was thoroughly amused.

"Objection," Scenario said as the bailiff led a blind man through the gate and helped him into the witness box. "This witness is not on the state's list."

Judge Ronald Adrine looked down on Stormie from his bench. Translation: *Explain yourself, Mister.*

"Your Honor," Stormie said, "Mr. Livingood just materialized."

Scenario said, "If Counselor Bishop wants to bullshit this Honorable Court, Your Honor, allow him to bullshit us in a sidebar."

The judge pointed an authoritative finger at Scenario. "Watch your mouth, Counselor. You're not beyond contempt of this court." He banged his gavel. "Sidebar."

Stormie and Scenario approached the bench. What a bummer, Chance thought. He really wished he was privy to their private talk.

Earlier that morning Scenario was elated the trial was winding down. She'd thrown so many loopholes in the case that no jury in the world would convict Chance. And because of that she couldn't wait until they were back together. She'd packed and shipped her belongings to Port Elizabeth and was now living out of a hotel like Chance had instructed her to do. She was ready. She dressed in an accentuating skirt and blouse, sprayed herself with her tailor-made perfume, Thin Air—per Chance's special request—and left the hotel to get her husband off. But now she was so pissed, she was shaking. *What in the hell is Chance doing?*

"Your Honor," Scenario said full of irritation, "the prosecution has a right to know who's testifying *prior* to them taking the stand. I also have the right to know the nature of their testimony in order to adequately prepare the appropriate defense."

"She is absolutely correct, Your Honor. But my investigator produced Mr. Livingood only ten minutes ago."

"You're stonewalling." Scenario's anger dissolved to tolerance. "If you weren't, this pop-up witness would not be the first to take the stand so the prosecution can have some time to prepare for his testimony. Point blank."

The judge said, "Is there a specific reason, Counselor Bishop, that Mr. Livingood is on the stand right now and not one of your other ten witnesses the prosecution has knowledge of?"

"Yes, Your Honor. Mr. Livingood's testimony can prove my client is an innocent man and significantly reduce the number of witnesses I'll have to put on the stand to prove the same point. Brevity, Your Honor."

As soon as they were alone, Scenario promised herself to strangle Chance for this.

"Proceed with your witness, Counselor."

Scenario rolled her eyes and turned her back on them in such a way that she hoped the judge and Stormie understood that she was telling both of them to kiss her light, bright, damn near white ass. She went to the state's table and prepared to take notes.

ONE HUNDRED SEVEN

Holding one of the twins in her lap made Aspen want to hold her own child all the more. Today she was clad in Vera Wang and her apple cap sat above a no-maintenance ponytail. On her left sat Africa Taylor, Gail Taylor, and the other twin. She couldn't tell the twins apart. To her right was Hakeem. He had a look etched in his face that matched her thoughts: the prosecution is down by a landslide in the fourth quarter, and they'll need all three-pointers from here to come back and win.

In the row behind them was the Smith family, a beautiful group of women from Ocean City, Maryland. Aspen wondered why Jazz hadn't returned to the proceedings after she left the stand weeks ago. And then there were Leon's parents and his illegitimate seven-year-old son, Leon Jr. Three different families who found the strength to come together and relive the details of their loved one's tragic death. Aspen closed her eyes and prayed to God to bless her with the man she was in love with and a child so she could start a family to surround herself with.

She gave the twin a loving squeeze, noting that Chance had looked at the clock for the sixth time, and then she leaned into Hakeem and whispered, "What's the blind guy's story?"

"Your guess is as good as mine. But it looks like we're about to find out."

Stormie said, "Mr. Livingood, in the streets you have a reputation of earning a living in a unique way. Would you state for the record how that is."

"Sure, sure. My grandpappy gave me an apartment building, sixteen units, when he went on to meets his Maker. Good man, my grandpappy. Anyhows, I rents my units out by the week."

"Can anyone rent an apartment from you, Mr. Livingood?"

"No siree. Only peoples who needs special help."

"Explain to us what you mean by *special* help."

"Womens who gets knocked upside theys head by no-good abusive men. I'm originally from Lodi, Mississippi, and wes don't play that in them parts. Anyhows, and peoples who's trying to hides theys childrens from nasty situations. I helps with that sorta thing."

"But you have an unusual renting procedure."

"Ifens that what you wanna call it. To me it's just my method causing I'm blind and all."

"Please state for the record what your method is, Mr. Livingood."

"I rely on two things only," Mr. Livingood said, touching his broad nose. "My nose and real names. And I knows ifen someone is fibbing about their name. Don't fool with liars under no circumstances. I never—ever—forget a smell or a name, sir. Sincing I'm blind and all, born this way, I can't keep books. Too much hassle. So, anyhows, I record names and smells in my mind. Tenants come through the door and I knows who theys is without either of us opening our mouths. My nose tells me."

"Where are your apartments located?"

"On Conventry. Sixteen forty-two Conventry."

"Mr. Livingood, have you heard about the Hieroglyphic Hacker?"

"Yup, some half-deck running 'rounds this fine city killin' and cuttin' up decent folks."

"Have the police questioned you in any way about any of your occupants in connection with the Hieroglyphic Hacker?"

Aspen started to feel uneasy. She felt Hakeem stiffen with tension.

"No, sir," Mr. Livingood said. "Never knew theys had cause to."

"Do you remember April sixteenth of this year?"

"Freshen my memory some. Needs a jump-start sometimes. Getting up in age."

"You rented Apartment 012."

"Yup, rented it to a lady running froms her husband. She was plain scared, I tell you."

"Does the lady you speak of still rent the apartment now?"

"Yup, paid up for twelve more weeks. Good business. Quiet. No problems. Parks her car in the lot next to mine."

"What kind of car is it, Mr. Livingood?"

"Course I ain't never seen it, but my help tells me it's one of them Infinitis. A red one."

Aspen's stomach flipped. Hakeem was all but ready to bolt from his seat.

"The woman you rented Apartment 012 to, Mr. Livingood. What's her name?"

"Cashmaire Fox."

Aspen was out her seat, headed for the door, on the phone getting a search warrant. Chance checked the clock again.

Stormie smiled a clean smile at Scenario. "Your witness."

Ninety-seven thousand words later, Jazz typed the words: *The End.* "So what did you think of it?" she said to Jaden as she emailed a PDF copy to her agent.

"It was tough."

"Tough, huh?" A brow raised over the rim of her sunglasses.

"Yeah, it was hard. Onica was the truth." He spun the basketball on a finger.

"Thanks. I kind of like her too."

"When it came to her family," Jaden said, "there was nothing she wouldn't do to protect them."

"Family means everything. But she took a stand to fight for what she believes in without crossing moral lines."

"I feel that, but she still was hard."

"I feel that too."

"I'm going outside to practice my jumpshot before it gets dark."

"I'll watch you from the window. You know I'm your number one fan, right?"

He nodded with a Kool-Aid grin. "As I am yours. Glad you're writing again."

"Me too. It feels good." Jazz dialed her agent as Jaden left the room.

"What's cracking?" Eric said on the third ring. Keyshia Cole and Monica's "Trust" played too loud in the background.

"Hi," Jazz said as the music settled to a decent level. "What are you doing?"

"Javenna and I are on our way to the airport. I'm taking her to Costa Rica to horseback ride in the rain forest and make love under the natural hot spring. Then we're shooting over to Hollywood to shop on Rodeo Drive for the weekend before flying into Columbus for the Oktoberfest."

"That's special."

"Got a special woman in my corner. What's up with you?"

"I have some good news for you."

"If it's not getting Simon and Schuster's lawyers off my answering machine every ten minutes, it ain't good."

Buank. Buank. Buank. Buank.

Jazz went to the window. "Well, tell them they can relax."

"You're writing again?"

"Yeah, I'm back," she said with power.

"Thank God. You had me worried. Damn the money. We could have given that back if we had to. I've been worried sick about you. Between Leon and the accident and the murders, you've been through too much. I was afraid that if you didn't find it in you to write for yourself to release some of that, you would implode." Then: "Javenna wants to say hi."

"Thanks for caring, Eric. I never thought you didn't. And I'm sorry for being mean while I was dealing with my confusion. We're a team."

"Don't worry about it. That's nothing between us. I know you pretty good by now. Didn't even notice you being mean."

"Thanks, Eric. Put Javenna on."

A couple seconds later, Javenna said, "Hey, girl."

"Hi. Must be nice to have a man like Eric."

"Your time is coming. Your heaven packaged in a man is coming. So you're writing?"

"Yeah, it's time I pick up the pieces of my life and put them back together."

"Girl, I've been rooting for you from day one. I knew you'd pull through. I'll be back in town in a couple of weeks. Let's get together and do something."

"Okay."

"Here's Eric."

Buank. Buank. Buank. Buank.

"So what are we calling this novel?" Eric said.

"Harm's Way."

"Like how that rings. Can't wait to read it. How long before you're finished?"

"I'm done. Check your email. Told you I'm back and I'm ready to grind."

ONE HUNDRED NINE

County Prosecutor Scenario Davenport was frustrated.

"Mr. Livingood, I don't have many questions for you," Scenario said.

"Good, good. Maybe I cans get myself home in time for kickoff. Ohio State is going alls the way to the national championship this season."

"I'm sure. You testified that you rented an apartment to a woman by the name of Cashmaire Fox."

"Yes, ma'am."

"And you've never seen this woman?"

"Ma'am, I don't think I'm liking your tone. Are you being funny?"

"No, I'm not. Answer the question, Mr. Livingood. Have you seen her? Can you describe her?"

"No, ma'am."

"You have no documentation that the court can view to substantiate your testimony."

"No."

"So we're supposed to take your testimony as credible because of your nose? Are you part bloodhound, Mr. Livingood?"

"No. But my nose knows. In fact, Ms. Davenport, you smell just like Cashmaire Fox. Bet you a dollar to a dime you's wearing a fragrance called Thin Air."

Scenario looked woozy. She clutched the witness box, as if she were trying to stay on her feet. "No...no further questions, Your Honor."

The bailiff rushed to her. "Let me help you, Ms. Davenport."

She made eye contact with Chance as the bailiff led her to the state's table and was chilled to the bone marrow. Evil—pure—crept from behind his gorgeous smile and poured out his engaging blue eyes. He looked at the clock just as the courtroom door swung open. A FedEx delivery man, bottom heavy with a receding hairline, walked straight to the state's table and handed Scenario a manila envelope. She opened the package and found a lone sheet of paper that read:

DEFENSE EXHIBIT A

Law 29: Plan All The Way To The End

Her eyes found Chance's again.

"Winner winner chicken dinner," he said.

Stormie stood up. "The defense calls the Hieroglyphic Hacker herself, Mrs. Cashmaire Fox, to the stand."

First the audience and jury gasped. Then they buzzed with excitement as their gazes bounced around the courtroom waiting for Cashmaire to step forward.

"What is going on here, Mr. Bishop?" Judge Ronald Adrine said, rubbing his temples. Scenario figured he was not happy with his court being made a mockery.

"I'll tell you, you shithead," Chance said, standing up behind the defense table. "You fuckin' jerks don't recognize my wife because she had reconstructive surgery on her face after a car accident and disappeared. She came back passing herself off as Scenario Davenport. Me and Stormie here figured it out." He turned to Scenario. "Ain't that right, honey? Tell these assholes how you fooled us all and killed my buddies."

Members of the press stood on their chairs to snap pictures of the expression on Scenario's face. Brilliant bursts of light flashed through the room. Whispers rose to the ceiling.

"Chance," Scenario said, "I thought…why—" She passed out.

"Your Honor, my serial killer wife here." He looked at Cash on the floor as the bailiff worked to revive her and Hakeem limped through the gate with cuffs in hand. "She has a condition called Androgen Insensitivity Syndrome, meaning she's got the guts of a dude on the inside like that track star bimbo Caster Semenya from South Africa who won the eight-hundred-meter competition at the world championship that everybody was making a fuss about. Check my wife's DNA against the DNA found at the crime scenes and I'm sure you assholes will figure the rest out. She set me up and was gonna prosecute the old Chancester to see it through." Then: "Now one of you ass wipes get these shackles off me. And I wanna press charges against Detective Eubanks for attacking me when I was only trying to warn Jazz."

They swarmed Apartment 012 like a school of honey bees. It was a modest one-bedroom dwelling outfitted with a three-piece couch and a Walmart dinette set.

"Son of a bitch," Hakeem said when he limped through the door and came face to face with a fifty-five-gallon, hexagon-shape aquarium. Its light illuminated the tiny deep gold and brown eight-armed mollusks. It was hard to believe the charming, cute little creatures were capable of murder. Hakeem tapped the glass. All eleven of them flashed bright iridescent blue rings, curling their tentacles as if they were prize-fighters raring back to deliver a knock-out blow. "Now we can say we actually saw a Blue-ring octopus."

Aspen looked on in astonishment. "We put the wrong person on trial."

"He was telling the truth about warning Jazz. I got a lame leg 'cause I attacked him."

"In here, you guys," Tony, the crime scene tech, called from the bedroom. "You gotta see this."

When Hakeem and Aspen entered the bedroom, Tony lifted a pillow on the bed to reveal a .45 automatic. "Same type used to murder Marcus. Think she was ambitious enough to murder for a promotion?"

"It wouldn't surprise me," Aspen said. "Nothing will ever surprise me after this." She opened the closet door and stood in front of a wardrobe of high-end clothes. "The bitch knows how to dress." Aspen pulled a bloody outfit from the closet. "Same outfit we got her wearing on camera going into her office the night Leon Page was killed."

"Okay," Hakeem said. "Print the place and bag and tag it." Then he froze.

"What?" Aspen followed his gaze to a perfume bottle on the dresser.

"Thin Air. The old man's nose knew. He called it."

"Check this out." Aspen gestured out the window.

Hakeem and Tony Adams joined her. They all looked to the building's parking lot at a red Infiniti.

"A female serial killer with male DNA." Aspen shook her head. "What this bitch did will be studied for years."

ONE HUNDRED ELEVEN

The October chill nipped at Jazz's ears as she stood in front of a burial plot in Lakeview Cemetery. Foliage covered the headstone. Tears leaked from beneath her sunglasses. In the distance a John Deer backhoe's entrenching shovel took hungry bits out of the earth. She hoped it wasn't the preparation of a gravesite for another child. She felt Jaden's eyes on her; his intense gaze heated her back.

"Well," Jaden said, "what are you waiting on?"

She didn't want him to see her tears. "I used to want this, now I don't," Jazz said without turning around.

He said, "It's been a whole year of—"

"Exactly what we both needed to grow. You changed my life, Jaden. Taught me how to open up and love again."

Jaden came up and stood beside her, basketball wedged between his arm and narrow body. "We taught each other a few things."

"Yeah. I know how to dribble a basketball with my eyes closed."

They laughed. It felt really good to laugh with Jaden.

"I'm not poisoning myself with anger anymore." He spun the ball on his finger. "I know the meaning of forgiveness because of you."

Jazz wiped her tears to make way for new ones.

"I forgive you," Jaden said. "Hope they got a basketball court up there. I'm ready."

"So am I." Jazz removed her sunglasses and Washington Wizards ball cap and placed them on the grave. "Ready for a new start." She cleared the leaves from the headstone.

IN LOVING MEMORY OF
JADEN EUBANKS
October 16, 1995 – October 16, 2010

"Happy birthday," Jazz whispered through the tears.

"Keebler," Jaden had said, "you wanna go outside and play some ball with me until Daddy gets home?"

She barked a let's get it on.

"Get the basketball, girl, get the ball while I finish this sandwich." He bit the peanut butter and jelly.

Keebler, tail wagging, left the kitchen and returned nudging the ball along with her nose.

"And don't you even try taking it easy on me because it's my birthday."

Keebler barked her agreement as Jaden threw on a thick sweat shirt. Outside, the cold air pushing off the lake made Jaden think that video games would've been a better choice. With the earbuds to his iPod in his ears and the music loud enough to cause damage, Jaden planted his feet and took a three-point shot. He watched it soar through the cold air and miss its mark. The ball ricocheted off the rim. It shot down the driveway like it was powered by gas and into the street of Spring Bank Lane. Keebler barked and took off after it. Jaden ran behind her. He stopped in his tracks at the end of the driveway, near the light pole on the tree lawn, when he saw a blue Mercedes about to plow into Keebler. He screamed, "Keebler!"

"Slow down, Danica Patrick," Cash had said, likening Jazz's driving to that of the famous female NASCAR driver.

"Girl, I'm not driving that fast." Jazz had it under control so she kept her eyes glued on Cashmaire. "Whoa, back up. How come you can't have babies? What's the matter with you?" Jazz had grown tired of pretending she didn't know Cash had complete AIS years ago. She hoped Cash came clean so Jazz didn't have to live with the secret of knowing any longer.

Jazz's foot was so deep on the pedal the residential houses blew by them at 56 mph.

"It's complicated." Tears fell out Cash's eyes. She'd been crying since they left the airport. "I'm—Jazz, watch out!"

Jazz's head snapped back to the road. A huge pitbull-looking dog was in the middle of the road less than three feet in front of her. The only way to avoid hitting the dog, she figured, was to try and dodge it. She jerked the steering wheel hard to the left and stood on the brakes with both feet. In that instance she made eye contact with a teenage boy as the Mercedes careened into and crushed him between her front end and a light pole, killing him instantly and throwing Cash through the windshield.

ONE HUNDRED TWELVE

akeem eased the Hummer away from the house as city workers replaced the crippled light pole on his tree lawn. He reached over to the passenger's seat and stroked Keebler, her head out the window, tongue hanging out her mouth. "Eventually everything changes," he said as the light pole came down in his rearview mirror.

Almost twenty minutes after leaving home, Hakeem heavily leaned on his cane and hobbled up on Jazz kneeling at Jaden's gravesite. His halting gait was more pronounced and painful now that the cold weather sunk its icy teeth into his injuries. Jazz's face was wet with tears. Keebler barked and started pulling hard on her leash.

"Keebler, what's gotten into you?" he said as she pulled away from him.

"It's Jaden," Jazz said. "She can see him."

"You're serious, aren't you?"

She nodded. "He's been with me since the accident. No one has ever believed me but Cash because she saw him too. She said right at the moment she came out of the coma, he was standing beside her, touching her hand. She said they made eye contact. I know it was him who saved her from Chance, because he was taking her off life support."

Hakeem leaned on the cane, keeping pressure off his aching leg.

"It baffled me for weeks how you were able to get by Keebler that day and make it to the second floor of my house. She would have mauled you to death if you weren't with me or Jaden. You see Chance had to shoot her to stop her." He paused to let a surge of pain pass. "Then I remembered something my grandmother told me when I was a little guy, much younger than Jaden."

Jazz looked at him as he pretended not to struggle with lowering himself to the ground to kneel beside her.

"Grandma told me that dogs can see human souls that roam the earth. Jaden was with you that day, wasn't he?"

She nodded, tears rolling off her face. "He showed me where you hide the spare key behind that false brick to the left of the door." Then: "He's here with us now. Right there with Keebler."

He cut his eyes to Keebler. She wagged her tail and ran in a circle and occasionally stood on her hind legs like she was playing with someone.

"Jaden is a fine young man. He's taken good care of me, you know."

Hakeem said nothing; his tears said it all.

Jazz gestured to the headstone next to Jaden's that read: *Gwynn Eubanks*. "Jaden's mother?"

"Yes," he whispered.

"I'm sorry."

"Don't be. My wife passed from breast cancer almost two years ago now." He collected himself and pointed. "My mother is right there and my grandparents are over there."

"You just try and stay out this ground for as long as you can."

"I'm working on it."

Jazz said, "I have a daughter here too. She was murdered in my belly."

"I didn't know."

"Wherever Leon is, he's answering for it." She wiped her tears, but the attempt was useless. "Mr. Eubanks, she didn't do it. Cash is a lot of things but a murderer she is not. So I need you to promise me that you will never stop searching for the truth because I know that something about the way it went down rubs you wrong. It's that irritation that I'm begging you not to ignore. If you do, an innocent woman is going to die and you'll break the promise you already made to me."

"Promise?"

"Yeah, you promised that you would not let anything happen to me. Cash didn't do it, and Chance is still out there. I'm the only one who wasn't punished for the wrong he feels we inflicted on his family."

Something did irritate Hakeem, but he didn't know what. But it was there in the caverns of his mind digging and clawing its way to the surface. An unformed thought that stubbornly refused to gel. And he needed to know what that something was no matter how long it took. "I promise." He studied Keebler's movements for a moment. "I come here once a week to talk to him. He would have been sixteen today."

"Well, you get to talk to him for real today."

He was quiet, then said, "What will I say to him?"

"Whatever you need to say, Mr. Eubanks. Whatever you can't live another day having not said to him, because he's ready to cross over. That's why we're here today."

"You're really serious, aren't you?" He watched her looking at someone he couldn't see. "Jaden, come over here."

ONE HUNDRED THIRTEEN

Jazz rubbed Keebler's head, impressed with the beautiful animal. "I almost hit you, you know that? You gotta stay out the street." She squatted and stroked Keebler's body. "Whenever you're ready, Mr. Eubanks, Jaden can hear you."

Jazz watched as Jaden stared at his father like he wished he could hug the man.

"Uh, where is he?" Hakeem was clearly nervous. His flushed skin perspired in spite of the cold.

"Standing in front of you."

Jaden said, "Tell him that I can tell he's stressing and not taking care of himself or sleeping like he did when Mom passed. Tell him to stop."

"Your son says not to stress and take better care of yourself and find a way to rest at night. That you can't do the same thing you did when your wife passed."

"It's hard," Hakeem said.

She knew he had to be feeling awkward about talking to someone who had passed away with the understanding that he was actually being heard.

"I miss you so much, son." His words got caught up in his throat. "I still come home and look forward to working on that jumpshot with you. My life is so empty without you and your mother. It's like there's this big hole in me and everything is spilling out."

Jaden told Jazz what to tell his father.

"He says he misses you too and that he's all right and that he didn't suffer. Never felt a thing."

Hakeem broke down in tears. "Thank God," he whispered to himself.

"He wants to know," Jazz said, still stroking Keebler, "that you won't let this beat you and that he'd be happy if you promise to live your life to the fullest for him and his mom."

Hakeem nodded and sobbed. "I promise, son. I promise."

"He wants to know if you used the season tickets y'all had for the Cavs' games?"

"I couldn't, son. I couldn't go without you."

Jaden said, "Tell him that I love you, Ms. Smith. That you've been like a mother to me, so I don't want him to be mad at you. You're special to me, Ms. Smith, so I want y'all to be friends and for him to look out for you when I'm gone."

"I'm not saying that, Jaden. I'm honored, but no." Her eyes watered, but she checked her emotions so the tears wouldn't fall.

"Tell him."

"No, I don't feel comfortable repeating that."

Jazz felt Hakeem watching her seemingly go back and forth with herself.

"Say what? What don't you feel comfortable saying?" Hakeem said.

She sighed. "He wants you to know that he looks at me like a second mom and he loves me. So he asks that you hold nothing against me for what happened." She looked to the tumbling leaves on the ground, feeling ashamed. "He wants us to be friends and look out for each other when he's gone."

Jaden said, "That's not exactly what I said, but I cosign it."

"Jaden, son, I love you with all I am. There hasn't been a single hour that I haven't thought about you. And there won't be a day that I won't miss you for as long as I live. Because of you, Jazz and I will always be bonded."

"Thank you," Jazz said, then listened to Jaden. "He says he loves you too and not to pay me any attention when I have my mean spells." She shook her head. "I'm not mean, Mr. Eubanks. He was deliberately trying to drive me crazy bouncing that darn ball in the house."

"Tell me about it." Hakeem chuckled.

Jaden pointed. "It's time for me to go."

Jazz saw a woman in the distance waving Jaden to her.

"That's my mother."

Keebler saw the woman and started barking and pulling, excited to near hysteria.

"What's wrong now, girl?" Hakeem tightened down on Keebler's leash, fighting to hold her back.

"It's Gwynn. She came for him." Jazz burst into tears as Jaden went to his mother.

Hakeem's tears flowed too. Keebler barked and barked. With his bad leg he fought to hold Keebler back. "He's leaving, isn't he?"

"Yes," she said through a cracked voice.

Jaden stood next to his mother and waved. "I love you, Dad. I love you, Ms. Smith."

"We love you too." To Hakeem, she said, "Wave bye, Mr. Eubanks."

They waved until Jaden and his mother were gone. Jazz turned to leave.

Hakeem gestured to Jaden's headstone. "Your sunglasses and cap."

"I won't be needing them anymore."

ONE HUNDRED FOURTEEN

Aspen stepped onto her bathroom scale; she weighed *perfect*. She smiled. A fresh pack of Newports sat on the vanity table among all the items that amplified her pretty. The sight of the cigarettes kicked her nicotine jones into overdrive. She tapped out a stick to feed the need. Then she saw it. The OB Complete starter kit. "It's one or the other. Can't have it both ways," she said, running a fingertip over the box of prenatal supplements. She gave herself a serious look in the mirror and found the cigarette pinched between her lips unattractive and unhealthy. "You can do this, Aspen," she said to herself, then tossed the cigarette in the toilet. Then she tapped the rest of the pack into the toilet. With her finger on the handle, she stared at the floating cigarettes. She pulled in a deep breath, then flushed, carving the decision in stone. Slipping out of her robe, she eased into a scented bubble bath in an in-floor tub that would make Tony Montana blush. Thinking of Jaden's sixteenth birthday, she wondered how Hakeem was doing. She swallowed a supplement, dialed his number, and relaxed against a cozy tub pillow.

Hakeem limped into the Homicide Unit with a new outlook on life. Allowing life to pass him by wouldn't be what Gwynn would accept from him. He had to thrive. That much he owed to the memory of his family as much as he owed it to himself. During the car ride from the cemetery to the office, Hakeem prayed and swore to God that he wouldn't break his promises to Jaden or Jazz. He was through feeling sorry for himself and beating himself up with blame. He'd left those negatives at Jaden's gravesite next to Jazz's sunglasses.

Keebler stretched out alongside his desk. He hung his leather coat on the back of the chair, then settled himself into it. He contemplated his cluttered desk. Among a stack of case files was a Priority Mail package addressed from Gus Hobbs. Hakeem almost got angry but thought better of it. He opened the mail with Aspen's letter opener and found a videotape inside. A note was rubber banded to the tape that read *Peace Offering.* Hakeem jerked his bottom drawer open and tossed the Priority package in with all the other junk he'd accumulated over the years that he had no use for. Reaching for the turned-down picture frame, Hakeem knew he was on the right track. He stood the picture right side up for the first time since the accident. He had almost forgotten what they looked like.

Jaden, a boyish version of Hakeem, wore a Cavaliers jersey, holding a game ball autographed by Boobie Gibson. Gwynn, hair framing her slender face and a splash of freckles covering her light skin, had her arm around Jaden as they posed for the picture in the Quicken Loans Arena. Hakeem remembered the moment he snapped the picture and smiled. Even from the picture, Gwynn's eyes penetrated Hakeem's soul.

He reached down and ruffled Keebler's head. "You miss them too, don't you, girl?"

Keebler whined.

Hakeem focused back on the picture. "I promise to live again, and I'll always love y'all."

His cell phone rang. After digging it out of his leather coat, Hakeem said, "Communicate."

"What are you doing?"

"Restoring order to my life. Figured I'd start by cleaning up my desk. Why? What are you up to?"

"Taking a bath."

He tried hard not to imagine that. "Aspen, you didn't call to tell me that."

"It doesn't bother you, does it?"

"It's awkward." He took the restraints off. He couldn't help himself. Now he pictured her chocolate skin wet with bubbles. Her hair pinned up in a bun…and those dimples.

She said, "Well, now you don't have to add *talk to Aspen while she's naked and in the tub* to your bucket list." Then: "A deal is a deal, Hakeem."

Hakeem said nothing.

"Get quiet all you want. I'm not letting you back out of this."

He leaned back and put his eyes on Jaden and Gwynn. "I'm not trying to."

"Okay, that was too damn easy. What in the hell did you do with the real Hakeem Eubanks?"

"When is the date, Aspen?"

"Tonight."

He pulled out a pen and found something to write on. "Phoenix Lovelace, right?"

"You remembered."

"Where?"

"X & O in the flats. Ten o'clock."

"How am I supposed to know what she looks like?"

"Don't worry about it. She knows what you look like. Just be there."

"Bye, Aspen." He clicked off and turned to Keebler. "Girl, what did I just get myself into?"

ONE HUNDRED FIFTEEN

She wasn't paying attention, but he was. She was too caught up in the relationship section in Barnes & Noble to notice. When he first saw her hit the aisle, he knew. He stood still, absent-mindedly flipping through the pages of the *The Truth About Love*.

She drew closer; his heart beat faster.

She was a tall and regal sister with a supermodel strut and the serene demeanor of an A-list celebrity. He observed every nuance of her: Long fingers, manicured nails, no wedding ring. Silky black hair tumbled down her back in loose curls. Skin the color of Werther's Original candy, and he was sure it tasted just as sweet. Her jeans and sweater were sensual and vibrant. Her long strides were efficient and arousing. This goddess was gorgeous enough to make a man look twice. But he only needed one glance. He was hooked. He put the book back on the shelf and reached for another.

That's when it happened.

They grabbed each other's hand. It felt sexy. It felt right. She looked up at him with eyes the color of old pennies. Clear. Calm. Steady. It was impossible to ignore the way her eyes bored into him. Instinctively he closed his eyes to pray this moment was real and caught a flashback of their initial eye contact. He opened his eyes because he had to see her again.

There you are, Jazz thought as she went to pluck a copy of Elizabeth Clare's *Soulmates and Twin Flames* from the shelf but grabbed a hand instead. She looked into his luminous black eyes. Then the energy of his touch registered. It surged through her body and landed down *there*. She giggled. Jazz had written about this intense feeling and look a thousand times. She intellectually knew it. She just never thought she would experience it or the look would truly be aimed at her during this lifetime. Love. Longing. Desire. Need. She loved it. The longer they held gazes, the deeper their souls connected.

"Whatever is happening here," he said, not one ounce of artifice, "I don't want it to stop. I'm really enjoying it."

Her pulse quickened. "Me too." She smiled a thousand watts of power.

"I'm Oasis."

She blushed. "Jazz."

"Well, Jazz, since we're already holding hands, how about you let me take you next door for lunch. See if we can figure this out, because I can't spend the rest of my life wondering about the what ifs of this moment."

She looked down at their hands, not even realizing they were still clenched together. It felt good. She threaded her fingers with his to test the fit. Her common sense screamed exchange numbers and build up to a lunch date, but her heart said this was God's doing. She squeezed his hand.

"Does that mean yes?"

She nodded, not sure if she was capable of words. "Yes."

"Your eyes," he said as they walked to the exit, "they're inspiring. Makes me enjoy smiling."

ONE HUNDRED SIXTEEN

akeem knew there was a crimp in his plan to be cordial to Ms. Phoenix Lovelace and leave without promises of another date when a curvy petite goddess in a couture Gucci Première gown with a thigh-high split sashayed into the room. She wore a Cartier necklace worth an MIT tuition. A V of naked flesh stretched from her delicate collarbone to her outie belly button. Usher's "There Goes My Baby" accompanied her spectacular entrance. The moment Hakeem met her gaze he knew it had fiery consequences. It flipped his switch. The intensity of it turned up his thermostat. Hakeem didn't know whether to approach Aspen or flee.

He had never seen Aspen more beautiful. She stopped and smiled at him under a chandelier; its light catching her diamond-drop earrings. He took a sip of wine the color of water, placed the glass on the bar, and went to her. Never once giving a conscious thought to his lilting gait.

"You look…wow, you're gorgeous."

"Thank you." Her voice sounded like a chorus of angels. "You look good yourself. But then again, you look good to me every day. Hakeem, you know you're this kitten's meow."

"What happened to your friend, Phoenix?"

She gave him a look. Translation: *Say the right thing, dammit.* "You sound disappointed."

His eyes flashed. "Try the opposite." A smile slid from one corner of his mouth to the other.

"I'm a Gemini, Hakeem. But you already know that. Phoenix Lovelace is my alter ego. So do I fit your requirements? Not too old, and I weighed in at a hundred twenty-five pounds this morning."

"You've always been perfect, Aspen." He took in her beauty again. "Let's dance."

"Hakeem, dancing is just a cheap trick so you can hold me and imagine screwing me without actually fucking me and cooling down this feminine moisture gathering between my legs. I say we get out of here and skip the imagination part."

A shot of adrenaline boiled his loins. He took her hand. "Where will our jobs end and our personal lives begin?"

"I don't think we can split it down the middle, but tonight our personal lives start in your bedroom. And in the morning, together, we'll decide what labeling you and me *we* will cost us."

With those words, their sexual tension became a tangible living thing. A goofy smile spread across his face.

The short hairs on their bodies coiled under the coitus sweat. Each time Hakeem pushed into Aspen's never-ending heat, she bit her bottom lip.

"Feels good," she whispered.

He nibbled her earlobe. "You like that, huh?"

"Yes, baby," she whispered. Her hands on his behind, pulling him in deeper. "Yes."

"Promise I won't stop until you feel how much I love you, how long I've been needing you."

"I feel it, Hakeem. I feel it. I feel all of it." She rolled him over and straddled him shamelessly. "I've been loving you a long time too." She cried and rode him. Rode him and moaned. Came and screamed his name like a spiritual mantra. "Hakeem, Hakeem, Hakeem. My God, Hakeem."

They slept in each other's arms with Keebler sleeping at the threshold of the room. Hakeem finally got a good night's sleep.

ONE HUNDRED SEVENTEEN

Oasis pushed an ottoman over to Jazz and put her feet on it, then slipped her heels off. "Just relax," he said. "Tonight is all about you."

"That smells really good. What are we eating?" Jazz had gotten used to this. In the last five months she'd experienced what it was like to be treated like a queen, to be the object of someone's affection.

Handing her a glass of lemon tea, he said, "How about you let me surprise you." He gave her a look that she'd told him made her feel ultra girly. "God, I love your eyes. I swear they drive me crazy, girl." He leaned in and kissed each of her eyelids, then slid down to her awaiting lips.

And their mouths made love while he gently stroked her face with the back of his fingers.

"I love you, Jazz. Thank you for showing up in my life."

She blushed. "You really mean that, don't you?"

"From the bottom of my heart."

"I love you too."

"Food will be done in, uh, give me twenty minutes."

"I'll wait for you as long as it takes."

The corner of his lips turned in to a smile. He put Monica's "Love All Over Me" on the sound system and went into the kitchen.

Jazz's cell phone rang. She fumbled through her purse for it. "Hello."

"Dudette."

The smile fell off her face. "Chance?"

"Winner winner chicken dinner."

"What?" Jazz said with venom. "What do you want?"

"How does it feel to be the lone survivor of a serial killer? Enjoy the feeling until we meet again. I got a bad habit of keeping my word."

The line went dead.

The weather along the shore of Port Elizabeth, South Africa, was upward of a hundred degrees. This was the type of heat that made people hate the greenhouse effect. Chance stood in his sandy backyard enjoying every bit of it.

Bridgette waddled up as Chance hung up the phone. "Who was that?"

"Just a loose end that needs tying up." He kissed her. "How are you this morning, Mrs. Fox?"

"Hungry."

Chance didn't have to imagine fucking the clerk of courts anymore. He rubbed her swollen belly. "Little Chance is hungry, huh?"

"So is his mother." Then: "And I'm ready to hear the raw truth."

Chance saw her anticipation. He recognized the unquenchable thirst of a predator lingering deep in her eyes. "Well, let's go inside and see what Daddy can do about that." He knew the time was right to invite his new wife into the dark side of his world.

They turned toward their bungalow. When they got to their patio, Chance called over his shoulder, "Come on, Champ. Come on, boy."

And their puppy Presa Canario came running.

EPILOGUE

Marysville State Penitentiary for women. Cashmaire Fox was one of sixteen women on death row. She was led into an interview room in shackles and cuffs where Brenda McGinnis, the FBI profiler she'd worked with as a prosecutor, waited. Brenda nodded at Cash, then she turned a portable camcorder on.

"How are you holding up?" Brenda adjusted the camera's view, then took her place at the table in front of Cash.

"I'm thankful I'm not dead yet."

"Can I get you something before we start the interview?"

Cash laughed, then stopped. "You can't get me what I want."

"As you know, I'm Brenda McGinnis. I work for the FBI's Investigation Support Unit. Today's date is May twenty-third, two thousand fourteen. I'm here to conduct a voluntary interview with you for research purposes and scientific studies into the mind of a female serial killer."

Cash nodded.

"Would you state your name for me?"

"Cashmaire Fox. I still use Fox even though I'm divorced. Habit. But my maiden name is Jones."

"What I'm going to do is tell you what we know about the events and evidence that led you to death row and you can freely talk along the way."

Cash nodded.

"You double majored in college. Graduated Summa Cum Laude. In combination with your law degree, you majored in Egyptology in which you learned the hieroglyphic language. Your term paper and dissertation was on ancient Egypt and the Nile Valley contribution to civilization."

"Chance majored in Egyptology. His term paper was similar to mine. We studied together."

"Three of your four Ohio victims, you went to school with and were friends with. The other was your boss."

"Chance went to school with them too. They were his friends."

"You hid the fact that you knew them from homicide investigators."

"I was trying to leave my old life behind. And I didn't kill Marcus."

"The gun that killed Marcus was found in your apartment with your fingerprints on it. Your fingerprints were also on hundreds of other personal items in the apartment."

"I'd planned on committing suicide, so I bought the gun off the streets because we didn't own one. That's how my prints are on it. I left that gun in Denver along with all my belongings that were found in that apartment that I never stepped foot in a day of my life. Chance murdered Marcus, and he transferred all that stuff from Denver to Cleveland."

"You were the last person seen with Yancee Taylor and Leon Page while they were alive."

"Chance disguised as me was last to see Yancee. Unfortunately, I was the last person to see Leon alive. But the woman on tape entering my office wasn't me. That was Chance in disguise."

"Yancee's urine and fecal matter was found in the trunk of your Infiniti."

"A car that I hadn't seen or thought twice about since October sixteenth twenty-ten when I walked away from Denver. I started my life over in Cleveland after the accident as Scenario Davenport. With that came a new everything, including a car."

"The killings in Denver stopped when you showed up in Cleveland."

"Chance followed me here."

"You assaulted Janice Carter for abusing a cat when you were thirteen. Each of your Denver victims was animal abusers."

"Chance hates people who harm animals. He protests against it. He became a veterinarian because of it."

"Your DNA was found at two of the Cleveland crime scenes. Leon's blood was found on an outfit in your closet."

"You mean planted by my husband. And I told you that wasn't my apartment."

"Coins with your fingerprints on them were found in the pay phone you used to call the police tip line."

"Ms. McGinnis, you mean coins that my husband took from my piggy bank in Denver and used when he called the hot line."

"You falsified documents with the Cleveland Metropolitan Bar Association to practice law in Ohio. Then you engaged in misprision of a felony and prosecutorial misconduct when you attempted to try your husband for the murders you committed."

"I. Did. Not. Kill. Anyone, Agent McGinnis. But, yes, I was trying to get my husband acquitted."

"Cashmaire, you volunteered for this interview under the pretense you were going to tell the truth. If you're going to combat everything I say with a justification, then why am I here?"

"You're here so that for once in my life, I can tell the truth and have that truth studied in order to save my life."

"And what is your truth, Ms. Fox?"

"That I have Complete Androgen Insensitivity Syndrome. I'm a female outwardly, but I have the chromosome pattern of a male. I don't have ovaries like you. I've never had a period. I have undescended testicles. Because of that, Agent McGinnis, I became a liar. A selfish habitual liar to conceal my freakishness. Those lies are the real reason I'm sitting here on death row." She paused. "So if you want to study something, study AIS. Study low self-esteem. Study what it feels like not knowing if people will see you as a woman or the mutation of a man if they discover your secret. Then maybe you, as a *complete* woman, can understand why I became a liar. So I'm guilty of being a liar, but that's no more. I'm guilty of deception. I'm through with that too." Cash turned to the camera and gave it a no-nonsense stare. "But I'm not guilty of murder. My husband, Chance Fox, set me up."

The End

Everything that deceives may be said to enchant.
—PLATO

AUTHOR'S EXIT

Writers know that some stories should wait to be born. *Wrong Chance* gestated within the deepest part of my mind for five years, a safe distance from a premature birth. But now it is time, my creative water has broken. Androgen Insensitivity Syndrome captured my attention during an episode of *House*. An accidental viewing, I must admit. Researching the subject further fascinated my creativity. Research (a headache word) revealed that 14 percent of the world's women live with this rare condition and the challenges it presents in their day-to-day journeys. AIS + "What if this were to happen?" = *Wrong Chance*.

It is not my intention to propagate any medical or terminology misrepresentations associated with AIS. Also it is not my intention to offend any person(s), any organizations, or any advocacy groups for women or couples living with AIS. It is my belief that all people are created exactly how they are supposed to be—perfect. So-called flaws are relative. My sole intent herein is to create compelling *fiction* with a fresh premise for my audience's enjoyment. Everyone, the key word here is "fiction." I'm clueless about half the *real* stuff I write about. So if something rings true and correct, trust me, I did it by mistake. And I take full responsibility and blame for whatever is incorrect and whatever police procedures, law practices, and medical situational rules I bent to make the plot work. It is not an oversight of any authority named below.

On that note (DRUM ROLL HERE!), the following individuals have been instrumental with their contribution to *Wrong Chance*. It is my honor to give my infinite thanks to the following:

My wife, Javenna, who has learned that dealing with the everyday life of a career writer is a difficult and sometime stressful undertaking. But she straps her pom-poms on and cheerleads for me through it all.

Brenda Hampton, my agent, the ride continues. No one else can ever roll shotgun with me but you.

My team, the entire staff at Strebor Books/Atria/Simon & Schuster for your encouragement and support.

My editorial guru, Docuversion. You're an integral part of the writing process. I'd be a hack without you.

I'm indebted to Alice Smith for all that you do for my projects. You're the world's unsung wonder.

Other important contributors: Charles Allen, K. Jones Bey, and Troy Cleveland, my no-nonsense test readers. Fernard Strowbridge, my human informational vault. My source inside Cleveland's law enforcement who wishes to remain anonymous. Officer A. Maresca, who schooled me on police procedures while I was locked in the hole of Fort Dix Correctional Institution. Antoinette A. Lakey, my infallible legal eagle. Thank you all for lending me your knowledge in order to make *Wrong Chance* a plausible tale.

I am deeply humbled by the family I'm surrounded by. Eric Jr., Rashaad, Rasheed, Braxton, Brooks, Brendyn, Brandyn, Linda, Alice, Mary, Billy Sr., Autum, Billy Jr., Walter Sr. (RIP), Bertha, Charlene, Marie, Jakhai, Terrance Sr., Ashley, Jamillah, Mokey, Jeanette, Betty Jean, Zabree, Jordan, Jessica, Jasmine, Austin, Renee, Mikey, Terrance Jr., Mellisa, Carmallita, Lisa, Freedie, Lil' Ronny, Silence, C-Mack, Eric Downs, and the most precious of them all: my adorable granddaughters, Khloei and Kaliyah.

Praise for E.L. Myrieckes (Writing as Oasis)

White Heat
(With Mrs. Oasis)

"Excellent storyline from beginning to end. Nonstop drama."

—Starred Review

"A must-read, action-packed novel that grabs your attention from the beginning and doesn't stop until the end. Oasis and Mrs. Oasis's writing is addictive."

—Brenda Hampton, bestselling author of *Naughty by Nature*

"Off the chain. Check this book out. Oasis and Mrs. Oasis weaved a perfect tale."

—Starred Review

"I recommend *White Heat.*"

—APOOO Bookclub

"Fast paced and well written. This one is HOT—careful while handling!"

—Starred Review

Push Comes To Shove

"Entertaining cautionary tale."

—*Publishers Weekly*

"Oasis is undoubtedly a creative genius. *Push Comes to Shove* proves it."

—TYRONE CLARY, PAROUSIA GALLERY ART

"Oasis is a refreshing voice for a new generation."

—RASHAAN ALI, *Essence* BESTSELLING AUTHOR OF *Nasty*

"Alas! Oasis is like a breath of fresh air to the literary industry, debuting with an entertaining and heartfelt family drama."

—JOYLYNN JOSSEL, AUTHOR OF *The Root of All Evil* AND *When Souls Mate*

"A multicultural-suspense novel, vibrant and rich in characters. A plot so intense it literally leaves wounds on the heart. A stunning debut."

—DAWNNY RUBY, MAHOGANY MEDIA REVIEW

"*Push Comes to Shove* has to be one of the best books I've read in a very long time! Its real life issues, believable characters, and its twists and turns have you laughing, crying, and shaking your head. Oasis is a talented author who is destined for great things in the literary world. This book is going to put him where he needs to be—at the top."

—KEILA MILLER, GROWN FOLKS CAFÉ

"In his newest novel, *Push Comes to Shove*, Oasis brings the drama right to his readers' face. His writing style is razor sharp, and the story line will cause your heart to skip a beat. I tremendously enjoyed this novel, and I look forward to more heart-throbbing stories in the future."

—BRENDA HAMPTON, *Essence* BESTSELLING AUTHOR OF *NAUGHTY BY NATURE*

"An engrossing story. *Push* is a mixed bag of life situations and hard knocks that will keep you turning the pages—never a dull moment. *Push Comes to Shove* is destined for bestseller status."

—NATALIE DARDEN, AUTHOR OF *All About Me*

"A positively compelling story that grabs you from the first paragraph and keeps you enthralled until the very end. A novel that [provokes] so many emotions: fear, anger, empathy, laughter, and tears. *Push Comes To Shove* is a tear jerker, but the end is oh so sweet."

—TINA BROOKS MCKINNEY, AUTHOR OF *All That Drama*

"*Push Comes to Shove:* Smart, well-paced, and vividly entertaining."

—OOSA ONLINE BOOKCLUB

"A heartfelt and laugh-out-loud book that had its tender moments. What an entertaining, powerful, and wonderful read."

—STARRED REVIEW

"This author always delivers fast-paced, cutting-edge drama. Great job!"

—STARRED REVIEW

Duplicity

"An engaging page-turner full of suspense and drama. Very entertaining."

—STARRED REVIEW

"Oasis has woven a hell of a good story, it's a nail biter."

—TINA BROOKS MCKINNEY, AUTHOR OF *Deep Deception*

"*Duplicity* is a beautifully orchestrated symphony of words. Oasis is ferocious with a pen."

—PITCH BLACK, AUTHOR OF *Code of Honor*

"One hell of a good read. Psychological suspense novels don't get any better than *Duplicity*."

—JAMES HENDRICKS, AUTHOR OF *A Good Day to Die*

"Grab a snack, this one is sure to keep you occupied."

—S. CULBERT, AUTHOR OF *Gutta Boyz*

"Literature at its best. A novel masterfully, artistically, and well written. *Duplicity* is a must-read. I stamp my approval with a guarantee—you will not be disappointed."

—BRENDA HAMPTON, *Essence* BESTSELLING AUTHOR OF
Naughty by Nature

"Oasis delivers a fascinating and gripping psychological suspense with masterful clarity. *Duplicity* seals his place as an innovative author and a mainstay in the genre."

—RAWSISTAZ LITERARY GROUP

"Psychodynamically witty! Oasis's *Duplicity* is a welcome respite in a literary desert."

—KAIYOS, DOCUVERSION CREATIVE WRITING INSTRUCTOR

"If you like suspense novels, *Duplicity* is perfect."

—OOSA ONLINE BOOKCLUB

"A well-written book; it had everything from drama to suspense."

—STARRED REVIEW

"*Duplicity* had me hooked. A quick and engrossing read."

—APOOO BOOKCLUB

"Oasis provides a very engrossing tale with *Duplicity*, guaranteed to keep readers guessing as to what's real and what's make-believe."

—THE URBAN BOOK SOURCE

"If you like stories that keep you guessing who the bad guy is, this is the book for you."

—ROMANCE READERS CONNECTION

"An excellent mystery novel; it will keep your mind working and turning until the last page. Get this book right now and don't get up until you are done."

—STARRED REVIEW